Pr

'An all too chilling

'Håkan Nesser [is
Van Veeteren novels have a puckishness and sprightliness
that too often elude his younger, gloomier pretenders . . .
Nesser has thus far only been a minor player in the British
Nordic crime scene: *Hour of the Wolf* should be the book to
change that'   *Metro*

'Nesser has something in common with another great
generator of suspense, Alfred Hitchcock: a preoccupation
with guilt and the way in which crime draws everyone
connected with it into a dark moral miasma . . . we are
reminded of the writer Ruth Rendell in the coolly method-
ical fashion in which lives are destroyed by a crime, those
of both the victims and the perpetrators . . . there is not a
single misstep as the grim implications of the narrative are
teased out'   *Independent*

'All the tropes of Scandinavian crime: physical and meta-
physical gloom, desolate landscapes and circumscribed
lives . . . The investigating cops are skilfully differentiated
and their banter is amusing. As for the plot . . . it contains
enough twists to keep you reading through the Bergman-
esque darkness'   *Evening Standard*

'Nesser has a style all his own, making him a writer who needs to be on the bookshelves of all crime fans'

Edinburgh Evening News

'The Swedish novelist Håkan Nesser is in another league, exhibiting a skill and consistency rare in crime fiction. *Hour of the Wolf* is one of his finest novels, starting with a road accident and unravelling its terrible consequences . . . a novel that combines a clever plot with authentic emotion'

Sunday Times

HOUR OF THE WOLF

Also by Håkan Nesser

BORKMANN'S POINT

THE RETURN

THE MIND'S EYE

WOMAN WITH A BIRTHMARK

THE INSPECTOR AND SILENCE

THE UNLUCKY LOTTERY

HÅKAN NESSER

HOUR OF THE WOLF

AN INSPECTOR VAN VEETEREN MYSTERY

Translated from the Swedish by
Laurie Thompson

PAN BOOKS

First published in Great Britain 2012 by Mantle

This paperback edition published 2012 by Pan Books
an imprint of Pan Macmillan, a division of Macmillan Publishers Limited
Pan Macmillan, 20 New Wharf Road, London N1 9RR
Basingstoke and Oxford
Associated companies throughout the world
www.panmacmillan.com

ISBN 978-0-330-51259-6

Originally published in 1999 as *Carambole*
by Albert Bonniers Forlag, Stockholm

1 3 5 7 9 8 6 4 2

A CIP catalogue record for this book is available from the British Library.

Typeset by Ellipsis Digital Limited, Glasgow
Printed and bound by CPI Group (UK) Ltd, Croydon, CR0 4YY

Visit **www.panmacmillan.com** to read more about all our books
and to buy them. You will also find features, author interviews and
news of any author events, and you can sign up for e-newsletters
so that you're always first to hear about our new releases.

'In the natural order of things, fathers
do not bury their sons.'

Paul Auster, *The Red Notebook*

ONE

1

The boy who would soon die laughed, and sat up straight. Brushed the remains of some crisps off his shirt and stood up.

'I must go now,' he said. 'I really must. The last bus is due in five minutes.'

'Yes,' said the girl, 'I suppose you must. I daren't allow you to sleep over. I don't know what Mum would say, she'll be home in a couple of hours. She's working late tonight.'

'That's a shame,' said the boy, pulling his thick sweater over his head. 'It would be great to spend the night with you. Couldn't we maybe . . . maybe . . .'

He hesitated about what to say next. She smiled and took hold of his hand. Held on to him. She knew he didn't really mean what he said. Knew he was only pretending. He would never dare, she thought. He wouldn't be able to cope with a situation like that . . . And for a brief moment she toyed with the idea of saying yes. Letting him stay.

Just in order to see how he reacted. See if he would go

along with it, or if he would chicken out.

Let him think just for a moment that she would agree to lie naked in bed with him.

It would be fun, no doubt about that. It could have taught her a lot about him. But she dropped the idea: it wouldn't have been fair, and she liked him too much to be as egotistic and scheming as that. She really did like him an awful lot, come to think about it, so sooner or later they would get to that stage no matter what. Lying in bed, both of them naked under the same duvet . . . Yes, that was what she had been feeling for the last few weeks, there was no point in shutting her eyes to the fact.

The first one. He would be her first one. But not tonight.

'Another time, then,' she said, letting go of him. Ran her hands through her hair to get rid of the static electricity from the silky cover of the sofa. 'You only ever think of one thing, you bloody stallions!'

'Huh,' he said, trying to produce an appropriately disappointed expression on his face.

He went out into the hall, she adjusted her jumper and followed him.

'We could be as quiet as mice and pretend you were asleep, then I could sneak out tomorrow morning before she wakes up . . .' he said, not wanting to seem to give up too easily.

'We can do it another time,' she said. 'Mum's working

nights next month – maybe then?'

He nodded. Put on his boots and started looking for his scarf and gloves.

'Oh, shit! I've forgotten my French book. Could you fetch it for me, please?'

She went back to get it. When he had buttoned up his duffle coat they started hugging again. She could feel his erection through all the layers of cloth: he hugged her close, and just for a moment her head spun. It felt good – like falling without having to worry about landing, and she realized that the link between reason and emotions, between mind and heart, was just as weak as her mother had said it would be when they sat at the kitchen table speaking seriously about such matters only the other day.

Not something you can rely on. Your reason is nothing more than a handkerchief you can blow your nose into afterwards, her mother had said, looking as if she knew what she was talking about.

Which she did, of course. Her mother had had three men, none of whom had been worth keeping, if she understood the situation correctly. Certainly not her father. She bit her lip and pushed him away. He laughed, sounding slightly embarrassed.

'I like you a lot, Wim,' she said. 'I really do. But you must go now, or you'll miss your bus.'

'I like you a lot as well,' he said. 'Your hair . . .'

'My hair?'

'You have such amazingly beautiful hair. If I were a little insect, I would want to live in it.'

'Oh, come on!' she said with a smile. 'Are you suggesting that I've got nits?'

'Of course not!' He grinned broadly. 'I just mean that if I die before you do, I hope to be resurrected as a little insect and come and live in your hair. So that we'd be together despite everything.'

She turned serious.

'You shouldn't talk like that about death,' she said. 'I like you so much, but please don't talk so casually about death.'

'I'm sorry,' he said. 'I didn't think . . .'

She shrugged. Her grandfather had died a month ago, and they had talked for a while about that.

'It's okay. I still like you a lot. I'll see you at school tomorrow.'

'Yes, I'll see you then. Anyway, I really must go now.'

'Would you like me to come to the bus stop with you?'

He shook his head. Opened the door into the porch.

'Don't be silly. It's only twenty metres from your front door.'

'I like you a lot,' said the girl.

'And I like you a lot as well,' said the boy who was about to die. 'An awful lot.'

She gave him one last hug, and he hurried off down the

stairs.

The man who would soon kill somebody couldn't wait to get home.

To his bed or his bath, he wasn't sure which.

Probably both, he decided as he stole a glance at his wristwatch. First a lovely hot bath, then bed. Why say either–or when you could have both–and? For God's sake, he'd been sitting with these wimps for over four hours now . . . Four hours! He looked around the table and wondered if anybody else was thinking what he was thinking. Anybody who was as bored as he was.

It didn't seem so. The expression on most faces was jolly and exhilarated – due to some extent to the alcohol, of course; but it was apparent that they enjoyed one another's company. Six men in their prime, he thought. Successful and prosperous, reasonably so at least, by normal worldly standards. Perhaps Greubner looked a bit on the tired side, worn out; but that was doubtless because his marriage was on the rocks again . . . or maybe problems at work. Or why not both?

No, I've had enough, he decided, knocking back the remains of his brandy. Dried the corners of his mouth with the table napkin and made to stand up.

'I think I ought to . . .' he began.

'Already?' said Smaage.

'Yes. Tomorrow is another day. There's nothing else on the agenda, is there?'

'Hmm,' said Smaage. 'Maybe another little conniyacky, how about that? Hmm?'

The man who would soon kill somebody stood up.

'I think I really must, no matter what . . .' he said again, purposely leaving the sentence unfinished. 'I wish all you gentlemen a very good night – don't sit up for too long.'

'Your very good health,' said Kuijsmaa.

'Peace, brother,' said Lippmann.

When he entered the foyer he suddenly felt he'd been right, he really had had enough. He had some obvious difficulties in putting his coat on, sufficiently obvious for the tattooed athlete behind the desk to come out and help him with it. It felt a little embarrassing, and he hurried down the steps and into the refreshing coolness of the night.

There was rain in the air, and the glistening black paving stones in the square bore witness to the fact that a shower had only just blown over. The sky seemed threatening; more rain was evidently on the way. He knotted his scarf, dug his hands into his pockets and started walking along Zwille towards Grote Square, where he had parked his car. A little walk is a good idea, he thought. A few hundred metres, and your head is a lot clearer. Just what the doctor ordered.

The clock on the Boodwick department store said twenty minutes past eleven as he passed by its lit-up entrance, but Ruyders Plejn was as dark and deserted as a forgotten churchyard. The mist had begun to settle on the Llanggraacht canal, and as he was walking over the Eleonora Bridge he slipped several times: the temperature must have fallen to zero or thereabouts. He reminded himself to be careful when he got to the car: slippery roads and alcohol in the blood was not a good combination. For a brief moment he considered hailing a taxi instead, but there was no sign of one and so he abandoned the thought. Besides, he would need the car tomorrow morning, and to leave it standing in Grote Square overnight was not an attractive prospect. Even if he had recently had a rather expensive alarm system installed, he had no illusions about what could happen. It would be a piece of cake for a few skilled thieves to break in, steal the stereo equipment and disappear into the night before anybody had a chance to stop them. That's a fact of life, he told himself with a sigh of resignation as he turned into Kellnerstraat.

Another thing to be taken into account was the fact that he had driven with a bit of alcohol in his blood before. More than once, to be honest, and he had never had any problems. As he crossed over the square and approached his red Audi, he tried to work out how much he had drunk during the evening, but he simply couldn't remember. He gave up, unlocked the car with the remote control and slumped down behind the wheel. Slipped four throat pastilles into his mouth and started thinking about that foam bath.

Eucalyptus, he decided he would choose. Checked his watch. It was twenty-eight minutes to twelve.

The bus zoomed past just as he emerged onto the pavement.

He raised his hand automatically, in an attempt to persuade the driver to stop. Then he launched into a long series of curses as he watched the rear lights fade away up the hill towards the university.

Shit! he thought. Why do they have to be dead on time tonight of all nights? Typical. Bloody typical.

But when he checked the time he realized that in fact he was five minutes late – so he had nobody to blame but himself.

Himself and Katrina. Mustn't forget her. Thinking of her made him feel better. He gritted his teeth and heaved up his rucksack, opened up his hood and adjusted it, then set off walking.

It would take him forty-five or fifty minutes, but he would be home by shortly after midnight no matter what.

No big deal. His mother would be sitting at the kitchen table, waiting for him – he could take that for granted, of course. Sitting there with that reproachful look she had perfected over the years, saying nothing but implying everything. But it was no big deal. Anybody could miss the last bus – it could happen to the best families.

When he came to the Keymer churchyard, he hesitated – wondering whether or not to take the short cut through it. He decided to skirt round it: it didn't look all that inviting in there among all the graves and the chapels, especially in view of the frosty mist creeping through the streets and alleys from the black canals. Intent on tucking the town into bed in its funeral shroud, it seemed. Once and for all.

He shuddered and started walking more quickly. I could have stayed, he thought out of the blue. Could have phoned Mum and stayed with Katrina. She'd have kicked up a fuss of course, but what could she have done about it? The last bus had already gone. A taxi would have been too expensive, and it was neither the time nor the weather for a young boy to be wandering around on his own.

Nor for his mum to be urging him to do so.

But these were mere thoughts. He pressed on notwith-standing. Through the municipal forest – along the sparsely lit path for cyclists and pedestrians, half-running if truth be told, and emerging onto the main road sooner than expected. He took a deep breath, and slowed down. Not far to go now, he thought. Just the long, boring walk along the main road – nothing to look forward to, to be honest. There wasn't a lot of room for pedestrians and cyclists. Just a narrow strip between the ditch and the road along which to walk the tightrope, and the cars travelled at high speed. There was no speed limit, and no street lighting to speak of.

Twenty minutes' walk along a dark road in November. He'd only walked a few hundred metres before a cold wind blew up and dispersed the mist, and it started pouring down.

Oh, shit! he thought. I could have been in bed with Katrina now. Naked, with Katrina pressed up against me, her warm body and caressing hands, her legs and her breasts that he had very nearly managed to touch . . . This rain must surely be a sign.

But he kept on walking. Kept on walking through the rain and the wind and the darkness, thinking about the girl who would be his first.

Would have been.

He had parked slightly askew, was forced to back out, and just when he thought he had managed it to perfection he bumped into a dark-coloured Opel, hitting it with his right rear wing.

Oh, bugger! he thought. Why didn't I take a taxi? He opened the door carefully and peered back. Realized that it was only a glancing blow and nothing to worry about. A mere bagatelle. He closed the door. Besides, he told himself, the windows were all misted up and he could hardly see out of them.

He didn't bother to work out just how relevant that was, but instead drove rapidly out of the square and down to Zwille with no difficulty. There wasn't much traffic about; he reckoned he would be home in a quarter of an hour, twenty minutes at most, and while he sat waiting for the traffic lights in Alexanderlaan to turn green he started wondering if in fact there was any of that eucalyptus bath gel left. He was slow to react when the lights changed, and stalled. Restarted in a hurry and raced the engine – this bloody dampness was causing havoc . . . Then he cut the corner as he turned and hit the traffic island.

Only with the front wheel, of course. Not much damage caused . . . None at all, to be precise. Keep a straight face and press on, he told himself – but it dawned on him that he was rather more drunk than he'd thought.

Damn and blast! he thought. I'd better make sure I don't drive off the road. It wouldn't be a good idea to . . .

He wound down the side window a couple of inches and turned the air conditioning up to maximum to get rid of the mist. Then drove commendably slowly for quite a while as he wormed his way through Bossingen and Deijkstraa, where there had not been a sighting of a traffic policeman for the last thirty-five years; and when he emerged onto the main road it became obvious that the danger of icy roads was non-existent. It had started to pour down: he switched on the windscreen wipers, and cursed for the fiftieth time that autumn for having forgotten to change the blades.

Tomorrow, he thought. I'll drive to the service station first thing tomorrow morning. It's madness, sitting here driving without being able to see anything properly.

Looking back, he could never work out if it was what he saw or what he heard that came first. But in any case, what persisted most clearly in his memory was the soft thud and the slight jerk of the steering wheel. And in his dreams. The fact that what flashed past in a fraction of a second on the extreme right of his visual field was linked with the bump and the minimal vibration he felt in his hands was not something that registered on his consciousness.

Not until he slammed on the brakes.

Not until afterwards – after the five or six seconds that must have passed before he drew to a halt and started running back along the soaking wet road.

As he ran, he thought about his mother. About an occasion when he was ill – it must have been just after he'd started school – and she'd sat there pressing her cool hand onto his forehead while he threw up over and over and over again: yellowish-green bile into a red plastic bucket. It was so devilishly painful, but that hand had been so cool and comforting – and he wondered why on earth he should think about that just now. It was a memory of something that had happened over thirty years ago, and he couldn't recall ever having remembered it before. His mother had been dead for more than ten years, so it was a mystery why she should crop up just now, and how he . . .

He saw him when he had almost run past, and he knew he was dead even before he'd come to a halt.

A boy in a dark duffel coat. Lying in the ditch. Contorted at impossible angles, with his back pressed up against a concrete culvert and his face staring straight at him. As if he were trying to make some kind of contact. As if he wanted to tell him something. The boy's face was partly concealed by the hood, but the right-hand side – the part that seemed to have been smashed against the concrete – was exposed like . . . like an anatomical obscenity.

He stood there, trying hard not to throw up. The same reflexes, the same old reflexes he'd felt thirty years ago, definitely. Two cars passed by, one in each direction, but nobody seemed to have noticed anything amiss. He had started shaking, took two deep breaths, and jumped down into the ditch. Closed his eyes, then opened them again after a few seconds. Bent down and tried to feel a pulse, on the boy's wrist and on his bloodstained neck.

No sign of a heartbeat. Oh hell, he thought, feeling panic creeping up on him. Bloody fucking hell – I must . . . I must . . . I must . . .

He couldn't work out what he must do. Cautiously, he slid his arms under the boy's body, bent his knees and lifted him up. He felt a stabbing pain at the bottom of his back: the boy was rather heavier than he'd expected. Perhaps the saturated clothes were adding to the problem. In so far as he'd expected anything at all. Why should he have done? The rucksack caused a bit of a problem. The rucksack and the boy's head. Both of them insisted on leaning backwards in a way that was quite unacceptable. He noted that the blood from the side of the boy's mouth was dripping straight down into his hood, and that he couldn't be more than fifteen or sixteen years old. A boy aged fifteen or sixteen . . . About the same as Greubner's son. You could tell by the sort of half-finished features of his face, despite the injuries. Quite a handsome boy, it seemed: no doubt he would develop into an attractive man.

Would have done.

He stood down there in the ditch with the boy's body in his arms for quite some time, while thoughts whirled around in his head. It was only a metre or so up to the road, but it was steep and the rain had made it slippery and treacherous: he doubted whether he would be able to get a sufficient foothold. No cars passed by while he stood there, but he heard a moped approaching. Or possibly a low-powered motorbike, he thought. When it passed by he could hear that it was in fact a scooter, and he was momentarily blinded by its headlight. Presumably – or so he thought later on with hindsight – presumably it was that very second of blinding light that started him functioning again.

Functioning, and thinking rational thoughts.

He lay the body down again next to the culvert. Wondered if he should wipe the blood from his hands onto the wet grass, but decided not to. Scrambled up onto the road, and hurried back to his car.

He noted that he must have automatically switched off the engine, but left the headlights on. Noted that the rain was pouring down like some sort of elemental force. Noted that he felt cold.

He slid down behind the wheel and closed the door. Fastened his safety belt and drove off. He could see rather better now through the windows, as if the rain had cleaned the inside of the glass as well.

Nothing has happened, he thought. Nothing at all.

He felt the first signs of a headache coming on, but

then he remembered his mother's cool hands again – and suddenly he was convinced that there was a drop left of that eucalyptus foam bath gel after all.

2

He woke up, and his first feeling was immense relief.

It lasted for three seconds, then he realized it had not been a nasty dream.

That it was reality.

The pouring rain, the sudden slight jerk of the steering wheel, the slippery ditch: it was all reality. The weight of the boy he was carrying in his arms, and the blood dripping into the hood.

He stayed in bed for another twenty minutes, as if paralysed. The only sign of life was the shudders that took possession of his body from time to time. They started in the ball of his foot, made their way up through his body and culminated in the form of white-hot flashes of lightning in his head: every time it felt as if some vital part of his brain and his consciousness had crumbled away. Frozen to death or burnt to a cinder, incapable of ever being revived to start working again.

Lobotomy, he thought. I'm being lobotomized.

When the insistent red figures on his clock radio had reached 07.45, he picked up the telephone and rang his place of work. Explained in a voice as fragile as newly formed ice on a mountain tarn that he was suffering from flu, and would have to stay at home for a few days.

Influenza, yes.

Yes, it was unfortunate – but that's life.

Yes of course, by all means ring if anything special cropped up.

No, he would stay in bed. Take a few tablets and drink lots of fluids.

Yes. Yes of course. No.

He got up half an hour later. Stood by the kitchen window and looked out at the gloomy suburban street, noting that the rain had faded away to be replaced by a heavy, grey, early-morning mist. As he stood there he entertained once more, slowly and gradually, a thought that he remembered from last night – and later, during the many hours he had lain awake, plagued by despair, before finally falling asleep.

Nothing has happened. Nothing at all.

He went out into the kitchen. There was an unopened bottle of whisky in the larder. Glenalmond, bought on holiday last summer. He unscrewed the top and took two large swigs. Couldn't remember having ever done that in his life before – drinking whisky straight from the bottle. No, never ever.

He sat down at the kitchen table, his head in his hands, and waited for the alcohol to spread throughout his body.

Nothing has happened, he thought.

Then started to make coffee and analyse the situation.

There was no mention in the morning papers. Neither in the *Telegraaf*, which he subscribed to, nor in the *Neuwe Blatt*, which he went out to buy from the kiosk. For a few seconds he almost managed to convince himself that it had all been a dream after all, but as soon as he remembered the rain and the ditch and the blood, he knew that it was wishful thinking. It was real. Just as real as the whisky standing on the table. As the crumbs around the toaster. As his hands, impotently and mechanically searching through the newspapers – he dropped them onto the floor, and returned to the bottle of whisky.

He had killed a young boy.

He had driven his car while under the influence of drink and killed an adolescent boy aged about fifteen or sixteen. He had stood there in the ditch and the rain with the boy's dead body in his arms – and then he'd abandoned him and driven home.

That's the way it was. Nothing to be done about it. No use crying over spilt milk.

It wasn't until a few minutes to ten that he switched on the radio, and heard confirmation in the ten o'clock news.

Young boy. Probably on his way home to Boorkhejm. Unidentified as yet.

But accurate details about the location.

Some time during the night. Probably between eleven and one. The body wasn't discovered until early this morning.

Death had most probably been instantaneous.

No witnesses.

Hit by a car – also most probably. The driver couldn't possibly have failed to notice what had happened. An appeal to all who had driven past the scene of the accident to come forward, and to anybody who thought they might have relevant information to tell. The police were very keen to contact everybody who . . .

The scene of the accident cordoned off, the rain had made police work more difficult, certain lines of investigation established . . . The police want to interview the driver who failed to stop . . . Renewed appeal to all who . . .

He switched off. Took two more swigs of whisky and went back to bed. Lay there for quite some time, his head swimming. But when he eventually got up again that misty Thursday morning, three thoughts had crystallized.

Three significant thoughts. Conclusions chiselled out in minute detail that he had no intention of compromising. Of abandoning, come what may. He had made up his mind, full stop.

First: the boy in the ditch was dead, and he was guilty of killing him.

Second: no matter what he did, he could not bring the boy back to life.

Third: there was nothing to be gained by giving himself up. Nothing at all.

On the contrary, he thought in connection with this number three. Why compensate for a ruined life by sacrificing another one? His own.

As he thought along these lines he knew that at long last he was on the right track. At long last he recognized himself again. At long last. It was just a matter of being strong. Not weakening.

That was all there was to it.

He devoted the afternoon to practical matters.

Washed the car in the garage, both inside and out. No matter how carefully he scrutinized the right side of the front and wing of the car, he could find no trace of any damage or marks: he assumed he must have hit the boy quite low down – at about knee height, with the bumper most probably, just a glancing blow. It seemed – when he tried to relive the scene down in the wet ditch – it seemed that the fatal outcome of the accident was due to the boy's hitting his head on the concrete culvert rather than contact with the car at road level. Which – in a rather strange, perverted way – made his guilt rather easier to accept. That's how it felt, at least. That's how he wanted it to feel.

Inside the car, on the driver's seat, was just one cause for concern: a dark oval-shaped stain, about the size of an egg, on the extreme right-hand edge of the beige-coloured upholstery. He had good reason to assume it must be blood, and he spent half an hour trying to scrub it away. But in vain: the stain would not go away, it had evidently penetrated the cloth through and through, and he decided to buy a set of seat covers before too long. Not immediately, but after a week or so, when the outcry after the discovery of the body had begun to fade away.

There were quite a lot of other traces of the boy's blood, on both the steering wheel and the gear lever, but it was no problem getting rid of them. As for the clothes he had been wearing the previous evening, he gathered them carefully together and burned them in the open fire in the living room, creating quite a lot of smoke. When he had finished, he was suddenly gripped by a moment of panic at the thought of somebody asking about them. But he calmed down quite quickly: it was of course highly unlikely that anybody would get onto his trail, or demand him to account for something so utterly trivial. A pair of ordinary corduroy trousers? An old jacket and a bluish-grey cotton shirt? He could have disposed of them in a thousand above-board ways – thrown them away, given them to a charity shop, all kinds of possibilities.

But most of all: nobody would get onto his trail.

Later in the afternoon, as dusk began to fall and it had started drizzling, he went to church. To the old Vrooms basilica a twenty-minute walk away from his home. Sat for half an hour in one of the side chancels, his hands clasped in prayer, and tried to open himself up to his inner voices – or to something more elevated – but nothing spoke to him, nothing made him feel uneasy.

When he left the deserted church, he realized how important it had been to make the visit, to take the trouble of sitting there in the chancel like that, with no specific intentions or aspirations. With no false pretences or motives.

Realized that it had been a sort of test, and that he had passed it.

It was remarkable, but the feeling was strong and unambivalent when he emerged from the dark building.

Something similar to catharsis. On the way home he bought two evening papers: both had a picture of the boy on their front page. The same picture, in fact, but in different sizes: a boy smiling cheerfully with dimples, slightly slant-eyed, dark hair combed forward. No hood, no blood. He didn't recognize him.

When he got home he read that the boy was Wim Felders, that he had celebrated his sixteenth birthday only a few days ago, and that he had been a pupil at Weger Grammar School.

Both newspapers were full of details, information and speculations, and the overall attitude that was perhaps summed up by the headline on page three of *Den Poost*:

HELP THE POLICE TO CATCH
THE HIT-AND-RUN DRIVER!

There was also a lot written about possible consequences if the police succeeded in tracing the culprit. Two to three years' imprisonment was by no means out of the question, it seemed.

He added in his alcohol consumption – which could no doubt be established by interviewing the restaurant staff – and increased the term to five or six years. At least. Drunken driving. Reckless driving and negligent homicide. Hit-and-run.

Five or six years under lock and key. What would be

the point of that? Who would gain from such a development?

He flung the newspapers in the rubbish bin and took out the whisky bottle.

3

He dreamt about the boy for three nights in a row, then he vanished.

Just as he'd vanished from the newspapers, generally speaking. They wrote about Wim Felders on Friday, Saturday and Sunday, but when the new working week began on Monday, reporting was restricted to a note saying that the police still had no leads. No witnesses had turned up, and no technical proof had been ascertained – whatever that meant. The young boy had been killed by an unknown driver who had then fled the scene, assisted in his efforts to remain anonymous by the rain and the darkness. This had been known from the start, and was still known four days later.

He also went back to work on Monday. It felt like a relief, but also an escape route to more normal routines. Life was trundling on once more along the same old pathways – familiar and yet also remarkably alien – and during the course of the day he was surprised to find himself pondering on how frail the link was between the mundane and the horrific.

How frail, and how incredibly easy to break. That link.

After work he drove out to the supermarket in Löhr and bought some new seat covers for his car. He found a set almost immediately in more or less exactly the same shade as the existing upholstery on the seats, and when he eventually managed to work out how to fit them in the garage later that evening, he had the feeling that he was home and dry at last. The parenthesis was over and done with now. The parenthesis around nothing. He had put in place the final element of the safety strategies he had evolved after long and careful consideration. All steps had been taken, all traces erased, and he was somewhat surprised to note that it was still less than a week after the accident happened.

And there was nothing for the police to hit on and follow up. He hadn't discovered the slightest thing to suggest that he ought to own up to what had happened during those fateful seconds on Thursday evening. Those horrific and increasingly unreal seconds that were rapidly hurtling away further and further into the darkness of the past.

He would pull through this. He took a deep breath and knew that he would pull through this.

To be sure, it had been claimed – both in some of the newspapers and in the television news broadcasts that he had happened to catch – that the police had certain leads that they were working on, but he realized that this was a lot of hot air. A heavy-handed attempt to give the impression that they knew more and were more competent than was really the case. As usual.

There had been no mention of a red Audi parked at the side of the road near the scene of the accident with its lights on. That is what he had been most afraid of: perhaps not that somebody would have noticed the colour or the make, never mind the registration number; but that they might have seen a vehicle parked there. Two cars had passed by while he was down in the ditch . . . or was it while he was still standing on the road? He couldn't remember that any more. But in any case he recalled quite clearly seeing two cars and a scooter. The driver of the car coming from the opposite direction to where he was heading – from Boorkhejm or Linzhuisen – might even had taken his Audi for an oncoming vehicle, he reckoned; but the other two surely must have registered that the car was parked on the edge of the road with its lights on.

Or was that the kind of thing that people forget all about? Bits of memory dust that only remain in the brain for a few seconds or half a minute at most, then vanish without trace for ever? Hard to say, hard to know, but definitely a question that kept him awake at night. These presumptive, latent pieces of evidence.

On Thursday, after a few days of silence in the media and a week after the accident, an appeal was made by the boy's family: his mother, father and a younger sister. They spoke on the television and the radio, and their pictures appeared in various newspapers. All they wanted was quite simply for the perpetrator to listen to his own conscience and make himself known.

Confess to what he had done, and take his punishment.

It seemed obvious that this move was yet another indication that the police were at a loss and had nothing to work on. No leads, no clues. When he watched the mother – a dark-haired, unexpectedly self-controlled woman of about forty-five – sitting on her sofa and looking him in the eye from his television screen, he felt distinctly uneasy; but the moment she disappeared from the screen, he immediately regained his composure. Acknowledged that from time to time he was bound to be subjected to such attacks of anxiety, but that he would always have the strength to pick himself up again. To find a way out of his weakness. As long as he kept his head.

It was good to know that he had it, that he possessed this essential quality. Strength of mind

Nevertheless he would have liked to talk to her.

Why? he had asked himself.

What would be the point of putting me in jail for five years?

I have killed your son, I regret it with all my heart – but it was an accident, and what would be gained by my contacting the police?

He wondered what her answer would have been. Would she have had anything to reproach him for? The whole business was an accident, and accidents don't have any culprits. No active participants at all, just factors and objects beyond control.

Later that evening he also toyed with the idea of sending an anonymous message to the family. Or just ringing them up and explaining his point of view. But he realized it was too risky, and he dismissed any such thoughts.

He also dismissed the alternative of trying to arrange for a wreath to be delivered for Wim Felders' funeral, which took place in a packed Keymer Church on the Saturday ten days after the accident.

For the same reason. The risks.

Apart from relatives and friends, the congregation comprised most of the pupils and teachers from Weger Grammar School plus representatives of various traffic organizations. He read about this in great detail in the

Sunday issue of the *Neuwe Blatt*, but that was also the final large-scale news coverage of the case.

To his surprise he found that on Monday he felt strangely empty.

As if he had lost something.

Like when I lost Marianne, he thought later on, similarly surprised; it was an odd comparison, but then, he needed to relate it to something. Something important in his life. For ten days the horrific happenings had been dominating his whole existence. Seeping into every nook and cranny of his consciousness. Even if he had managed to take control of his panic relatively quickly, it had been present all the time. Lurking, ready to break out. His thoughts had been centred on that hellish car journey almost every second. That slight thud and the jerk of the steering wheel; the rain, the lifeless body of the boy and the slippery ditch . . . Always present in the background, day and night: and now at last when he was starting to have periods when he didn't think about it, it felt in a way as if something was missing.

A sort of emptiness.

Like after an eleven-year-long childless marriage . . . Yes, there were definitely similarities.

During this period it occurred to him that he must be

some kind of hermit. Since Marianne left me, nobody has really meant anything to me. Nobody at all. Things happen to me, but I don't make anything happen. I exist, but I don't live.

Why haven't I found myself a new woman? Why have I hardly ever asked myself that question? And now, suddenly, I'm somebody else.

Who? Who am I?

The fact that such thoughts should start occurring to him after he'd run over a young boy was remarkable in itself, of course, but something prevented him from digging too deeply into the situation. He decided instead to take things as they came, and to do something about it for once, and break new ground. And before he knew where he was – before he'd had time to think about it and perhaps have second thoughts – he had invited a woman round for dinner. He happened to meet her in the canteen: she had come to sit at his table – there was a shortage of space, as usual. He didn't even know if he'd seen her before. Probably not.

But she'd accepted his invitation.

Her name was Vera Miller. She was cheerful and red-haired, and on the Saturday night – just over three weeks since he had killed another human being for the first time in his life – he made love to another woman for the first time in almost four years.

*

The next morning they made love again, and afterwards she told him that she was married. They discussed it for a while, and he realized that the fact worried her much more than it worried him.

The letter arrived on Monday.

Some time has passed since you murdered the boy. I have been waiting for your conscience to wake up, but I now realize that you are a weak person who doesn't have the courage to own up to what you have done.

   I have irrefutable evidence which will put you in jail the moment I hand it over to the police. My silence will cost you ten thousand – a piffling amount for a man of your stature, but nevertheless I shall give you a week (exactly seven days) to produce the money. – Do the necessary.

   Looking forward to hearing from you.

   A friend

Handwritten. With neat, sloping letters. Black ink.

He read it over and over again, five times.

4

'Is something bothering you?' Vera Miller asked as they were eating their evening meal. 'You seem a bit subdued.'

'No.'

'Are you sure?'

'It's nothing,' he assured her. 'I just feel a bit out of sorts. I think I have a temperature.'

'I hope it's nothing to do with me? With us, I mean.'

She swirled the wine in her glass and eyed him solemnly.

'No, of course not . . .'

He tried to laugh, but could hear that he produced a rasping sound. He took a swig of wine instead.

'I think it's all started so well, you and me I mean,' she said. 'I so much want there to be a second chapter, and a third as well.'

'Of course. Forgive me, I'm a bit on the tired side – but it's nothing to do with you. I think the same as you . . . I promise you that.'

She smiled and caressed his arm.

'Good. I'd almost forgotten that making love could be as enjoyable as this. It's incredible that you've been lying fallow for four years. How could that happen?'

'I was waiting for you,' he said. 'Shall we go to bed?'

When she left him on Sunday, he found himself longing for her almost immediately. They had made love until well into the early hours, and it was just as she had said: it was almost incredible that it could be as satisfying as this. He crept back into bed and burrowed his head into the pillow. Breathed in her scent and tried to go back to sleep, but in vain. The vacuum was too vast. This really was amazing, bloody amazing.

The biggest difference in the world, he thought. That between a woman still in your bed, and a woman who has just left. A woman you love. A new woman?

He gave up after a while. Went to collect the newspaper, had breakfast and then took out the letter again.

It wasn't necessary, of course. He knew it off by heart. Every single formulation, every single word, every single letter. Nevertheless, he read it through again twice. Felt the paper – high-quality stuff, no doubt about it; and the letter paper and envelope the same design. Thick, hammered paper: he guessed it had been bought in one of the bookshops in the city centre where you could buy by the sheet rather than in packs.

Sophisticated nuances as well. Pale blue. Stamp with a sporting motif – a woman swinging round before throwing a discus. Meticulously placed in the top right-hand corner of the envelope. His name and address handwritten with the same slightly sloping letters as in the message itself. The name of the place underlined.

That was all. All there was to say about it. Nothing, in other words. Or almost nothing, to be precise. It didn't even seem possible to establish the writer's sex. He tended to think it was a man, but that wasn't much more than a guess. Could be either.

Ten thousand? he thought for the hundred-and-fiftieth time since Monday evening. Why only ten thousand?

It was a considerable sum of money, to be sure, but still – as the letter-writer very rightly pointed out – not exactly a preposterous demand. He had more than twice that in the bank, and he owned a house and various other assets worth ten times that amount. The blackmailer had also used the expression 'a man of your stature', suggesting that he was familiar with his circumstances and financial status.

So why only ten thousand? Perhaps not 'a piffling amount', but a cheap price even so. Very reasonable, considering what was involved.

A pretty well-educated person too, it seemed, this letter-writer. The handwriting was neat and tidy, there were no grammatical errors, the wording was clear and concise. No doubt the person concerned ought to have (must have?) known that he would have been able to squeeze out more. That the price for his silence was low.

He kept returning to that conclusion. And looking back, he was also surprised by how easy he found it to sit there reasoning with himself along such comparatively rational lines. The letter had arrived like a bomb; but as soon as he'd been able to get used to and accept the fact of its existence, it was the logical and relevant questions arising that occupied his mind.

All week, and now on Sunday afternoon.

So, why only ten thousand?

What were the implications? Was it just a first instalment?

And who? *Who* had seen him, and was now exploiting the opportunity of earning money from his accident? And the boy's?

Was it the scooter rider, or one of the two motorists who had passed by while he was standing in the ditch, holding the lifeless body in his arms? Or up on the road.

Were there any other possibilities? He didn't think so.

In any case, what gave him away must have been the car, his red Audi – he soon decided that this must be the case. Somebody had seen it parked in an unusual place, memorized the registration number and traced the owner via the licensing authority.

He was convinced that this is what must have happened. Increasingly convinced. He soon decided that there was no other possibility – until a dreadful thought struck him.

Perhaps the boy hadn't been alone that evening. Perhaps there had been two young people, for instance, walking along the side of the road, but it was only Wim who had hit his head against the concrete culvert.

A bit further away, perhaps a couple of metres on the other side of the culvert, there might have been a girlfriend lying dazed . . . No, not a girlfriend: he'd read in the paper that the boy's girlfriend had stayed behind in town. More likely a friend, or somebody he'd just met, walking in the same direction . . . Lying there unconscious, hidden in the darkness. Or in a state of shock, and scared stiff by the sight of the dead boy and the man holding his body in his arms, with blood dripping down into the boy's hood . . .

It was an horrific scenario, of course, and even if he managed to convince himself eventually that it wasn't all that likely, it kept on recurring. He made a purely clinical effort to erase this macabre variation – this unlikely possibility – since it was of no consequence, no matter what.

Irrelevant. It didn't matter who it was who'd seen him that fateful night, nor exactly how the person concerned had found out what had happened. It was the other questions that demanded his attention and concentration.

And resolve.

So, could he be sure that this would be all that was demanded?

Ten thousand. That he would be able to pay that off, then not need to worry about it any more?

Aye, there's the rub. What guarantee did the letter-writer intend to give, proving that when he (she?) had collected and vanished with the cash, there wouldn't be a demand for a bit more after a month or so? Or a year?

Or that the blackmailer wouldn't simply go to the police and report him in any case?

Would any guarantee be given? What could such a guarantee be like?

Or – and this was of course the most important question – should he not accept that the situation was impossible? Should he not realize that the game was up, and it was time to hand himself in to the police?

Was it time to surrender?

By Sunday evening he still hadn't answered any of these questions. The fact that on Friday he'd slunk into the Savings Bank and withdrawn eleven thousand from his account could not necessarily be regarded as a decision.

Merely as a sign that he was still keeping all doors open.

He also had in the back of his mind the conversation they'd had on Saturday.

'Your husband?' he'd asked as they came back to the car after their stroll along the beach. 'Have you told him?'

'No,' she'd said, letting her hair hang loose after having it tucked away inside her woolly hat. Ran her hands through it and shook it in a movement he thought she was exaggerating in order to give herself time to think. 'I didn't know how serious things were going to become with you . . . Not to start with, that is. Now I know. But I haven't had a chance to talk to him yet. It sort of needs time and space.'

'Are you quite sure?'

'Yes.'

'That you want to divorce him?'

'Yes.'

'Why haven't you got any children?'

'Because I chose not to have any.'

'With your husband, or at all?'

She made a vague gesture with her head. He gathered she'd rather not talk about it. They stood in silence for a while, watching the choppy sea.

'We've only been married for three years. It was a mistake from the very beginning. It was idiotic, in fact.'

He nodded.

'What's his job?'

'He's unemployed at the moment. Used to work for Zinders. But they closed down.'

'That sounds sad.'

'I've never said it was especially funny.'

She laughed. He put his arm round her shoulders and hugged her close.

'Are you sure you're not wavering?'

'No, I'm not,' she said. 'I don't want to live with him, I've known that all the time.'

'Why did you marry him in the first place?'

'I don't know.'

'Marry me instead.'

It slipped out before he could stop himself, but he realized immediately that he actually meant it.

'Wow,' she said, and burst out laughing. 'We've been together a couple of times, and at long last you ask me to marry you. Shouldn't we go home and have a bite to eat first, as we'd planned to do?'

He thought it over.

'I suppose so,' he said. 'Yes, you're right. I'm ravenous.'

★

During the rest of the evening he hadn't repeated his offer

of marriage – but nor had he retracted it. He liked the idea of it hanging in the air, as it were, without their needing to address it or comment on it. It was a sort of string between them that didn't need to be plucked, but which was there nevertheless, binding them together. He also had the impression that Vera had nothing against it. That she felt more or less the same.

A sort of secret. A link.

And when they had sex later, it was as if they had drunk from the well of love.

Incredible. In a way, it was incredible.

How could life take off in entirely different directions without warning? Directions which turned all the habits one had acquired, all one's powers of reason and all one's worldly wisdom upside down? How was it possible?

And to cap it all, in just a few weeks. First that horrific Thursday evening, then Vera Miller and true love. He couldn't understand it. Was it possible to understand it?

He spent most of the rest of that Sunday evening lying on the sofa with just one candle lit, thinking about how he seemed to be being hurled from one extreme to the other. Between feelings of doubtful, confusing, inadequate conceptions of reality on the one hand, and a very calm and rational interpretation of his existence on the other.

Reason and emotions, but without connections, without synapses.

He eventually decided that despite appearances to the contrary, there was only one reality and that applied constantly: his feelings regarding it and his attempts to control it might vary, but it was only the point of view that varied. The perspective.

Two sides of the same coin, he thought. Like a toggle-switch. The mundane and the incomprehensible. Life and death? The thin band that separated them.

Remarkable.

After the eleven o'clock news on the radio he took out the letter again. Read it one more time before sitting down at his desk again. Sat there for a good while in the darkness, giving free rein to his thoughts, and soon – very soon – he began to discern another way of approaching things when he had previously comprehended only two.

A third way. It appealed to him. He sat there for a long time, trying to weigh up its advantages and disadvantages.

But it was still too soon to choose. Much too soon. Until he had received more detailed instructions from 'A friend', all he could do was wait.

Wait for the next day's postal delivery.

5

He was twenty minutes early. While he waited behind the wheel of his car in the almost empty car park, he read the instructions one more time. Not that it was necessary – he'd been rereading them all day: but it was a way of passing the time.

The money: *banknotes in bundles of fifties and one hundreds packed in double plastic bags and placed inside a carrier bag from the Boodwick department store.*

Place: *Trattoria Commedia at the golf course out at Dikken.*

Time: *Tuesday, six p.m. exactly.*

Instructions: *Sit down in the bar. Order a beer, take a few swigs, go to the gents after about five minutes. Take the carrier bag containing the money with you, leave it well camouflaged by paper towels in the rubbish bin. If there are others in the gents, wait until they have gone. Then leave the toilets, go straight out to your parked car and drive away.*

That was all.

The same sort of paper as last time. The same hand-writing, presumably the same pen.

The same signature: *A friend*.

No threats. No comments about his weakness.

Nothing but the necessary instructions. It couldn't be any simpler.

At two minutes to six he opened the side window and got out of the car. He had parked as far away from the restaurant as possible, next to the exit. Without seeming to hurry, he walked quickly the fifty or so metres over the windswept gravel to the restaurant. It was low and L-shaped, its façade plastered with dark pebble-dash. Gaudi windows with black steel frames. He opened the imitation jacaranda door and went in.

It looked pretty deserted, but nevertheless inviting. He had never set foot in the place before: he assumed it was probably a favourite haunt of golfers, and that it could hardly be high season, given the chilly late-autumn weather. The bar was on the left as you entered: a lone woman in her forties sat smoking in the company of an evening newspaper and a green drink. She looked up when he came in, but decided that the newspaper was more interesting.

Before sitting down he peered into the restaurant sec-tion. It branched off at right-angles to the bar, and most of the tables he could see were empty. An unaccompanied man was busy eating a pasta dish. A fire was crackling away in the hearth. The furniture and fittings were a mixture of dark brown, red and green, and a piano sonata was struggling to find its way out of hidden speakers. He put the carrier bag down at his feet and ordered a beer from the bartender, a young man with a ponytail and a ring in one ear.

'Still windy, is it?' asked the barman.

'It certainly is,' he replied. 'You're not exactly jam-packed this evening, it seems.'

'You can say that again,' said the barman.

His beer was served in a tapered effeminate-looking glass. He paid, drank about half of it and asked where the gents was. The bartender pointed towards the open fire, he thanked him, picked up the bag and made his way there.

It smelled of pine forests and was strikingly empty. And clean. The bin between the two washbasins was only a third full of used paper towels. He put the Boodwick carrier bag into the bin and covered it over with new paper towels that he pulled out of the holder one by one, crumpling them up slightly. All in accordance with the instructions. The whole procedure took ten seconds. He remained standing there for another ten, contemplating with some surprise his reflection in the slightly scratched mirror over the washbasin. Then he left the room. Nodded to the barman as he made his way to the door and continued to his car. There was a tang of frozen iron in the air.

So far so good, he thought as he sat down again behind the wheel. A piece of cake, dammit.

Then he opened the glove box and took out the metal pipe.

He only needed to wait for exactly six-and-a-half minutes.

The man who emerged from the restaurant seemed to be in his thirties. He was tall and lanky, carrying the bag with his right hand and dangling a set of car keys from his left. He was obviously heading for an old Peugeot about twenty metres away from his own car. One of the total of five vehicles standing in the large car park.

Before the man opened the car door, he had time to reflect on how amateurish the procedure was. Waiting for such a short time and then marching out into the car park with the bag in full view – surely that indicated pretty poor judgement? It seemed obvious that his opponent was easy game, despite what he had thought previously – and most importantly, that the man had seriously underestimated his own calibre.

He caught up with him just as he was about to insert the keys into the lock.

'Excuse me,' he said. 'I think you dropped something.'

He held up his cupped hand half a metre in front of the man's face.

'What is it?'

He glanced quickly around the car park and beyond. It was growing darker by the second now. There was not a soul in sight. He hit the man on the head with the pipe, using all his strength. Caught him just over his left ear. He fell to the ground without a sound. Flat on his stomach with his arms underneath him. This time he aimed at the back of the man's head, and hit him with full force once again. There was a short crackling sound, and he knew the man was dead. If he hadn't already died from the first blow. Blood was pouring profusely from the man's head. He carefully detached the casualty from the carrier bag and the car keys, stood up straight and looked around.

Still no sign of life. The place was dark and deserted. After a couple of seconds' thought, he took hold of the man's feet and dragged him into the thick undergrowth that surrounded the car park. There were clear marks left in the gravel, but he assumed that the rain would soon cover them up. He took a few steps backwards and established that nothing could be seen from a few metres away. At least, not for somebody who didn't know what he was looking for. Or that there was anything to look for in the first place.

He nodded in satisfaction and returned to his own car.

It would do no harm if it was a few days before anybody came across the body. The more days, the better, in fact. He wrapped the pipe in a newspaper and put it into the carrier bag together with the money.

Started the engine and drove off.

He kept his bushy black hair, his beard and his blue-tinted spectacles on until he had passed that fateful concrete culvert on the main road to Boorkhejm, and half an hour later when he was pouring himself a tot of Glenalmond in a plain glass tumbler in his kitchen at home, he offered up thanks to those Sobran tablets – those little blue miracle pills that had kept him calm and in complete control of himself all afternoon. And the previous few days as well. It was not a disadvantage to have a certain degree of insight into one's own mind and its need of psychopharmacological drugs, he thought. No disadvantage at all.

He emptied his glass.

Then took a long, relaxing bubble bath.

Then he phoned Vera Miller.

TWO

TWO

6

It was a certain Andreas Fische who found the body.

It happened on the Thursday afternoon. Fische had been visiting his sister in Windemeerstraat out at Dikken (a pain in the neck if truth be told, but blood is thicker than water and she had managed to marry a pretty wealthy lawyer), and he had taken a shortcut over the car park at the Trattoria Commedia, stopped for a pee, and noticed that there was something lying in among the bushes.

Fische finished peeing, and looked around. Then he bent aside some thorny branches and peered into the undergrowth. There was a man lying there. A body. A dead body.

Fische had seen dead bodies before. On several occasions during his rather colourful life; and having overcome his first impulse – which was to get the hell out of there – he allowed his better and more practically inclined self to take command. He checked once again to make sure there was nobody around in the dimly lit car park, then bent down carefully and moved aside several more branches – making a point of not treading on the soft, damp soil and leaving a footprint – he was no wide-eyed innocent – and took a closer look at the corpse.

Quite a young and rather tall man. Lying on his stomach with his arms stretched out peacefully over his head. Dark-green jacket and blue jeans. The side of his face turned upwards was covered in dark, dried-out stains, and Fische guessed that somebody had put an end to the man's life by hitting him on the head with something hard and heavy. Just like that, without any fuss. He'd seen that sort of thing before, even if it was quite a few years ago now.

Checking once again to make sure there was nobody about, he leaned down and started going through the man's pockets.

It only took a few seconds, and his booty was rather meagre. He established this fact after putting a couple of hundred metres between himself and the body. A battered wallet containing no credit cards and a small amount of cash in notes and coins. An almost empty packet of cigarettes and a lighter. A bunch of four keys and a business card from some pharmaceutical company or other. That was all. He threw it all into a litter-bin apart from the money and the cigarettes, made a rapid calculation of his current financial situation and decided that despite everything, he had a decent sum to get by on. Together with the hundred he'd wheedled out of his sister, he had more than enough for a night out at the pub, and he was feeling quite pleased with himself when he boarded the number twelve tram to the town centre. Without a ticket, of course. Andreas Fische hadn't bought a tram ticket for the past thirty years.

Klejne Hans, on the northern side of Maar, was one of his favourite haunts. That was where Fische usually spent the evening when he had enough money to paint the town red, and that was where he headed for that drizzly Thursday in November. The place was almost empty – it was only just turned six, and he sat by himself at one of the long tables with a beer and a whisky. Tried to make the drinks last as long as possible while he smoked the dead man's cigarettes and wondered whether he ought to inform the police straight away. One has duties as a citizen, as they used to say. Then three or four of his friends turned up, and as usual Fische put the matter off until later. No point in rushing things, he told himself. God didn't create hurry, and there's no way the bloke's going to come back down to earth to create it now.

And when Fische tumbled into his rickety bed in the run-down lodging house in Armastenstraat at getting on for one o'clock in the morning, he had various things buzzing around inside his head – but none of them was a dead body in a deserted car park out at Dikken, nor did he hear any stern voices from what remained of his withering conscience.

The next day, a Friday, was wet and miserable. He spent most of it in bed, feeling ill and hungover; and so it was Saturday morning before Andreas Fische rang the police from one of the free public telephones at Central Station, and asked them if they were interested in a tip-off.

Yes, of course they were, he was told – but they were not prepared to pay for it, he should be quite clear about that from the start.

Fische considered the odds briefly. Then his sense of civic responsibility took over and he informed them without charge that there was a dead body out at Dikken. In the car park near the golf course, outside that restaurant whose name he bloody well couldn't remember.

Murdered, if he wasn't much mistaken.

When the police officer began asking for his name and address and all that stuff, Fische had already hung up.

'How long?' asked Chief Inspector Reinhart.

'Hard to say,' said Meusse. 'I can't say for certain yet.'

'Have a guess,' Reinhart suggested.

'Hmm,' said Meusse, glancing at the body on the large marble slab. 'Three or four days?'

Reinhart considered.

'So Tuesday or Wednesday, then?'

'Tuesday,' said Meusse. 'But that's pure speculation.'

'He looks pretty worn out,' said Reinhart.

'He's dead,' said Meusse. 'And it's been raining.'

'Yes, yes,' said Reinhart.

'But I expect you've been indoors, Chief Inspector?'

'Whenever possible,' said Reinhart. 'Only two blows, you said?'

'Only one is needed,' said Meusse, running his hand over his own bald head. 'If you know where to aim.'

'And the murderer knew that?'

'Perhaps,' said Meusse. 'But it's only natural that you would hit him about there. Near his temple. The other blow, on the back of his head, is more interesting. Rather more professional. Broke the cervical spine. You can kill a horse with a blow like that.'

'I'm with you,' said Reinhart.

Meusse went over to the washbasin in the corner of the room and washed his hands. Reinhart remained by the slab, contemplating the dead body. A man in his thirties, it seemed. Perhaps slightly younger. Quite thin and quite tall – 186 centimetres, Meusse had said. The man's clothes were lying on another table and seemed to be very ordinary: blue jeans, a green half-length windcheater, a thin and quite worn-out woollen jumper that had once been light grey and still was here and there. Simple brown deck shoes.

No identity papers. No wallet, no keys, no personal belongings at all. Somebody had emptied his pockets, that was obvious.

Somebody had killed him by hitting him on the temple and the back of his head with a blunt instrument, that was equally obvious.

Ah well, Reinhart thought. Here we go again.

Meusse cleared his throat and Reinhart gathered it was time for him to go and leave the pathologist in peace. Before leaving he took a final look at the dead man's face.

It was long and thin. Rather haggard with a broad mouth and heavy features. Long hair, pulled back from behind the ears and tied in a ponytail at the back of his head. Dark stubble and a little scar just underneath his left eye. There was something familiar about him.

I've seen you before, Reinhart thought.

Then he left the Forensic Laboratories and returned to the police station.

Detective Inspector Ewa Moreno put the photographs back into the folder and slid it across the table to Reinhart.

'Nope,' she said. 'He's not on the list. We've only had notice of three disappearances this week, incidentally. A senile old woman from a care home in Löhr and a fifteen-year-old boy who's run away from home.'

Rooth finished chewing away at a biscuit.

'Three,' he said. 'You said three.'

'Yes, I did,' said Moreno. 'But the third one's a snake. I think we can exclude that one as well.'

'A snake?' said Jung.

'A green mamba,' explained Moreno. 'Apparently it escaped from a flat in Kellnerstraat during the night between Monday and Tuesday. Highly dangerous, according to the owner. But friendly. It can kill a human being in two seconds. Answers to the name of Betsy.'

'Betsy?' said Rooth. 'I used to have a girlfriend called Betsy. She wasn't very friendly, but she went missing as well . . .'

'Thank you for that information,' said Reinhart, tapping his pipe on the table. 'I think that's enough to be going on with. Tropical snakes are unlikely to survive for several days in this kind of weather, no matter what. But you'd have thought that somebody would have missed the young man we've found by now. If Meusse is right, that is . . .'

'Meusse's always right,' insisted Rooth.

'Don't interrupt,' said Reinhart. 'If Meusse is right, our

man has been lying there in that undergrowth since last Tuesday – most people don't wait for more than a day or two at most before they ring us . . . The nearest and dearest, that is.'

'If there are any,' said Moreno. 'Nearest and dearest, I mean.'

'Lonely old blokes can lie dead for six months before anybody notices nowadays,' said Jung.

'Yes, that's how it is now,' said Reinhart with a sigh. 'And not only old blokes. I read about a woman in Gosslingen who continued to receive her pension for two-and-a-half years after she died. She was lying in the cellar, and her pension was paid directly into her bank account . . . Huh, that's the world we live in . . . Jung, what did they have to say for themselves at that restaurant?'

Jung opened his notebook.

'I've only spoken to a few of the people who work there,' he said 'Nobody recognized him from the photographs, but tomorrow afternoon we're due to meet a couple of the staff who were on duty last Tuesday. If that's really when it did happen, it's not impossible that they might be able to identify him. Or at least to tell us whether he's been there for a meal.'

'Anything else?' asked Reinhart, lighting his pipe.

'Yes, that car,' said Jung. 'There's apparently been an old Peugeot parked there since last Tuesday or Wednesday.

We've checked up on it and it's owned by somebody called Elmer Kodowsky. Unfortunately we haven't been able to get hold of him. According to the caretaker in the block of flats where he lives, he works on an oil platform somewhere out in the North Sea.'

'Brilliant,' said Reinhart. 'It's probably lovely weather out there at this time of year. Any volunteers?'

'Mind you, the caretaker indicated that he might be a bit closer to home in fact,' said Jung. 'But in any case it wasn't Kodowsky lying there in the undergrowth.'

'What do you mean?' wondered Rooth. 'Talk so that we can understand what you're on about.'

'Jail,' said Jung. 'Kodowsky isn't one of God's chosen few, according to the caretaker, so it's not impossible that the business of being away on an oil platform is just another way of saying that in fact he's in prison somewhere. It's happened before, it seems.'

'Hmm,' said Reinhart. 'That sounds better. Check up on all the prisons . . . Or maybe Krause should do that. But if he is in clink, this Kodowsky, he'd presumably have found it a bit hard to drive his car out to Dikken and park there, wouldn't he?'

'Parole,' said Jung. 'Or he might have lent it out . . . Or somebody might have stolen it.'

'Not impossible,' admitted Reinhart, blowing out a cloud of smoke. 'Although if it's an old banger it's unlikely anybody would want to pinch it. Car thieves are pretty choosy nowadays. No, I don't think we're going to get any further right now. Or has anybody got anything they want to say?'

Nobody had. It was a quarter past five on Saturday afternoon, and there were better times for small talk and speculations.

'Okay, we'll meet again for a couple of hours tomorrow morning,' Reinhart reminded them. 'If nothing else the fingerprints should be sorted out by then. Not that there's likely to be any that will be of use to us. But let's hope we get a bit more info from Meusse and the forensic boys in any case. By the way . . .'

He took the photographs out of the yellow folder once again and eyed them for a few seconds.

'Does anybody think they recognize him?'

Jung and Rooth looked at the pictures and shook their heads. Moreno frowned for a moment, then sighed and shrugged.

'Maybe,' she said. 'There might be something there I recognize, but I can't put my finger on it.'

'Okay,' said Reinhart. 'Let's hope the penny drops. There's no denying that it's an advantage if you know who the victim is. That applies to all types of investigation. Here's wishing all my colleagues a perfect Saturday evening.'

'Thank you, and the same to you,' said Moreno.

'The first of many,' said Rooth.

'Can I offer you a beer?' asked Rooth a quarter of an hour later. 'I promise not to rape you or to make advances.'

Ewa Moreno smiled. They had just emerged from the main entrance of the police station, and the wind felt like an ice machine.

'Sounds tempting,' she said. 'But I have a date with my bathtub and a third-rate novel – I'm afraid it's binding.'

'No hard feelings,' Rooth assured her. 'I also have a pretty good relationship with my bathtub. She's as bad at the tango as I am, so I assume we'll end up together again. It makes sense to make the best of what you've got.'

'Wise words,' said Moreno. 'Here comes my bus.'

She waved goodbye and scampered over the parking area. Rooth checked his watch. He might just as well go back in and sleep in his office, he thought. Why the hell should anybody want to go wandering around out of doors at this time of year? Sheer madness.

Nevertheless, he started walking towards Grote Square and his tram stop, wondering how long it was since he'd last cleaned his bathtub properly.

Well, it certainly wasn't yesterday, he decided.

7

The phone call came at 07.15 on Sunday morning, and it was Constable Krause who took it. He thought at first that it was a strange time to ring the police – especially as he began to suspect what it was all about and that she must have been holding back for at least four days – but then he gathered from her voice that she couldn't have had very many hours' sleep during that time. If any.

So perhaps it wasn't all that odd.

'My name's Marlene Frey,' she began. 'I live in Ockfener Plejn, and I want to report a missing person.'

'I have a pen in my hand,' said Krause.

'It was last Tuesday evening,' explained Frey. 'He said he was just going out to see to something. He promised he'd be back later in the evening, but I haven't heard from him since and he doesn't usually . . . It's not like him to—'

'Hang on a minute,' interrupted Krause. 'Could you please tell me who it is you are referring to? His name and appearance, what he was wearing, that sort of thing.'

She paused, as though she was composing herself. Then he heard her take a deep breath, heavy with anxiety.

'Yes, of course, forgive me,' she said. 'I'm rather tired, I haven't slept a wink . . . Not for several nights, I'm afraid.'

'I understand,' said Constable Krause, and then he received all the details he needed. It took two minutes at most, but after the call was completed Krause remained seated at his desk for five times as long, staring at the information he had written down and trying to make sense of it.

When he was forced to accept that this was not possible, he picked up the phone again and rang Chief Inspector Reinhart.

Synn put her hand over the receiver for a moment before handing it to Münster. Mouthed a name, but he couldn't make it out. He forced himself up into a half-sitting position, and took the receiver.

'Reinhart here. How are things?'

'Thanks for asking,' said Münster. 'It's been quite a while.'

'Are you still in bed?' Reinhart asked.

'It's Sunday,' Münster pointed out. 'It's not even nine o'clock yet. What's on your mind?'

'Something bloody catastrophic has happened,' said Reinhart. 'I need your help.'

Münster thought for a couple of seconds.

'Are you *that* short of staff?' he asked. 'I'm still tied up with that inquiry, have you forgotten that? I won't be back at work until February at the earliest.'

'I know,' said Reinhart.

'What's it all about, then?'

There was silence for a few seconds. Then Chief Inspector Reinhart cleared his throat and explained what had happened.

'Hell's bells!' said Münster. 'I'll be with you in a quarter of an hour. Of course I shall help.'

'Let's take the long way there,' said Reinhart. 'I need a bit of time.'

'So do I,' said Münster. 'How did it happen?'

'A heavy blow to the head,' said Reinhart. 'Manslaughter or murder, probably the latter.'

'When?'

'Tuesday, it seems.'

'Tuesday? It's Sunday today.'

'They only found him yesterday. He didn't have any papers on him that could identify him. I thought I recognized him, but I've only ever seen him once or twice . . .

Anyway, that woman rang this morning to report him missing. She's already been to identify him. There's no doubt about it, unfortunately.'

Münster said nothing, studied the movement of the windscreen wipers.

Oh hell! he thought. Why did something like this have to happen? What's the point?

He knew they were futile questions, but the fact that they always cropped up might indicate something even so. Something to do with hope and positivism. A sort of refusal to surrender to the powers of darkness? Perhaps that was a way of looking at it, perhaps that was how one should interpret that eternal *why*.

'Have you had much contact with him lately?' Reinhart asked when they had crossed the river and started to approach the high-rise apartment buildings out at Leimaar.

Münster shrugged.

'A bit,' he said. 'About once a month. We usually have a beer now and again.'

'No badminton?'

'Twice a year.'

Reinhart sighed deeply.

'How is he?'

'Not too bad, I think. So far. He's found himself a woman as well.'

Reinhart nodded.

'I'm grateful to you for agreeing to join me.'

Münster made no reply.

'Bloody grateful,' said Reinhart. 'I don't know if I'd be able to cope with it on my own.'

Münster took a deep breath.

'Let's get it over with,' he said. 'There's nothing to be gained by putting it off any longer. Have you rung to check that he's at home?'

Reinhart shook his head.

'No. But he's at home all right, I can feel it. This isn't something we can avoid.'

'No,' said Münster. 'We can't. Nor can he.'

There was a shortage of parking places around Klagenburg. After circling the block a few times Reinhart finally found a space on the corner of Morgenstraat and Ruyder Allé, but they had to walk a couple of hundred metres through the rain before they were able to ring the bell on the door of number four.

At first there was no reaction from inside; but after a second more insistent ring, they could hear somebody coming down the stairs. Before the door opened, Münster noted that despite the wet conditions his mouth was absolutely dry, and he began to wonder if he would be in a fit state to force even a single word past his lips. The door opened slightly.

'Good morning,' said Reinhart. 'May we come in?'

Van Veeteren was dressed in something dark blue and red that presumably was – or had been – a dressing gown, and something brown that was certainly a pair of slippers. He didn't look as if he had just woken up, and was carrying a newspaper folded up under his arm.

'Reinhart?' he exclaimed in surprise, and opened the door wide. 'And Münster? What the hell?'

'Yes,' Münster managed to utter, 'you can say that again.'

'Come in,' said Van Veeteren, gesturing with the newspaper. 'All this bloody rain is a pain. What's the matter?'

'Let's sit down first,' said Reinhart.

They all walked up the stairs, the visitors were ushered into the cosy-looking living room and flopped down into armchairs. Van Veeteren remained standing. Münster bit his lip and plucked up courage.

'It's your son,' he said. 'Erich. I'm sorry, but Reinhart says he's been murdered.'

Looking back, he was convinced that he'd closed his eyes as he said that.

8

When Jung and Rooth parked outside the Trattoria Commedia at about two o'clock on Sunday afternoon it had stopped raining for the moment. Two forensic officers were still working on the abandoned Peugeot, supervised by Inspector le Houde: the car had been cordoned off by red-and-white police tape, as had the spot where the body was found some ten metres away. Plus a narrow corridor between the two. Rooth paused and scratched his head.

'What do they think they'll find in the car?'

'I've no idea,' said Jung. 'He'd had it on loan for a few months from that jailbird mate of his – maybe he's involved as well in some way?'

'It can't have been Elmer Kodowsky who bashed his head in,' said Rooth. 'He hasn't been out on parole for eight weeks – it would be hard to get a better alibi than that.'

'I dare say you're right,' said Jung. 'Shall we go in and attack the barman then, or do you intend standing here and searching for nits a bit longer?'

'I've finished now,' said Rooth. 'God, but I don't like this bloody business. I don't like it when crimes affect one of us. Somebody like VV should have the right to immunity, for fuck's sake.'

'I know,' said Jung. 'Don't go on about it. Let's go in and do our job, then we can go for a coffee somewhere.'

'All right,' said Rooth. 'I'm with you there.'

The barman's name was Alois Kummer, and he looked anything but happy.

He was young, suntanned and athletic-looking, so Jung didn't really understand why. They sat down opposite him in the bar, which was deserted – as long as no customers turned up they might just as well sit here and talk. Both Jung and Rooth agreed on that, and apparently herr Kummer as well, as he made no objection.

'So you were on duty last Tuesday evening, is that right?' Jung began.

'Only until nine o'clock,' said Kummer.

'Let's concentrate on that time,' said Rooth. 'Did you have many customers?'

Kummer displayed his teeth. They looked strong and healthy, and presumably were expressing an ironic grin.

'How many?' asked Jung.

'A dozen or so,' said Kummer. 'At most. Can I get you anything?'

Jung shook his head. Rooth laid out the photographs on the counter.

'What about this person?' he asked. 'Was he there? Don't answer until you're sure.'

The barman studied the pictures for ten seconds, pulling at his earring.

'I believe so,' he said.

'You believe so?' echoed Rooth, 'Are you religious?'

'I like it,' said Kummer. 'Yes, he was here. He sat eating at one of the tables through there. I didn't pay much attention to him.'

'At what time?" asked Jung.

'Between five and six, or thereabouts . . . Yes, he left at about a quarter past six, just before Helene arrived.'

'Helene?' said Jung.

'One of the girls in the kitchen.'

'Have you got something going with her, then?' Rooth wondered.

'What the hell has that got to do with it?' said Kummer, starting to look annoyed.

'You never know,' said Rooth. 'Life is a tangle of remarkable connections.'

Jung coughed and changed the subject.

'Was he alone, or was there anybody else with him?' he asked.

'He was on his own,' said Kummer without hesitation.

'All the time?' Rooth asked.

'All the time.'

'How many diners did you have altogether? Between five and six o'clock, that is.'

Kummer thought for a moment.

'Not many,' he said. 'Four or five, perhaps.'

'It doesn't seem to be high season just now, does it?' said Rooth.

'Would you like to play golf in weather like this?' Kummer wondered.

'Golf?' said Rooth. 'Isn't that a sort of egg-rolling on a lawn?'

Kummer made no reply, but the tattoo on his forearm twitched.

'He didn't come over here to sit in the bar, then?' said Jung, trying to get the interview back on course. 'For a drink or whatever?'

Kummer shook his head.

'How many were there in the bar?'

'Two or three, perhaps . . . I don't recall for certain. One or two customers popped in and only stayed for a couple of minutes, I think. As usual.'

'Hmm,' said Jung. 'When he left – this lone diner, that is – you didn't notice if anybody followed him, did you? Very soon afterwards, I mean?'

'No,' said Kummer. 'How the hell would I be able to remember that?'

'I don't know,' said Jung. 'But the fact is that he was killed out there in the car park only a few minutes after leaving here, so it would help us a lot if you could try to remember.'

'I'm doing my best,' Kummer assured them.

'Excellent,' said Rooth. 'We don't want to demand the impossible of you. Is there anything at all that evening that you recall? Something that was different, somehow or other? Or remarkable?'

Kummer pondered again.

'I don't think so,' he said. 'No, everything was as usual. It was pretty quiet.'

'Had he ever been here before, this person?' asked Jung, tapping his pen on the photographs.

'No,' said Kummer. 'Not while I've been working here, at any rate.'

'You seem to have a good memory for faces.'

'I usually remember people I've met.'

'How long have you been working here?'

'Three months,' said Kummer.

Rooth noticed a bowl of peanuts a bit further along the

bar counter. He slid off his chair, and went to take a hand-ful. The bartender observed him with a sceptical frown. Jung cleared his throat.

'That car,' he said. 'The Peugeot out there in the car park – that's been there all the time since Tuesday, has it?'

'They say so,' said Kummer. 'I never gave it a thought until today.'

'You're better at faces than at cars, is that right?'

'That's right,' said Kummer.

'What was the weather like last Tuesday evening?'

Kummer shrugged.

'Overcast, I suppose. And windy. Mind you, the bar is indoors, as you may have noticed.'

'You don't say,' said Rooth, taking the rest of the peanuts.

'How do you get here?' Jung asked. 'Do you also use the car park? I mean, you don't live in Dikken, do you?'

Kummer shook his head and displayed his teeth again.

'I generally come by tram,' he said. 'I sometimes get a lift with Helene or one of the others. But none of the staff uses the car park. There are a few private parking places round the back.'

'How many staff are there here?' Rooth asked.

'A dozen or so,' said Kummer. 'But only three or four of us are on duty at any one time. As we've already said, it's low season at this time of year.'

'Yes, as we've already said,' said Rooth, looking round the deserted bar. 'So you don't know who the murderer is, then?'

Kummer stood up straight.

'What the hell do you mean? Of course I don't bloody well know. It's not our fault if somebody gets attacked in our car park.'

'Of course not,' said Rooth. 'Anyway, thank you for your cooperation, but we'd better be moving on now. We might well be back.'

'Why?' asked Kummer.

'Because that's the way we work,' said Jung.

'Because we like peanuts,' said Rooth.

Moreno and Reinhart went together to Ockfener Plejn on Sunday evening. It was only a few blocks from the police station, and despite the wind and the driving rain, they went on foot.

'We need to give our minds a good soaking and blow away all the dust,' explained Reinhart. 'And it would be no bad thing if our internal and external landscapes were in harmony.'

'How did he take it?' Moreno asked.

Reinhart thought it over before answering.

'I don't know,' he said. 'I'll be damned if I know. But he

didn't have much to say for himself, that's for sure. Münster found it hard to cope. It's such a bloody mess.'

'Was he on his own?'

'No, he had his new woman with him, thank God.'

'Thank God for that,' agreed Moreno. 'Is she okay?'

'I think so,' said Reinhart.

They came to the old square, and located the property. One of a row of cramped houses with high, narrow gables: pretty run-down, filthy frontages and badly maintained window frames. A few steps led up to the front door, and Moreno pressed the bell push next to the hand-printed name plate.

After half a minute and a second ring, Marlene Frey opened the door. Her face seemed to be a little swollen, and her eyes were about three times as red and tearful as they had been when Moreno interviewed her in her office at the police station that morning. Nevertheless, the frail-looking woman displayed signs of willpower and strength.

Moreno noted that she had changed her clothes as well. Only a different pair of jeans and a yellow jumper instead of a red one, it was true: but perhaps that indicated that she had begun to accept the situation. Understood that life must go on. Nor did she give the impression that she had been taking sedatives – although that was hard to judge, of course.

'Hello again,' said Moreno. 'Have you managed to get any sleep?'

Marlene Frey shook her head.

Moreno introduced Reinhart, and they went up the stairs to the second floor.

Two small rooms and a cramped, chilly kitchen, that was all. Wine-red walls and a minimum of furniture, mainly big, colourful floor cushions to sit or lie down on. A few big, green plants and a couple of posters. In the bigger room two wicker chairs and a low stool stood in front of a calor gas stove. Marlene Frey sat down on the stool, and invited Moreno and Reinhart to sit on the wicker chairs.

'Can I offer you anything?'

Moreno shook her head. Reinhart cleared his throat.

'We know that this is extremely difficult for you,' he said. 'But we have to ask you a few questions even so. Say if you don't feel up to it, and we can come tomorrow instead.'

'Let's get it over with now,' said Marlene Frey.

'Have you got anybody staying with you?' Moreno asked. 'A girlfriend, for instance?'

'A friend is due this evening. I'll get by, you don't need to worry.'

'So you lived here together, is that right?' Reinhart asked, moving a bit closer to the stove. It was evidently the only source of heat in the whole flat, so it was important not to be too far away from it.

'Yes,' said Frey, 'we live here. Or lived . . .'

'How long had you been together?' Moreno asked.

'Two years, more or less.'

'You know who his father is, I take it?' said Reinhart. 'It's not relevant, of course, but it makes it all rather more unpleasant from our point of view. Even if—'

'Yes, I know,' said Frey, interrupting him. 'They didn't have much contact.'

'We'd gathered that,' said Reinhart. 'Was there any at all? Contact, that is?'

Frey hesitated before answering.

'I've never met him,' she said. 'But I think . . . I think things were getting a bit better recently.'

Reinhart nodded.

'Did they meet at all?' Moreno wondered.

'Erich went to see him a few times during the autumn. But that's irrelevant now.'

Her voice shook a little, and she stroked the palms of her hand quickly over her face, as if to switch it off. Her red hair looked dyed and not very well cared for, Moreno noted, but there were no obvious signs of drug abuse.

'Let's concentrate on last Tuesday,' said Reinhart, taking out his pipe and tobacco, and receiving an encouraging nod from Marlene Frey.

'Erich drove out to that restaurant in Dikken,' said Moreno. 'Have you any idea why?'

'No,' said Frey. 'No idea at all. As I said this morning.'

'Was he working?' Reinhart asked.

'A bit of this, a bit of that,' said Frey. 'He did odd jobs as a carpenter and painter and labourer . . . On various building sites and similar. Most of it was the black economy, I'm afraid, but that's the way it is nowadays. He was good with his hands.'

'What about you yourself?' Moreno asked.

'I'm attending a course for the unemployed. Economics and IT and that kind of crap, but I get a grant for doing it. I do the odd hour in shops and supermarkets when they're short-staffed. We get by in fact . . . Or got by. Financially, that is. Erich worked at a printing works as well now and then. Stemminger's.'

'I understand,' said Reinhart. 'He had a bit of form, if one can put it like that . . .'

'Who doesn't?' said Frey. 'But we were on the straight and narrow, I want you to be quite clear about that.'

It looked for a moment as if she were about to burst into tears; but she took a deep breath and blew her nose instead.

'Tell us about last Tuesday,' said Reinhart.

'There's not a lot to say,' said Frey. 'I attended my course in the morning, then I worked for a few hours in the shop in Kellnerstraat in the afternoon. I only saw Erich here at home between one and two – he said he was going to help somebody with some boat or other, and then he had something to see to in the evening.'

'A boat?' said Reinhart. 'What sort of a boat?'

'It belongs to a good friend,' said Frey. 'I assume he was helping with fitting it out.'

Moreno asked her to write down the friend's name and address, which she did after consulting an address book she fetched from the kitchen.

'That something he had to see to in the evening,' said Reinhart when the boat business was over and done with. 'What was that about?'

Marlene Frey shrugged.

'I don't know.'

'Was it a job?'

'I assume so.'

'Or something else?'

'What do you mean by that?'

'Well . . . Something that wasn't a job.'

Frey took out her handkerchief and blew her nose again. Her eyes narrowed.

'I understand,' she said. 'I understand exactly what's going on. It's only for his celebrated father's sake that you're sitting here being so damned polite to me. If it weren't for that you'd treat him like any other yob you care to name. And you'd treat me like a drugged-up whore.'

'Steady on . . .' said Moreno.

'You don't need to put on a show,' said Frey. 'I know the score. Erich had a lot on his conscience, but he's packed all that in during the last few years. Neither of us shoot up nowadays, and we're no less law-abiding than anybody else. But I suppose it's a waste of time trying to make the fuzz believe that?'

Neither Moreno nor Reinhart responded. Marlene Frey's outburst remained hanging for a while in the warm silence over the calor gas stove. But this was shattered when a tram clattered past in the street outside.

'Okay,' said Reinhart. 'I understand what you're saying and you may be right. But now we're where we are, and it's a bit bloody annoying if we get told off for treating people decently for once . . . I think we know where we stand now, without going on and on about it. Shall we continue?'

Marlene Frey hesitated for a moment, then nodded.

'Dikken,' said Reinhart. 'Why did he have to go there? You must have some idea, surely?'

'It could've been anything at all,' said Frey. 'I suppose you're fishing for something to do with drugs, but I can swear that it had nothing to do with that. Erich gave all that stuff up even before we started living together.'

Reinhart gave her a long, hard look.

'All right, we'll accept that,' he said. 'Was he going to

get something out of it? Money, I mean . . . Or was he just going to meet a friend out there, for instance? Or do somebody a favour?'

Frey thought for a while.

'I think it was a job,' she said. 'Some sort of job.'

'Did he say he was going out to Dikken?'

'No.'

'Nor what it was about?'

'No.'

'Not even a hint?'

'No.'

'And you didn't ask?'

Frey shook her head and sighed.

'No,' she said. 'Erich and I could have seven or eight different jobs in any given week – we hardly ever talked about it.'

'Did he say when he'd be back?' asked Moreno.

Frey thought that over again.

'I've been thinking about that, but I'm not sure. I had the impression he'd be back home at around eight or nine in any case, but it's not definite that he actually said that. Who bloody cares anyway?'

She bit her lip, and Moreno saw that her eyes had filled with tears.

'Cry,' she said. 'It's possible to cry and talk at the same time, you know.'

Frey immediately heeded this advice. Moreno leaned forward and stroked her arm somewhat awkwardly, while Reinhart squirmed uncomfortably in his chair. Fumbled with his pipe and managed to light it.

'Names?' said Moreno when the sobbing became less violent. 'Did he name any names in connection with what he was going to do last Tuesday evening?'

Frey shook her head.

'Do you know if he'd been there before? If he went there regularly?'

'To Dikken?' She couldn't help laughing. 'No, it's not exactly our kind of place out there, wouldn't you say?'

Moreno smiled.

'Had he been worried about anything recently? Had anything special happened that you could possibly link with the accident?'

Frey wiped her eyes with the sleeve of her jumper and thought again.

'No,' she said. 'Nothing I can think of.'

'Had he met any new acquaintances lately?'

'No. Erich knew an awful lot of people . . . Of all kinds, you might say.'

'I understand,' said Reinhart. 'This Elmer Kodowsky, for instance, whose car he borrowed?'

'For instance, yes,' said Frey.

'Have either of you had any contact with him lately?'
She shook her head.

'He's inside. I don't know where. He was an old friend of Erich's, I've never met him. I've only seen him once or twice.'

'And you yourself haven't felt threatened in any way?' Moreno asked.

'Me?' said Frey, looking genuinely surprised. 'No, definitely not.'

There followed a brief silence. Frey leaned forward, closer to the stove, and rubbed the palms of her hands together in the waves of heat floating upwards.

'You waited for rather a long time before contacting the police,' said Reinhart.

'I know.'

'Why?'

She shrugged.

'Perhaps it's the way it is in cases of this sort. Or what do you think?'

Reinhart said nothing.

'Had either of you any contact with Erich's mother?' asked Moreno.

'No,' said Frey. 'None at all. But I would like to speak to his father – please tell him that if you happen to see him.'

'Really?' said Reinhart. 'What do you want to say to him?'

'I'll tell him that when I see him,' said Frey.

*

Afterwards they spent some time in Cafe Gambrinus, trying to sum up their impressions.

'Not much in the way of lines to follow up yet,' said Reinhart. 'Or what do you think? Damn and blast.'

'No, not a lot,' said Moreno. 'Although it does seem as if he had a date with his murderer out at Dikken. Even if he didn't really know what was going to happen. The odd thing is that he sat in the restaurant by himself, waiting. Assuming we can trust what Jung and Rooth say, that is. That could suggest that the person he was waiting for didn't turn up according to plan.'

'Possibly,' said Reinhart 'But it could have happened much more straightforwardly, we mustn't forget that.'

'What do you mean?' said Moreno, taking a sip of her mulled wine.

'A no-frills robbery,' said Reinhart. 'A junkie with a hammer who thought he could do with a bit of cash. The victim's pockets were emptied, even his fags and keys were nicked – that ought to tell us something.'

Moreno nodded.

'Do you think that's what happened?' she asked.

'Maybe, maybe not,' said Reinhart. 'Besides, it doesn't need to have been the same person – the one who killed him and the one who went through his pockets, that is. The character who rang to report finding the body didn't exactly give the impression of being a blue-eyed innocent, did he?'

'Hardly,' said Moreno. 'But in any case, I'm inclined to think it wasn't just a case of a mugging that went wrong. I reckon there's more to it than that – but whether or not I think that because of who the victim was, I don't know . . . I suppose it's a bit warped to think along those lines.'

'A lot of thinking is warped when you look closely at it,' said Reinhart. 'Intuition and prejudice smell pretty much alike in fact. But we can start off with this, no matter what.'

He took out the well-thumbed address book Marlene Frey had lent them – on condition they returned it as soon as they had copied it.

'This must mean that they really were on the straight and narrow path nowadays,' said Moreno. 'Who hands a whole address book over to the police of their own accord if they have something on their conscience?'

Reinhart leafed through the book and looked worried.

'There's a hell of a lot of people in here,' he said with a sigh. 'I think we'd better talk to her again and get her to narrow it down a bit.'

'I'll do that tomorrow,' Moreno promised. 'Anyway, I think I ought to be moving on. I don't think we're going to lay any golden eggs this evening.'

Reinhart looked at the clock.

'I'm sure you're right,' he said. 'But one thing is crystal clear in any case.'

'What's that?' wondered Moreno.

'We must solve this. If we don't solve another single bloody case between now and the next century, we must make absolutely certain that we sort out this one. That's the least we can do for him.'

Moreno leaned her head on her hands and thought.

'If it were anybody else, I'd think you were nattering on in the spirit of romanticized boy scout mentality,' she said. 'But I must admit that I agree with you. It's bad enough as it is, but it'll be even worse if we let the murderer get away with it. Will you be contacting him tomorrow? I suppose he'll want to know how things are going.'

'I've promised to keep him informed,' said Reinhart. 'And I shall do just that. Whether I want to or not.'

Moreno nodded sombrely. Then they emptied their glasses, and left the cafe and the town and the world to their fate.

For a few hours, at least.

9

He woke up and looked at the clock.

A quarter to five. He had slept for twenty minutes.

Erich is dead, he thought. It's not a dream. He's dead, that's reality.

He could feel his eyes burning in their sockets. As if they wanted to force their way out of his head. Oedipus, it occurred to him. Oedipus Rex . . . Wandering around blind for the rest of my life, seeking God's grace. Perhaps that would be an idea. It might give things a meaning. Erich is dead. My son.

It was remarkable how the same thought could fill up the whole of his consciousness, hour after hour. The same three words – not even a thought, strictly speaking: just this constellation of words, as impenetrable as a mantra in a foreign language: Erich is dead, Erich is dead. Minute after minute, second after second; every fraction of every moment of every second. Erich is dead.

Or perhaps it wasn't remarkable at all. Presumably this

was exactly as it had to be. As it would always be from now on. This was the keystone for the rest of his life. Erich was dead. His son had finally taken possession of him: thanks to his death he had finally captured the whole of his father's attention and love. Erich. That's how it was. Quite simply.

I shall fall short, Van Veeteren thought. I shall fall to pieces and sink to the bottom, but I don't care. I ought to have made sure I died at the right time.

The woman by his side stirred and woke up. Ulrike. Ulrike Fremdli. The one who had become his woman despite all the uncertainties and convulsions of the mind. His convulsions, not hers.

'Have you slept all right?'

He shook his head.

'Not at all?'

'Half an hour.'

She stroked his chest and stomach with her warm hand.

'Would you like a cup of tea? I can go and make you one.'

'No thank you.'

'Do you want to talk?'

'No.'

She turned over. Crept up closer to him, and after a while he could hear from her breathing that she had fallen asleep again. He waited for a few more minutes, then got up cautiously, tucked the covers round her, and went out into the kitchen.

The red digital numbers on the transistor radio in the window said 04.56. It was still pitch black outside: only a few faint streaks of light from a street lamp fell onto the corner of the building on the opposite side of the street. Guijdermann's, the bakery that had closed down. The objects he could make out in the kitchen were wreathed in this same pale, shadowy half-light. The table, the chairs. The cooker, the sink, the shelf over the larder, the pile of copies of the *Allgemejne* in the basket in the corner. He opened the refrigerator door, then closed it again. Took a glass from a cupboard and drank some ordinary tap water instead. Erich is dead, he thought. Dead.

He went back to the bedroom and got dressed. As he did so, Ulrike moved restlessly in the bed but she didn't wake up. He stole out into the hall, closing the door behind him. Put on his shoes, a scarf and an overcoat. Left the flat and tiptoed down the stairs and out into the street.

Light rain was falling – or rather, drifting around to form a soft curtain of floating, feathery drops. The temperature must have been seven or eight degrees above freezing. No wind to speak of either, and the streets deserted – as if a long-awaited bomb attack were now imminent. Dark and self-absorbed, caught up in the all-embracing sleep of the surrounding buildings.

Erich is dead, he thought, and started walking.

He returned an hour and a half later. Ulrike was sitting in the murky kitchen, waiting for him with her hands wrapped round a cup of tea. He could sense an aura of reproachful worry and sympathy, but it affected him no more than a wrong number or a formal condolence.

I hope she can cope, he thought. I hope I don't drag her down with me.

'You're wet,' she said. 'Did you go far?'

He shrugged and sat down opposite her.

'I walked out towards Löhr and back,' he said. 'It's not raining all that hard.'

'I fell asleep,' she said. 'I'm sorry.'

'I needed to get out.'

She nodded. Half a minute passed: then she stretched her hands out over the table. Left them lying half-open a few centimetres in front of him, and after a while he took hold of them. Wrapped his own hands round them and squeezed them tentatively. He realized that she was waiting for something. That he needed to say something.

'There was an old couple when I was a little boy,' he began. 'They were called Bloeme.'

She nodded vaguely and looked enquiringly at him. He contemplated her face for a while before continuing.

'Maybe they weren't that old in fact, but they gave the impression of being the oldest people in the whole world. They lived in the same block as we did, just a few houses away from ours, and they hardly ever went out. You only ever saw them very occasionally on a Sunday afternoon . . . And when they appeared all games and all signs of life in the street came to a standstill. They always walked arm in arm on the shady side of the street, the husband always wore a hat, and there was an aura of deep sorrow around them. A cloud. My mother told me their story – I was no more than seven or eight, I should think. The Bloemes used to have two daughters, two pretty young daughters who travelled to Paris together one summer. They were both murdered under a bridge, and ever since, their parents stopped associating with other people. The girls came back home, each of them in a French coffin. Anyway, that was the story . . . We children always regarded them with the greatest possible deference. A hell of a lot of respect, in fact.'

He fell silent and let go of Ulrike's hands.

'Children shouldn't die before their parents.'

She nodded.

'Would you like a cup of tea?'

'Yes please. If you add a drop or two of rum.'

She stood up. Went over to the work surface and switched on the electric kettle. Searched round among the bottles in the cupboard. Van Veeteren remained seated at the table. Clasped his hands and rested his chin on his knuckles. Closed his eyes and once again felt his eyes throbbing in their sockets. A burning sensation inside them and up into his temples.

'I've experienced it before.'

Ulrike turned to look at him.

'No, I don't mean at work. It's just that I've imagined Erich's death many times . . . That it would be me who had to bury him instead of vice versa. Not lately, but a few years back. Eight or ten years ago. Imagined it pretty tangibly . . . The father burying his son − I don't know, perhaps it's something all parents do.'

She put two steaming hot cups down on the table, and sat down opposite him again.

'I didn't,' she said. 'Not in detail like that, at least. Why did you torture yourself with that sort of thing? There must have been reasons.'

Van Veeteren nodded, and took a cautious sip of the strong, sweet tea.

'Oh yes.' He hesitated a moment. 'Yes, there were reasons all right. One at least . . . When Erich was eighteen he tried to commit suicide. Swallowed enough tablets to have accounted for five or six fully grown people. A girlfriend found him and rushed him to hospital. But for her he would have died. That's over ten years ago now. I dreamt about it every single night for quite a while. Not just that vacant, desperate, guilt-laden expression on his face as he lay in bed at Gemejnte . . . I dreamt that he had succeeded in taking his own life, that I was putting flowers on his grave. And so on. It feels as if . . . as if I was practising for what's happened. It's reality now, and during those years I knew that it would be, one of these days. Or thought so, at least. I had almost managed to forget it, but we're there now. Erich is dead.'

He fell silent again. The newspaper boy or some neighbour or other passed by on the landing outside. Ulrike made as if to say something, but changed her mind.

'I tried to get into Keymerkyrkan while I was out walking,' Van Veeteren continued, 'but it was locked. Can you tell me why we need to keep our churches locked up?'

She stroked his hands gently. A minute passed. Two minutes. She was sitting there digesting his words, he realized that.

'Erich didn't die because he wanted to die,' she said eventually. 'That's an important difference.'

He didn't answer. Let go of her with his right hand and took a sip of tea.

'Perhaps,' he said. 'Perhaps that does make an important difference. I find it hard to decide that just now.'

Then silence again. The grey light of dawn had begun to creep in through the window. It was a few minutes past seven. The street and the town had woken up. To yet another November day. Life was about to start moving again.

'I don't have the strength to talk about it any more,' said Van Veeteren. 'I can't see the point of wrapping it up in a mass of words. Forgive me if I say nothing. I'm very grateful that you are here. Eternally grateful.'

'I know,' said Ulrike Fremdli. 'No, it's not about words. It's not about you and me at all. Shall we go back to bed for a while?'

'I wish it was me instead.'

'It's futile, thinking like that.'

'I know. Futility is the playing field of desire.'

He emptied his cup and followed her into the bedroom.

Renate rang at lunchtime: his ex-wife, the mother of his dead son. The call lasted twenty minutes: sometimes she was speaking, sometimes crying. When he replaced the receiver, he thought about what Ulrike had said.

It's not about you and me at all.

He decided he would try to bear that comment in mind. Ulrike had lost her husband in circumstances reminiscent of these: that was three years ago, and that was how they had first met. Van Veeteren and Ulrike Fremdli. There was a lot to suggest that she knew what she was talking about.

In so far as it was possible to know. At two o'clock he got into his car and drove out to Maardam's airport to collect Jess. She was overcome by despair even as she walked towards him in the arrivals hall: they fell into each other's arms and remained standing in the middle of the floor like that – for what seemed hours. Just stood there, in the midst of the usual hustle and bustle that was the norm at Sechshafen, swaying back and forth in wordless, timeless, mutual sorrow.

He and his daughter Jess. Jess with the seven-year-old twins and a husband in Rouen. Erich's sister. His only remaining child.

'I don't want to meet Mum yet,' she admitted when they came to the car park. 'Can we just drive somewhere and sit down for a bit?'

He drove to Zeeport, the little pub out at Egerstadt. Phoned Renate and explained that they would be a little late, then they spent the rest of the afternoon sitting opposite each other at one of the tables with a view over the dunes and the rain. And of the lead-grey sky that formed a sort of weighty dome over the windswept, barren stretch of coast. She insisted on keeping the fingers of one hand intertwined with his, even while they were eating; and like

Ulrike Fremdli she seemed to have understood that what was needed was not words.

That it wasn't about the two of them. That it was Erich, and what mattered was clinging on to him.

'Have you seen him?' she asked eventually.

Yes, he had been to the Forensic Science Clinic briefly on Sunday. He thought Jess should also go there. If she felt she wanted to. Possibly the next day – he would gladly go with her.

She also asked who had done it, and he explained that he didn't know.

Why?

He didn't know that either.

They left Egerstadt at half past five, and forty-five minutes later he dropped Jess off outside Renate's house in Maalerweg, where she would be staying for the time being. Renate came out onto the steps and hugged her daughter, sobbing loudly; but Van Veeteren merely took Jess's luggage out of the back seat, and arranged for the three of them to meet the following day. In the morning, so that perhaps they could go and take a look at Erich. Renate hadn't got round to doing that either; or perhaps hadn't had the strength.

When he got back home, there was a message from Ulrike on the kitchen table. It said that she loved him, and that she would be back by about nine o'clock. He made himself a wine toddy and sat down in the dark living room. Put a Penderecki CD on the hi-fi system, but switched it off after a couple of minutes.

Not words, he thought, and not music either. Erich is dead. Silence.

After three-quarters of an hour, Reinhart rang.

'How are things?' he asked.

'What do you expect?' said Van Veeteren.

'Are you on your own?'

'Just for the time being.'

There was a pause while Reinhart worked out what to say next.

'Would you like to talk about it? We could meet briefly tomorrow.'

'Maybe,' said Van Veeteren. 'I'll phone you in that case. Do you know who did it yet?'

'We have no idea,' said Reinhart.

'I want you to find him,' said Van Veeteren.

'We shall find him . . . There was another thing as well.'

'Another thing?' said Van Veeteren.

'Marlene Frey. His girlfriend. Have you met her?'

'I've spoken to her on the telephone.'

'She wants you to get in touch with her,' said Reinhart.

'I'll do that,' said Van Veeteren. 'Of course. Can I ask you to do me a favour?'

'I'm at your service.'

Van Veeteren hesitated for a few seconds.

'When you've got him . . . When you've found the killer, that is . . . I'd like to meet him.'

'Why?' Reinhart asked.

'Because that's the way things work. I'll let you know if I change my mind.'

'All right,' said Reinhart. 'Of course. You will meet him face to face, I promise you that.'

'The sooner, the better,' said Van Veeteren.

'I'll do whatever I can.'

'Thank you. I have faith in you,' said Van Veeteren.

10

'I couldn't care less what else you are busy with,' said Reinhart. 'I couldn't care less if you have to work three hundred hours overtime a week. I couldn't give a toss whatever you say or think – but this takes priority over everything else! *The Chief Inspector*'s son has been murdered: if somebody shoots the minister of home affairs or somebody rapes the Pope, those cases are mothballed until we've solved this one. Is that clear? Have you understood? Does anybody object? In which case he or she had better apply for a move somewhere else without more ado! Fuck, fuck, fuck! Off the record, that is.'

'I agree,' said Rooth.

Presumably everybody else did as well. At any rate, nobody spoke up. The atmosphere round the table was already stuffy. Reinhart had managed to cram four extra chairs into his office – there were plenty of larger rooms in the police station of course, but nowhere else where he could smoke to his heart's content: since their daughter was born he had come to an agreement with his wife only to smoke outside their home.

Anyway, there were seven officers leading the investigation. Inspectors Moreno, Rooth and Jung. Constable Krause, just as young and promising as usual. Intendent deBries and a newly appointed Detective-Sergeant Bollmert, on loan from Aarlach until Intendent Münster returned from his duties in connection with the official inquiry: Münster was taking it easy after being stabbed in the kidney while on duty ten months ago. And working too many long hours.

Plus himself, of course: Chief Inspector Reinhart, as he now was. Although whenever anybody spoke about the chief inspector, they were never referring to him – unless Chief of Police Hiller was trying to be ironic, or even simply amusing. *The Chief Inspector* always meant Chief Inspector Van Veeteren, who had been in charge of the Maardam CID for fifteen years, and its leading light for twice as long as that. But for over two years now he had descended from the Judicial Parnassus in order to freewheel down the path to his retirement as part-owner and shop assistant in Krantze's antiquarian bookshop in Kupinskis Gränd.

And good luck to him: nobody begrudged him the peace and quiet and the books, and nobody failed to miss him with a mixture of fear and trembling, respect and admiration.

And now he was once again involved in a case. *The Chief Inspector*. In the worst possible way . . . Not as a victim, but very nearly. His son had been murdered. Bloody hell! Reinhart thought. Bloody, fucking hell! Many times during his so-called career he had thought that things couldn't get any worse, nothing could be worse than this. But what had happened now was indeed worse. More infernally awful that he could ever have imagined.

I must try to suppress my personal fury, he thought. Must try to keep it at arm's length, otherwise it will only get in the way.

'We must try to ignore the involvement of *The Chief Inspector*,' he said. 'The way in which we are personally involved in this case through him. We must go about things in exactly the same way as we would do in any other case . . . Although we can give it the highest priority, of course. We *must* solve it. Or there'll be hell to pay. But we must be professional.'

He fumbled around and eventually produced the right sheet of paper from the piles on the table in front of him, and cleared his throat.

'Erich Van Veeteren was killed by two blows to the head with a blunt instrument. Either of the two blows could have been fatal. Especially the second one, which hit the back of his head, Meusse says . . . He ascribes to it a touch of professionalism. The weapon seems to have been rather heavy . . . Made of metal and with no protruding edges – perhaps a piece of piping or something of the sort. We haven't recovered it.'

'A pity,' said deBries. 'It would have made things easier.'

Reinhart stared at him for a moment before continuing.

'Time: Tuesday evening. In view of observations made in the Trattoria Commedia, probably shortly after 18.15. It seems that the killer struck in the car park, then dragged his victim into the bushes. The body lay there until Saturday, when we received a tip-off from a telephone caller. We can only guess what happened to whatever the victim had in his pockets. Either the murderer took them himself, or somebody else did. The somebody else could well be synonymous with our anonymous telephone caller. Clues? Leads? Motives? Not a thing! Any comments?'

'Was there any trace of drugs in his clothes?' wondered Sergeant Bollmert. Presumably in an attempt to make an impression, Reinhart thought. The ruddy-faced sergeant had only been in post in Maardam for a couple of weeks, and was especially keen to distinguish himself. That was nothing to hold against him, of course.

The fact that he had never met *The Chief Inspector* could perhaps also be seen as an advantage. Given the circumstances.

'Not in his clothes,' said Reinhart. 'Not in his blood, not in his hair or nails. We can no doubt confirm that his girl-friend was telling the truth about that. It's a pity he didn't tell her what he was going to do out at Dikken, so that we could have had her word on that as well.'

'The fact that he didn't do so suggests that whatever he was going to do wasn't entirely above board, don't you think?' said Rooth. 'He said nothing about it to the girl, nor to Otto Meyer, whose boat he had been working on earlier that afternoon.'

'Didn't he even say he was going to Dikken?' asked Moreno. 'To that Meyer character, that is.'

'Nope,' said Jung. 'Just that he'd have to leave at half past four as he had a little job to do.'

'Job?' said Reinhart. 'Did he actually use that word?'

Jung nodded.

'We pressed Meyer pretty hard on that point. Yes, he called it a "job". No doubt about it. Anyway, he left the boathouse down at Greitzengraacht a few minutes after half past four. They'd been doing some sort of refurbish-ing work in the cabin, and the intention was that they'd continue this week. It's a pretty smart boat, I have to say – eighteen metres, six bunks, teak panels, bar cupboard, the whole caboodle. Meyer's a bloody crook, of course, but one of the socially acceptable kind, nothing for us.'

'And he didn't have anything more he could tell us?' asked Reinhart.

'Not a squeak,' said Rooth.

Jung shrugged and looked apologetic. Reinhart sighed.

'Brilliant,' he said. 'Our case is about as substantial as a vegan on laxatives. Has anybody anything else to add?'

He knew the answer already, but looked round the room even so and tried to seem optimistic.

'The address book,' said deBries in the end.

'Precisely,' said Reinhart. 'On the ball as usual. How's it going?'

DeBries thrust his arms out wide and narrowly missed hitting Rooth on the chin.

'No need to converse in semaphore, you bloody idiot,' said Rooth.

Bollmert laughed nervously.

'It's going like clockwork,' said deBries, unrepentant. 'There are a hundred and forty-six private individuals listed in the book, and about fifty institutions or similar. Plus a dozen or so incomprehensible entries – crossings out, vague scribbles and suchlike. He's evidently had the book for six or seven years, that's what his girlfriend estimates anyway – although she's only known him for three. She's been able to identify thirty-five people so far: we'll start checking tomorrow.'

'Are there any people the pair of them knew who aren't in the book?' asked Jung.

DeBries shook his head.

'Not really. He's been pretty scrupulous, it seems. A bloke they met at a party only a few weeks ago is duly listed, for instance.'

'Hmm,' said Reinhart. 'So you reckon the murderer is in there somewhere, among all those names?'

'If it was somebody he knew, there's a pretty good chance.'

'Good,' said Reinhart. 'You have Moreno, Krause and Sergeant Bollmert to help you – and make bloody sure you are careful and don't miss anything. Meet 'em all face to face and record every single conversation. A bit of idle chatter on the phone isn't good enough, remember that. Prepare a list of questions to ask them all, and show it to me first. What their alibi is for last Tuesday, and so on. No kid gloves, right? Is that clear? It's all we've got to go on for the time being.'

'Crystal clear,' said deBries. 'I'm not an idiot.'

'That can be an advantage sometimes,' muttered Reinhart. He lit his pipe and blew a few thick clouds of smoke over those present.

'What about this girlfriend of his?' said Jung. 'Hadn't we better have a session with her? About the last few days, what they were doing and so on?'

'Of course,' said Reinhart. 'I'll look after that. Rooth and Jung can go back to the restaurant again – that should suit Rooth down to the ground. We'll have a press release tomorrow that will require every bastard who set foot in that restaurant to come forward. That always produces some kind of results . . . If you can't fish deep down, you have to cast your nets out wide.'

'Wise words,' said Rooth. 'Mind you, ugly fish swim deep, if I'm not much mistaken. Cod, for instance.'

'True,' said Bollmert, who was almost born on a trawler, but didn't think that was something to bring up here and now.

'What the hell have codfish got to do with this?' wondered Reinhart.

There followed a few seconds of silence while the team leader exhaled more clouds of smoke and the others watched.

'What do you think?' said deBries eventually. 'Surely we need to have some kind of theory as well? Why was he killed?'

Reinhart cleared his throat.

'I'll tell you that when I've mapped out this last week in rather more detail,' he promised. 'Young Van Veeteren was going to meet somebody out at Dikken. He was presumably going to earn a bit of pocket money as a result, and

I don't suppose he was going to sell Christmas magazines. That is what we have to sort out just now.'

'And he was clobbered,' said Rooth.

'By whoever he was going to meet, or by somebody else.'

'Could it be the geezer he borrowed the car from?' wondered Bollmert.

'I reckon we can count him out,' said Reinhart after two seconds' thought. 'He's in Holte jail, and as far as we know he and young Van Veeteren haven't been in touch for several months. And he hasn't been out on parole for ages either.'

'What's he in for?' asked Rooth.

'All kinds of things,' said Reinhart. 'Robbery and white slave trading, among other things. Illegal possession of weapons. Four years. Two-and-a-half left. More or less.'

'Okay,' said deBries. 'We'll count him out. Anything else? I'm hungry, I haven't eaten since last week.'

'Same here.' said Rooth.

Reinhart laid his pipe in the ashtray.

'Just one other thing,' he said, in a serious tone of voice. 'I spoke to *The Chief Inspector* yesterday evening and I promised him that we would solve this case. I hope you all understand how extraordinary this business is. I mean what I said at the start. We must sort it out. *Must!* Is that understood?'

He looked round.

'We're not idiots,' said deBries. 'As I said before.'

'It'll sort itself out,' said Rooth.

It's good to have a team with self-belief, Reinhart thought: but he didn't say anything.

Van Veeteren paused in the south-west corner of the long, narrow square. Ockfener Plejn. Shuddered, dug his hands down deeper into his overcoat pockets. Looked around. Until Saturday he hadn't known that this was where Erich lived – or had he in fact known in some subconscious way? They had met twice during the autumn: once at the beginning of September, and then again just over three weeks ago. Despite everything, he thought as he groped around after his cigarette roller, despite everything he had socialized a little with his son. Recently. He had received Erich in his home, and they had talked to each other like civilized human beings. That was definitely the case. Something was on its way: it wasn't clear exactly what, something confused and obscure of course, but something nevertheless . . . Erich had talked about Marlene Frey as well, but only in terms of a nameless young woman, as far as he could remember, and of course he might well have mentioned where they lived as well – why not? It was just that he couldn't remember.

So he lives here . . . Or lived here. Almost in the centre of the old town, in this run-down nineteenth-century block of flats whose dirty façade Van Veeteren was now staring at. On the second floor, almost at the top of the building. There was a faint light in the window overlooking the tiny balcony with its rusty iron railings. He knew that she was at home, and that she was expecting him: his dead son's fiancée whom he had never met, and he also knew – suddenly but with overwhelming certainty – that he wouldn't be able to go through with it. That he wouldn't be able to summon up the strength to ring the bell on that shabby front door with the paint flaking off. Not today.

Instead he looked at his watch. It was almost six. The darkness that had begun to envelop the town seemed to him to be freezing cold and hostile. There was a strange smell of sulphur or phosphorus in the air. He didn't recognize it, it somehow didn't belong here. There was a temporary breathing space in the otherwise constant downpour, but of course rain was never far away at this time of year. He lit a cigarette. Lowered his gaze, preferring not to ask himself if it was due to shame or to something else . . . and having done so he noticed a cafe on the opposite corner of the square, and when he had finished his cigarette, that is where he headed. Sat down with a glass of dark beer at a table by one of the windows where it was impossible for anybody to see out or in. Rested his head on his hands and thought back over the day.

Today. The third day he had woken up in the knowledge that his son was dead.

First of all an hour at the antiquarian bookshop, where he explained the situation to Krantze and they rearranged their working hours. He didn't dislike old Krantze, but they would never be more than business partners. Certainly not, but that's just the way it was.

Then he paid another visit to the Forensic Laboratories, this time together with Renate and Jess. He had stayed outside the door when they went into the refrigerated room. You only need to look at a dead son once, he had told himself. And he still thought that, as he sat in the cafe and tasted the beer. Only once: there were images that time and forgetfulness would never retouch. Which never needed to be reawoken because they never slept. Jess had been in control of herself when they came out again – with a crumpled handkerchief in each hand, but controlled all the same.

Renate was just as numb and apathetic as she had been when she went in. He wondered what tablets she was on, and how many.

A few minutes' conversation with Meusse as well. Neither of them had performed especially well. Meusse had looked as if he were about to burst into tears, and he didn't usually behave like that.

Soon afterwards he had introduced Jess to Ulrike. It was a bright spot in all the darkness, a meeting that went exceptionally well. Only half an hour in the living room at Klagenburg with a glass of wine and a salad, but that was enough. What mattered was not the words themselves, as had been said before . . . But there was something between women that he would never understand. Between certain women. When they said their goodbyes out in the hall, he had felt almost like a stranger: he was able to smile in the midst of all the grief.

Then he had rung Marlene Frey and arranged a meeting. She had sounded pretty much in control of herself, and said he was welcome to call round any time after five o'clock. She would be at home, and was looking forward to speaking to him. There was something she wanted to say, she said.

Looking forward? Something she wanted to say?

And now he was sitting here with feet colder than his beer. Why?

He didn't know. Knew only that it wouldn't work today, and after he had finished his beer he asked if he could use the telephone. Stood there between the ladies and gents toilets surrounded by a faint smell of urine, and rang his dead son's living fiancée to tell her that something had cropped up.

Would it be okay if he came tomorrow instead? Or the day after?

Yes, that was okay. But she had difficulty in hiding her disappointment.

So did he as he left Ockfener Plejn and started walking back home. Disappointment and shame.

I don't understand myself any more, he thought. It's not me that it's all about. What am I scared of, what the hell is happening to me?

But he went straight home.

Reinhart was woken up by Winnifred whispering his name. And placing a cold hand on his stomach.

'You're supposed to be putting your daughter to bed, not yourself.'

He yawned, and tried to do some stretches for a couple of minutes. Then he eased himself cautiously out of Joanna's narrow bed and out of the nursery. Flopped down on the sofa in the living room instead, where his wife was half-lying under a blanket at the other end.

'Let's hear it,' she said.

He thought for a while.

'Triple-headed and Satanic,' he said. 'Yes, that's exactly what it is. Would you like a glass of wine?'

'I think so,' said Winnifred. 'As we know, the Devil is triple-headed in Dante already, so all is in order.'

'In Dante's time women who knew too much were burnt at the stake. Red or white?'

'Red. No, it was later than Dante. Well?'

Reinhart got up and went into the kitchen. Poured out two glasses and came back. Lay down on the sofa again and started his narration. It took quite a while, and she didn't interrupt him a single time.

'And the three heads?' she said when he'd finished.

Reinhart took a drink before answering.

'In the first place,' he said, 'we haven't the faintest idea who did it. That's bad enough in routine cases.'

'I'm familiar with that,' said Winnifred.

'In the second place it's *The Chief Inspector*'s son who's the victim.'

'Nasty,' said Winnifred. 'And the third?'

Reinhart paused once more to think.

'In the third place, he was presumably mixed up in something. If we find a killer, we shall presumably also find that Erich Van Veeteren was mixed up in something illegal. Yet again. Despite what his girlfriend says . . . That's unlikely to be something to warm the cockles of his father's heart, don't you think?'

'I understand,' said Winnifred, swirling her wine round in its glass. 'Yes, it's three-headed all right. But how certain is it that he was involved in something illegal? That doesn't necessarily have to be the case, surely?'

'Certain and certain,' said Reinhart, tapping his forehead with his middle finger. 'There are signals in here that can't be ignored. Besides . . . besides, he's asked to be left alone face to face with the murderer when we eventually find him. *The Chief Inspector*, that is. Hell's bells . . . But I think I understand him.'

Winnifred thought for a moment.

'It's not a nice story,' she said. 'Could it be much worse, in fact? It sounds almost as if it's been stage-managed in some way.'

'That's what he always says,' said Reinhart.

11

The police's appeal for help in the Dikken case was plastered all over the main newspapers in Maardam on Tuesday, exactly a week after the murder, and by five o'clock in the afternoon ten people had rung to say they had been at the Trattoria Commedia on the day in question. Jung and Rooth were delegated to look into the tip-offs, and eliminated six of them as 'of secondary interest' (Rooth's term), as the timing didn't fit in. The remaining four had evidently been in the restaurant during the period 17.00–18.30, and all four were kind enough to turn up at the police station during the evening to be interrogated.

The first was Rupert Pilzen, a fifty-eight-year-old bank manager who lived in Weimaar Allé in Dikken, and had slipped into the Commedia and sat in the bar for a while. A little whisky and a beer, that's all. A quarter past five until a quarter to six, roughly speaking. While he waited for his wife to prepare the evening meal – he sometimes indulged in that pleasure after a hard day's work, he explained. When he had time.

He lifted up his spectacles while he studied the photographs of Erich Van Veeteren carefully. Then stated that he had never seen the man before, neither at the Commedia nor anywhere else, and he looked ostentatiously at his glistening wristwatch. He had presumably planned to pay another well-deserved visit to the bar, which was now becoming less likely a possibility, Jung reckoned.

Was there anything else he had noticed that he thought could be of relevance to the case?

No.

Any faces he recalled?

No.

Had there been any other customers in the bar?

Pilzen furrowed his brow and retracted his double chins into deep folds. No, he had been alone there all the time. Oh, hang on, a woman had come in just before he left. Short hair, about forty, probably a feminist. She'd sat at the bar and ordered a drink. Quite a long way away from him. With a newspaper, he seemed to recall. That was all.

'If there had been a second bar, she would no doubt have sat there instead,' said Rooth when herr Pilzen had waddled out on his unsteady legs. 'You fat slob.'

'Hmm,' said Jung. 'People get like that when they've too much money and no lofty interests. You'd become like that as well. If you had any money, that is.'

'Go and fetch the next one,' said Rooth.

The next one turned out to be a couple. Herr and fru Schwarz, who didn't live in Dikken but had been visiting somebody they knew out there to discuss business. Exactly what was irrelevant. On the way back they had stopped off at the Commedia for a meal, a little luxury they granted themselves occasionally. Going out for a meal. Not just to Trattoria Commedia, but to restaurants in general. Especially now, when they had more or less retired. Yes indeed. Just once or twice a week.

They were both around sixty-five, and recognized Erich Van Veeteren immediately when Jung produced the photographs. He had been eating – a simple pasta dish, if fru Schwartz remembered rightly – at a table a few metres away from their own. They had ordered fish. Turbot, to be precise. Yes, the young man had been on his own. He had paid and left the restaurant at more or less the same time as they were being served their dessert. Shortly after six.

Were there any other guests while they were eating?

Just a young couple sitting further back in the restaurant section. They arrived shortly before six and probably ordered that same cheap pasta dish. Both of them. They were still there when herr and fru Schwartz had finished.

Half past six or thereabouts.

Had they noticed anything else of interest?

No – such as?

Had they noticed any customers sitting in the bar?

No, they couldn't see the bar from their table.

Was there anybody there when they passed through on the way out?

Maybe, they weren't sure. Oh yes, a little man in a dark suit, that's right. A bit dark-skinned, in fact. An Arab, perhaps. Or an Indian or something like that.

Rooth ground his teeth. Jung thanked them, and promised – in response to fru Schwartz's pressing request – that they would make sure they had the murderer under lock and key in a trice.

Because it was terrible. In Dikken of all places. Did they recall that whore who was crucified there a few years ago?

Yes, they did – but thank you very much, they must now talk to the next representative of that great detective, the general public.

Her name was Lisen Berke. She was in her forties, and had been in the bar at the Trattoria Commedia between a quarter to six and half past, approximately. She declined to explain why she had gone there – she had the right to go for a drink wherever she liked if she felt like it, for God's sake.

'Of course you do,' said Jung.

'Or two,' said Rooth. 'Come to that.'

'Do you recognize this person?' Jung asked, showing her the photographs.

She studied them for three seconds then shook her head for four.

'He was sitting at one of the tables in the restaurant, between—'

'Is he the one who's been killed?' she interrupted.

'Yes,' said Rooth. 'Did you see him?'

'No. I was sitting reading my paper.'

'I see,' said Rooth.

'You see?' said Berke, eyeing Rooth over the top of her octagonal spectacles.

'Hmm,' said Jung. 'Were there any other customers in the bar?'

She dragged her eyes away from Rooth, and thought that one over.

'Two, I think . . . Yes, first of all there was a fat managerial type hanging around, but he didn't stay long. Then a very different type appeared. Long hair and beard. Dark glasses as well, I seem to remember . . . Looked like some kind of rock star. Macho, out and out. Depraved.'

'Did you speak to him?' Jung asked.

Lisen Berke snorted contemptuously.

'No,' she said. 'Of course I didn't.'

'And he didn't try to talk to you?' said Rooth.

'I was reading my newspaper.'

'Quite right too,' said Rooth. 'You shouldn't get involved with men you don't know in bars.'

Jung gave him a withering look to shut him up. For Christ's sake, he thought. Why don't they send him on a diplomacy course?

Berke gritted her teeth and glared at Rooth as well, as if he were an unusually nasty piece of dog shit she had accidentally trodden on and which was difficult to scrape off the sole of her shoe. A male dog, needless to say. Rooth looked up at the ceiling.

'How long did he stay?' asked Jung. 'This depraved rock musician.'

'I don't remember. Not all that long, I don't think.'

'What did he drink?'

'I've no idea.'

'But he left the bar before you did, is that right?'

'Yes.'

Jung pondered.

'Would you recognize him again?'

'No. He didn't have any features. Just a mass of hair and glasses.'

'I understand,' said Jung. 'Many thanks, fröken Berke: I'll be getting back to you, if you don't mind. You've been extremely helpful.'

'What did you mean by that last remark?' Rooth asked when they had closed the door after Lisen Berke. '"Extremely helpful"? What kind of crap is that?'

Jung sighed.

'I was just trying to apply a bit of balsam after your charm offensive,' he explained. 'Besides, this character in the bar could well be of interest. We must ask if the barman remembers him as well.'

'Once chance in ten,' said Rooth. 'But maybe those are the best odds we can hope for in this match.'

'Have you anything else to suggest?' asked Jung.

Rooth thought that one over.

'If we drive out there, we can take the opportunity of having a bite to eat,' he said. 'So that we can work out a few new angles of approach and so on.'

'Depraved?' said Jung. 'Is "depraved" the word she used?'

Ewa Moreno flopped down in the visitor's chair in Reinhart's office.

'So you're still at work, are you?'

Reinhart looked at the clock. Half past six. He wished it

had been a bit less.

'I need to summarize a few things. I didn't get hold of fröken Frey until quite late. How are things going for you?'

'Not all that well,' said Moreno with a sigh. 'To tell you the truth, I don't think the strategy we're following is exactly top-notch.'

'I know,' said Reinhart. 'But if you have a better one you should have come out with it before you crossed the threshold. Correct me if I'm wrong.'

'Yep,' said Moreno. 'No doubt I should have done. But whatever: it's pretty hard going. We've chatted to sixteen friends of Erich Van Veeteren so far . . . In accordance with the list of priorities his fiancée gave us. All of them here in Maardam – we've sent Bollmert out into the sticks, and he's due back on Friday. Nobody has come up with any-thing of interest yet, and nobody seems to be hiding anything. Nothing to do with the case, that is.'

'Alibis?' said Reinhart.

'How nice of you to ask,' said Moreno. 'You don't exactly make yourself popular when you ask people to pro-vide alibis – but then, maybe it isn't our job to make ourselves popular, as The Chief Inspector used to say. Anyway, everything seems above board so far. We haven't had a chance to check anything yet, of course – but I sup-pose that's not the point?'

'Not so long as we don't suspect there's something nasty hiding in the woodwork,' said Reinhart. 'I take it there are a few dodgy characters among these names?'

'There are all sorts,' said Moreno. 'No doubt some of them are not exactly pleased at the fact that Marlene Frey handed the address book over to the enemy without further ado. But we are ignoring everything that has nothing to do with the case. As instructed.'

'As instructed,' agreed Reinhart. He leaned back in his desk chair and thought for a while with his hands clasped behind the back of his neck. 'If you'd like to have a session with Marlene Frey instead, that's fine by me,' he said. 'There are two things that have wounded her in life: police officers and men. At least you're only half of that.'

Moreno nodded and said nothing for a while.

'What do you think?' she said eventually. 'What do you think happened to Erich?'

Reinhart bit the stem of his pipe and scratched his temples.

'I don't know,' he said. 'I haven't the slightest idea, that's the worrying bit. We usually have some kind of suspicion of what's going on . . . An indication, at least.'

'But you haven't a clue?'

'No,' said Reinhart. 'Do you?'

Moreno shook her head.

'Does Marlene Frey know something that she's holding

back?' she asked.

Reinhart pondered again. Tried to replay the afternoon's conversation for his inner ear.

'No,' he said. 'I don't think so. Mind you, you might have a different impression – who knows what to make of female intuition?'

'I know all about that,' said Moreno. 'Have you spoken to *The Chief Inspector* again?'

'Not since yesterday,' said Reinhart. 'I might ring him this evening. It feels really uncomfortable, poking our noses into his son's dealings. I mean, he hasn't exactly been your blue-eyed innocent. It's not nice, sifting through that dirty linen, and it can't be much fun for him sitting at home mourning, and knowing what we're up to. Holy shit, what a mess!'

'Is it really all that dirty nowadays?' Moreno asked. 'His linen, I mean.'

'Maybe not,' said Reinhart, standing up. 'It was a bit dirtier a few years ago at any rate. It's possible that it's exactly how she says it is, fröken Frey – that they are following the straight and narrow nowadays. It's just a pity that he didn't get a bit further along that path. But then, you have to agree with Strindberg and feel sorry for the human race.'

He went over to the window. Prised apart a couple of the slats in the Venetian blind and looked out over the town and the dark sky.

'How many of the people he met last week – who we *know* he met last week – have you been in contact with?'

'Seven,' said Moreno without hesitation. 'And as many again tomorrow, if all goes to plan.'

'All right,' said Reinhart, letting go of the slats. 'What we're looking for is just the end of a thread that we can follow up. We'll find one sooner or later, it's just a question of being patient . . . That's not exactly unusual, is it?'

'Not unusual at all,' agreed Moreno. 'Although it would help if things started moving pretty soon. So that we get an indication, as we've said.'

'Some hopes,' said Reinhart. 'Anyway, that'll do for today. I seem to remember that I have a family. At least, I had one this morning. How are things with you nowadays?'

'I'm married to my work,' said Moreno.

Reinhart looked at her with raised eyebrows.

'You must file for a divorce,' he said in all seriousness. 'Can't you see that he's just exploiting you?'

On Thursday evening they made the first rather more formal attempt to sum up the state of the investigation. Five-and-a-half days had passed since Erich Van Veeteren's body had been found in the bushes at the car park out at Dikken. Nine days since it had been put there – unless they were much mistaken. So it was high time. Even if they hadn't discovered very much so far.

They started with the victim's fiancée.

Marlene Frey had been pinned down several times by both Reinhart and Moreno – and been shown the greatest possible amount of consideration and respect, of course – and as far as both of them could judge, she had done everything in her power to supply them with information and assist the police in every way. There were no grounds at all for complaining about her willingness to cooperate. Especially if one took the circumstances into consideration, and they did just that.

The number of interviews with friends and acquaintances of the deceased had risen to the considerable total of seventy-two – a rather motley collection of interviews if one were to be honest, as one should, but with two constants common to all of them: nobody had been able to suggest anybody who might want to remove Erich Van Veeteren from the face of the earth, and nobody had the slightest idea about why he might have gone to Dikken that fateful Tuesday evening.

As for the evidence gathered from the Trattoria Commedia itself, Inspectors Jung and Rooth were able to report that it had increased – very slightly – in volume, and eventually it had been possible to suggest a lead: only one, but the first and only one so far in the investigation as a whole. The male person with long, dark hair and a beard who had been noticed by Lisen Berke in the bar shortly before six p.m. on the Tuesday evening in question had had his existence confirmed by two further witnesses: the barman Alois Kummer and the chef Lars Nielsen – both of them were a hundred per cent certain (two hundred per cent in toto, Rooth pointed out optimistically) that a person of that description had been seated at the bar in front of a beer for a few minutes at about the time stated.

As certain as amen in church and the whores in Zwille, as they generally say in Maardam.

The description was about all that could be wished for – at least, as far as agreement among the witnesses was concerned. Dark hair, dark beard, dark clothes and dark glasses. The chef also thought he recalled seeing a plastic carrier bag standing alongside the bar stool, but questions on that score produced only neutral shrugs from Kummer and Berke. So no confirmation, but then again, no denial either.

When Jung and Rooth had finished reporting on these vital facts – the only ray of hope after five days of arduous investigation in fact – Rooth felt the urge to stick his neck out.

'It was the murderer sitting there, I'll bet my bloody life on that. Remember that I was the one who recognized the fact first!'

Nobody was willing to express support for this prognosis as yet, but nevertheless it was decided to send out a description of the man and issue a Wanted notice.

In order to establish the facts, if nothing else.

And to be able to say they had made at least one decision during the day's run-through.

12

He woke up shortly before dawn – in the hour of the wolf.

He did that occasionally. Nowadays.

Never when he had Vera Miller with him, or when she had just left or was soon due. Never then. As things had turned out, they met once a week and spent Saturday and Sunday together. It was in the intervening period when he missed her most that it usually happened. That he woke up in a cold sweat. In the hour of the wolf.

And it was while he was lying awake, between three and four in the morning, during those merciless, never-ending minutes while the rest of the world was asleep, that he peered through the protective membrane that surrounded him. Saw the horrific things he was guilty of having done in the cold light of retrospection, and became fully aware of how the delicate membrane could give way at any moment. At any moment. He wasn't aware if he had dreams as well. Or at least was unable to recall any images from them. Didn't even try, naturally enough, neither this night nor any other night. Got up in the darkness instead, tiptoed over to his desk and switched on the lamp. Flopped down on the chair and started counting the days in his diary: found that twenty-five had passed since he killed the boy. Ten since he killed the blackmailer. It would soon be a new month. Everything would soon be forgotten.

Out of mind and out of this world. The newspapers weren't writing about it any longer. They had done so at the beginning of the week. The police had found the body of the young man last Saturday, but by now the media had already lost interest. There had been nothing on either Thursday or Friday.

That's the way it was. People in the twenty-first century would be ephemeral – here today and gone tomorrow, he thought. Draw a line, work out a sum of money if there is any. Forget and carry on as usual. That would be the order of the day. Actually, that was what he was like himself, he realized. A good representative of the future, yes indeed. It was only these sleepless hours that anchored him in the past and provided continuity. In fact.

Nevertheless, nothing was the same as it had been. It was paradoxical how that evening with the light thud and the boy in the muddy ditch could change everything. Could change the perspective to that degree. Open the door. Cut through the moorings. Let Vera Miller in, let his new life in. Yes indeed, the word is paradoxical, and chaos is the neighbour of God, as the poet said.

The murder out at Dikken did not weigh in as heavily. Not at all, that was merely a consequence. Something he had been forced to carry out, an inexorable consequence of having been accidentally observed that first evening. Billiard balls that had been set in motion and had no alternative but to roll in a given direction – he had read about theories of that kind in scientific journals not so long ago. A sort of neo-mechanical conception of the world, if he had understood it correctly . . . Or psychology. But at the same time a retribution applied to his own life, of course. After only a day or so the Dikken event had ceased to trouble him. The man he had killed out there had tried to line his own pocket at the expense of the bad luck of others, his own and the boy's . . . You could even argue that he had deserved to die. Tit for tat, as they say. A simple blackmailer who had grown into a terrible threat in the space of a week, but whom he had met on his own ground and liquidated. Simply and painlessly. The path to further development was open again.

The development with Vera Miller. He no longer had any doubt at all that this would be how things would go. Not for a fraction of a second, not even while he was awake again and again during the hour of the wolf. She hadn't yet told her husband that she had found another man and that they must divorce, but that was only a matter of time. A question of a few weeks and a bit of consideration. Andreas Miller was not a strong person, she didn't want to crush him. Not yet. But soon.

While they were waiting for this to happen they refrained from making any plans. But they were there all the same, they were in the air all the time they were together. While they were making love, while he was inside her, while he was sucking her nipples and making them hard and stiff and tender. While they were sitting opposite each other, eating and drinking wine, or simply lying together in his big bed, breathing and listening to music in the darkness. All the time. Plans – hitherto unexpressed hopes for the future and a new life. Somewhere else. Him and Vera Miller. He loved her. She loved him. They were both mature adults, and nothing could be simpler. They would live together. Half a year from now. A month. Soon.

He tried to imagine it in secret. Strong images, warm and satisfying. Images of a future in which he would never need to lie awake in the hour of the wolf.

Never need to peer through that membrane that was on the point of splitting.

Never need to wipe foul-smelling cold sweat from his body.

Vera, he thought. For your sake I could kill again.

He featured in a police Wanted notice printed in Saturday's *Neuwe Blatt*. He read it at the breakfast table, and after an initial moment of apprehension he burst out laughing. It was not a threat. On the contrary. He had been expecting it, in fact. After all, it would have been unreasonable to think that nobody had noticed him during the few minutes he had spent in the bar, totally unreasonable – and he soon realized that the information given in the newspaper, far from putting him in danger in some way or other, was more of an assurance. An assurance that the police investigation had come up against a brick wall, and he had no reason to fear anything that they might come up with. No reason at all.

Why else would they come up with such laughable information?

A man of an uncertain age. Dressed in dark, probably black clothes. Long, dark, probably black hair. Beard and glasses. Possibly disguised.

Possibly? He smiled. Did they expect him to put it all on again and go out to be seen in public? Return to the scene of the crime and call in at the Trattoria Commedia once again? Or what? He had never entertained an especially high regard for the competence of the police, and it became no higher that Saturday morning.

Detectives? he thought. Stupid country bumpkins.

Vera arrived in the afternoon. She had bought some wine and food from the covered market in Keymer Plejn, but they hadn't seen each other for six days and were forced to start making love out there in the hall. How amazing that there could be such passion. How amazing that such a woman could exist.

They eventually got round to the food and wine. She stayed the whole night, and they made love several times, in various different places, and instead of waking up in the hour of the wolf he fell asleep more or less in the middle of it.

Tired out and satisfied. Full of love and wine and with Vera Miller as close to him as could be.

She stayed until Sunday afternoon. They spent a serious hour talking about their love: about what they ought to do with it, and about their future.

It was the first time.

'Nobody knows you exist,' she said. 'Not Andreas. Not my sister. Not my workmates and friends. You are my secret, but I don't want it to be like that any more.

He smiled, but made no reply.

'I want to have you all the time.'

'Your husband?' he asked. 'What do you intend to do about him?'

She looked at him long and hard before answering.

'I shall deal with that,' she said. 'This week. I've thought it through, there aren't any short cuts. I love you.'

'I love you,' he replied.

He worked late on Monday. On his way home in the car – just as he was passing the concrete culvert in the ditch – he realized he was singing along to the car radio, and it dawned on him that it was still less than a month since that evening. It was still November, but everything had changed to a far greater extent than he would have believed possible.

It was unreal. Totally unreal. But that was life.

He smiled, still humming away as he took the day's post out of the letter box. But he stopped only a few seconds later as he sat at the kitchen table and read the letter. As far as he could recall – if he remembered rightly: he had disposed of the others – it was written on exactly the same type of writing paper and was in exactly the same sort of envelope as the two earlier ones. It was handwritten, and no more than half a page long.

Two lives.
You now have two lives on your conscience. I have given
you plenty of time to come forward, but you have hidden
yourself away like a cowardly cur. The price for my silence
is now different. One week (exactly seven days) is available
to you for producing 200,000. Used notes. Low values.

I shall get back to you with instructions. Don't
make the same mistake twice, you won't have another
opportunity to buy your freedom. I know who you are, I
have incontrovertible evidence against you, and there are
limits to my patience.

A friend

He read the message twice. Then he stared out of the
window. It was raining, and he suddenly sensed the smell
of cold sweat in his nostrils.

THREE

THREE

13

Erich Van Veeteren was buried after a simple ceremony on Monday, 30 November. The service took place in a side chapel of the Keymer Church, and in accordance with the wishes of his closest relatives – especially his mother – only a small circle of mourners were present.

Renate had also chosen both the officiating clergyman and the hymns – in accordance with some sort of obscure principles she claimed were important for Erich, but which Van Veeteren had difficulty in believing. Besides, it didn't really matter as far as he was concerned: if Erich had felt the need for spirituality, it was hardly likely he would have found it within the realm of these high-church ceremonies and under these menacing spires reaching heavenwards, he was convinced of that.

The vicar seemed comparatively young and comparatively lively, and while he spoke and proceeded through the rituals in a broad accent revealing his origins in the offshore islands, Van Veeteren spent most of the time with his eyes closed and his hands clasped in his lap. On his right was his ex-wife, whose presence he found difficult to tolerate even in these circumstances; on his left sat his daughter, whom he loved above everything else on this earth.

Directly in front was the coffin holding the mortal remains of his son.

It was difficult to look at it: perhaps that's why he kept his eyes closed.

Kept his eyes closed and thought of Erich when he was still alive instead. Or rather, allowed the thoughts to flow freely: and it seemed that his memory picked out images completely at random. Some incidents and memories from Erich's childhood: reading him stories on a windy beach, he wasn't at all sure which; visits to the dentist, visits to the skating rink and Wegelen Zoo.

Some from the difficult period much later on: the years when he was a drug addict, the times in prison. The suicide attempt, the long, sleepless nights at the hospital.

Some from their last meeting. Perhaps these were the most important and frequent of all. As these more recent images rolled past, he was also uncomfortably aware of his own egotistical motives – his compulsion to derive something positive from that meeting; but if it is true that every new day carries with it the sum of all the preceding ones, he thought, perhaps he could be excused.

Today, at least. Here, at least, in front of the coffin. He had sat with Erich at the kitchen table at Klagenburg on that final occasion. Erich had come to return an electric drill he'd borrowed, and they had sat down to drink coffee and discuss things in general, he couldn't recall precisely what. But it had nothing to do with his addiction to this and that, nothing to do with his ability (or inability) to take responsibility for his own life, or with social morality versus private morality. Nothing at all to do with those difficult topics, which had been discussed before at enormous length.

It was just chat, he told himself. Nothing to do with matters of guilt. A conversation between two people, it could have been anybody at all; and it was precisely that, the simplicity and insignificance of what they discussed, which provided the positive outcome of the situation.

Something positive among all the negatives. A faint light in the eternal darkness. He recalled yet again Gortiakov's walk through the pond carrying a candle in *Nostalghia*. He did that often. Tarkovsky's *Nostalghia* . . . And now, as he sat there in that ancient cathedral, in front of his son's coffin, with his eyes closed, with the vicar's measured litany floating up to the Gothic arches above them, it was as if . . . as if he had achieved a sort of kinship. Perhaps that was too much to expect; but nevertheless a kinship with so many weighty things. With Erich; with his own incomprehensible father who had died long before Van Veeteren had the slightest chance of getting to understand and become reconciled with him; with suffering and with art and with creativity – all possible kinds of creativity – and eventually also with a belief in something beyond this world of ours, and in the visions and ambitions of those who had built the church in which they were sitting . . . With life and death, and the never-ending passage of time. With his daughter Jess, who was leaning heavily on him, and occasionally seemed to be convulsed by a shudder. Kinship.

It works, he thought. The ritual works. The forms overcome doubts. We have learned over the centuries to weave meaning around emptiness and pain. A meaning and a pattern. We have been practising that for a very long time.

The spell was not broken until he processed past the coffin with Jess clinging to his arm – not until he had turned his back on it all and started to leave the chancel. Then he was hit by an ice-cold stab of despair instead; he almost stumbled, and had to cling on to his daughter in order not to fall. He was supporting her, she was supporting him. It seemed a vast distance to Renate on Jess's other side, and he wondered why he found it necessary to keep her so far away. Why?

And once they were outside the heavy church door,

standing in the drizzle, his only thought was: Who killed him? I want to know who it was that killed my son.

Who blew out the flame.

'I haven't finished sorting stuff out yet,' said Marlene Frey. 'Separating his things from mine, that is. I don't know what is the usual thing to do in these circumstances. Is there anything you'd like to have?'

Van Veeteren shook his head.

'Of course not. You lived together. Erich's things are yours now, naturally.'

They were sitting at a table in Adenaar's. Marlene Frey was drinking tea, he had a glass of wine. She wasn't even smoking. He didn't know why that surprised him, but it did. Erich had started smoking when he was fifteen . . . probably earlier than that, but it was on his fifteenth birthday that he'd caught him at it.

'Please feel free to come and have a look a couple of days from now, in any case,' she said. 'There might be something you'd like as a souvenir.'

'Photographs?' it occurred to him. 'Do you have any photos? I don't think I have a single one of Erich from the last ten years.'

She smiled fleetingly.

'Of course. There are some. A few, at least.'

He nodded, and eyed her guiltily.

'I apologize for not having called round to see you yet. I have . . . There's been so much to do.'

'It's never too late,' she said. 'Call in when you have time, and I'll give you a few pictures. I'm at home in the evenings. Usually, that is – maybe it would be an idea to ring first. We don't need to make a big thing of it.'

'No,' he said. 'We don't.'

She took a drink of her tea, and he sipped his wine as a sort of half-hearted gesture of agreement. Stole a glance at her and decided that she was good-looking. Pale and tired, of course, but with clean-cut features and eyes that met his without deviating as much as a centimetre. He wondered what she had been through in her life. Had she had the same kind of experiences as Erich? It didn't seem so: the tribulations always seemed to leave deeper traces on women. She'd been through her fair share, of course, he could see that: but there was nothing in her demeanour that suggested a lack of strength.

Strength to see her through life. Yes, he could see that she had that.

It's disgraceful, he thought. Disgraceful that I haven't met her until now. In circumstances like these. Obviously, I ought . . .

But then the *Erich-is-dead* constellation took possession of him with such force that he almost fainted. He gulped down his wine and took out his cigarette-rolling machine.

'Do you mind if I smoke?'

She smiled briefly again.

'Erich smoked.'

They sat in silence while he rolled, then lit up.

'I ought to give it up,' he said. 'Using this thing helps to cut down at least.'

Why the hell am I sitting here, he thought, going on about smoking? What difference does it make if the father of a dead son smokes too much?

She suddenly placed her hand on his arm. His heart missed a beat and he almost choked on his cigarette. She observed his reaction, no doubt, but did nothing to pretend it was an accident. Nothing to gloss over it. Simply left her hand where it was while looking hard at him with probing, slightly quivering eyes.

'I think I could get to like you,' she said. 'It's a pity things turned out as they did.'

Turned out as they did? he thought. A pity? Talk about understatement . . .

'Yes,' he said, 'I'm sorry I didn't have more contact with Erich. Naturally, it ought to—'

'It's not your fault,' she said, interrupting him. 'He was a bit . . . Well, how should one describe it?' She shrugged. 'But I loved him. We had good times together, it was as if being together made us grow up, as it were. And then of course there was that special thing.'

He had forgotten all about that.

'Er, yes,' he said. 'What special thing?'

She let go of his arm and gazed down at her cup for a few seconds. Stirred it slowly with her spoon.

'I don't know how you're going to take this, but the fact is that I'm expecting a child. I'm pregnant, in the third month. Well, that's how things stand.'

'Good God!' he exclaimed, and now the smoke really did spark off a coughing fit.

Early on Tuesday morning he drove Jess out to Sechshafen. He had told both her and Renate about the conversation with Marlene Frey: Jess had phoned her on the Monday evening and arranged to meet her the next time she came to Maardam. With a bit of luck around New Year.

The intention had been that Renate should also accompany them to the airport, but apparently she had woken up with a temperature and what seemed to be tonsillitis. Van Veeteren thanked God for the bacilli, and suspected that Jess didn't have anything against them either.

She held his hand that morning as well as they crawled through the fog enveloping Landsmoor and Weill: it was a warm hand, and occasionally gave his a hard squeeze. He was aware that the squeezes were indications of daughterly love, and the familiar old anxiety that goes with parting. Stronger than ever on a day like this, of course. Separation from her roots in this flat, north European landscape. From Erich. Perhaps also from him.

'It's hard to say goodbye,' he said.

'Yes,' she said. 'It's hard.'

'You never get used to it. But I suppose there's a point to that as well.'

Parting is a little death, he almost added, but he managed to keep that thought to himself.

'I don't like airports,' she said. 'I'm always a bit frightened when I'm going to travel somewhere. Erich was the same.'

He nodded. He hadn't known that, in fact. He wondered how much there was he didn't know about his children. How much he had missed over the years, and how much could still be repaired or discovered.

'But I didn't know him all that well,' she said after a while. 'I hope I'll grow to like Marlene – it feels as if through her he's left traces of himself behind. I hope to goodness all goes well. It would be awful if . . .'

She didn't complete the sentence. After a while he noticed that she had started crying, and he gave her hand a long squeeze.

'It feels better now, at least,' she said when it had

passed. 'Better than when I came. I'll never get used to it, but I occasionally feel almost calm now. Or maybe one just feels numb after all the crying. What do you think?'

He muttered something in response. No, he thought. Nothing goes away, it all just gets worse as time passes. Worse every day as you grow older.

As they began to approach the airport she let go of his hand. Took out a paper handkerchief and dried her eyes.

'Why did you really pack up being a police officer?'

The question came out of the blue, and for a moment he felt on the spot.

'I don't really know,' he said. 'I'd just had enough . . . I suppose that's the simplest explanation. I felt that quite clearly, I didn't have to think deeply about it.'

'I understand,' she said. 'I suppose there's quite a lot one doesn't need to think deeply about.'

She paused, but he could hear that she had more on her mind. Had a good idea of what it was as well – and after a minute she started again.

'It's odd, but I've started to think about something I didn't think at first would worry me at all . . . In the beginning, when I first heard that Erich was dead.'

'What exactly?' he asked.

'The murderer,' she said. 'The one who did it. I want to know who it was, and why he did it. I want to know that more and more. Do you think that's odd? I mean, Erich's gone, no matter what . . .'

He turned his head to look at her.

'No,' he said. 'I don't think it's odd at all. I think it's one of the most natural reactions you could possibly imagine. There's a reason why I packed up being a police officer, but there was a reason why I started as well.'

She looked at him and nodded slowly.

'I think I understand. And you still think that?'

'Yes, I still think that.'

She paused before her next question.

'How's it going? For the police, I mean. Do you know anything? Are they in touch with you?'

He shrugged.

'I don't know much. I've asked about it, but I don't want to poke my nose in too far. When they get anywhere they'll let me know, of course. Perhaps I'll give Reinhart a ring and ask how they're getting on.'

They arrived. He turned into the multi-storey car park, up the narrow ramp, and pulled up in front of a grey concrete wall.

'Do that,' she said. 'Find out how far they've got. I want to know who killed my brother.'

He nodded, and they got out of the car. Twenty minutes later he watched her walk off between two uniformed airline staff and disappear into the security-check area.

Yes indeed, he thought. When all's said and done, that's the big question that still needs to be answered.

Who?

14

He found it incomprehensible to start with.

His first reaction – the first attempt to explain it – was that he had survived.

That the man in the car park had somehow or other come back to life after being struck down. Crawled out of the bushes and into the restaurant, and been taken to hospital. Pulled through.

With a broken parietal bone and smashed cervical vertebrae?

Then he remembered the facts. That there had been articles in all the newspapers. That there had been reports on the radio and television. There was no doubt about it, of course. That lanky young man he had killed at the golf course was dead. Finally and irrevocably dead.

Ergo? he thought. Ergo I've killed the wrong person. That had to be the explanation. Was there any alternative?

Not as far as he could see. It must be the case that . . . that yet again he had killed somebody by mistake.

That didn't make it any less incomprehensible.

It had been asking too much, far too much, for him to sleep that Monday night, and after a few fruitless hours he got up. It was two a.m. He drank a cup of tea with a drop of rum in the kitchen, then took the car and drove out to the sea. Sat for an hour and a half by himself with the windows open in a lay-by between Behrensee and Lejnice and tried to think things through while listening to the mighty waves breaking on the shore. The wind was blowing hard from the south-west, and he could hear that the rollers must be several metres high.

The wrong person? He had killed the wrong man. It wasn't the blackmailer who had emerged from the Trattoria Commedia that evening with the Boodwick carrier bag dangling from his hand. It was somebody else.

Somebody who had gone to the gents and happened to discover the bag in the rubbish bin? Could it be as simple as that?

A coincidence? Somebody who had found it by sheer bad luck before the blackmailer? Could that be what happened?

He excluded that possibility more or less straight away.

It was too improbable. Too far-fetched. No, the truth was different, quite different. It didn't take him long to find the solution.

There was an assistant. Had been. That was who he'd killed. The anonymous letter-writer had chosen to send an assistant to collect the spoils, instead of doing it himself. So as not to run any unnecessary risks. Good thinking, no doubt about it, and not really surprising in the circumstances. He ought to have anticipated that. Ought to have made allowances for that.

In fact it was an inexcusable blunder: the more he thought about it, the more obvious it was. A terrible blunder. While he had been thinking sarcastically about the amateurish conduct of his opponent out there at Dikken, in fact he was up against an exceptionally prudent person. Somebody who had acted with much more caution and precision than he had.

And who had now made his next move. Two hundred thousand, he was demanding. Two hundred grand!

Oh, hell! He swore out loud and hammered his hands on the steering wheel. Fucking hell!

In the wake of his anger came fear. Fear with regard to what he had done, and for the future. The future? he thought. What future? In so far as his life hadn't already been compromised by what had happened in the last few weeks, it would be in the next few. The next *one*. It was blindingly obvious. A matter of days, there was no other way of assessing the situation.

Another crucial encounter was in store.

He opened the door and got out of the car. Offered himself up to the mercy of the wind, and started walking along the road. Waves crashed on the beach.

Am I still me? he suddenly asked himself. Am I still the same person as I was before? Am I still a person, in fact?

A billiard ball rolling towards an inevitable fate? Two cannons, two changes of direction . . . And then what?

Images of the boy in the ditch and of the young man as he raised his eyebrows in surprise a second before the first blow kept recurring increasingly rapidly in his mind's eye. Intertwining, merging, over and over again, leaving no room for anything else. He tried to think about Vera Miller instead, the laughing, lively, red-haired Vera: but without success.

As he walked, leaning forward into the darkness – and in the hour of the wolf, he reminded himself with feelings of weary resignation – hunched up to protect himself from the cold and the salt-laden wind, he felt over and over again the urge to simply give up. Powerful urges to deliver himself into the lap of the sea or the hands of the police, and put an end to it all.

To follow the faint whispering of what must of course be the voice of his conscience – which in some remarkable way seemed to both harmonize with and drown out the thunder of the waves. Very impressive, he thought. They blend in together like the soundtrack of a film. Extremely impressive. The thundering and the whispering.

But in the end it was Vera Miller who won. In the end it was her laughing face with those glittering green eyes, and her warm, wet pussy welcoming his stiff penis, that brushed aside the fear and hopelessness, and choked the whispering. The inexorable power of her love. Of *their* love.

And the future.

I can't give up, he thought. Not now. I must take Vera into consideration as well.

It was five minutes to five in the morning by the time he came home. He had calmed down to some extent during the return journey – although it could simply be that he was tired out. What's done is over and done with, he thought. No point crying over spilt milk. It was the future that was important. The immediate future to start with, and then the next stage – life with Vera.

Mind you, if he didn't manage to sort out 'A friend', there wouldn't be any future with Vera, of course. The future would be a week at most, no more, that was beyond all doubt. He would have to devise a strategy. A defence, a counter-move. What should he do?

Yes indeed, what? If he simply decided to pay the 200,000 requested, that would mean that all his resources had been used up. His savings and his house – and it still wouldn't be enough. He would have to negotiate a loan for another 50,000 at least. And what then?

And then? Even if he bankrupted himself in this way, what guarantees would he have? The blackmailer would still have the knowledge, and would doubtless not forget it. And anyway, was there anything to suggest that he'd be satisfied with what he'd been paid?

No, nothing, was the answer to his rhetorical question. Nothing at all.

And how would he be able to explain it away to Vera, if he was suddenly bankrupt? How?

Ergo?

There was only one possibility.

Kill him.

Kill the right person this time. Although for a few moments, as he wound his way through the narrow suburban streets of Boorkhejm, it occurred to him that perhaps he had killed the right person after all. Despite everything

The right one in a way, at least. Because there could have been two of them. *Could have been*. There was virtually no doubt that the letters he'd received so far must have been written by the same person; but of course it was just possible that it could be . . . could be the handwriting of a wife, for instance. He couldn't exclude that possibility, he told himself. The wife of a dead blackmailer who had now taken over on her own account.

Taken over and raised the stakes.

No, this was a possibility that couldn't be ignored. He decided to find out the name of the man he'd killed outside the Trattoria Commedia, and use that as the starting point of further investigations. In any case there had to be a link – some kind of a link – between him and the other one.

The other one? he thought.

His opponent.

I'd give my right hand for his identity.

Time seemed to be both for and against him.

Naturally he needed time to prepare himself and plan ahead. Even if he had no intention of raising the money that 'A friend' had demanded. No, a different sort of time. Time in which to act. Time to find things out, and to prepare himself.

But it wasn't long before the respite designated ('Exactly seven days' – a phrase used in both the latest letters, one might wonder why) seemed to have the opposite implications from those at first thought. It seemed a long time. Exactly what ought he to do? *What?* Sort out what plans? Make what preparations?

The only thing he eventually managed to find out was the name of his second victim. Erich Van Veeteren. He memorized the name – placed him in the same box as Wim Felders. The dead persons' box. But actually taking the next step – starting to investigate and poke around into this unknown person's private life: that was too much. He didn't have the strength. He found his home address in the telephone directory, of course, and on the Wednesday evening he stood for a while in Ockfener Plejn staring up at the grimy façade, wondering which of the flats it could be. Stood there shivering in the wind, but without being able to summon up the will to cross over the tramlines, walk up six steps and read the list of names beside the doorbell.

Having killed him is enough, he thought. That's bad enough, I don't need to invade his home as well.

That same evening he gave up all thought of playing the detective. He'd begun to realize that doing so could be dangerous: he might attract the attention of the police – they must be working all out to try to find the murderer of the young man. No, it would be better to wait, he decided. Wait for the further instructions that were a hundred per cent certain to arrive with Monday's post.

Wait for that pale-blue letter, and then work out how to solve the problem on the basis of how the handover was supposed to take place this time.

Because that would have to take place, he reasoned. At a certain place and at a certain time there would have to be physical contact between himself and the blackmailer.

Or rather, between himself, the money and the black-mailer – there were three links in the chain, and of course it was probable that this time his opponent would be even more careful about his own safety than he had been on the previous occasion. Highly probable: he wasn't dealing with an amateur, that was now crystal clear. But that opponent would have to acquire the money somehow or other, and in some way or other he would have to be outfoxed.

Only time would tell how this was to be done. Time and the next letter.

After visiting Ockfener Plejn he spent the whole evening in front of the television in the company of a new bottle of whisky, and when he retired shortly before midnight, both the bed and the bedroom were spinning round.

But that was the intention. He really must sleep through the hour of the wolf tonight at least. Thursday was his day off.

Thursday was the day when Vera Miller was due to phone him.

Three days without contact, that was what they had agreed. A short time that she would use to discuss matters with her husband. Tell him about their affair. Liberate herself.

It was seven p.m. when the call came, and he could still feel the effects of his excessive drinking the night before.

She sounded sad. That was unusual.

'It's so hard,' she said.

She didn't usually say that. He didn't respond.

'He's going to take this very badly, I can see that.'

'Haven't you told him yet?'

She said nothing for a couple of seconds.

'I've started,' she said. 'I've hinted at it . . . He knows what's coming. He's keeping out of the way. He's gone out tonight, I'm sure he's only done that because of this business . . . He's running away from it.'

'Come round to me.'

'That's not on,' she said. 'Andreas will be back home in a couple of hours. I have to treat him above board from now on. I'll see you on Saturday, as we agreed.'

'I love you,' he said.

'And I love you,' she said.

'You're not changing your mind, I hope?' he said.

'You must give me time,' she said. 'No, I'm not changing my mind. But you can't rush something like this.'

Time? he thought. Three days. Then it would be Monday. Just think if she knew . . .

'I understand,' he said. 'The main thing is that things

turn out as we've planned. And that I can see you on Saturday.'

'I shall be attending my course on Saturday.'

'Eh?'

She laughed.

'My course. Come on, you know about that. It's the fourth weekend in a row. I love that course.'

He thought about what she'd said with regard to treating Andreas above board, but he didn't follow it up.

'I love it as well,' he mumbled instead. 'I need you.'

'You've got me,' she said.

When they'd hung up he started crying. He remained seated in the armchair for quite some time, until it had passed over and he'd had a chance to think about when he had last wept.

He couldn't remember.

He took two Sobran tablets instead.

15

'We're not exactly making progress,' said Reinhart, eyeing the investigation team. Five of the original seven were left: Krause had been hijacked by Hiller, and Bollmert was still tracking down obscure candidates for interrogation in the provinces.

'But on the other hand, we're not going backwards,' said Rooth. 'What we knew a week ago we still know today.'

Reinhart ignored him.

'Moreno,' he said. 'If you would be so kind as to summarize the situation, the rest of us can lean back and enjoy the sound of a beautiful voice for a change.'

'Thank you,' said Moreno. 'Man's ability to keep on inventing new compliments never ceases to amaze us females. However, let's get to the point.'

Reinhart smiled slightly, but said nothing. She flicked through her notebook until she found a summary. Noted that Jung was wearing a tie for some inexplicable reason, and that deBries had a sticking plaster over the bridge of his nose. For some other inexplicable reason. She took a deep breath, and began.

'What we know more or less for certain is as follows: Erich Van Veeteren was killed by a powerful blow to the temple and the back of his head with a blunt instrument shortly after six p.m. on Tuesday, the tenth of November. I won't go into the weapon, which was presumably some kind of metal pipe. But as we haven't found it, it is hardly of much importance at this stage. There were no witnesses to the actual attack: the car park was deserted, it was dusk, and the murderer had time to drag the body of his victim into the surrounding bushes. We have interviewed everybody who was in the Trattoria Commedia at – and before – the time of the murder. All but two, that is – the victim and the killer, assuming the latter had also been in there. Ten customers and four members of staff, at any rate: we've spoken to all of them. Nobody had anything of direct importance to tell us, apart from the fact that three of them saw a strange-looking character sitting in the bar for a short time. Between six and a quarter past, roughly speaking. We have a pretty detailed description of him, and it seems highly likely that he was disguised, with a wig, a beard and dark glasses. It also seems highly likely that he was the murderer.'

'As I seem to recall somebody saying a week ago,' said Rooth.

'That's true,' said Moreno. 'We advertised his description and a Wanted notice several days ago, but he hasn't contacted us, so I suppose we can give a brownie point to Rooth. Anyway, none of the witnesses noticed any kind of contact between this Mr X and Erich Van Veeteren – who was sitting in the restaurant section, and left the premises shortly after Mr X. They might well have been in eye contact; Erich was sitting at a table with quite a good view of the bar.'

'Hmm,' said Reinhart. 'He sits there waiting for an hour. And when the man appears he does nothing, but the man follows him out into the car park, and kills him. There we have it in a nutshell. Can you tell me what the hell it's all about?'

'Drugs,' said deBries after a while.

'Any other suggestions?' asked Reinhart.

'I'm not convinced that deBries is right,' said Jung. 'But if we assume it was in fact a delivery of some kind of goods, there are two things I wonder. First of all: did they know each other? Did they both know who the contact person was that they would be meeting in the restaurant? Or was there just one of them who knew the other's identity?'

'Was that one or two wonderings?' asked Rooth.

'One,' said Jung. 'The other is: which of them was delivering, and which was receiving?'

Nobody spoke for a couple of seconds.

'Another question, in that case,' said deBries. 'If it was a delivery, where did it take place?'

'It wasn't a delivery,' said Rooth. 'He murdered him instead.'

'Where *would* it have taken place, then?' said deBries, fingering his plaster in irritation.

'The car park, it has to be the car park,' said Moreno. 'It's also obvious that Erich must have identified Mr X. He recognized him when he came in and sat in the bar, then followed him out as had been agreed.'

'Possible,' said Reinhart, lighting his pipe. 'Very possible. But that arrangement seems to me more like the meeting of a couple of secret agents than a drugs deal. But I agree with deBries in principle, and I also agree that it must have been Mr X who was delivering the stuff . . .'

'. . . and that he didn't have anything to deliver, in fact, but killed his contact man instead.'

There followed a few more seconds of silence. Reinhart closed his eyes and blew out smoke with full force.

'But where exactly is this getting us?' wondered Rooth. 'And what the hell could it have been about if it wasn't drugs? Is there anybody apart from me who votes for a postage stamp? One of those bloody misprinted ones that sell for eighteen million . . .'

'A postage stamp?' said deBries. 'You're out of your mind.'

Reinhart shrugged.

'Could be anything,' he said. 'It could have been stolen goods . . . Something that was dangerous but useful in the right hands . . . Or it could have been money, that's surely the simplest explanation. One of them was going to pay the other for something or other. Something that needed a degree of discretion, as it were. But I don't think we're going to get much further than this at the moment. Maybe it's time to change the perspective a bit. As long as we can't work out what he was doing out there, we're stymied and just marking time – I agree with Rooth on that score.'

'So do I,' said Rooth.

'Okay, let me sum up where the brains trust has got to so far,' said Moreno. 'Erich knew that the contact person was Mr X when he arrived and sat down in the bar. And when he left he followed him out in order to collect something from him, and instead was given a blow to the side of his head and another to the back of it. Fatal. Have I got that right?'

'I would think so,' said Reinhart. 'Any objections? No? Well, remember for Christ's sake that this is no more than speculation. Right, let's go over to the Western Front. We've got no end of information there. Marlene Frey and the address book. Who wants to start? DeBries has volunteered.'

It took an hour and twenty minutes to deal with the Western Front. A hundred and two interviews had taken place with people who had known Erich Van Veeteren in one context or another, according to the list in the black address book.

All of them had been duly recorded: deBries and Krause had spent all Wednesday afternoon and a good part of the night listening to every one of them. They had also produced a list of the people who had been in contact with Erich Van Veeteren during the weeks immediately before his death, a list so far comprising twenty-six names. But several further interviews were still outstanding, so the list could well expand before the end of the road was reached.

The result of all this was not too bad, from a quantitative point of view: but as they were not involved in a macro-sociological investigation, as deBries pointed out, the real result was very meagre indeed.

To be frank, so far – sixteen days after the murder and twelve since the body had been found – they had not succeeded in digging up anything looking remotely like a lead or a suspicion. Not with the best will in the world. It was enough to drive one up the wall. However, with the aid of the interviews and above all of Marlene Frey, they had begun to establish what her boyfriend had been up to during the last days of his life. It had been a very tiring process, and as far as being fruitful was concerned, it had not yet produced so much as a gooseberry. As Detective Inspector Rooth chose to put it.

Nobody seemed to have the slightest idea why Erich Van Veeteren had driven out to Dikken that fateful day.

Not his fiancée. Not the police. Not anybody else.

'How reliable is Marlene Frey?' asked Jung. 'Bearing in mind drugs and all that stuff.'

'I believe her,' said Reinhart after a few moments' thought. 'It might be a misjudgement, of course, but I have the impression that she's on our side one hundred per cent.'

'It's not really very odd if we don't discover anything right away,' said Moreno. 'If we have in fact stumbled upon the killer somewhere among all these interviews, it would be a bit much to expect the person concerned to break down and confess simply because we'd switched on a tape recorder. Don't you think?'

'Why bother to do it, then?' Rooth wanted to know. 'Doesn't the law say people must tell the police the truth?'

'Hmm,' said Reinhart. 'You haven't seen the point of spending a dark night in front of a tape recorder trying to catch on to a murderer's slight slip of the tongue . . . But perhaps you couldn't be expected to? Anyway, let's press on! What do you all think? There must surely be one of us – and for the moment I'm discounting Rooth's postage stamp theory – one of us with an idea of some sort? We're getting paid for doing this, for Christ's sake. Or is it just as black in your bird-like brains as it is in mine?'

He looked round the table.

'Pitch black,' said deBries eventually. 'My tape recordings are available to anybody who's interested. It only takes eighteen hours to listen to them all. No doubt there's one-tenth of a clue somewhere among them, but Krause and I have given up.'

'I'll pass for the time being,' said Rooth.

'It might be an idea to have another chat with one or two of those closest to him,' suggested deBries. 'With Erich's best friends – there are three or four who knew him pretty well. Get them to speculate a bit, perhaps?'

'Could be,' said Reinhart with a sombre nod. 'Why not? Does anybody else want to raise anything?'

Nobody did. Rooth sighed and Jung tried to conceal a yawn.

'Why are you wearing a tie?' Rooth asked. 'Doesn't your shirt have any buttons?'

'Opera,' said Jung. 'Maureen has won two tickets at work. I won't have time to go home and change, I'll have to drive straight there after work.'

'Make sure you don't get dirty this afternoon, then,' said Rooth.

Jung made no comment. Reinhart lit his pipe again.

'No,' he said, 'we're certainly not making any progress. But we're bloody brilliant at being patient.'

'How poor are they that have not patience,' said Rooth.

'Have you spoken to *The Chief Inspector* lately?' asked Moreno.

'Not for a few days,' said Reinhart.

Van Veeteren took the tram out to Dikken. There was something about the car park there that prevented him from even thinking about taking the car.

Perhaps it was the risk that he would happen to park at the very spot where his son was killed.

It was just as empty and deserted as it usually was at this time of year, apparently. Only four cars, plus a chocked-up trailer from a long-distance lorry of which there was no trace. He didn't know precisely where the body had been found – there were several hundred metres of undergrowth to choose from. He didn't want to know anyway. What would have been the point?

He hurried across the empty space and into the Trattoria Commedia. The bar was immediately in front of the entrance door. Two elderly men in crumpled jackets were sitting there, drinking beer. The bartender was a young man in a yellow shirt, with a ponytail: he was busy, but nodded to Van Veeteren.

Van Veeteren nodded back and continued into the restaurant section. Three of the eighteen tables were occupied; he chose one with a good view of the bar and sat down.

Maybe this is the very table that Erich was sitting at, he thought.

He ordered the dish of the day from a waitress with blonde plaits: lamb cutlet with potatoes au gratin. And a glass of red wine.

It took half an hour, waiting to be served and then eating the meal. It didn't taste bad at all, he decided. He had never set foot inside the place before, and for obvious reasons would never do so again; but as far as he could see they served decent food. Golfers in general probably couldn't be fobbed off with any old rubbish, he assumed.

He gave the dessert a miss. Ordered a coffee and a little cognac in the bar instead.

Perhaps this is exactly where the murderer sat, he thought. Maybe I'm sitting on the very chair my son's killer had occupied.

When the yellow-shirted barman came to top up his coffee, he took the opportunity of asking if he'd been on duty that evening.

Yes, the young man admitted. He had been. Why was he asking?

Van Veeteren thought for a moment before replying.

'Police,' he said.

'What, another one?' said the barman, looking somewhat amused.

'Hmm,' said Van Veeteren. 'I can imagine they've been here like a swarm of flies. I'm from a quite different branch.'

'Which branch?' the barman wondered.

'Special Branch,' said Van Veeteren. 'Maybe we could have a friendly little chat?'

The bartender hesitated for a moment.

'Okay, I'm not exactly rushed off my feet at the moment,' he said.

'This sausage is a gift from the gods to mankind,' said Rooth.

'I can see you're enjoying it,' said Jung, eyeing his colleague who was chewing away with his eyes half-closed and an expression of celestial bliss. 'I'm glad to see you have a spiritual side as well.'

'It's the garlic that does it,' said Rooth, opening his eyes. 'An excellent old medicinal plant. I have a theory.'

'You don't say?' said Jung. 'Is it the postage stamp again?'

'Better than that,' said Rooth, shovelling some potato salad into his cheek pouches.

Jung waited.

'Can you make up your mind whether you're going to eat or to talk?' he said. 'That would make it easier to eat my lunch.'

Rooth nodded and chewed away.

'All right,' he said. 'Something occurred to me as we were sitting upstairs, discussing the case.'

'Go on,' said Jung.

'Blackmail,' said Rooth.

'Blackmail?' said Jung.

'Exactly. It would fit. Listen. Erich Van Veeteren is the blackmailer. He has some kind of hold on somebody, and has named a price for his silence. He drives out to Dikken in order to collect his cash. But his victim doesn't want to pay up, and kills him instead. It's as plain as a pikestaff, correct me if I'm wrong.'

Jung thought it over.

'It's not impossible,' he said. 'It's a credible theory. Why didn't you say anything about it during the run-through?'

Rooth looked a bit embarrassed.

'I only thought of it towards the end,' he said. 'You lot didn't seem all that amenable. I didn't want to drag things out.'

'You mean you were hungry?' said Jung.

'You said that, not me,' said Rooth.

16

'If you regard it as a sort of cancer,' said Reinhart, 'it becomes quite clear.'

'White man, he speak with forked tongue,' said Winnifred, who was a quarter aboriginal.

'What do you mean by that?'

'Explain.'

They were lying in the bath. The fact that Winnifred Lynch, born in Australia but grown up and awarded a doctorate in England, had moved in with Reinhart and given birth to his child was largely due to that bath. At least, that's what she usually claimed when he asked her if she really loved him.

It was big and deep. And built-in. Adorned with an irregular mosaic pattern of small green and blue ceramic tiles on the outside, and fitted with an impressive array of copper taps in the middle. Big enough for two adults to half-lie in. One at each end. Like now. With their legs and bodies nicely intertwined. It had cost Reinhart two months' wages to refurbish his bathroom twelve years ago.

But it had been worth it, obviously.

'Cancer,' he said again. 'A cancerous growth forms metastases – if it doesn't do so it often escapes detection. It's the same with a lot of criminal cases, that's what I mean. This business involving *The Chief Inspector*'s son, for example. Are you with me?'

'I'm with you,' said Winnifred.

'Good. We've established everything that can reasonably be established regarding what happened. But even so we've got nowhere, and that doesn't bode well for our chances of solving the case . . . Unless it produces a few buds.'

'Produces a few buds?'

'Metastases,' said Reinhart. 'Something else has got to happen. That's what I'm trying to explain. If you just commit an isolated crime – kill somebody, rob a bank or whatever – and leave it at that, well, you have a pretty good chance of getting away with it. Especially if you are a pretty law-abiding citizen otherwise. But generally speaking it doesn't stop at the initial growth stage. The crime gives birth to metastases, we discover them and trace them to where they came from, and so we solve the bloody case. Are you with me?'

Winnifred sighed.

'Brilliant metaphorics,' she said, and started wiggling her toes in his armpits. 'Criminality as a cancer in the body of society. Clever stuff, I give you that. I haven't heard anything quite as telling for several hours.'

'Hmm,' said Reinhart. 'It was mostly that business of the metastases that I was after.'

'All right,' said Winnifred. 'It has to produce a few buds, otherwise you won't find Erich's murderer – is that the point you're making?'

'More or less,' said Reinhart. 'We're marking time at the moment. Or treading water if you want a more appropriate—'

He broke off because Winnifred had bitten him in the calf.

'Ouch,' said Reinhart.

'Is there anything to suggest the production of a bud?'

Reinhart thought that one over.

'How the hell should I know? Cancer is a mystery, isn't it?'

'Of course,' said Winnifred. 'But if you massage my feet and give me a few facts about the case, I'll see what I can suggest.'

'Fair deal,' said Reinhart. 'Remove them from my armpits.'

*

Ulrike Fremdli was displaying a new trait that he hadn't seen before. A sort of caution. He had been thinking about it for several days, and when she collected him from the antiquarian bookshop at closing time on Thursday evening, he said as much.

'Caution?' she said. 'What do you mean?'

'You look at me as if I were a patient,' said Van Veeteren. 'Stop it. My son has been murdered: if I go out of my mind as a result, I'll get more than enough of that bloody therapist's look in the loony bin.'

'What the hell . . . ?' she said. Then they walked in silence, arm in arm, past Yorrick's Cafe before she stopped dead.

'All right, you may be right. No more being unnecessarily considerate – but in that case you really must open your mouth now and again as well.'

'Hmm,' said Van Veeteren.

Ulrike looked at him with a vertical furrow between her eyebrows.

'I'm with you in that grief doesn't need to be expressed in words,' she said, 'but I refuse to believe that not doing so is the best way of honouring the dead. We ought to celebrate them instead of mourning them . . . Like they do in Mexico, or wherever it is. The Day of the Dead and all that. Silent grief is only of benefit to somebody who wants to wallow in it.'

Van Veeteren thought that over for a while.

'You may be right,' he said eventually. 'Yes, if life has to go on it's presumably necessary to open your cake-hole now and again.'

She suddenly burst out laughing. Threw her arms round him and hugged him so tightly that he wondered if he could be completely confident of winning if he took her on in an arm-wrestling match. If it was going to come to that.

'I give in,' he said. 'Do you think . . .'

'Do I think what?' she said, letting go of him.

'Do you think we can find a sort of compromise position . . . somewhere between patient and sparring partner? I think that would be of benefit for our relationship.'

She smiled. Linked arms with him again and started walking.

'What you are trying to describe is the ideal man,' she said. 'But he doesn't exist. I'll have to put up with you as you are. Sometimes patient, sometimes sparring partner – but it doesn't matter. I've never expected anything else. Come on, then, let's go up to Marlene's and see if she's found any photographs.'

They had finally got round to visiting her together for the first time, and it didn't last long. Marlene Frey had been having problems with her stove: the temperature in the flat hovered between ten and twelve degrees, and she was just about to go to a friend's place for the night.

However, she had dug out a dozen photographs of Erich – some of them featured both Erich and herself, in fact. Obviously she would like to keep some of them – perhaps they could meet on another occasion and come to some agreement. When it wasn't so damned cold. One could always have copies made if one still had the negatives – and she did have them. Most of them, at any rate.

'How's it going with . . . ?' he wondered, glancing for a fraction of a second at her stomach.

'All's well,' she assured them. 'He's still hanging in there.'

It was obvious that she was stressed, and he didn't think she was quite herself, compared with when they'd met at Adenaar's. She merely shook hands with Ulrike and gave her a quick smile, and the brief visit left a somewhat insipid taste in the mouth.

'You mustn't read too much into it,' said Ulrike when they had found a table at Kraus's half an hour later. 'It's easy to do that when you're not on top form yourself.'

'Top form?' said Van Veeteren. 'I haven't been on top form since I started school.'

*

While waiting for Reinhart he rolled four cigarettes and smoked two of them. Vox wasn't a place he usually frequented: it was Reinhart's choice, and he was afraid they might start playing jazz music if they stayed there too long. It had said something to that effect on a poster in the entrance, and there was a little stage right at the back of the dirty-brown, smoke-filled premises.

Not that he had all that much against jazz as such. Reinhart used to maintain that when you listened to – and above all if you could play, of course – modern, improvised jazz, you increased your IQ to record levels. As an exponential function of time, concentration and alcohol intake . . . or something like that: he didn't always listen too carefully to what Reinhart said. But not tonight, thank you, he thought. It's too soon. He had barely felt up to coping with his own music. He couldn't even stomach William Byrd and Monteverdi, so the barbed-wire tones of saxophones didn't seem particularly appropriate for the occasion.

He sipped away at his dark beer while waiting, and thought things over. Asked himself just what was happening to his thoughts and his mind nowadays. All the mood swings. It was not pleasant. Grappling with all the different states he found himself in. His usual attitude born of experience: his chastened – not exactly optimistic but nevertheless bearable – belief that there was something logical behind all the darkness. Certain patterns. Positive resignation, to borrow a term from old Borkmann. But on the other hand this new feeling: the totally black resignation. To be sure, he'd occasionally had a sniff of it – especially in connection with his professional life – but it had never been able to retain its grip on him as it was doing now.

Not like this. For hours on end. Sometimes half a day. Incapable of action. Incapable of thought.

Incapable of living?

I must put a stop to it, he thought. I must get a grip. It's Erich who's dead, and me who's still alive. All lives come to an end, some too soon, others too late. Nothing can change that eternal truth. And I don't want to lose Ulrike.

Reinhart turned up at half past nine, half an hour late.

'Sorry about that,' he said. 'Joanna has earache. Terribly painful, it seems. Did they have that in your day as well?'

Van Veeteren nodded. Reinhart noticed his half-empty glass, and signalled for two new ones.

'How's it going?' Van Veeteren asked when the goods had been delivered, and each had taken a swig. Reinhart lit his pipe, and scratched his short, greying hair.

'So-so.'

'So-so?' said Van Veeteren. 'What the devil does that mean? Have you been stricken by aphasia?'

'We haven't made all that much progress,' said Reinhart. 'What do you expect? Do you want me to spell out every bloody detail?'

Van Veeteren tapped a cigarette against the table top, then lit it.

'Yes,' he said. 'Every bloody detail. Please.'

It took quite a while, and when Reinhart had finished the music had started on the stage. Only a pianist and a dark-skinned lady singing in quite a low voice, so it wasn't difficult to make oneself heard. Van Veeteren established that his earlier prejudices had been wide of the mark: the woman had a pleasantly low voice that reminded him of simmering velvet (in so far as velvet could possibly simmer, and produce sounds . . .), and while Reinhart was speaking the singing produced an attractive distancing effect. It seemed to swathe Erich's death and all the associated circumstances in a sort of soft, almost sensuous shroud. It occurred to him that Erich would have liked that.

Grief and suffering, he thought. We can't avoid that. All we can do is welcome it with open arms and treat it in the right way. Swathe it in art or rituals or whatever else we have at our disposal. But for goodness' sake don't just leave it lying in a corner like a ball of dust.

'Anyway, that's more or less it,' said Reinhart. 'We've got the killer surrounded – that character in the bar. It's got to be him, everything suggests it's him; but we don't have any plausible hypotheses regarding what Erich was doing out there. Or was intending to do. You could speculate about various possibilities, of course: but I'd be misleading you if I claimed there was anything more to it than that.'

'I understand,' said Van Veeteren.

'You're still pretty keen on our nailing him, I take it.'

Van Veeteren glanced at the singer before answering. She was saying thank you for the sporadic applause, and announcing that there would be a brief interval.

'Yes,' he said. 'Keener for every day that passes. I didn't understand it properly at first, but it seems to be more or less rooted in one's genes . . . You have to find your son's murderer.'

'Rooted in our culture, in any case,' said Reinhart. 'And in our mythology.'

'Bollocks to whether it's mythology or not,' said Van Veeteren. 'I want you to catch him. Are you going to do that?'

'I've already promised you I'll do that,' said Reinhart.

Van Veeteren thought for a moment.

'Are you annoyed because I'm interfering?' he asked. 'For Christ's sake say so if you are.'

Reinhart raised his glass.

'I'd think it was damned odd if you didn't. Cheers.'

'Cheers,' said Van Veeteren, and drained his glass. 'Anyway, go home now and look after your daughter. I think

I'll sit here a bit longer and listen to that singer.'

'Good for you,' said Reinhart, getting to his feet.

17

After work on Friday he went to visit his father. It was over two months since he'd last been, and it was a way of passing the time. The Oesterle Care Home was in Bredenbuijk, just outside Loewingen: he took the route via Borsens in order to avoid the worst of the traffic, and arrived just after the evening meal had finished.

As usual, his father was sitting in his bed, gazing at his hands. It often took some time to get him to look up, but on this occasion he did so more or less immediately. He had barely managed to move the chair to the side of the bed and sit down before his father slowly raised his head and looked at him with those bloodshot, watery eyes of his. Just for a second there was a sign of recognition, but perhaps that was wishful thinking.

Why should he recognize him today when he hadn't done so for the last six years?

After half a minute his father's chin sank gradually down towards his chest, and he returned to studying his hands, which were lying on top of the blue blanket and slowly rotating around each other.

He sat there for ten minutes. He couldn't stand it any longer than that. He couldn't see a nurse or care assistant he recognized, and didn't bother to ask about his father's condition.

How is he? Is he all right?

Such questions were pointless. Had been pointless for several years; it felt better not to ask them. He had often wondered what the point was of keeping him alive, but nobody at the care home had so much as whispered the word euthanasia, and he didn't want to be the first to do so. Besides, his sister in America would be against it, he knew that without needing to ask.

So his father just sat there. Never spoke to anybody, never read a book or a newspaper. Never watched television or listened to the radio. Didn't even get up nowadays to go to the toilet. The only sign he gave of being in some sort of a conscious state was that he opened his mouth when a spoonful of food was approaching.

My father, he thought. One of these days I shall be like you are now. Nice to see you.

And he made up his mind that he would make the most of life while he still could.

*

That Friday night became very difficult. Bearing in mind that Vera would be coming the next day, he gave the whisky a miss. He didn't want it to become a habit. And he didn't want to overdo the Sobran tablets either. He took a weak sleeping tablet instead, but it only made him feel sluggish and slightly sick.

His decision to wait for Monday's letter before deciding what to do next was of course the right one – the only conceivable one: but in no way did it mean that he could stop thinking about it.

Those persistent gloomy thoughts and images of what would happen to him. Speculations about what kind of scenario 'a friend' would propose for handing over the money this time. And about what he would be forced to do. Again.

Whether there was going to be any possibility of doing it.

Killing him.

Killing one last time and drawing a line once and for all under his former life. Without needing to sum it all up or look back at all. Simply waking up to a new, blank day.

He wished he were already at that point.

Wished it were all over. So he could make the most of his life while he still could?

The last time he looked at the clock it was ten minutes to six.

★

It was raining when he woke up a few hours later. Persistent rain, and a strong wind hurling it at the windows. He stayed in bed for a while, listening to it. Then he got up and had a shower.

He spent the morning and the early afternoon preparing the evening meal. Did some vacuuming and tidying up, and opened some bottles of wine to breathe. Sorted out the laundry as well. Shortly after two he had a call from Smaage, reminding him that the next meeting of the Fraternity was due to take place the coming Friday; they chatted for a while, and afterwards he was surprised at how easy he had found it. How uninhibited he'd been. After all, it had been immediately after the previous meeting that it had all begun. After that damned meeting of the 'brothers' his old, secure life had been brought to a halt, and everything had shot off in different directions. He promised Smaage that he would be there, provided nothing unforeseen cropped up – and it was when he said 'unforeseen' that he suddenly felt a flash of dizziness. Smaage wished him a pleasant weekend, and hung up.

Then there was one more hour during which he had nothing to do but sit around, waiting for her. Between four and five, as darkness was falling and the wind seemed to ease off a little. But the rainbows kept coming and going. He spent quite a long time by the bedroom window, looking up at the low, restless sky over the strip of trees planted along the back of the row of terraced houses.

Stood there wrestling with a completely new thought.

I'll tell her, he thought. She would understand. Then we'd both be in it together, and could give each other strength. Surely that would be a good thing.

She rang the doorbell at exactly five o'clock. When he went to open the door he suddenly felt weak at the knees.

It was their most difficult evening so far. At least at the beginning there was something reserved about her behaviour, and even though she didn't say so straight out, it was evident that she was tormented by the situation between herself and Andreas.

Tormented by the need to tell her husband that she was in the process of leaving him for somebody else. He understood her difficulties. Realized that she still hadn't put him on the spot, even though she had promised to do so. But he didn't press her. Didn't allow any impatience or disappointment he was feeling come up to the surface. Nevertheless there was a cloud hanging over them, something that he had never felt before; and it wasn't until they had drunk almost three bottles of wine that they began to make love.

It was just as enjoyable as ever. Perhaps even better: for a brief moment he had the feeling that it was due to the bitter whiff of disaster in the air, but the feeling went just as quickly as it had come. He managed to give her four or five orgasms, and afterwards she lay with her head on his chest, weeping. His own head was as empty as if an atom bomb had exploded inside it.

They eventually shared yet another bottle of wine: it felt as if the blood was finally starting to flow through his veins again. Soon afterwards he took her one more time – slightly brutally, as she liked it – on the kitchen table, and then they each drank a glass of Glenlivet to round things off.

He would regret that glass of whisky for the rest of his life, as that is what made him lose his sense of judgement and embark on the path to ruin. He never thought there was any other explanation.

There couldn't possibly be any other explanation.

As he stood in the bathroom, getting washed, he realized that he was quite drunk – more drunk than he had been that evening, for instance – but that there was something he must do. He needed to do it. The doubts that had plagued him earlier in the week seemed to have been blown away, and when he examined his face in the mirror all he saw was strength.

Strength and determination.

He grinned at his own image and went back into the bedroom. Sat down on the edge of the bed and played for a while with one of her nipples between his thumb and forefinger.

I'll tell her now, he thought.

He realized that it had been a terrible mistake the moment he saw the look on her face.

FOUR

FOUR

18

Jochen Vlaarmeier had been driving buses between Maardam and Kaustin for more than eleven years.

Six trips in each direction. Every day. Apart from his days off in accordance with the company rota. And the occasional week's holiday, of course.

The first and last trip of every day were pointless, in a way. But only in a way. There was no sensible reason to drive out to Kaustin at half past six in the morning, and no sensible reason to drive back from there twelve hours later. But the bus spent its nights in the garage in Leimaar Allé, and Vlaarmeier had nothing against driving an empty bus now and then. Nothing at all. Over the years he had begun more and more to regard passengers as an annoying aspect of his work, and he reckoned the evening drive back to Maardam among the best parts of his life. No traffic on the roads. An empty bus and another day's work over and done with. What more could anybody ask for?

On Sundays the number of trips was reduced to four. Two in each direction. He drove out to Kaustin at nine a.m. – an empty bus was always guaranteed – and returned at ten o'clock with a cargo of four farmers' wives on their way to morning service in Keymer Church. Because their own church wasn't good enough, for some reason. Or perhaps their village church wasn't functioning any more. Vlaarmeier had no time for things sacred ever since he lost a girlfriend to a callow theology student thirty years ago.

At two o'clock he would drive the farmers' wives back home again. By then they would have partaken of coffee and cakes at Heimer's cafe in Rozenplejn.

Always the same four. Two dumpy little women, two emaciated and hunched up. He had often wondered why the company didn't arrange for a taxi instead. It would have been much cheaper.

This cold Sunday – 29 November – there were only three, as fru Willmot, one of the dumpy ones, had flu. This was announced by the windswept fru Glock when she clambered aboard outside the school.

Thirty-eight degrees and two swollen tonsils, she informed him. A running cold and aches and pains all over. Just so that he knew.

It was also fru Glock who screamed so loudly that he almost drove into the ditch. It happened shortly before the long bend into the village of Korrim, and it sounded as if a seagull had flown into Vlaarmeier's ear.

He managed to get the bus back on course, and glanced at the inside mirror. The old lady was half-standing and hammering away with her hand on the side window.

'Stop the bus!' she screeched. 'Oh my oh my, stop for God's sake!'

Jochen Vlaarmeier slammed on the brakes and pulled up at the side of the road. Oh hell, he thought. One of them has had a stroke.

But when he looked at the back of the bus he could see that all of them were hale and hearty. Or at least, in no worse a condition than usual. The two sitting further back were gaping open-mouthed at fru Glock who was still hammering on the window and yelling incomprehensibly. He sighed, left his cabin and walked towards her.

'Calm down now,' he said. 'Take it easy. What on earth's got into you?'

She stopped screaming. Swallowed twice, making her false teeth click, and stared at him.

'A body,' she said. 'A woman . . . Dead.'

'What?' said Vlaarmeier.

She pointed towards a black-looking field behind the bus.

'Over there. At the side of the road. A body.'

Then she flopped down on the seat with her head in

her hands. The other two ladies came striding along the centre aisle and started crossing themselves somewhat doubtfully.

'A body?' said Vlaarmeier.

She knocked on the window again and pointed. Vlaarmeier thought for a moment. Then he opened the pneumatic door, got out of the bus and started walking back along the edge of the road.

He found her after about twenty-five metres. Diagonally over the shallow ditch that separated the road from the newly ploughed field was the body of a woman. It was wrapped up in what looked like a sheet . . . A very dirty sheet, its edges flapping slightly in the breeze, that left one leg and part of her upper torso bare. Two large, white breasts and arms spread out at unnatural angles. She was lying on her back, her face staring straight up at the sky but largely hidden by her wet, reddish hair that seemed to have stuck fast to it somehow.

Oh Christ, thought Vlaarmeier. For Christ's bloody sake. Then he sicked up the whole of his substantial breakfast – both the porridge and the sausage and eggs – before staggering back to the bus in order to telephone for help.

By the time Chief Inspector Reinhart and Inspector Moreno got to the village of Korrim it had started snowing. Large white flakes were floating diagonally down and melting on the wet, black soil.

A patrol car with two constables, Joensuu and Kellermann, was already on the spot. Joensuu was standing on the road next to the dead woman, with his back towards her and his arms folded over his chest. Legs wide apart, and uncompromising. Kellermann was standing beside the bus, pen and notebook in hand, talking to the driver and passengers. Three old women were standing pressed up against each other by the side of the yellow bus, as if they were trying to keep one another warm. All three were wearing dark-coloured overcoats and ghastly hats. They reminded Reinhart of crows, their feathers ruffled, jumping around on the road looking for scraps of food. The driver was marching nervously up and down, smoking.

Why don't they sit inside the bus instead? Reinhart wondered. Haven't they noticed that it's snowing?

He ordered Moreno to go and assist Kellermann, and approached Joensuu in order to look at what he needed to look at.

For two seconds at first. Then he closed his eyes for five. And then looked once more.

That was what he always did. He didn't know if it made things any easier, but it had become a sort of ritual over the years.

Anyway, a dead woman. Almost certainly naked, but

inadequately wrapped up in something looking like a sheet, exactly as Vlaarmeier had said on the telephone. She was lying more or less flat on her back, her head resting on a clod of earth, her feet just reaching as far as the narrow strip of grass verge. Red toenails in the midst of all the mess, he noted: it looked almost surreal, or at any rate intensified the impression of unreality. Quite a well-built body, as far as he could judge. Somewhere between thirty and forty, it seemed, but that was only a guess, of course. Her face was largely hidden by her longish, dark red hair. Snowflakes were falling on the woman as well – as if the sky had wanted to cover up what it preferred not to see, it struck him. A tactful shroud. That was typical of the thoughts that usually occurred to him on occasions like this. Words, phrases, images: the same vain attempt to cover up the truth that the sky was busy with, more or less.

'What a bloody mess,' said Joensuu. 'A good-looking woman. Not now, of course . . .'

'How long have you two been here?' asked Reinhart.

Joensuu checked his watch.

'Fourteen minutes,' he said. 'We got the call at ten thirty-nine. We were here by fifty-eight.'

Reinhart nodded. Clambered down from the road, bent over the body and studied it for a few seconds.

'Blood,' said Joensuu without turning round. 'There's blood on the sheet. And on her head. Somebody's clocked her one there.'

Reinhart stood up and clenched his fists in his pockets. The sheets – for there seemed to be two – were stained not only by soil and dirt: there was a series of stripes and drops of blood over one of her shoulders, and as Kellermann had said, her hair on the left side of her head and face was clogged with something that could hardly be anything else but blood.

Although he supposed it could possibly be brain substances.

Two more cars arrived. Reinhart greeted Intendent Schultze, who weighed 120 kilos and was acting head of the scene-of-crime team.

'It's snowing,' he said grimly. 'That's a damned nuisance. We'll have to set up a canopy.'

Reinhart stayed there for a while and watched Schultze's assistants hammering thin metal poles into the soft ground, then stretching a thin sheet of canvas a metre over the body. He wished them good luck with their analyses and went to the bus. Told Kellermann to go and help Joensuu and to cordon off the scene of the crime.

And also to do whatever they could to assist Schultze and his men.

Moreno seemed to have already squeezed out of the bus driver and his passengers what little contribution they could make. They had travelled past in the bus, and one of them had happened to see the body, that was about it. After checking their names and addresses, Reinhart told them they could continue on their way. But a bit of a palaver ensued, since none of the women wished to continue to Keymer Church – the service was already under way – and eventually Vlaarmeier rolled over and agreed to turn the bus round and take them back to Kaustin instead.

The timetable had gone to pot ages ago anyway, and there were no other passengers to take into consideration. There never were on a Sunday.

Half an hour later Reinhart and Moreno also left the scene. They had with them a record of the first oral report from Schultze: the dead victim was a red-headed woman of average height, round about thirty-five years old. She had been killed by several blows to the side and back of the head, probably during the night or in the early hours of the morning. It couldn't have been any later than four a.m. in view of the state of rigor mortis. She was completely naked, apart from the two sheets she had been wrapped up in, and it seemed highly likely that the body had been dumped on the verge from a car. Nothing that could be of value for the investigation had been found, but the scene-of-crime team were still creeping around and searching, and would continue to do so for several more hours yet.

Both underneath and around the canopy that had been

set up.

Just as Reinhart and Moreno were clambering into their car, the green body bag was being lifted into another car for transport to the Forensic Laboratory in Maardam. No unauthorized spectators had turned up at the scene, and the few cars that had passed by during these godforsaken Sunday hours had been waved on authoritatively by Joensuu or Kellermann. Or both.

The snow continued to fall.

'The first of Advent,' said Reinhart. 'It's the first of Advent today. A nice setting. We ought to light a candle.'

Moreno nodded. The thought occurred to her that Good Friday and death on the cross might be more appropriate; but she said nothing. She turned her head and looked out over the barren landscape and the occasional large snowflakes drifting down over the dark soil. Grey. Only shades of grey for as far as the eye could see. And hardly any light. She'd intended to have a lie-in this morning. Then sit up in bed with a newspaper, and spend two hours over breakfast. Go for a swim in the afternoon.

Had intended. That's not the way things turned out. She would have to spend the day working instead. All day, most probably: especially if they succeeded in identifying the dead woman. Interrogations and interviews with her nearest and dearest. Questions and answers. Tears and despair. It wasn't especially difficult to see the whole thing in her mind's eye. While Reinhart led the way over the narrow, wet road, muttering and cursing to himself, she began to hope that they wouldn't find out who she was . . . That the anonymous dead woman would remain anonymous for a few more hours. A whole day, even. It was probably a thought that would make things easier for those nearest and dearest, whoever they might be; but hardly compatible with her work as a detective officer. It didn't fit in with the long-established rule that the first few hours of an investigation were always the most important ones – fitted in better, much better, she had to admit, with a vague hope that she might be able to spend a few hours at the swimming baths in the afternoon despite everything.

It was wrong to falsify one's motives, Moreno thought with a sigh. That had been one of *The Chief Inspector*'s favourite sayings, one she found it impossible to forget. Why is it that I always want to take a shower after looking at a dead body? she wondered out of the blue. Especially if it had been the body of a dead woman. Must have something to do with empathy . . .

'I wonder why he left her there,' said Reinhart, interrupting her train of thought. 'In the middle of this flat plain. It would make more sense to have hidden her up in the forest instead.'

Moreno thought that one over.

'Maybe he was in a hurry.'

'Could be. In any case, there must surely be blood in his car. He must have had a car. If we can find it, there must be proof of his guilt there. What do you think?'

'Nothing at all at the moment,' said Moreno with a shrug.

'We can always hope,' said Reinhart. 'Hope that her husband, or whoever it was that did it, has rung to confess. It seems to be . . . Yes, I have the feeling that he's sitting in Krause's office at this very moment.'

'You think so?' said Moreno.

'Yes, I do,' said Reinhart. 'Sitting there, waiting for us. Hungover and half crazy . . . Saturday night, a bit too much to drink . . . A quarrel, some infidelity, and then he appears with the iron in his hand. Yes, the poor bastards. You have to feel sorry for the human race.'

'Yes, you're right,' said Moreno. 'Perhaps we ought to light a candle.'

There was no killer waiting for them, either in Krause's office or anywhere else in the police station. Nor did anybody report a missing woman with red toenails and red hair during the next few hours. At half past one Reinhart and Moreno received a set of photographs from the scene of the crime, and shortly afterwards came a rather more detailed report from the doctors and forensic officers.

The dead woman was 172 centimetres tall and weighed 62 kilos. She had dark red hair, both on her head and round her pudenda; she had never given birth, but she had partaken of sexual intercourse in close proximity to the murder. *Before the murder*, thought both Reinhart and Moreno without needing to discuss the matter. There was a lot of sperm in her vagina – another piece of certain proof for when they caught the perpetrator. Freeze the sperm and run a DNA test. Mind you, it didn't necessarily follow that they were the same person of course – the man who had sex with her not long before she died, and the man who made sure that she did. Die. But of course it was highly likely that the two were identical. That was the view of both Reinhart and Moreno.

Healthy teeth and no obvious distinctive features. She had been killed by three heavy blows to the side of her head and one to the back of it. The relatively large amount of blood was due to the fact that one of the blows to the side of her head had split an artery in her temple. The location of the murder was unknown, but it was definitely not the place where she was found. The exact time of death could not yet be established for certain, but it appeared to be somewhere between two o'clock and four o'clock in the early hours of Sunday morning. No clothes or belongings had been discovered at the place where the body was found, nor any other objects. The alcohol content in the woman's blood was 1.56 per thousand.

'She was drunk, then,' said Reinhart. 'Let's hope that made it less horrendous for her. Fucking hell.'

Moreno put down the report from the Forensic Laboratory.

'We'll get a more detailed report this evening,' said Reinhart. 'Meusse is pulling out all the stops. Shall we take a few hours off?'

By the time Moreno set off on foot for the swimming baths in Birkenweg, the snow had turned into rain. Dusk was beginning to descend over the town, even though it was only three o'clock, and she thought once again about what Reinhart had said about lighting a candle.

But when she saw the body of that unknown woman lying out at Korrim in her mind's eye, it seemed to her that she preferred the darkness.

It was one of those days, she decided. A day that couldn't cope with opening up properly. Or a day when she herself couldn't cope with opening up properly. A day that could be survived best by keeping your senses and consciousness as much in the dark as possible, leaving only narrow cracks through which to communicate with reality.

One of those days. Or perhaps it was the time of year?

The life of an oyster, she thought as she opened the heavy entrance door of the swimming baths. I wonder what her name was. I wonder if she could have been me.

19

'He's in here with me,' said Krause. 'We've just got back.'

'Who?' asked Reinhart. 'From where?'

'Andreas Wollger,' said Krause. 'Her husband. Identification positive.'

Reinhart stared at the telephone. Then he stared at the clock. It was two minutes past eight, it was Monday morning.

'Have you found the man who did it and not informed me?'

Krause coughed down the line.

'Not the man who did it. Her husband. He's here in my office, with Probationer Dobbermann. He's not feeling very well – we've just been to the Forensic Laboratory and had a look at her. There's no doubt. Her name's Vera Miller.'

'Vera Miller?' said Reinhart. 'Why are you only ringing now? How can you be certain that he wasn't the man holding the iron?'

'The iron?' wondered Klause.

'Or whatever the hell it was . . . How do you know he's not the one?'

He could hear Krause shifting a piano over his office floor. Or perhaps it was just a sigh.

'It's only eight o'clock,' he said. 'Wollger turned up at a quarter to seven and we drove straight out to take a look at her. Does the chief inspector intend to come to my office and talk to him, or is he going to continue to interrogate me over the telephone? Besides, I'm pretty sure there was no iron involved.'

He's getting cheeky, Reinhart thought after he'd hung up. Constable Krause.

The suggestion that Wollger wasn't feeling very well was a perfectly correct observation on Krause's part. When Reinhart entered the room he was sitting stiffly erect on a chair with his hands clenched in his lap. Staring straight ahead with a vacant expression on his face, with Probationer Elise Dobbermann standing by his side, looking as if she had no idea what to do next. She was wearing the latest – not especially inspired – uniform issued to women police officers. It occurred to Reinhart that he was glad he wasn't a woman. At least, not a female police officer at uniform level.

'Hmm,' he said. 'Herr Wollger, I'm Chief Inspector Reinhart.'

He held out his hand. After a few seconds Wollger stood up and shook it. Then he sat down again and resumed staring into the void. Reinhart remained standing, looking at him: this didn't seem to disturb Wollger. Quite a tall, well-built man, barely forty years old, in Reinhart's judgement. Jeans, dark blue polo shirt, crumpled grey jacket. Rather a large head, beginning to go bald. Eyes pale behind metal-framed spectacles. Signs of weakness in his mouth and chin.

He didn't do it, was Reinhart's first reaction.

But one shouldn't jump to conclusions, was his second.

'Are you up to answering a few simple questions?'

'Questions?' said Wollger.

'Would you like something to drink? Tea, coffee?'

Wollger shook his head.

'Excuse me a moment,' said Reinhart and took Probationer Dobbermann to one side. Lowered his voice and asked her about the situation in general. She replied in a whisper that Wollger had drunk some juice and half a cup of coffee at the Forensic Laboratory after having seen his wife's dead body. But she hadn't got many words out of him. Neither before nor after the identification. Neither her nor Krause. Reinhart nodded and asked her to go and fetch Dr Schenck from his office on the ground floor. Then he turned back to herr Wollger.

'I'm afraid I need to gather some information. Then a doctor will come and make sure that you can have a good rest. Your name is Andreas Wollger, is that right?'

Wollger nodded.

'I'd be grateful if you would answer in words.'

'Yes, I'm Andreas Wollger.'

'Your wife has been the victim of a terrible accident. You have just identified her as' – he checked with his notebook – 'Vera Miller. Is that right?'

'Yes.'

'What's your address?'

'Milkerweg 18.'

'Do you have any children?'

'No.'

'How long have you been married?'

'Three years.'

'What's your job?'

'I'm unemployed.'

'For how long?'

'Six months.'

'And before that?'

'Zinder's Industries. They closed down.'

Reinhart nodded and fumbled for his pipe and tobacco. Zinder's used to make components for mobile phones, if he remembered rightly. Forced out of business by the Japanese. Or possibly the Koreans.

'And your wife?'

'Her job, do you mean?'

'Yes.'

'She's a nurse.'

'What were you doing last Saturday evening?'

'I was having dinner with a good friend.'

'Where?'

'At the Mefisto restaurant.'

'In Lofters Plejn?'

'Yes.'

'Was your wife with you?'

'My wife was attending a course.'

'What sort of a course?'

'For nurses. She's a nurse.'

'At which hospital?'

'Gemejnte.'

'And the course was held in Gemejnte Hospital?'

'No. It was in Aarlach.'

'Aarlach?' said Reinhart, making a note. 'That's a long way from here.'

Wollger said nothing.

'So it was a course for nurses in Aarlach. When did she go there?'

'On Saturday morning.'

'When was she due back?'

'On Sunday afternoon. As usual.'

'As usual? What do you mean by that?'

Wollger took a deep breath.

'She's been attending that course for several Saturdays. It's some kind of further education.'

'Always in Aarlach?'

'Always in Aarlach,' said Wollger. 'But she didn't come home.'

'I understand,' said Reinhart. 'And when she didn't come home, you reported that to the police?'

'She's dead,' said Wollger. 'For Christ's sake, Vera's dead!'

His voice rose half an octave at the end of the sentence, and Reinhart realized that Wollger was close to breaking point.

'How did she get there?' he asked. 'To Aarlach, I mean.'

'By train,' said Wollger. 'She took the train, of course. For Christ's sake, she's dead: why are you sitting here asking me how she got to Aarlach?'

Reinhart waited for a few seconds.

'Your wife has been murdered,' he said. 'Somebody killed her during the night between Saturday and Sunday. Have you any explanation for why her body was found here just outside Maardam when she was supposed to be a couple of hundred kilometres away from here?'

Wollger had no explanation. Instead, he slumped down on his chair, sunk his face into his hands and started sobbing, swaying backwards and forwards. There was a discreet knock on the door, and Dr Schenck's curly grey locks came into view.

'How's it going?'

Reinhart sighed, and moved out of earshot of the man who had just become a widower.

'As you might expect. I think you'd better take over. I don't know who his next of kin is, but we'd better get somebody here PDQ. We need to talk to him, of course, the sooner the better. But that's not possible the way things are at the moment.'

'Okay,' said Schenck. 'I can see how things stand. Let's see what I can do.'

'Thank you,' said Reinhart, leaving the room.

When he arrived at the Forensic Laboratory it was more or less lunchtime, so he suggested that they should nip over the road to Fix. Meusse had nothing against that: he took off his soiled white coat and exchanged it for the jacket he'd tossed onto his desk.

Fix bar was just over the street. It was quite full when they entered, but with the aid of a touch of diplomacy Reinhart managed to find a fairly secluded table. He asked

Meusse if he would like something to eat, but the patholo-gist merely shook his bald head. That was not exactly unexpected. If you could believe the gossip it was years since any solid food had crossed his lips. Reinhart ordered two dark beers, sat down opposite him and waited.

'Well?' he said. 'I gather you've come up with some-thing.'

Meusse took a deep swig, and dried his lips carefully with his serviette.

'It's a circumstance.'

'A circumstance?' said Reinhart.

'Precisely,' said Meusse. 'You are obviously paying at-tention.'

Reinhart let that pass.

'It's a decidedly uncertain observation. But I'd like you to bear it in mind.'

'I see,' said Reinhart.

'It's about those blows.'

'Blows?'

'The blows to the side and back of the head,' said Meusse. 'There is a concordance with *The Chief Inspector*'s boy.'

It was a couple of moments before Reinhart realized that this expression referred to Erich Van Veeteren.

'Hell's bells!' he said.

'You can say that again,' said Meusse, taking another

drink of beer. 'Don't forget that it's only a superficial observation.'

'Of course not,' said Reinhart. 'I've got quite a good memory. Are you suggesting that it could be the same person?'

'Hmm,' said Meusse.

'That the same person killed both Erich Van Veeteren and this woman. Is that what you're saying?'

'I'm not excluding the possibility,' said Meusse after a pause for thought. '*That's* what I'm saying. If you listen carefully, I'll explain . . . What we are dealing with is a somewhat unusual blow. There's nothing to suggest that it couldn't be the same weapon used in both cases, either. A length of iron pipe, for instance. Pretty heavy. I've got no comment to make about the blows to the side of the head, apart from the fact that the killer was right-handed. I'm basing the concordance on the blow to the back of the head. Broke the cervical spine in both cases. Hit more or less exactly the same place. Causing instant death. It could be a coincidence, of course, but I thought you ought to know.'

'Thank you,' said Reinhart.

He sat quietly for a while, trying to clarify the reasoning for himself by drawing a column of vertebrae in the notebook on the table in front of him. It wasn't all that successful.

'But there were several blows to the side of the head this time?'

Meusse nodded.

'Three. Quite unnecessary. The blow to the back of the head would have been sufficient, but that assumes that the victim was the right way up . . . as it were.'

'Would you say it was professional?' Reinhart asked.

Meusse hesitated before answering.

'Whoever delivered the blow must have known what to aim at, and what the result would be,' he said. 'Is that what you mean by professionalism?'

Reinhart shrugged.

'There could well be two different killers,' said Meusse. 'Or there could well be just the one. I just wanted to keep you informed. Thanks for the beer.'

He emptied his glass and wiped his mouth again.

'Hang on a minute,' said Reinhart. 'I want a judgement as well. Nobody could be better placed than you to give it. Are we in fact looking for the same killer? There's no bloody point in summoning me here and then just offering me an either–or.'

Meusse contemplated his empty glass with a furrowed brow. Reinhart beckoned a waiter and ordered two more beers. When they had been delivered the little pathologist stroked the palm of his hand over his bald head and gazed out of the window for a while. He must have dreamt about

becoming an actor, Reinhart thought. When he was young
. . . Two or three hundred years or so ago.

'I don't want to pass a definite judgement,' said Meusse
eventually. 'But I wouldn't be sitting here telling you this if
I didn't have certain suspicions . . . Provided there's nothing to prove that it's not the case, of course.'

'So highly probable?' said Reinhart. 'Is that your opinion?'

'I just wanted to do my bit,' said Meusse.

They sat for a while in silence, drinking their beer.
Reinhart lit his pipe.

'There are no connections between Vera Miller and
Erich Van Veeteren. Not as far as we know, at least – but
we haven't been looking for any, of course.'

'You only need one,' said Meusse. 'But that's not my
job.'

'Absolutely right,' said Reinhart. 'Anyway, thanks for
this, we'll see what we can make of it.'

'Let's do that,' said Meusse, standing up. 'Thanks for
the beers.'

20

'There is no course in Aarlach,' said Moreno, sitting down opposite Reinhart. 'At least, not at the weekend for nurses, every week. How is he?'

'Fragile,' said Reinhart. 'I'd put money on that Aarlach business being a bluff. He doesn't want to go home, Wollger. He's lying downstairs in Schenck's office: a good friend has been to see him, but Schenck had already tranquillized him. Poor sod. The parents are coming this evening – two seventy-five-year-olds coming by car from Frigge. *His* parents, that is. We haven't been in touch with hers yet. We'll have to see how it goes, but no matter what happens we have to get him on his feet so that we can talk to him. Tranquillized or not.'

'So she was being unfaithful to him, was she?' said Moreno. 'Are we to take that for granted?'

'I'd have thought so,' said Reinhart. 'Why else would she lie to him and disappear every Saturday?'

'There could be other explanations.'

'Really? Give me one.'

Moreno thought for a moment, then put off answering.

'What's he like?' she said instead. 'Naive?'

Reinhart stroked his chin and looked thoughtful.

'Yes,' he said. 'Naive's probably the right word. Van Berle, that good friend of his, didn't have much he could tell us about his wife, in any case. She'd evidently entered his life quite recently. She used to live in Groenstadt. Van Berle and Wollger are childhood friends, or so he maintains. He was the one Wollger used to go to the pub with while his wife was out getting screwed by somebody else. If that was what she was doing.'

'Hmm,' said Moreno. 'Perhaps there's another side to the coin as well. But what the hell does this have to do with Erich Van Veeteren? I don't get it.'

'Nor do I,' said Reinhart. 'But you know what one of Meusse's guesses is usually worth.'

Moreno nodded.

'What do we do now?'

Reinhart stood up.

'We do this,' he said. 'Jung and Rooth talk to her workmates and friends. And relatives, if we can find any. You and I will have another try with Wollger. I think we might as well go down and see him now. There's no point in waiting for his mum and dad to come – or what do you think?'

'I don't think anything at all at the moment,' said

223

Moreno, following Reinhart to the lift. 'Are you going to tell him about the course in Aarlach, or shall I do it?'

'You,' said Reinhart. 'I bow to your feminine cunning and empathy. Maybe it doesn't matter all that much now that she's been murdered. Maybe he'll take it like a man.'

'Of course he will,' said Moreno. 'I'm looking forward to meeting him.'

Jung had arranged to meet Liljana Milovic in a cafeteria at Gemejnte Hospital. She had no idea why he wanted to talk to her, and he had the less than uplifting task of informing her that her friend and colleague had unfortunately been murdered, and that was why she hadn't turned up for work this gloomy Monday.

Liljana Milovic was beyond doubt a beautiful woman, and in different circumstances he would have had nothing against holding her in his arms and trying to control her fit of sobbing. Come to think of it, he had nothing against it even in these circumstances – and in fact he spent most of their meeting doing just that. She slung her arms around him and simply wept, that was all there was to it. Slid her chair next to his and hung onto his neck. He stroked her slightly awkwardly over her back and her long, black hair which smelt of honeysuckle, rosewater and God only knew what else.

'Forgive me,' she sniffled over and over again. 'Forgive me, I can't help it.'

Nor can I, thought Jung, noticing that he had a large lump in his throat as well. Her flow of tears eventually ebbed away and she began to get a grip of herself, but she didn't break off bodily contact with him. Not completely.

'I'm sorry,' said Jung. 'I thought they'd already told you.'

She shook her head and blew her nose. He noticed that the other cafeteria customers at nearby tables were glancing furtively at them. He wondered what they imagined was going on, and asked her if she'd prefer to move somewhere else.

'No, no, it's okay here.'

She had only a slight foreign accent, and he guessed she had emigrated from the Balkans when she was a teenager and her homeland was still called Yugoslavia.

'Did you know Vera well?'

'She was my best workmate.'

'Did you meet outside working hours as well?'

She took a deep breath and looked sad. That made her even more beautiful. Under her high cheekbones were faint suggestions of shadow, something that always made Jung go weak at the knees for some reason. He bit his tongue and tried to become a police officer again.

'Not so much,' she said. 'We've only been working on the same ward for a few months. Since August. What happened to her? In detail.'

She squeezed his hands tightly in anticipation of his answer.

'Somebody hit her and killed her,' he said. 'We don't know who.'

'Murdered her?'

'Yes, murdered her.'

'I don't understand.'

'Nor do we. But that's how it is.'

She looked him straight in the eye, from fifteen centimetres away.

'Why?' she asked. 'Why would anybody want to kill Vera? She was such a lovely person. What exactly happened?'

Jung looked away and decided to spare her the details.

'It's not quite clear,' he said. 'But we want to talk to everybody who knew her. Have you noticed at all that she seemed a bit worried lately in some way or other?'

Milovic thought for a while.

'I don't know, but these last few days perhaps . . . On Friday she was a bit . . . I don't quite know how to put it. A bit sad.'

'Did you speak to her then, on Friday?'

'Not so much. I didn't really think about it at the time, but now that you ask I do recall that she didn't seem as happy as she usually was.'

'You didn't talk about that?'

'No. We were very busy, we didn't have time. Just think, if I'd known . . .'

The tears started to flow again, and she blew her nose. Jung looked hard at her and thought that if he didn't have his Maureen he would have invited Liljana Milovic to dinner. Or to the cinema. Or to anything at all.

'Where is she now?' she asked.

'Now?' said Jung. 'Oh, you mean . . . She's at the Forensic Medicine Laboratory. They're busy with the post-mortem . . .'

'And her husband?'

'Her husband, well . . .' said Jung. 'Did you know him as well?'

She looked down at the table.

'No, not at all. I've never met him.'

'Are you married yourself?' he asked, and thought about what he'd read in one of Maureen's weekly magazines the other day concerning Freudian slips.

'No.' She gave a little smile. 'But I do have a boyfriend.'

He's certainly not worthy of you, Jung thought.

'Did she usually speak about her husband? How they

were getting on together and so forth?'

'No,' she said. 'Not often. I don't think they had so good.'

That was the first time she had made a linguistic slip, and he wondered if it was a sign of something.

'Really?' he said, and waited.

'But she didn't say anything about it to me. She just said that things weren't always so good. If you understand?'

Jung nodded and assumed he understood.

'So you didn't talk about . . . private matters?'

'Sometimes.'

'Do you think she might have been interested in another man? That she was having a relationship with somebody else?'

Milovic thought that over before replying.

'Maybe,' she said. 'Yes, she may have been. Just recently, there was something.'

'But she didn't say anything about it?'

'No.

'And you don't know who it could have been?'

Milovic shook her head and started crying again.

'The funeral,' she said. 'When will the funeral be?'

'I don't know,' said Jung. 'It probably hasn't been decided yet. But I promise to tell you as soon as I hear about it.'

'Thank you,' she said and smiled through her tears. 'You are a very nice policeman.'

Jung swallowed twice, but couldn't think of anything else to say.

21

He slept until eight o'clock on Sunday evening.

When he woke up his first reaction was that something had broken inside his head. That the way he perceived the world had burst. He had dreamt about billiard balls rolling about non-stop on an enormous table without pockets or holes. Unfathomable patterns; collisions and changes of direction, a game in which everything seemed to be just as uncertain and yet as predetermined as life itself. The speed and direction of every ball as it scudded over the moss-green table was the secret code which contained within itself all future events and collisions. Together with all the other balls' directions and codes of course; but in some mysterious way each individual ball also contained within itself the future of all the others in its own private Möbius curve – at least the ball that was himself did . . . An infinity of programmed future, he thought as he lay in bed, still trying to find a starting point and something to hold on to . . . This enclosed infinity. Some time ago he had read some

articles on chaos research in one of the journals he subscribed to, and he knew that what was regulated by laws
and what was incapable of being calculated could both
very well be contained within the same theory. Compatible
opposites. The same life.

The same marionette, dangling from those millions of
strings. The same sloping plane. This accursed life. The
images were legion.

The explosion itself, for that is what had produced the
new direction, had happened when he hit Vera Miller on
the head with the pipe. As he did so, he could see with
absolute clarity that it had been inevitable from the
beginning, but also that he couldn't possibly have known
about it.

Not until he was standing there, having done it. A
consequence, quite simply; a development which with
hindsight was predictable and completely logical . . . Just as
natural as night following day, or sorrow following happi-
ness, and just as unaware as dawn must be about dusk. An
effect of causes that had been outside his control all the
time, but which were there nevertheless.

A necessity.

Another infernal necessity, then, and when he aimed
those desperate blows at her temples and the back of her
head, that desperation was no more than a vain confronta-
tion with necessity itself. Nothing more. They were both

victims in this accursed, predetermined dance of death known as life, both he and Vera; but in addition, he was the one who had been forced to act as the executioner. *In addition*: a sort of extra, thank you very much . . . Stage-managed and ordered, and carried out in accordance with all these hopeless codes and tracks. The big picture. With the key in his hand, he could see that it was required of him, and now he had done it.

Shortly before he woke up he had also dreamt about his mother's hand on his forehead, on that occasion when he had sicked up yellow bile . . . And images of the course taken by all the balls of various colours . . . And the bucket with a drop of water in the bottom . . . And his mother's constant tenderness . . . And the collisions . . . Over and over again until the moment when everything was finally drenched by a flood of red blood flowing out of Vera Miller's temples where the first blow had hit her with horrific force, everything in accordance with what was ordained by fate, over and over again, that macabre melo-drama, that hyper-intense whirlwind of madness . . . And it was when all this had transmogrified into repugnance that he woke up and knew that something had broken. Something else.

That membrane. It had finally split.

★

When he got up he saw that there was plenty of real blood everywhere. In the bed. On the carpet on the floor, on the clothes lying around here and there. On his own hands and on the piece of pipe that had rolled under the bed and that he couldn't find at first.

In the car in the garage as well. The back seat. Full of Vera Miller's blood.

He took two tablets. Washed them down with a glass of water and a thumb's breadth of whisky. Lay down on the sofa, on his back, and waited until he could feel the first blessed effects of the alcohol.

Then he began to get to grips with it all.

The follow-up work. Calmly and methodically, as far as possible. Washing away what it was possible to wash away. Rubbing and scraping and trying various concoctions. He didn't feel any agitation, no regret, no fear any more. Nothing but ice-cold calm and clarity: he knew that the game was still continuing according to the rules and patterns over which he had no control. Over which nobody had any control, and which one should always be wary of opposing.

The inevitable direction. The code.

When he had done what he could, he drove into town. Sat for two hours in Lon Pejs restaurant down at Zwille, had a Thai meal, and wondered what the next move in this unavoidable game would be. Wondered how much room for manoeuvre he would have in whatever came next.

He reached no conclusions. Drove back home the same way as he'd come. Noticed to his surprise that he felt calm. Took another pill to see him through the night, and flopped down into bed.

The sun never rose on Monday. He rang work in the morning and advised them that he was unfit for work. Read in the *Neuwe Blatt* about the woman who had been found murdered in the village of Korrim, and found it difficult to accept that it was her. And that it was him. His memories of the car drive on Saturday night through the seemingly endless fields were dim: he had no idea which route he had taken or where he eventually stopped and dragged her out of the car. He had never heard the name Korrim before.

There were no witnesses. Despite the open countryside he had been able to dispose of the body under cover of darkness, and assisted by the late hour. The police had very little to say about it. The reporter assumed they had no significant clues.

So there we are, he thought. No need to worry. The game is still on, and the balls are still rolling.

The postman arrived shortly before eleven. He waited until he had left in the direction of the day nursery before going out to empty the letter box by his gate.

It was there all right. The same blue envelope as always. The same neat handwriting. He sat at the kitchen table with it in his hands for a while before opening it.

The letter was a little longer this time, but not much. Half a page in all. He read it slowly and methodically. As if he were not much good at reading – or afraid of missing something hidden or merely implied.

It's time to get down to the details of our little transaction.

If you do not follow the instructions to the letter this time I shall have no hesitation in informing the police. I think you realize that you have tried my patience rather too much.

Do as follows:

1) Place 200,000 in a white plastic carrier bag and tie it securely.

2) At exactly four o'clock in the morning on Tuesday, the first of December put the carrier bag in the rubbish bin beside the statue of Hugo Maertens in Randers Park.

3) Go straight home and wait for a telephone call. When it comes, answer with your name and follow the instructions you receive.

You will have no further opportunity of avoiding justice. This is the last one. I have deposited an account of all your doings in a safe place. If anything happens to me that account will arrive in the hands of the police.

Let us get this business out of the way with no more faux pas.

A friend.

Well thought-out.

He had to acknowledge that. It somehow felt satisfying to be up against a worthy opponent.

And yet he felt that in the end, he would be able to out-manoeuvre him and win. But doing so would doubtless require a considerable effort.

For the moment – sitting here at the kitchen table with the letter in his hand – it was not possible to see what form that solution would take. A game of chess, he thought: a game of chess in which the pieces had a clear profile, but the required moves were nevertheless difficult to analyse. He didn't know why this metaphor occurred to him. He had never been more than a very average chess player: he'd played quite a lot but had never been able to summon up the necessary patience.

However, his skilful opponent had now stage-managed an attack whose consequences he was unable to discern. Not yet. While he waited for the penny to drop, all he had to do was to make one move at a time and wait for an opening. A weak spot.

A sort of delaying tactic. Were there any other possible

solutions? He didn't think so, not for the moment. But time was short. He looked at the clock and saw that there were fewer than seventeen hours left before he was required to put a small fortune in a rubbish bin in Randers Park.

His opponent seemed to have a predilection for rubbish bins. And plastic carrier bags. Didn't this suggest a certain lack of imagination? A certain simplicity and predictability that he ought to be able to exploit?

Seventeen hours? Less than a full day. Who? he thought. Who?

For a while the identity of his opponent pushed to one side the question of what he was going to do. Now that he came to think of it, he realized that so far he had devoted surprisingly little time to that problem. *Who?* Who the hell was it who had seen him that evening? Was it possible to read anything into the way he was going about things? From the letters? Shouldn't he be able to get some idea of who it might be by examining the premises he was in possession of?

And it suddenly struck him.

Somebody he knew.

He stored this insight away in his consciousness as if it were made of glass. Afraid of shattering it, afraid of placing too much reliance on it.

Somebody he knew. Somebody who knew him.

The latter above all. His opponent had known who he

was even when he saw him with the dead boy that evening. As he stood there holding the boy in his arms in the rain. That must surely be the case.

Yes, he convinced himself. That must be right.

It wasn't a matter of having registered and memorized the number of his car. The blackmailer had known straight away. He had driven past without stopping, and then when he had read in the newspapers about what had happened, he had put two and two together and made his move. He or she. *He*, presumably, he decided without really understanding why.

Yes, that's how it happened. When he thought about it now he realized how implausible his earlier explanation had been. How far-fetched. Who the hell notices and memorizes a car registration number when they are merely driving past a parked vehicle? In the dark, and the rain? Impossible. Out of the question.

So: somebody who knew him. Somebody who knew who he was.

He noticed that he was smiling.

He was sitting there with a pale-blue letter that could ruin his life in less than a day. He had killed three people within a month. But even so, he was smiling.

*

But who was it?

It didn't take him long to run through his sparse circle of friends and exclude it.

Or rather, *them*: all those who, with a modicum of goodwill, he might consider inviting to his wedding or his fiftieth birthday party. Or his funeral. No, none of those: he couldn't believe that was possible. Of course there were perhaps one or two whom he couldn't exclude quite as straightforwardly as the others, but there was nothing that made him stop and think. Nobody he suspected.

And there was another thing. To be sure, he wasn't exactly a well-known name in Maardam, not a local celebrity; but nevertheless there were a few people who knew who he was and recognized him in the street. That was sufficient, of course. Every day he came into contact with people in town without being able to remember later whether he'd seen them or not; but obviously, they knew who he was. Some of them even said 'hello' – and were often somewhat embarrassed when they realized that he had no idea who they were.

One of those. It must be one of those, somebody like that, who was his opponent. He found himself smiling again.

Then he cursed out loud when he realized that the elimination process and conclusions were not much help, given the shortage of time.

No help at all. If he allowed himself to assume that the

blackmailer lived somewhere in Maardam, that meant he had reduced the candidates from about 300,000 to 300. Perhaps.

Excluding old dodderers and children: from 200,000 to 200.

A considerable reduction, certainly, but futile even so. The plain fact was that there were still too many left.

Two hundred possible blackmailers? Seventeen hours to play with. Sixteen and a half, to be precise. He sighed and eased himself out of his armchair. Went to check the medicine chest and established that there was enough there to keep him going for another ten to twelve days at least.

In ten to twelve days' time the situation would be quite different. No matter what.

Game over. A draw out of the question.

Then he phoned the bank. The loan he had applied for on Thursday was still not granted. It would take a few more days – but he needn't worry, he was assured. It was a mere formality. He was a valued customer, and the bank looked after their valued customers.

He said thank you and hung up. Remained standing for a while, looking out of the window at the gloomy suburban street and the rain. So he wouldn't have the cash by that evening. In no circumstances.

So something else was needed.

A strategy was called for.

He read the letter one more time, and tried to think of one.

22

The picture of the murdered Vera Elizabeth Miller became somewhat clearer during the course of Monday.

She was born in Gellenkirk in 1963, but grew up in Groenstadt. She had three siblings – two brothers and a sister – all of whom still lived in that southern province. Her father died in 1982, her mother married again and was now working as a domestic science teacher in Karpatz: she had been informed of her daughter's death via the school, and was expected in Maardam together with her new husband at some time on Tuesday.

Vera Miller had trained to be a nurse in Groenstadt, and worked there until 1991, when she divorced a certain Henric Veramten and moved up to Maardam. Her marriage to Veramten had not produced any children of their own, but in 1989 they had adopted a little girl from Korea – she died in a tragic road accident the following year. According to Vera's mother and two of her siblings, the divorce from Varamten was a direct result of the girl's death. It was not stated in so many words, but reading between the lines it seemed that the husband could well have been responsible for the accident. Directly or indirectly. No official investigation had taken place.

In Maardam Vera Miller had started work at Gemejnte Hospital in the spring of 1992, and two-and-a-half years later she married Andreas Wollger. Neither her mother not her siblings knew anything at all about this second marriage. They hadn't been to a wedding celebration – didn't even know that there had been one – and had only been in sporadic contact with Vera in recent years.

Andreas Wollger's condition was unchanged. At about seven o'clock on Monday evening it had still not been possible to interrogate him any further about his relationship with his wife as he was still in shock after what had happened. However, both Moreno and Reinhart had the strong impression that relations between the two had probably not been of the best.

And probably not second-best either.

What still needed to be done, of course, was to get these assumptions confirmed via conversations and interrogations with people who had known the couple in some connection or other.

And via herr Wollger himself.

As far as Vera Miller's general character was concerned, it soon became clear that she was a very much admired and liked woman, in the view of both friends and colleagues. Most notably of all, a certain Irene Vargas – who had known Vera since they were both knee-high to a grasshopper down in Groenstadt, and now lived in Maardam – had expressed her shocked sorrow and regret at losing, as she put it, 'one of the warmest and most honest people I've ever known, it's a bloody tragedy'. Fru Vargas and Vera Miller had evidently been close friends for many years, and Reinhart assumed that if there was anybody at all who might possibly have insight into the darker sides of Vera's life – possible extra-marital relations, for instance – she was the one.

No such information had emerged from the first conversation with her, but of course there was good reason to talk to her again about it.

Very good reason. By all accounts it seemed that Vera Miller had begun two-timing her husband round about the end of October/beginning of November. According to what she had told her husband, she would be attending a further education course for nurses in Aarlach for several weekends to come, at least eight.

Where she actually spent those Saturdays and Sundays – and with whom – was still an unanswered question.

*

'Bloody blockhead,' said Reinhart. 'Fancy letting her go off every weekend without checking up on what she was doing. How naive can you get?'

'Are you telling me that you would check up on Winnifred if she announced she was enrolling for a course?' Moreno wondered.

'Of course not,' said Reinhart. 'That's something entirely different.'

'I don't see the logic,' said Moreno.

'Intuition,' said Reinhart. 'Healthy male intuition. Anyway, are we in agreement that he's not the one who did it? Wollger, that is.'

'I think so,' said Moreno. 'We'd better not eliminate the possibility altogether, though it seems highly unlikely. But what we can say about the link with Erich Van Veeteren . . . well, I haven't a clue about that.'

While deBries and Rooth were talking to people who knew the Miller-Wollgers, Moreno had been concentrating on Marlene Frey and some of Erich Van Veeteren's friends, but nobody had been able to supply any information that seemed remotely relevant.

Nobody had recognized Vera Miller from the photograph they had borrowed from Irene Vargas, and nobody could recall ever having heard her name before.

'I don't know where I stand on that either,' said Reinhart, blowing out a cloud of smoke. 'I have to admit that. I'll be meeting *The Chief Inspector* tomorrow, and I think I'll raise it with him . . . The *possible* link. That would mean we had something concrete to talk about. It gets so bloody depressing, just sitting there philosophizing about death.'

Moreno thought for a moment.

'You're very fond of theories,' she said. 'I mean, is it possible to find a motive for killing both Erich Van Veeteren and Vera Miller based on the assumption that they didn't know one another? Can you think up a story that hangs together?'

'A story . . . ?' said Reinhart, scratching his forehead with the stem of his pipe. 'Without their knowing each other? Hmm, it could be as far-fetched as you like, and yet still be crystal clear if you could see the actual threads . . . Assuming of course that we're not dealing with an out-and-out lunatic, because that would be a different kettle of fish altogether. Yes, of course I could think up a chain of events that hang together – I could churn out ten if you wanted me to. But where would that get us?'

Moreno smiled.

'Do that,' she said. 'Spend the night thinking up ten threads linking the deaths of Erich Van Veeteren and Vera Miller. Then tell me about them tomorrow, and I promise I'll pick out the right one.'

'Good God,' said Reinhart. 'I have a lovely wife to devote the nights to. And a daughter with inflammation of the ear to see to when she hasn't got any strength left. Are you still married to your work?'

'It seems like it,' said Moreno.

'Seems like it? What the hell is that for an expression?' He leaned forward over the table and stared at her with a vertical furrow between his eyebrows.

'It's something to do with Münster. Isn't it?'

Inspector Moreno stared back at him for three seconds.

'Go to hell,' she said, and left the room.

'Do you know what I am?' said Rooth. 'I'm the worst hunter in Europe.'

'I've no reason to doubt that,' said Jung. 'Mind you, I didn't know you did any hunting.'

'Women,' sighed Rooth. 'I'm talking about women. Here's me busy chasing after them for twenty years . . . twenty-five, in fact . . . And I haven't captured a single one. What the hell am I supposed to do?'

Jung looked around the bar, which was full of men. They had just dropped in at the Oldener Maas in order to gild the day (Rooth's term), and it didn't appear to be especially good hunting ground.

'You've got yours nailed down,' said Rooth. 'Maureen's a bloody marvellous woman. If she throws you out I'd be only too happy to take over.'

'I'll tell her that,' said Jung. 'That should guarantee that she'll hang on to me.'

'Kiss my arse,' said Rooth, and took a justifiable swig of his beer. 'But perhaps it's due to the ammunition.'

'Ammunition?' said Jung.

'I'm beginning to think I've been using too big a calibre of buckshot all these years. I'm thinking about reading some poetry – what do you think about that?'

'Good,' said Jung. 'Just the thing for a man like you. Can't we talk about something else instead of women?'

Rooth assumed an expression of utter astonishment.

'What the hell could that possibly be?'

Jung shrugged.

'I don't know. Work, perhaps?'

'I prefer women,' said Rooth with a sigh. 'But since you ask so nicely . . .'

'We could just sit and keep our traps shut,' said Jung. 'Perhaps the best choice.'

Rooth really did sit quietly for quite a while, digging deep into the bowl of peanuts and chewing away thoughtfully.

'I've got a hypothesis,' he said eventually.

'A hypothesis?' said Jung. 'Not a theory?'

'I don't really know the difference between them,' Rooth admitted. 'Who cares, in any case? . . . Now listen to this . . .'

'My ears can't wait.'

'Good,' said Rooth. 'But don't keep interrupting me all the time. Anyway, this Vera Miller . . . If she was having an affair with another man, it would make sense if we found the bloke in question.'

'You're a genius,' said Jung. 'How do you do it, Constable?'

'I haven't finished yet. There's no doubt it would make things easier if we knew where to look for him.'

Jung yawned.

'This is where the hypothesis bursts out into full bloom,' said Rooth. 'It's obvious that we're looking for a doctor.'

'A doctor? Why the hell . . . ?'

'It's as clear as a summer's day. She worked at a hospital. Sooner or later all nurses fall for a man in a white coat with knick-knacks round his neck. The stethoscope syndrome. It affects all the women who work in that line of business. We should be looking for Dr X, it's as simple as that. At Gemejnte Hospital. Perhaps I should have studied medicine . . .'

Jung succeeded in grabbing the last of the peanuts.

'How many are there? Doctors at the Gemejnte, I mean.'

'God only knows,' said Rooth. 'A few hundred, I assume. But it must surely be somebody she came into contact with . . . In the line of work, as they say. On the same ward, or whatever. What do you think?'

Jung thought for a moment.

'If we believe what Meusse has told us,' he said, 'how does this fit in with the postage stamp theory and the blackmailer theory?'

Rooth belched discreetly into his armpit.

'My young friend,' he said with a fatherly smile. 'You can't just mix theories up with hypotheses as the whim takes you – I thought you knew that. Was it the police college you attended, or the dog handlers' college?'

'Go and buy a couple of beers,' said Jung. 'But don't mix them up.'

'I'll do my best,' said Rooth, standing up.

He's not as stupid as he looks, thought Jung when he was alone at the table.

Thank God for that.

Why do I do this? Moreno thought when she had come home.

She kicked off her shoes in irritation and threw her jacket into the basket chair.

Why do I tell Reinhart to go to hell and slam the door behind me? Am I becoming a man-hater? A bitch?

He was right, after all. Absolutely right. There had been

something going with Münster – even if she couldn't be more precise about it than Reinhart had been.

Only *something*. It had come to an end when Münster had been stabbed up in Frigge last January, and very nearly lost his life. Since then he had been in hospital for months, and was now mixed up in some dodgy inquiry at the ministry, filling in time until he was fit for battle again. That would be a few more months yet, if rumour was correct.

Hell and damnation, she thought. And when he's back on duty, what then? Presumably in February. What would happen then?

Nothing at all, of course. Intendent Münster had gone back to his wife and children – and he had never left them in the first place, not for a second. What had she imagined? What was she waiting for? Was she really waiting for something? She had only met him a couple of times since it happened, and there hadn't been the slightest trace of any vibrations. Not even a flutter in the air . . . Well, maybe a little one that first time, when she and Synn were both sitting at his bedside . . . There had been something in the air then.

But no more than that. A slight flutter. Once.

And who the hell was she to come between Münster and his wonderful Synn? And the children?

I'm losing the plot, she thought. I'm becoming just as dotty as all the rest of the lonely spinsters. Did it really take no longer than that to become an old maid? Was it really as simple as that? To be sure, when she left that shithead Claus she had been furious with him, and the wasted five years she'd spent with him. But she hadn't tarred all men with the same brush. Not Münster, at least. Certainly not him.

But now she had more or less told Reinhart to fuck off. Just because he had happened to tread on the right toe. To be sure, Reinhart was not her type (was there such a creature?), but she had always regarded him as a good person and a good police officer.

And a man.

I must do something about all this, she told herself as she turned on the shower in the hope of washing all the horrors away.

Maybe not right away, but in the long run I really must. Thirty-one and an embittered man-hater?

Or a desperate hunter? Even worse, much worse. No, there are – there must be – better strategies for the future.

But not just at the moment. This evening she had neither the time nor the strength. And no ideas, either. Better to get down to something different. To the challenge she had presented him with, perhaps?

Ten possible links between Erich Van Veeteren and Vera Miller.

Ten? she thought. What hubris.

Let's see if I can find three.

Or two.

Or even one, at least?

Winnifred had just started her period, and Joanna had finally accepted the blessings bestowed by penicillin, so as far as Reinhart was concerned it was neither one thing nor the other. Instead he sat down on the sofa to watch an old Truffaut film while Winnifred prepared the next day's seminar in the study. She woke him up when the film had finished. They spent a quarter of an hour comparing the relative attractions of Leros and Sakynthos with an eye to a possible trip at Easter, and when they eventually went to bed he was unable to sleep.

Two thoughts were buzzing around in his head.

The first concerned Van Veeteren. He was due to meet *The Chief Inspector* the next day and would be forced to admit that they were still marking time on square one. That after three weeks' work they still hadn't a single lead, not even the slightest sniff of one, in their hunt for his son's murderer. Needless to say he would report on the strange circumstance regarding the blow to the back of Vera Miller's head, but there wasn't a lot to say about that.

We simply don't know what lay behind it, he would have to admit. What a bloody mess, Reinhart thought.

The other thought concerned Ewa Moreno.

I'm a cretin, he thought. Not always, but now and then. He had promised her ten plausible scenarios to explain a connection he hadn't the slightest idea about, and then he had insulted her.

Insulted her and stuck his nose into matters that were nothing at all to do with him.

Another bloody mess.

He got up at two o'clock and phoned her.

'Were you asleep?' he asked. 'It's Reinhart.'

'I can hear that,' said Moreno. 'No, I was awake in fact.'

'I want to apologize,' said Reinhart. 'I mean, I'm ringing to apologize . . . I'm a bloody cretin.'

She said nothing for a moment.

'Thank you,' she said. 'For the apology, that is. But I don't think you're all that much of a cretin. I wasn't myself, it was my fault.'

'Hmm,' said Reinhart. 'Very clever. And uplifting. Two grown-up people exchanging apologies on the telephone in the middle of the night. It must have something to do with sun-spots – I'm sorry I rang . . . No, for Christ's sake! Now I've put my foot in it again.'

Moreno laughed.

'Why aren't you asleep?' Reinhart asked.

'I'm trying to think of ten plausible connections.'

'Oh dear. How many have you got?'

'None,' said Moreno.

'Excellent,' said Reinhart. 'I'll see what I can come up with. Goodnight. I'll see you tomorrow under a cold star.'

'Good night, Chief Inspector,' said Moreno. 'Why aren't you asleep, incidentally?'

But Reinhart had already hung up.

23

Van Veeteren stared at the phosphorescent second hand making its leisurely way round the face of the clock. He had been doing that for quite some time, but every new circuit was a new experience even so. He suddenly remembered that a long time ago, in pre-puberty – if he had in fact ever been through such a phase – he used to occupy himself when he couldn't sleep by taking his pulse. He decided he'd try that now.

Fifty-two the first minute.

Forty-nine the second one.

Fifty-four the third.

Good Lord, he thought. My heart is collapsing as well.

He lay there for a few more minutes without taking his pulse. Wished he'd had Ulrike by his side, but she was sleeping over with her children out at Loewingen. Or at least, with one of them. Jürg, aged eighteen, and the last one to fly the nest. She obviously needed to spend some time with him as well, he realized that. Even if he seemed to be an unusually level-headed young man. As far as he could judge, at least: they had only met three times, but everything seemed to point in that direction.

Apart from the fact that he wanted to become a police officer.

Van Veeteren sighed, and rolled over in order to avoid having to look at the confounded clock. Put one of the pillows over his head.

A quarter past two, he thought. I'm the only person in the whole world who's awake.

He got up an hour later. It was impossible to sleep – the last few nights he had managed no more than two to three hours on average, and no known medicines helped.

Nor did beer. Nor wine. Nor even Handel.

It was just as bad with other composers, so it wasn't Handel's fault.

It's not possible, he thought as he stood in the bathroom, splashing cold water into his face. It's not possible to sleep – and I know why, for Christ's sake. Why don't I just admit it? Why don't I stand on the mountain-top and shout it out so loudly that all mankind can hear it?

Revenge! Show me the father who can lie at peace in his bed while the search for his son's murderer is going on out there!

It was as simple as that. Embedded deep down in the black hole of biology. He had known that when he wrote about it in his diary a few hours ago, and he knew it now. Action was the only effective antidote. Homo agentus. In all situations. Illusory or real. Do something, for God's sake!

He got dressed. Checked the weather through the kitchen window, and went out. It felt freezing cold, but no rain and hardly any wind. He set off walking.

Southwards to begin with. Down over Zuijderslaan and Primmerstraat towards Megsje Plejn. When he came to the Catholic cemetery he hesitated for a moment, then decided to skirt round it: but when he came to the southeastern corner he felt that he'd had enough of all that asphalt and turned off into Randers Park, which was a sort of natural extension of the cemetery. Or perhaps the cemetery was a natural extension of the park, it wasn't clear which. No doubt there was a history to explain it, but he wasn't aware of it.

He thought the darkness in there among all the trees and bushes felt almost like a sort of embrace, and the silence was striking. The park is listening, he thought as he proceeded slowly . . . Further into the heart of darkness – that was an image that seemed unusually apt. Mahler used to claim that nature is alive during the night. During the day she sleeps and allows herself to be observed: but during the night she comes to life, and invites you to go out there and really feel her presence.

Absolutely right, no doubt about it. Van Veeteren shook his head to break that chain of thought and get away from all that verbosity. Tossed up inside his head and turned right when he came to a fork, and after a minute found himself in front of the statue of Hugo Maertens. It was lit up not very brightly by a single spotlight in the flower bed that surrounded the heavy pedestal, and he wondered why. Tourists in the park at night? Hardly. He checked his watch.

Ten to four.

Action? The only effective antidote? Give me a bit of space in which to act then, Mother Nature! Release me from captivity!

He shrugged, and lit a cigarette.

I'm just wandering around in the night in order not to go mad, he thought. For no other reason. Then he heard a twig breaking somewhere out there in the darkness. So I'm not alone, he thought. Animals and lunatics wander about during the night.

By three o'clock he felt unable to wait any longer. He went out to the garage, slung the plastic carrier bag on the passenger seat and clambered into the car. Started the engine and began the drive to the town centre. He didn't meet a single car all the way along the unlit road, and as he passed by the concrete culvert he thought no more about it than he would have done about any other familiar old landmark. There was nothing to think about it. What had happened seemed now to be so far in the past that it was beyond recall. He couldn't remember it. Even if he'd wanted to.

He turned left after the Alexander Bridge, followed Zwille as far as the Pixner Brewery and came up to Randers Park on its southern side. Parked outside the entrance where the minigolf courses were situated – they were not open at this time of night, of course. Nor at this time of year. He remained sitting in the car for a while. It was just short of half past three. The park looked dark and brooding, lost in its own deep winter slumbers. Nature closes down at night, he thought, and he wondered why his opponent had chosen this particular place. Did he live nearby, or was it the very inaccessibility of the place that had been decisive? If so that indicated excessive caution: at this time of night there must be hundreds of empty rubbish bins that were easier to get to. Last time he had chosen to carry out the transaction in a restaurant, with an abundance of possible witnesses, so tonight's venue may have been chosen to avoid that.

There would be no assistant to collect the bag tonight. It would be the blackmailer himself, and he would know that his victim was of a different calibre than he had thought from the start. A very different calibre.

The thought almost made him smile, and no doubt the fact that he could sit here in his car and wait in the darkness without feeling worried at all indicated stability and self-control. If the blackmailer didn't accept his conditions, the result could be that the police would be knocking on his door as soon as tomorrow morning. In just a few hours from now. It was not impossible.

He felt the package. Wondered whether his opponent would be able to tell immediately that it didn't contain all the money he was expecting, or would he only find out when he got home? The two old newspapers he had torn up and stuffed into the plastic carrier bag were not intended to create the illusion of money. They were merely to give it a certain amount of bulk.

Two old newspapers and an envelope.

Five grand and a request for a delay of three days – that is what his opponent would receive for his night's work.

The amount was carefully considered. It was exactly half of what had been demanded the previous time, and he would never receive any more. He would believe that 200,000 would be waiting for him on Thursday night instead, and surely he would swallow the bait? Three extra days to wait plus a bonus of 5,000 – what the hell did he have in the way of choice? Go to the police and collect nothing at all? Hardly likely.

He checked his watch. A quarter to four. He picked up the carrier bag, got out of the car and entered the park.

He had checked up earlier on the precise location of the Hugo Maertens statue, and that proved to be a good move. The darkness inside the overgrown park made it feel like a black hole, and it was not until he glimpsed the faint beam from the spotlight aimed at the statue that he was sure he hadn't gone astray. He paused briefly before stepping out into the little opening where paths converged from four or five different directions.

He stood there listening to the silence. Thought that his opponent was presumably somewhere in the vicinity: perhaps he was also standing on tenterhooks with his mobile phone out there in the darkness, waiting. Or perhaps in a nearby telephone box.

Billiard balls, he thought again. Balls rolling towards each other, but avoiding a collision by no more than a couple of millimetres. Their paths cross, but the clash is avoided by minutes. Or even seconds.

Ridiculously short fractions of time.

He walked over to the rubbish bin and pressed down the plastic carrier bag.

*

On the way back to Boorkhejm he wondered what would happen if his car broke down. It was not a particularly pleasant thought. Standing by the side of the road and trying to hail some early bird of a driver to ask for help. It would be difficult to explain what he'd been doing, out at that time, to a police officer, especially if they started investigating. Supposedly off work sick, but on his way back home at half past four in the morning. And the back seat covered in traces of blood, which would hardly escape a trained eye.

Not to mention the consequences if he wasn't at home to answer the telephone. No, not a pleasant thought at all.

But his car didn't break down. Of course it didn't. His four-year-old Audi performed immaculately today as on every other day. It had just been an idea he'd played with. He had lots of ideas these days . . . Bizarre thoughts that had never troubled him before, and he sometimes wondered why they had suddenly turned up in his head. Just now.

He parked the car in the garage, took one-and-a-half tablets and crept down into bed to wait for the call. Wondered rather vaguely if the blackmailer was intending to say anything, or if he would simply hang up. The latter seemed more likely, of course. There was no reason to risk the slight possibility of being unmasked. One's voice is always naked. It was more likely that he would ring back later – when he had checked the contents of the bag and read the message. Much more likely. When he realized that he hadn't been paid as much as he'd expected for all his efforts. For all his evil machinations.

If his clock radio was accurate the call came at exactly five seconds past five. He let it ring three times before answering – if for no other reason, to demonstrate that he wasn't sitting by the telephone, tense and nervous. It could be important to make that clear.

He picked up the receiver and said his name.

For a few seconds he could hear the presence of the caller, then the line went dead.

Okay, he thought. Let's hear what you have to say for yourself next time.

He rolled over in bed, adjusted the pillows and tried to sleep.

He succeeded very well. When he was woken up by the telephone ringing again, it was a quarter past eleven.

During the brief moment that passed before he picked up the receiver he began to realize that something had gone wrong. That things had not proceeded as he had expected. What had happened? Why had his opponent waited for several hours? Why had . . . ?

It was Smaage.

'How are you, brother?'

'Ill,' he managed to say.

'Yes, I'd heard. The priest curses and the doctor's ill. What sort of an age are we living in?'

He laughed in a way that made a rasping noise in the receiver.

'Just a touch of flu. But it looks as though I'll be off all week.'

'Oh dear. We thought we'd have a little session on Friday evening, as I said. Will that be too much for you? At Canaille.'

He coughed and managed to produce a few heavy breaths. They sounded pretty convincing.

'I think so,' he said. 'But I'll be back at work by Monday.'

When he had said that, and when Smaage had expressed the hope that he'd soon be well again and hung up, it occurred to him that his prognosis had been one hundred per cent wrong.

Whatever happened – no matter how the balls rolled over the next few days – one thing was absolutely clear. Only one. He would not be going to the hospital on Monday.

He would never set foot inside the place again.

There was something extremely attractive about that thought.

24

'Right then, let's kick off this brainstorming session,' said Reinhart, placing his pipe, tobacco pouch and lighter in a neat row on his desk in front of him. 'I'll be meeting *The Chief Inspector* this evening, and as you can well imagine he's more than a little interested in how things are going for us. I intend to give him a tape recording of this run-through, so that I have at least something to deliver. So think about what you say.'

He pressed the button and started the recorder running. Immediately, Van Veeteren's presence was felt in the room as something almost tangible, and a respectful silence ensued.

'Hmm, okay,' said Reinhart. 'Tuesday, the eighth of December, fifteen hundred hours. Run-through of the cases Erich Van Veeteren and Vera Miller. We'll take them both even though the connection is far from definite. Let's hear your comments.'

'Have we anything more than Meusse's guess to suggest that the two cases are linked?' wondered deBries.

'Nothing,' said Reinhart. 'Apart from the fact that our esteemed pathologist's guesses can usually be taken as dead-certs. But I suppose even he will have to get something wrong one of these days.'

'I doubt that,' said Moreno.

Reinhart opened the zip of his tobacco pouch and sniffed the contents before continuing.

'Let's start with Vera Miller,' he suggested. 'We have no new technical evidence relevant to her case. Unfortunately. Apart from the time being slightly more precise now. She evidently died some time between a quarter past two and half past three in the early hours of Sunday morning. It's difficult to say when she was dumped out there at Korrim. If she'd been there long, you might think she ought to have been discovered sooner: but we must remember that the body was hidden and there's hardly any traffic on those roads. Not at the weekend at this time of year, at least. Oh, we've spoken again to Andreas Wollger . . . That is, Inspector Moreno and I have spoken to him. The gods should be aware that he didn't have much to tell us – like everybody else we've talked to. But at least he's begun to admit that their marriage wasn't entirely idyllic. I think in fact that he's only just beginning to realize that . . . He seems to be a bit handicapped when it comes to the labyrinth of love – something else the gods ought to be aware of.'

'He was thirty-six when he got married,' Moreno explained. 'He doesn't seem to have had many relationships earlier in his life. If any.'

'A peculiar chap,' said Rooth.

'Yes, he gives the impression of being a bit of a wimp,' said Reinhart, 'and I don't think he's the type who would commit murder on grounds of jealousy. I suspect he'd prefer to cut off his testicles and give them away as a peace offering if a crisis arose. He has an alibi until one o'clock on Sunday morning, which was when he left a restaurant he'd been at with a good friend . . . And who the hell has an alibi for the small hours?'

'I do,' said Rooth. 'My fish are my witnesses.'

'So we can clear him of any suspicion – for the moment, at least,' said Reinhart.

'How many does that leave, then?' asked deBries. 'Assuming we can exclude Rooth as well.'

Reinhart looked as if he had a retort on the tip of his tongue, but he glanced at the tape recorder and suppressed it.

'Perhaps Rooth can tell us what Vera Miller's mother had to say for herself,' he said instead.

Rooth sighed.

'Not so much as the shadow of a chicken's fart,' he

said. 'To make things worse she was a domestic science teacher and hysterical about calories. I wasn't even allowed to eat my Danish pastry in peace and quiet. Not my type.'

'We all feel sorry for you,' said deBries. 'But I have to say I think we're missing something in this connection.'

'What?' said Moreno.

'Well, listen to this,' said deBries, leaning forward over the table. 'We know that Vera Miller was two-timing her wimp of a husband. We know there must be some other bloke involved. Why don't we make an appeal via the media? Issue a Wanted notice for the bastard in the newspapers and on the telly – I mean, somebody must have seen them out together . . . If they'd been carrying on for four or five weekends in a row.'

'That's not certain,' said Reinhart. 'I can't believe that they were prancing around in pubs and restaurants. Or canoodling in public. Besides . . . Besides, there are certain ethical aspects we must take into account.'

'You don't say?' said deBries. 'And what might they be?'

'I know that this isn't your strong point,' said Reinhart, 'but we haven't had it confirmed yet. The infidelity, that is. Her mythical courses might have been a cover for something quite different – though I have to say I find it hard to understand what. But in any case, she's been murdered, and I think we ought to be a bit careful about adding adultery to her obituary. In public, that is . . . Bearing in

mind the feelings of her husband and other next of kin.
I wouldn't want to be held responsible if it turned out
that we'd hung her out to dry in the press, but then discovered that she was innocent.'

'All right,' said deBries with a shrug, 'I give in. Did you
say it was a matter of ethics?'

'Exactly,' said Reinhart, pressing the pause button on
the tape recorder. 'I think it's time for a coffee break now.'

'We don't have much that's new regarding Erich Van
Veeteren either, I'm afraid,' said Reinhart when fröken
Katz had left the room. 'A few interviews of course, mainly
conducted by Detective-Sergeant Bollmert who's been out
and about. Anything of interest?'

'Not as far as I can see,' said Bollmert, fiddling nervously with a propelling pencil. 'I've spoken to welfare
officers and probation officers and old friends of Erich's,
but it was mainly people who haven't had much to do
with him in recent years. He'd been walking the straight
and narrow, as you know. I mentioned Vera Miller to the
ones I spoke to as well, but nobody took the bait there
either.'

'Yes, that seems to be the way things are,' said Reinhart.
'No winning tickets. You'd think that somebody – just one
individual would do – would be acquainted with both our

victims . . . from a purely statistical point of view. We've spoken to hundreds of people, for God's sake. But no . . .'

'Unless of course the murderer is acquainted with both of them,' Rooth pointed out, 'but is being crafty and not letting on.'

'Not impossible,' said Reinhart offhandedly. 'Incidentally I've spent some time trying to find a plausible link between Erich Van Veeteren and fru Miller – how they might theoretically be connected – but I have to say it's not easy. Mainly airy-fairy hypotheses . . . Cock and bull stories . . .'

He made eye contact with Moreno, who smiled and shook her head: he understood that she shared his opinion. He raised his hand to switch off the tape recorder, but paused. Jung was waving a pencil and looking thoughtful.

'With regard to hypotheses,' he said, 'I've been looking into Rooth's hypothesis.'

'Rooth?' said Reinhart, raising his eyebrows. 'Hypothesis?'

'Which one do you mean?' wondered Rooth.

'The postage stamp gang,' said deBries.

'No, the stethoscope syndrome,' said Jung.

Now Reinhart switched off the tape recorder.

'What the devil are you on about?' he said. 'Wait while I wind the tape back.'

'Sorry,' said deBries.

'I'm serious,' said Jung. 'It's like this . . .'

He waited until Reinhart had pressed the record button again.

'What Rooth suggested was that this bloke – always assuming that Vera Miller did have another bloke – would most probably be a doctor. You know what they say about nurses and men in white coats and all that . . .'

He paused and looked round to see if there was any reaction.

'Go on,' said Reinhart.

'Well, I thought it might be worth looking into whether she might have been having an affair with one of the doctors at the Gemejnte. Nearly everybody who's unfaithful does it with somebody at work, according to what I've read . . . So I went to hear what Liljana had to say this morning.'

'Liljana?' said Reinhart. 'Who the hell is Liljana?'

He could have sworn that Jung blushed.

'One of Vera Miller's workmates,' he said. 'I spoke to her for the first time yesterday.'

'I've seen her,' said Rooth. 'A veritable bombshell . . . From the Balkans as well, but not in that way . . .'

Reinhart glared at him and then at the tape recorder, but let it pass.

'Go on,' he said again, 'What did she have to say?'

'Not a lot, I'm afraid,' said Jung. 'But she reckons it's

not impossible that Vera Miller had something going with a doctor. She had the impression that another colleague had hinted at that, but she wasn't absolutely sure.'

'Another colleague?' said Moreno. 'And what did she have to say? I assume it's a she.'

'Yes,' said Jung. 'A trainee nurse. But I haven't been able to get hold of her. She's off work today and tomorrow.'

'Shit,' said Reinhart. 'Anyway, we'll dig her out, of course. We might as well get to the bottom of this. I have to say that it sounds quite likely, when you think about it. A nurse and a doctor – we've heard about that before.'

'They say there are quite a few white coats at the Gemejnte,' said deBries.

Reinhart sucked at his pipe and looked ready to kill.

'This is what we'll do,' he said after a few seconds' thought. 'I'll phone the head doctor, or the hospital's CEO, or whatever the hell he's called. He can supply us with the full list of employees – let's hope he's got photographs as well. It would be a bit of a bugger if we didn't get a bit of joy out of this . . . I don't suppose Inspector Rooth has a little theory about a possible link to Erich Van Veeteren as well?'

Rooth shook his head.

'I seem to recall that I did have,' he said. 'But I can't remember what it was.'

DeBries sighed loudly. Reinhart pressed the stop button, and the run-through was finished.

He had chosen Vox again – bearing in mind Van Veeteren's positive memory from the previous time – but this evening there was no velvet-voiced chanteuse to look forward to. No music at all, in fact, as it was a Tuesday. Monday and Tuesday were low season, and apart from Reinhart and Van Veeteren there was only a handful of listless customers sitting at the shiny metal tables. *The Chief Inspector* was already installed when the chief inspector arrived. For the first time – the first time ever, as far as he could remember – Reinhart thought he was looking old.

Or perhaps not old, rather resigned in that way a lot of elderly people gave the impression of being. As if some strategic muscles in the spine and the back of the head had finally had enough and contracted for the last time. Or snapped. He assumed Van Veeteren must be sixty by now, but he wasn't sure. There were a lot of mysterious circumstances surrounding *The Chief Inspector*, and one of them was the question of his real age.

'Good evening,' said Reinhart, sitting down. 'You look tired.'

'Thank you,' said Van Veeteren. 'No, I don't sleep at night any more.'

'Oh dear,' said Reinhart. 'When the Good Lord robs us of our sleep, he doesn't exactly do us any favours.'

Van Veeteren opened the lid of his cigarette-rolling machine.

'He stopped doing us favours hundreds of years ago. The devil only knows if he ever did us any.'

'Could well be,' said Reinhart. 'I've just been reading about God's silence after Bach. Two Dunckel, please.'

The latter request was addressed to a waiter who had just emerged from the shadows. Van Veeteren lit a cigarette. Reinhart started filling his pipe.

Hard going, he thought. It's going to be hard going this evening.

He took the tape out of his jacket pocket.

'I'm afraid I don't have a Gospel for you either,' he said. 'But if you want an indication of where we are, you can always listen to this. It's a recording of today's discussions. Not exactly a climactic experience, of course, but you know what it's usually like. The voice you won't recognize is a detective-sergeant called Bollmert.'

'Better than nothing,' said Van Veeteren. 'Ah well, I'm not finding it easy to keep my nose out of things.'

'Perfectly understandable,' said Reinhart. 'As I've said before.'

He took out the photograph of Vera Miller.

'Do you recognize this woman?'

Van Veeteren looked at the picture for a couple of seconds.

'Yes,' he said. 'I do, in fact.'

'What?' said Reinhart. 'What the devil do you mean by that?'

'If I'm not much mistaken,' said Van Veeteren, handing the photograph back to Reinhart. 'A nurse at the Gemejnte. Looked after me when I had my colon operation a few years ago. A very pleasant woman – how have you come across her?'

'That's Vera Miller. The woman who was found murdered out at Korrim last Sunday morning.'

'The woman who's linked with Erich somehow or other?'

Reinhart nodded.

'It's only a hypothesis. Extremely shaky so far – but perhaps you can confirm it?'

The waiter came with the beers. They each took a swig. Van Veeteren looked at the photograph again, then slowly shook his head and looked sombre.

'No,' he said. 'It's sheer coincidence that I happen to remember her. Have I understood it rightly, and that it's Meusse who has indicated this link?'

'Meusse, yes. He thinks the blow to the back of the head suggests a connection. It indicates a degree of expertise, he says. In both cases . . . Well, you know Meusse.'

Van Veeteren was lost in silence. Reinhart lit his pipe and allowed him to ponder to his heart's content. Suddenly felt extreme anger bubbling up inside himself. A fury directed at whoever had killed *The Chief Inspector*'s son. Who had killed Vera Miller.

Was it the same person, or two different ones? Who cares? A fury directed at this murderer or these murderers, but also at all killers, whoever they might be . . . And so the coldest and darkest of all his memories began to stir. The murder of Seika. Of his own girlfriend. Seika, whom he should have married and built up a family with. Seika, whom he had loved like no other. Seika with the high cheekbones, the half-Asian eyes and the most beautiful laugh the world has ever heard. It was almost thirty years ago now: she had been lying in that accursed grave out at Linden for three decades. Nineteen-year-old Seika who ought to have been his wife.

If it hadn't been for that evil killer, a knifeman on that occasion, a drugged-up madman who had stabbed her to death one evening in Wollerims Park without the slightest trace of a reason.

Or at least, nothing more than the twelve guilders she had in her purse.

And now *The Chief Inspector*'s son. Bloody hell, Reinhart thought. He's absolutely right, it was a long time ago that the Good Lord stopped doing us favours.

'I went out to Dikken to have a look around,' said Van Veeteren, interrupting his train of thought.

'What?' said Reinhart. 'You?'

'Me, yes,' said Van Veeteren. 'I took the liberty – I hope you'll forgive me.'

'Of course,' said Reinhart.

'I spoke to a few people at that restaurant. It's more like a sort of therapy really. I don't expect to find anything that you lot won't find, but it's so damned hard just sitting around, doing nothing. Can you understand that?'

Reinhart paused for a few seconds before answering.

'Do you remember why I joined the police?' he asked. 'My fiancée in Wollerims Park?'

Van Veeteren nodded.

'Of course I do. Okay, you understand. But anyway, there's one thing I wonder about.'

'What?' said Reinhart.

'The plastic carrier bag,' said Van Veeteren. 'That plastic carrier bag that changed owners. Or was supposed to change owners.'

'What bloody plastic bag are you on about?' said Reinhart.

Van Veeteren said nothing for a moment.

'So you don't know about it?'

Oh, shit, Reinhart thought. Now he's put us on the spot again.

'There was somebody who said something about a plastic carrier bag,' he said, trying to sound offhand about it. 'That's true.'

'It seems that this Mr X, who is presumably the killer . . .' said *The Chief Inspector*, noticeably slowly and in a tone of voice that sounded to Reinhart painfully like some pedagogue explaining the obvious to ignorant pupils, '. . . had a plastic carrier bag by his feet when he was sitting in the bar. And it appears that Erich was carrying that bag when he left the restaurant.'

He raised an eyebrow and waited for Reinhart's reaction.

'Oh, shit,' said Reinhart. 'To tell you the truth . . . Well, to tell you the truth I'm afraid it looks as if we'd missed this. The second half, that is. Several witnesses said Mr X had a plastic carrier bag with him, but we haven't heard anything about Erich having taken it over. How did you find out about that?'

'I happened to meet the right people,' said Van Veeteren modestly, contemplating his newly rolled cigarette. 'One of the waitresses seemed to recall having seen him carrying a plastic bag when he left the restaurant, and when she said that the barman remembered it as well.'

And you *happened* to ask the right questions as well, no doubt, Reinhart thought, and felt a flood of deep-rooted admiration surging through his consciousness, removing all trace of anger and embarrassment. Admiration for that psychological insight that *The Chief Inspector* had always been blessed with, and which . . . which could cut like a scalpel through a ton of warm butter faster than a hundred riot police in bullet-proof vests could work out the whiff of a suspicion.

Intuition, as it was called.

'So what conclusion do you draw?' he asked.

'Erich was there to collect something.'

'Obviously.'

'He drove out to the Trattoria Commedia in order to collect the plastic carrier bag in an agreed location – perhaps in the gents.'

Reinhart nodded.

'He didn't know who Mr X was, and it was not the intention that he should know.'

'How do you know that?'

'If it had been possible for them to meet without concealing their identities, they could just as well meet anywhere at all. In the car park, for instance. Why mess about with that bloody masquerade if it wasn't necessary?'

Reinhart thought that over.

'Mr X was disguised,' he said.

'He was going to murder my son,' Van Veeteren pointed out. 'And he did so. Of course he was going to be disguised.'

'Why hand over the carrier bag if he was going to kill him anyway?' said Reinhart.

'You can answer that yourself,' said Van Veeteren.

Reinhart sucked twice at his pipe, which had gone out.

'Oh, shit,' he said. 'He didn't know who he was. Neither of them knew who the other was. He didn't know who it was until he saw him with the carrier bag in his hand . . . He'd be out in the car park, waiting for him, of course.'

'Presumably,' said Van Veeteren, rolling another cigarette. 'That's the conclusion I've drawn as well. What else? What do you think it was all about? Who's calling the shots, and who's obeying?'

A good question, Reinhart thought. Who is calling the shots and who is obeying?

'Erich calls the shots, and Mr X obeys,' he says. 'To start with, at least. Then Mr X reverses the roles. That's why . . . Yes, that's why he does it. That's why he kills him.'

Van Veeteren leaned back on his chair and lit the cigarette. His son, Reinhart thought. For Christ's sake, we're talking about his murdered son.

'And what do you think it was all about?'

The narcotic cloud hung in the way, and blurred Reinhart's thinking for five seconds: then he hit on the answer.

'Blackmail,' he said. 'It's as clear as bloody day.'

'He maintains that Erich had never indulged in anything like that,' Reinhart explained to Winnifred an hour later. 'I believe him. Besides, it seems incredible that he'd be so bloody stupid simply to drive out to that restaurant and sit there waiting for the money . . . Not if he knew what it was all about. Erich was a messenger boy. Somebody else – the real blackmailer – had sent him out there: when you come to think about it it's pretty obvious. Everything falls into place.'

'What about this Vera Miller woman, then?' said Winnifred. 'Was she behind it all, somehow or other?'

'It's very possible,' said Reinhart. 'The murderer thought it was Erich who was the blackmailer, and killed him quite unnecessarily. Maybe he got the right person when he killed Vera Miller.'

'Did Erich know Vera Miller?'

Reinhart sighed.

'Unfortunately not,' he said. 'That's where it all comes to a stop for the moment. We haven't found a single little thing to link them together. But there might be one. If we assume that he – the murderer, that is – is a doctor at the Gemejnte, it's quite possible that Vera Miller had some kind of hold over him. An operation that he made a mess of, something of that sort perhaps. Could be any damned thing. It's unforgivable for a doctor to make a mistake. He might have killed a patient through sheer carelessness, for instance. She saw an opportunity to earn a bit of cash, and took it. That it turned out as it did is another matter altogether, of course. Anyway, it's a theory at least.'

Winnifred looked sceptical.

'And why did she have to go to bed with him? That's what she did, isn't it?'

'Hmm,' said Reinhart. 'Were you born yesterday, my lovely? That's where a man reveals his true self. It's in bed that a woman gets to know all a man's merits and short-comings.'

Winnifred laughed in delight and snuggled up close to him under the covers.

'My prince,' she said. 'You are so right, but I'm afraid you'll have to wait for a few days before you can demon-strate your merits to me.'

'That's life,' said Reinhart, and switched off the light. 'And I have hardly any shortcomings.'

A quarter of an hour later he got up.

'What are you doing?' wondered Winnifred.

'Joanna,' said Reinhart. 'I thought I heard something.'

'You didn't at all,' said Winnifred. 'But go and fetch her so that we can lie here, all three of us. That's what you were thinking, isn't it?'

'More or less,' admitted Reinhart and tiptoed over to the nursery.

My wife knows what I'm thinking before I do, he told himself as he lifted up his sleeping daughter. How the hell does she do that?

25

On Wednesday, 9 December it was plus ten or eleven degrees, and the sky was high and bright.

The sun seemed to be surprised, almost embarrassed at having to display itself in all its somewhat faded nudity. Van Veeteren phoned Ulrike Fremdli at work, was informed that she would be finished by lunchtime, and suggested a car trip to the seaside. They hadn't seen the sea for quite some time. She accepted straight away: he could hear from her voice that she was both surprised and pleased, and he reminded himself that he loved her. Then he reminded her as well.

The living must look after one another, he thought. The worst possible outcome is to die without having lived.

As he sat in the car outside the Remington dirt-brown office complex he wondered if Erich had lived. If he had managed to experience the fundamentals of life, whatever they might be. He had read somewhere that a man must do three things during his life: raise a son, write a book and plant a tree.

He wondered where that had come from. In any case, Erich had not achieved the first two of those requirements. Whether or not he had planted a tree he had no idea, of course: but it didn't seem all that likely. Before he had time to think about how far he himself fulfilled those requirements, he was interrupted by Ulrike flopping down in the seat beside him.

'Isn't it lovely?' she said. 'What a marvellous day!'

She kissed him on the cheek, and to his surprise he found that he had an erection. Life goes on, he thought, somewhat confused. Despite everything.

'Where would you like to go?' he asked.

'Emsbaden or Behrensee,' she said without hesitation. She had evidently been thinking about it ever since he'd rung.

'Emsbaden,' he said. 'I have a bit of a problem with Behrensee.'

'Why?'

'Hmm,' he said. 'Something happened there a few years ago. I'd rather not be reminded of it.'

She waited for an explanation, but there wasn't one. He started the car and drove off instead.

'My secretive lover,' she said.

★

They spent an hour wandering around the dunes, then had a late lunch at the De Dirken inn, almost adjacent to the lighthouse in Emsbaden. Lobster tails in dill sauce, coffee and carrot cake. They spoke about Jess and Ulrike's children and their future prospects.

And eventually also about Erich.

'I remember something you said,' Ulrike told him. 'Then, when you'd found the woman who murdered Karel.'

Karel Innings was Ulrike's former husband, but not the father of her children. They had been the product of her first marriage to an estate agent, who had been a good and reliable paterfamilias until his inherited alcoholism got the better of him.

'We never found her,' Van Veeteren pointed out.

'But you found her motives,' said Ulrike. 'In any case, you maintained that from her point of view – in one sense at least – killing my husband had been justified. Do you remember that?'

'Of course,' said Van Veeteren. 'But it was only true in a way. From a very individual, limited point of view. It's a distortion if you put it like you did.'

'Isn't that always the case?'

'What do you mean?'

'Isn't it always the case that the murderer – or any other criminal, come to that – thinks that his crime is justified? Doesn't he have to think that to himself anyway?'

'That's an old chestnut,' said Van Veeteren. 'But you are right in principle, of course. A murderer always justifies his motives – acknowledges them also, naturally. Mind you, it's a different matter if somebody else points them out. There are reasons for everything we do, but the dogma of original sin never seems to convince members of the jury nowadays. They are much more thick-skinned than that.'

'But you believe in it?'

He paused for a moment and gazed out over the sea.

'Naturally,' he said. 'I don't defend evil deeds, but if you can't understand the nature of crime . . . the motives of a criminal . . . well, you won't get very far as a detect-ive. There is a sort of twisted logic which is often easier to discover than the logic that governs our everyday actions. As we all know, chaos is the neighbour of God: but every-thing's usually neat and tidy in hell . . .'

She laughed, and took a bite of her carrot cake.

'Go on.'

'All right, since you ask me so nicely,' said Van Veeteren. 'Anyway, this malicious logic can affect us all when we are trapped in a corner. It's not a problem to understand why an Islamic brother murders his sister because she's been going to discotheques and wants to be a Westerner. No problem at all if you are familiar with the background. But the fact that the deed itself is so disgusting that the very thought of it makes you want to throw up, and that your spontaneous reaction is to take the killer and demolish a skyscraper on top of him – well, that's something else. Something completely different.'

He fell silent. She eyed him gravely, then took hold of his hand over the table.

'A crime is born in the gap between the morality of society and that of the individual,' said Van Veeteren, and immediately wondered if that really was generally true.

'And if they find Erich's murderer,' said Ulrike. 'Will you understand him as well?'

He hesitated before answering. Gazed out over the beach again. The sun had gone away, and the weather was as it presumably was before some god or other hit on the idea of creating it. Plus eight degrees, slight breeze, white cloud.

'I don't know,' he said. 'That's why I want to meet him face to face.'

She let go of his hand, and frowned.

'I can't understand why you want to expose yourself to something like that,' she said. 'Sitting opposite your son's murderer. Sometimes I just don't understand you.'

'I've never claimed that I do either,' said Van Veeteren.

And I've never said that I wouldn't want to put a bullet between those eyes either, he thought; but he didn't say so.

*

On the way home Ulrike came up with a suggestion.

'I'd like us to invite his fiancée to dinner.'

'Who?' said Van Veeteren.

'Marlene Frey. Let's invite her to dinner tomorrow evening. At your place. I'll ring and talk to her.'

Such a thought had never struck him. He wondered why. Then he felt ashamed for two seconds before saying yes.

'On condition that you stay the night with me as well,' he said.

Ulrike laughed and gave him a gentle punch on the shoulder.

'I've already promised that,' she said. 'Thursday, Friday and Saturday. Jürg's away at a school camp.'

'Excellent,' said Van Veeteren. 'I sleep so damned badly when you're not there.'

'I don't come to you in order to sleep,' said Ulrike.

'Excellent,' said Van Veeteren again, unable to think of anything better to say.

Chief of Police Hiller clasped his hands on the pigskin desk pad and tried to establish eye contact with Reinhart. Reinhart yawned and looked at a green, palm-like thing that he seemed to recall he knew the name of, once upon a time.

'Hmm, well,' said Hiller. 'I happened to bump into the

chief inspector this morning . . . I mean *The Chief Inspector*.'

Reinhart shifted his gaze to a benjamin fig.

'It's taken its toll on him, this business with his son. I think you should be aware of that. Not so strange. After all these years and all the rest of it . . . Anyway, I think it's a point of honour, this business. We really *must* solve this case. It mustn't slip though our fingers. How far have you got?'

'Quite a way,' said Reinhart. 'We're doing all we can.'

'Well, yes,' said Hiller. 'I don't doubt that for a moment, of course. Everybody – and I mean *everybody* – must feel the same way about it as I do. That it's a point of honour. If we have to allow a few murderers to go free, one of them must on no account be this one. Not in any circumstances. Do you need more resources? I'm prepared to lean over backwards, a long way backwards. Just say the word.'

Reinhart said nothing.

'As you know I never interfere in your operational work, but if you want to discuss the way things are going with me, just say the word. And resources, as I said. No limits. Point of honour. Is that clear?'

Reinhart got up from the spongy visitor chair.

'Crystal clear,' he said. 'But you don't solve equations by using tanks.'

'Eh?' said the chief of police. 'What the devil do you mean by that?'

'I'll explain some other time,' said Reinhart, opening the door. 'I'm in a bit of a hurry, if you'll excuse me.'

Jung and Moreno were sitting in his office, waiting for him.

'Greetings from the Fourth Floor,' said Reinhart. 'The master gardener has a new suit again.'

'Has he been on the telly?' Jung wondered.

'Not as far as I know,' said Moreno. 'But perhaps he's going to?'

Reinhart flopped down on his chair and lit his pipe.

'Well?' he said. 'What's the situation?'

'I still haven't got hold of her,' said Jung. 'She's with her boyfriend somewhere. She won't be back at work until tomorrow afternoon. I'm sorry.'

'Damn and blast,' said Reinhart.

'Who are you talking about?' asked Moreno.

'Edita Fischer, of course,' said Reinhart. 'That nurse who implied to the other nurse that Vera Miller had implied something . . . Huh, what a wishy-washy set-up, for Christ's sake! Any luck with the list of doctors?'

'Tip-top,' said Moreno, handing him the file she'd had on her knee. 'You have there the names and photographs of all the hundred-and-twenty-six doctors who work at the Gemejnte. Plus a handful who left during the last year – they are all marked. Date of birth, date of appointment, medical qualifications, specialist training and everything else you could possibly want to know. Even civil status and family members. They are well organized at Gemejnte Hospital.'

'Not bad,' said Reinhart, leafing through the files. 'Not bad at all. Are they split up according to clinic and ward as well?'

'Of course,' said Moreno. 'I've already put a cross by those who worked on Ward Forty-six, Vera Miller's ward. There are six doctors permanently linked, and another seven or eight who work there from time to time. There's quite a lot of movement from ward to ward, not least among the specialists – anaesthetists for instance.'

Reinhart nodded as he continued thumbing through the documents, studying the series of smiling faces of men and women in white coats. It was evidently part of the routine to be photographed in this way. The background was the same in most of the pictures, and everybody – the vast majority in any case – were sitting with their heads at the same angle and their mouths fixed in a broad smile. Apparently the same photographer: he wondered what awful joke he must have told them to make them all roar with laughter the way they seemed to be doing.

'Not bad,' he said for the third time. 'So here we have the murderer complete with photograph and personal details down to shoe size. It's just a pity we don't know which of them it is. Which one of the hundred-and-twenty-six . . .'

'If we're still sticking to Rooth's hypothesis,' said Moreno, 'we can eliminate forty of them.'

'Really?' said Reinhart. 'Why?'

'Because they are women. But I don't know how we should proceed with this – it seems a bit much to interrogate the whole lot of them, rather than thinning them down a little. Even if they look friendly enough in the photos, they might well be rather more difficult to deal with in reality. Especially when they catch on to what we suspect them of . . . Not to mention *esprit de corps* and goodness knows what else.'

Reinhart nodded.

'Let's start with those most closely connected,' he said. 'Only them for the time being. What was it you said? Six attached to the clinic and a few more who keep dropping in. We ought to be able to deal with them before Jung's witness turns up again. Who should we send to deal with this?'

'Not Rooth,' said Jung.

'Okay, not Rooth,' said Reinhart. 'But I can see two reliable police officers before my very eyes just now. Get on with it – good hunting.'

He closed the file and handed it back. As Jung left the room first, he was able to put a question to Inspector

Moreno.

'Have you been sleeping well lately?'

'Better and better,' said Moreno, and she actually smiled. 'What about you?'

'I get my deserts,' said Reinhart, cryptically.

26

Tuesday's post comprised a few bills and a couple of letters.

One was from the Spaarkasse, informing him that his loan had been granted. The sum of 220,000 had already been credited to his account.

The other letter was from his opponent.

A different kind of envelope this time. Simpler, cheaper. The letter paper itself was a folded page, apparently torn out of a spiral pad. Before he began reading he wondered if this in itself was a sign of something, if it had some sort of significance, this reduction in quality.

He failed to find a satisfactory answer; and the instructions were just as simple and clear as before.

Your last chance. My patience is soon at an end. The same procedure as last time.

Place: the rubbish bin behind the grill bar at the junction of Armastenstraat and Bremers Steeg.

Time: the early hours of Friday, 03.00.

Stand by your telephone in your home at 04.00. Don't try transferring calls to your mobile – I have taken measures to protect myself from that. If I don't have my money by Friday morning, you are a goner.

A friend

This business concerning his mobile phone had already occurred to him. He'd rung and investigated the possibility of doing that, but it gradually became clear to him that the caller could always establish whether the call had been diverted from one number to another. Otherwise, of course, he would have been very tempted to hide himself some twenty metres into Bremers Steeg, which he knew was a dark, narrow alley . . . To stand there and wait for his opponent, with the pipe hidden inside his overcoat. Very tempted.

Another thing that struck him when he read the instructions again was the sheer damned self-confidence of the blackmailer. How could he be certain, for instance, that his victim wouldn't use an assistant, just as he had done out at Dikken? How could he be so sure of that? It was even possible that he could arrange for the assistance of a good friend without needing to reveal what it was all about. He could get somebody else to answer the telephone, for instance. Or did his opponent know his voice so well that he would recognize such a move immediately? Was he so well acquainted with him?

Or had he refined his tactics this time? Polished them in some way? It looked like it. Perhaps the telephone call would involve further instructions to guarantee that the money could be collected behind the grill bar in peace and quiet.

But how, in that case? What instructions might they be, for Christ's sake? Would he be armed?

That last point cropped up without his having thought about it, but it soon became clear that it was the most significant of them all. Would his opponent have a weapon, and – in the worst-case scenario – would he be prepared to use it in order to collect his money?

A pistol in his jacket pocket in a dark corner in Bremers Steeg?

He put the letter back into its envelope and checked the clock.

Eleven thirty-five. Less than sixteen hours left.

Time was short. Very short, and this was the last round now. No further delays were conceivable.

Time to run away? he thought.

27

Moreno and Jung spoke to a dozen doctors on the Thursday morning. Including three women – if for no other reason than to avoid raising suspicions.

Suspicions that the police had suspicions about their male colleagues. Or one of them, at least.

Instead, the ostensible starting point of the conversations was that they needed information about the murdered nurse, Vera Miller. General impressions of her. Her relations with patients and colleagues – everything that might, in some way or other, contribute to a more complete all-round picture of her. Especially with regard to her work.

As far as Moreno and Jung could judge, all the doctors told them without reservation all they knew about Nurse Miller. Some had quite a lot to say, others naturally enough rather less, due to the fact that they hadn't had so much to do with her. But impressions and judgements were remarkably unanimous: Vera Miller had been an outstanding nurse. Knowledgeable, positive, willing to work hard – and with that little bit extra feeling for patients that was so very important: if only everybody who worked in health care had that little bit extra!

De mortuis . . . Moreno thought; but it was only an automatic thought that seemed hardly appropriate in this case. Nurse Miller had been well liked and much appreciated, it was as simple as that. Nobody had any idea as to who might have wanted to kill her in the way that she was killed – nor in any other way, come to that. Not the slightest idea.

Nor did Moreno and Jung after they had finished their questioning, and sat down for lunch in the restaurant in Block A. Not the slightest idea.

They had finished their unusually substantial pasta meal by a few minutes past one, and decided that they might as well wait for Edita Fischer up in Ward 46. She was due to come on duty at two o'clock – after two-and-a-half days' leave. Time off she had spent with her boyfriend at some unknown location. His name was Arnold, but that was all they knew about him. When Jung had finally succeeded in contacting fröken Fischer that morning, after no end of trials and tribulations, she had declined to disclose where they had been, and what they had been doing.

Not that he was especially interested, but even so . . .

'Presumably they were robbing a bank,' he explained to Moreno, 'but so what? The important thing is that we can talk to her. In any case, it had nothing to do with Vera Miller.'

Moreno thought for a moment, then agreed.

The important thing was that they could talk to her.

Edita Fischer was young and blonde, and looked more or less how a nurse in an American television series was supposed to look. With the possible exception of the fact that she was slightly cross-eyed: but Jung at least thought that made her even more charming.

She was obviously embarrassed by what she had set in motion. Blushed and apologized several times, even before they had settled down in the pale-green reception room that had been placed at their disposal thanks to the ward sister's determined efforts. It was usually reserved exclusively for discussions with the next of kin after a patient had died, she explained: green was said to have a calming effect.

'For Christ's sake,' exclaimed Fischer, 'it was nothing! Nothing at all. I gather it was Liljana who told you about this?'

Jung admitted that the matter had cropped up during one of his conversations with Liljana Milovic.

'Why couldn't she hold her tongue?' said Fischer. 'It was just a throwaway remark I made as we sat talking.'

'If everybody held their tongues, we wouldn't find many criminals,' said Jung.

'What sort of a throwaway remark was it?' asked Moreno. 'Now that we're sitting here.'

Fischer hesitated a little longer, but it was obvious that she was going to come clean. Jung exchanged glances with Moreno, and they both refrained from asking questions. All they needed to do was wait. Wait, and gaze at the comforting green walls.

'It was over a month ago . . . Nearly one-and-a-half, in fact.'

'The beginning of November?' said Moreno.

'About then. I don't think I've ever cried as much as I did when I heard that Vera had been killed. It's so awful – she was such a happy, lively person . . . You don't think anything like that could happen to a person you know so well. Who did it? – It must be a madman.'

'We don't know yet,' said Jung. 'But that's what we're going to find out.'

'Did you socialize outside working hours as well?' asked Moreno.

Fischer shook her head.

'No, but she was a wonderful colleague – ask all the others.'

'We have done,' said Jung.

'Yes, of course,' said Fischer, with a sigh. 'But you must understand that it was of no importance, in fact. Liljana tends to blow things up out of all proportion . . . She's okay, but that's just the way she is.'

'Let's hear it now,' said Jung. 'We can usually work out what's important and what isn't. But we like to know as much as possible before we do that.'

'Of course,' said Fischer. 'Forgive me. Anyway, the fact is that Vera made that visit to Rumford.'

'The New Rumford Hospital?' wondered Moreno.

'Yes, there was a patient who needed to be transferred there. That happens sometimes. A woman with pulmonary emphysema – they have better resources at Rumford for dealing with that than we have here. Sometimes we transfer patients to them, and sometimes they send patients to us . . .'

'Sounds sensible,' said Jung.

'Yes,' said Fischer. 'It is sensible. Anyway, Vera accompanied this patient, and she stayed half a day at Rumford. To make sure that the patient was all right, felt she was being properly looked after and so on. Vera was very particular with that kind of thing – that's why she was such a good nurse. When she came back that afternoon we were having our coffee break, and we pulled Vera's leg a bit. Asked her why it had taken her so long – whether it was because they have such handsome doctors at Rumford. They do, in fact . . .'

She seemed embarrassed again, and squirmed on her chair.

'Much younger than ours in any case,' she added. 'And that's when Vera said what she said. "You've hit the nail on the head," she said.'

'Hit the nail on the head?' said Moreno.

'Yes, she laughed and said: "You've hit the nail on the head, Edita." That was all. I don't know if she was joking or if there was more to it than that. Good God, have you been sitting and waiting here all this time just to hear that?'

'Hmm,' said Jung. 'We're used to sitting and waiting, you don't need to worry about that.'

Moreno pondered as she scribbled something in her notebook.

'What do you think?' she said. 'What did you think she meant when Vera Miller said that? Don't be afraid of misleading us, it's better if you tell us your spontaneous reaction.'

Fischer bit her lip, looked down at her hands which were clasped in her lap, and squirmed again.

'I thought there was something going on,' she said eventually. 'Yes, when I look back now, I really did think so.'

'You know that she was married?' Jung asked.

'Of course.'

'But you don't think it's out of the question that . . . that she'd met a doctor at Rumford she'd fallen for?'

Fallen for? he thought. I'm talking like an actor in a B-movie. But so what?

'I don't know,' she said with a shrug. 'How the hell could I know that? It was just what she said . . . And the way she said it.'

'And it never cropped up again?' Moreno asked. 'No more insinuations like that, for instance?'

'No,' said Fischer. 'None at all. That's why I said it was a throwaway remark.'

Jung thought for a while.

'All right,' he said. 'Many thanks for your cooperation. You can get on with your work now.'

Edita Fischer thanked them, and left. Jung stood up and walked twice around the room. Then sat down again.

'Well,' said Moreno. 'That was that. What do you think?'

'Think?' said Jung. 'I know what we have to do next, in any case. A hundred new doctors. We'll have enough work to keep us going until Christmas . . . But I suppose we have to be grateful that we're not left twiddling our thumbs.'

'Thus spake a real police officer,' said Moreno.

28

It was twenty minutes to three when he left the Spaarkasse branch in Keymer Plejn with almost a quarter of a million in his pockets. They'd looked a bit doubtful when he'd said that he wanted the whole amount in cash. It was a deal to buy a boat, he'd explained . . . An eccentric seller who insisted on having ready cash. Otherwise there would be no deal.

He wondered if they'd swallowed it. Maybe, maybe not. But it didn't matter either way. The main thing was that he had the money. When it was time to pay off the loan, he would be nowhere near Maardam. Not even on the extreme edge of nearness. Exactly where in the world he would be, he didn't know yet. There were only twelve hours to go before the money was due to be handed over, and he still didn't have a strategy.

I'm too calm, he thought as he clambered into his car. I've taken too many pills, they're making me dozy.

He took the usual route to Boorkhejm. The mild

weather from yesterday was holding its own, and he drove unusually slowly since it had struck him that this might be the last time he would ever make this trip. Which he had made thousands of times . . . Yes, it must be thousands. It was nearly fifteen years since he'd moved into the modern terraced house with Marianne, and now he was going to leave it. It was high time, too.

It really was high time.

Perhaps it was the low speed and the feeling of making this journey for the last time that made him notice the scooter.

An ordinary, red scooter parked outside one of the doors to the block of flats just before the row of terraced houses where he lived. No more than twenty-five metres from his own house, in fact.

A red scooter.

The realization came to him in a flash. The scooter.

The scooter.

He parked on the drive to his garage as usual. Got out of the car and started walking slowly back along the street. Thoughts were exploding like fireworks inside his head, and he had to apply all his strength to prevent himself from stopping and staring at the vehicle, which was glittering in the pale sunshine.

He walked past it. Continued to the kiosk and bought a newspaper. Passed by the magical two-wheeler again and returned to his house. Glanced over his shoulder and discovered that he could in fact see it from where he was standing. On the drive, next to his car. He thought for a moment, then tried to see if he could see it just as well from inside the car.

He couldn't, not really: but after backing out into the street, turning round and reversing up the drive, he found he had a perfectly good view from the driver's seat. He remembered that he possessed a pair of binoculars, went in and fetched them.

Sat down in the car again, but before starting his surveillance in earnest he got out and made another trip to the kiosk. Bought two beers that he knew he would never drink, paused briefly outside the block of flats and memorized the registration number.

Then he sat down in the car with the binoculars. Sat there on guard for forty-five minutes and tried to think if there could be any doubt. To examine the conclusions he'd drawn in the space of only a few seconds, and which felt as definite as an axiom.

Everything fitted. A scooter had passed by that evening. It had been on the way to Boorkhejm. He had already worked out that the blackmailer must be somebody who recognized him, who knew who he was . . . The answer was quite simply that it must be a neighbour. Not somebody he spoke to every day – in any case, the only people

in that category were his neighbours on both sides: herr
Landtberg and the Kluumes.

But somebody in the block of flats.

There were only three floors. There couldn't be more
than ten or a dozen flats. Three entrances. And a red
scooter outside the door nearest to his own house.

It was as clear as day. Boorkhejm was not a large hous-
ing estate, and people knew one another. Or recognized
one another, at least. He doubted if there were any other
scooters around here. The fact that he'd never seen this
one before – or at any rate not noticed it – must be due
to the fact that the owner normally parked it at the rear
of the building. He realized that his opponent must not
be aware that his vehicle could give him away: if he was,
it seemed implausible that he would be so careless today
of all days, and leave it out in full view.

Today of all days. When there were only a few hours
left.

He checked his watch. Just turned four. Eleven hours
left.

He felt he had goose pimples on his arms.

Felt that a strategy was beginning to take form.

Three-quarters of an hour. That is how long he sat in the
car, waiting and planning. Then the owner emerged. The

owner of the red scooter. In the binoculars his face seemed to be only a few metres from his own. A cheerless, very ordinary face. About his own age. He recognized him.

A member of staff in the prosthesis workshops at the hospital. He seemed to recall having spoken to him once, but they never used to greet each other.

He couldn't remember the man's name. But that was irrelevant. His strategy evolved at record speed. The goose pimples were still there.

The dinner with Marlene Frey was quite a tense occasion to begin with. Van Veeteren noticed that she was on edge when he opened the door for her, and his clumsy attempts to make her feel welcome didn't exactly improve matters.

Ulrike was perhaps a little more successful in this respect, but it was only when Marlene burst into tears halfway through the soup that the ice was well and truly broken.

'Damn,' she snivelled. 'I thought I'd be able to cope, but I can't. Please forgive me.'

While she was in the bathroom Van Veeteren drank two glasses of wine, and Ulrike observed him with a worried expression on her face.

'I miss him so much,' said Marlene when she came back. 'I realize that you do as well, but that doesn't make it any easier. I miss him so much, I'm scared I'm going out of my mind.'

She stared at Van Veeteren with her inadequately spruced-up eyes. Unable to think up anything better, he stared back at her – then walked round the table and gave her a big hug. It wasn't easy as she was sitting down, but as he did so he felt something inside himself loosening its grip.

A clenched fist letting go. Releasing him. Remarkable, he thought.

'Jesus,' said Ulrike. 'Just think how far it can be between people's hearts at times.'

Marlene burst out crying again, but it was sufficient to blow her nose into her paper napkin this time.

'I've felt so lonely,' she said. 'And I've been quite scared of meeting you.'

'He's not all that dangerous,' Ulrike assured her. 'I've begun to realize that more and more.'

'Hmm,' said Van Veeteren, who had sat down on his chair again. 'Cheers.'

'I'm going to bear his child,' said Marlene. 'It feels so horrendously unreal, and I don't know how things are going to turn out. It had never occurred to us that only one of us would be around to look after it.'

She sighed deeply and tried to smile.

'Forgive me. It's just that it's so hard. Thank you for giving me a hug.'

'Good Lord,' said Van Veeteren. 'Dammit all. Cheers! I promise to look after you. You and the child, of course. Hmm.'

'I should jolly well think so,' said Ulrike Fremdli. 'Let's finish off the soup now – there's a bite of meat to follow.'

'What about your parents?' he asked cautiously an hour later. 'Do you get any support from them?'

Marlene shook her head.

'I was a druggie. My mum does her best, but it's not exactly what you could call support. I hope you believe me when I say I've put all that behind me now . . . Because it's true: I really have. We both did it together, Erich and I. Mind you, it sometimes feels as if you manage to lift yourself up and the reward is to get knocked down again . . .'

'Life is much overrated,' said Van Veeteren. 'But it's better if you don't discover that too soon.'

Marlene looked at him with eyebrows slightly raised.

'Hmm,' she said. 'Perhaps it is. Erich said you'd never been much of an optimist – but I like you even so. I hope you'll allow me to carry on doing so.'

'Of course,' said Ulrike. 'He has a certain grumpy charm, you're absolutely right there. More coffee?'

Marlene shook her head.

'No, thank you. I must go now. I'd love to invite you round, but you know what it's like at my place . . . Although the heating is much better now.'

'We expect to see you here for Christmas,' said Van Veeteren. 'And New Year. Them as can do it, does it . . . And all that.'

Ulrike laughed and Marlene smiled. He wondered how long it had been since he last put two women in such a good mood at the same time. And concluded that it had never happened before. As they stood in the hall Marlene remembered something.

'Oh yes,' she said. 'There was that note . . .'

'What note?' said Ulrike, helping her on with her duffel coat.

'I found a note,' said Marlene. 'When I was doing the cleaning the other day. Erich always used to leave notes all over the place . . . With times and names and addresses and suchlike.'

'Really?' said Van Veeteren, and realized that he had just become a CID officer again for a second.

'The police went through all the bits of paper Erich had left lying around these last few weeks, but they didn't find this one. It was under a table mat in the kitchen. I know he wrote it recently, because there was also a note about a job he did one of the last days as well.'

'What else did it say?' asked Van Veeteren.

'Just a name,' said Marlene. 'Keller.'

'Keller?'

'Yes, Keller. It's not exactly an unusual name, but I don't know anybody called that. And it's not in the address book. Anyway, that was all. Do you think I should phone the police and tell them about it?'

Van Veeteren thought for a moment.

'Yes, do that,' he said. 'Keller? Keller? No, I don't know anybody of that name either. But phone them, as I said. Give Reinhart a buzz – they need all the help they can get. Have you got his number?'

Marlene nodded. Then she hugged them both, and after she'd gone it felt as if she'd left a vacuum behind her.

It was remarkable. A big vacuum.

'You're going to be a granddad,' said Ulrike, sitting down on his knee.

'Ouch,' said Van Veeteren. 'I know. Was it three days you said?'

'Nights,' said Ulrike. 'I'm working during the day. Tomorrow, at least.'

Aron Keller saw the red Audi drive past in the street outside. Then he watched it park on the drive up to number seventeen. He was able to do that because his living room had a bay window on the front of the building. That was where he was standing. It was where he often stood. On the second floor, half-hidden by the two magnificent hibiscus bushes. It provided him with a first-class view of what was going on outside.

Which was not normally very much. Nevertheless, he often stood there. It had become a habit as the years passed. Standing in the bay window for a while, now and then.

A bit later he thanked his lucky stars that he had done so. That he had stayed there for a minute or so after he'd watched the murderer-doctor pass by in his shiny-clean car.

He came back. The doctor came walking back again. Went to the kiosk and bought a newspaper. He didn't usually do that. Not normally.

Aron Keller remained standing in the bay window, waiting. Just as motionless as the hibiscus bushes. Watched the Audi back out into the street, then reverse back up the drive. Then the doctor got out of the car, and disappeared into his house to fetch something – Keller couldn't see what it was. Came back and sat behind the wheel again. Sat there in the car in front of his house. Keller felt the sweat in the palms of his hands. After only another minute or so the doctor got out of the car and started walking to the kiosk again. Just outside the entrance door, Keller's own entrance door, he slowed down and stared at the scooter. Then continued to the kiosk. Bought something he put into a brown paper carrier bag and came back once more. Keller took two paces backwards into the room until the doctor had gone past. Then returned to his position in the bay window, and watched the doctor sit down behind the wheel of his car again.

Sit there and stay there. The minutes passed. Still he sat there in the front seat, doing nothing.

Bugger, Keller thought. He knows. The bastard knows.

When he walked past number seventeen quite a long time later, the doctor was still sitting in the car. That was the final proof he needed. Keller went round the back of the row of terraced houses and returned to his flat from the rear. Took a beer from the refrigerator when he was back inside, and emptied it in three swigs. Stood in the bay window. The Audi outside number seventeen was empty. The sun had set.

But *he* doesn't know, he thought. The murderer-doctor doesn't know that I know that he knows. I'm one step ahead. I'm still in control.

FIVE

29

If you look at it from a purely quantitative point of view, Chief Inspector Reinhart thought during a brief smoking break at about eleven o'clock on Saturday morning, we don't need to be ashamed of the work we've put in.

There was plenty of evidence to back up that thought. After hearing what Edita Fischer had to say, they suddenly found themselves with so many doctors to interview that Rooth, deBries and Bollmert were all pressed into duty as well. To be sure, if he were honest with himself Reinhart regarded the whole rigmarole as grasping at straws: but as there were no other straws lying around (and in view of Chief of Police Hiller's generous promise of unlimited resources), they had to follow everything up, of course. Nobody called the operation 'Rooth's hypothesis' any more – least of all Rooth himself once it had become clear that he would have to work on both Saturday and Sunday.

The New Rumford Hospital was rather smaller than

the Gemejnte, but even so it employed 102 doctors – 69 of whom were men. With this new group, they were naturally unable to pretend they were simply looking for impressions of the murdered nurse Vera Miller – among other reasons due to the simple fact that nobody could be expected to have any impressions.

With the possible exception of the murderer himself, as deBries very rightly pointed out: but he would presumably not be especially keen to unburden himself simply because he'd been asked a few polite questions. Everybody in the investigation team was agreed on that score.

Instead, Reinhart decided to proceed with all his cards laid on the table. There was information to suggest that Vera Miller might have been having an affair with a doctor at one of the two hospitals: did anybody know anything about this? Had anybody heard any rumours? Could anybody contribute any guesses or speculations?

The latter question was perhaps on the borderline of bad taste, but what the hell? If you asked a hundred people to guess, Reinhart thought, there could well be somebody who guessed right.

For his part Inspector Jung had never counted this type of mass interrogation among his favourite tasks (informal conversations like the one he'd had with Nurse Milovic were an entirely different category, of course), and when he met Rooth for a well-earned coffee break in the afternoon, he took the opportunity of thanking him for the weekend's stimulating work.

'A pity you picked on the doctors, of all people,' he said.

'What are you on about?' said Rooth, swallowing a bun.

'Well, if you'd hit upon a shop-assistant hypothesis instead, we'd have had ten times as many nice interviews to carry out. Or a student hypothesis.'

'I've already told you I don't know what a hypothesis is,' said Rooth. 'Am I not allowed to drink my coffee in peace?'

As had been the case with conversations with Erich Van Veeteren's friends and acquaintances, all the new interviews were recorded; and when Reinhart contemplated the pile of cassettes on his desk on Sunday evening – especially if he were to combine them with those from the earlier interviews – the material began to acquire a scope comparable to that in the investigation into Prime Minister Palme's murder.

Borkmann's point? he thought. *The Chief Inspector* had talked about that some time ago. Was it not true to say that the quantity of evidence had long since superseded the quality? Without his having noticed. Did he not already know what he needed to know? Surely the answer . . . or answers? . . . were contained (and hidden) in the vast mass of investigation material already collected? Somewhere.

Perhaps, he thought. Perhaps not. How could one possibly know? Intuition as usual? Bugger that for a lark.

A little later on the Sunday evening they had a run-through meeting. Reinhart bore in mind Hiller's insistence that there should be no holding back of resources, and in order to help his colleagues survive had purchased four bottles of wine and two large savoury sandwich layer cakes. Since there were only six officers involved, he felt he had followed the chief of police's exhortations to the letter.

Not even Rooth was able to eat the last half of the sandwich layer cake.

It was always possible to summarize work done in terms of quantity. And they did just that.

In the course of two-and-a-half days six detective officers had interviewed 189 doctors, 120 of them male, 69 female.

None of those questioned had confessed that he (or she) had murdered Vera Miller – or even that they had had a sexual relationship with her.

Nobody had fingered anybody else as a possible candidate (although it was not clear if this was a result of the legendary so-called *esprit de corps*). Not so much as a guess, so Reinhart had no need to worry about taking into consideration the ethical aspect of it all. Something for which he was grateful.

None of the six police officers had conceived any direct suspicions in the course of their conversations – at least, not in connection with what they were trying to discover. If Chief Inspector Reinhart wanted to check the judgement of his colleagues in this respect, all he needed to do was to listen to the tapes. On the assumption that he restricted himself to just one run-through of each interview, that would take him in round figures a total of fifty-two hours.

Not counting pauses while cassettes were changed, visits to the toilet and sleep. In the aftermath of the sandwich layer cakes, he thought he might well be able to cut back on breaks for refreshments.

'It's not a lot,' said Rooth. 'To coin a phrase. The results, I mean.'

'Never in the history of human endeavour have so few had so many to thank for so little,' said Reinhart. 'Hell's bells. How many have we left?'

'Twenty-eight,' said Jung, checking with a document. 'Five on secondment somewhere else, six on holiday, nine on days off and not in town . . . Seven on sick leave and one about to give birth in half an hour's time.'

'Shouldn't she be added to the list of those on sick leave?' wondered Rooth.

'She's certainly not on holiday, that's for sure,' said Moreno.

There was also another arithmetical sum to be solved, involving rather fewer unknowns. The so-called Edita Fischer trail. Moreno and Jung, who had shared responsibility for the Rumford Hospital investigation, had worked out exactly which day it was that Vera Miller had gone there with the pulmonary emphysema patient. And precisely how many male doctors had been on duty that day, and on which wards. Unfortunately Vera Miller had taken the opportunity of having lunch in the large staff canteen, where she could theoretically have met anybody at all – but the sum of all their efforts had been a comparatively small number of doctors.

Thirty-two, to be precise. Jung was in favour of eliminating all those who had passed their fifty-fifth birthday, but Moreno refused to go along with such a prejudiced suggestion. Grey temples were not to be underestimated. Especially if they were on doctors. In any case they had met twenty-five of this 'high potency' group (Jung's term), none of whom had behaved in a remotely suspicious manner nor had anything of interest to say.

That left seven. One on holiday. Four on days off, not in town. Two off sick.

'It must be one of them,' said Jung. 'One of those seven. It sounds like a film – shall we lay bets?'

'You'll have to find somebody else to bet against,' said Moreno. 'I agree with you.'

When the others had gone home, Reinhart shared the last bottle of wine with Moreno. Rooth was also present, but had fallen asleep in a corner.

'This is a right bugger,' said Reinhart. 'I don't know how many times I've said it during this investigation . . . Sorry, *these investigations*! . . . But we're getting nowhere. I feel as if I were working for some bloody statistics institute. If we'd thought of asking them about their political views and drinking habits as well, we could no doubt have sold the material to *The Gazette*'s Sunday supplement. Or some public opinion firm or other.'

'Hmm,' said Moreno. '*The Chief Inspector* used to say that one had to learn how to wait as well. To have patience. Perhaps we ought to think along those lines.'

'He used to say something else as well.'

'Really?' said Moreno. 'What?'

'That you need to solve a case as quickly as possible. Preferably on the very first day, so that you don't have to lie awake thinking about it all night. For Christ's sake, it's five weeks now since we discovered the body of his son. I don't like admitting it, but the last time I met Van Veeteren I felt ashamed. Yes, ashamed! He explained to me that the whole thing was based on a blackmailing scam . . . There's no doubt that he's right, but still we're not getting anywhere. It's a right bug— No, I'll just have to learn to live with it.'

'Do you think she was the blackmailer?' asked Moreno. 'Vera Miller, that is.'

Reinhart shook his head.

'No, for some reason or other I don't think so. Despite the fact that the story about her being linked to a doctor rings true. Why should a woman about whom nobody has a bad word to say stoop to something like that?'

'Blackmail involves a weakness of character,' said Moreno.

'Exactly,' said Reinhart. 'Both axe murderers and wife beaters have a higher status in prison. Blackmail is one of the most . . . immoral crimes there is. Not the worst, but the lowest. Cheap, if that word still exists in this context.'

'Yes,' said Moreno, 'I think you're right. So we can exclude Vera Miller. And we can also exclude Erich Van Veeteren. Do you know what we have left?'

Reinhart poured out the last drops of wine.

'Yes,' he said, 'I've thought about that as well. We're left with a blackmailer. And his victim. The victim is the murderer. The question is: has the blackmailer been paid yet?'

Moreno sat quietly for a while, swirling her glass.

'I don't understand how Vera Miller became involved in this,' she said. 'But if we establish that she's linked with Erich, well we have . . . I suppose we have somebody who has murdered twice in order to avoid paying. If the black-mailer isn't as daft as the proverbial brush, he will have raised the price a bit and . . . Well, I'd suppose he was living a bit dangerously.'

'I'd have thought so,' agreed Reinhart.

He emptied his glass and lit his pipe for the tenth time in the last hour.

'That's what's so bloody annoying,' he said. 'That we don't know what's behind it all. The motive for the black-mail. We have a series of events, but we don't have the first link in the chain . . .'

'Nor the last,' said Moreno. 'We presumably haven't seen the last round between the blackmailer and his victim yet, don't forget that.'

Reinhart looked at her with his head resting heavily on his hands.

'I'm tired,' he said. 'And a bit drunk. That's the only reason why I haven't said that I'm quite impressed. By your reasoning, that is. A bit, anyway.'

'In vino veritas,' said Moreno. 'But we could be quite wrong as well. It doesn't have to be blackmail, and there doesn't have to be a doctor involved . . . And perhaps there's no connection at all between Vera Miller and Erich Van Veeteren.'

'Oh, don't start that,' groaned Reinhart. 'I thought we were just getting somewhere.'

Moreno smiled.

'It's midnight,' she said.

Reinhart sat up on his chair.

'Ring for a taxi,' he said. 'I'll wake Rooth up.'

When he got home both Winnifred and Joanna were sound asleep in the double bed. He stood in the doorway for a while, looking at them and wondering what he had done to deserve them.

And what the payment would be . . .

He thought about *The Chief Inspector*'s son. About Seika. About Vera Miller. About what would happen to Joanna in fifteen to twenty years' time when young men began to take an interest in her . . . All kinds of men.

He noticed that the hairs on his lower arms were standing on end when he tried to imagine that, and he carefully closed the door. Took a dark beer out of the refrigerator instead, and flopped down on the sofa to think things over.

To think about what, if anything, there was he could be absolutely sure about regarding the Van Veeteren and Miller cases.

And what he could be fairly sure about.

And what he thought.

Before he had got very far, he fell asleep. Joanna found

him on the sofa at six o'clock the following morning.

30

Winnifred had only one seminar on Monday morning, and would be home by noon. After a short discussion with himself, Reinhart phoned the childminder and gave her the morning off. Then devoted himself exclusively to Joanna. Brushed her teeth and hair, drew pictures and flicked through books, and had a nap between nine and ten. Ate yoghurt with bananas, danced and flicked through more books between ten and eleven. Strapped her into the child seat in the car at half past eleven and twenty minutes later collected mother and wife from the university.

'Let's go for a drive,' he said. 'I think we need it.'

'Terrific,' said Winnifred.

It was not difficult to decide to leave the police station to its own devices after the work put in over the last few days. On that December Monday the weather comprised equal doses of wind and a distinctly dodgy absence of rain. Nevertheless, they chose the coast. The sea. Walked along the promenade at Kaarhuis and back – Reinhart with a singing and shouting Joanna on his shoulders – and enjoyed some fish soup at Guiverts restaurant, the only one in town that was open. The tourist season seemed to be further away than Jupiter.

'Ten days to Christmas,' said Winnifred. 'Will you really have a whole week off, as you tried to trick me into believing?'

'That depends,' said Reinhart. 'If we solve the case we're busy with, I think I can promise you two.'

'Professor Gentz-Hillier is keen to rent us his cottage up at Limbuijs. Shall I accept? . . . Ten to twelve days over Christmas and New Year? It would be nice to live the simple life out in the wilds – or what does the chief inspector think about that?'

'The simple life out in the wilds?' said Reinhart. 'Do you mean a log fire, mulled wine and half a metre of books to read?'

'Exactly,' said Winnifred. 'No telephone and a kilometre to the nearest native. If I've understood it correctly, that is. Shall I clinch the deal?'

'Do that,' said Reinhart. 'I shall sit down tonight and solve these cases. It's about time.'

When he entered his office in the police station it was half past five. The pile of cassettes on his desk had grown a little, since during the day Jung, Rooth and Bollmert had been in contact with ten more doctors. There were also a few scribbled notes to the effect that nothing especially exciting had emerged from any of those interviews. Krause had submitted a report after having spoken to the Pathology Laboratory – the contents of Vera Miller's stomach had been analysed and it had been established that she had consumed lobster and salmon and caviar during the hours before she died.

Plus a considerable quantity of white wine.

So he fed her pretty well before killing her at least, Reinhart thought as he lit his pipe. Every cloud . . . Lets hope she was a bit numb after drinking all that wine as well – but they'd known about that earlier.

He sat back in his chair and tried to recall the previous day's conversation with Moreno. Cleared an area of his desk and took a sheet of paper and a pencil and began recapitulating with iron-hard, systematic logic.

At least, that was what he intended doing, and he was still hard at work half an hour later when the telephone rang.

It was Moreno.

'I think I've found him,' she said. 'Are you still in your office? If so, I'll be there shortly.'

'Shortly?' said Reinhart. 'You have three minutes, not a second longer.'

He screwed up his iron-hard thoughts and threw them into the waste-paper basket.

Van Veeteren didn't think the temperature in the flat had become much better than the previous time he'd been there, but Marlene insisted that there had been a significant improvement. She served tea, and they shared fraternally the apple strudel he had bought in the bakery on the square. The conversation was somewhat inhibited, and he soon realized that there was not going to be a straightforward lead-in to what he really wanted to talk to her about.

'How are things for you?' he asked in the end. 'Financially and so on, I mean?'

That was heavy-handed, and she buttoned up immediately. Went out into the kitchen without answering, but came back half a minute later.

'Why do you ask?'

He thrust out his arms and tried to adopt a mild, disarming expression. That was not something that came naturally to him, and he felt like a shoplifter who had been caught red-handed with six packets of cigarettes in his pockets. Or condoms.

'Because I'd like to help you, of course,' he admitted. 'Let's not beat about the bush – I'm bloody useless when it comes to beating about the bush.'

That was much more disarming than any facial expression, it seemed, for she smiled at him after a moment's hesitation.

'I can manage,' she said. 'So far, at least . . . And I have no desire to become a burden on anybody. But I like the fact that you exist. Not with regard to money, but because of Erich, and this.'

She stroked her stomach, and for the first time Van Veeteren thought he could discern a slight bump there. A trace of a protuberance that was just a little bit more than a normally rounded female stomach, and he felt a faint wave of dizziness surge through him.

'Good,' he said. 'I'm glad you exist as well. Do you think we know where we stand now?'

'I think so,' said Marlene.

Just before leaving, he remembered another thing.

'That note,' he said. 'That scrap of paper with the name. Did you phone the police about it?'

She raised her hand to her forehead.

'I forgot all about it,' she said. 'I didn't give it another thought . . . But I've still got it, if you'd like to look at it.'

She went back into the kitchen, and returned with a small piece of lined paper, evidently torn out of a notebook.

'I'll take care of it,' said Van Veeteren, putting it in his inside pocket. 'Don't worry about it. I'll phone Reinhart tomorrow morning.'

When he got back home he checked the telephone directory. There was half a column of people with the surname Keller in the Maardam section. Twenty-six, to be precise. He wondered whether he ought to ring Reinhart straight away, but as it was a quarter past nine by now, he let it be.

No doubt they are up to the eyes in it, he thought. I'd better not keep poking my nose in all the time.

It was three quarters of an hour before Moreno put in an appearance. Meanwhile Reinhart had managed to drink three cups of coffee, smoke the same number of pipefuls, and started to feel queasy.

'I'm sorry,' she said. 'I really had to gobble a sandwich and take a shower first.'

'You look like a young Venus,' said Reinhart. 'Well, what the hell do you have to say for yourself?'

Moreno hung up her jacket, opened the window and sat down opposite Reinhart.

'A doctor,' she said. 'It could well be him . . . Although I'm afraid I had second thoughts after I'd rung. I mean, I could be quite wrong.'

'Don't be silly,' said Reinhart. 'Who is he, and how do you know it's him?'

'His name's Clausen. Pieter Clausen. But I haven't spoken to him . . . He seems to have disappeared.'

'Disappeared?' said Reinhart.

'Well, disappeared might be an exaggeration,' said Moreno. 'But he can't be contacted, and he wasn't at the hospital today, despite the fact that he ought to have been.'

'Rumford?'

'New Rumford, yes. He was off sick all last week, but he should have been back on duty today. This morning. But he didn't turn up.'

'How do you know all this? Who have you spoken to?'

'Doctor Leissne. The doctor-in-charge of general medicine. He's Clausen's boss. Obviously, I didn't tell him all my suspicions, or what we were really looking for and so on; but I thought . . . Well, I thought I was on to something. Leissne was annoyed, obviously – his secretary had been trying to phone Clausen all morning but nobody had answered. And nobody on his ward knows where he is. There might be something fishy about his week on sick leave as well, but I'm only guessing, of course.'

'Family?' said Reinhart. 'Is he married?'

Moreno shook her head.

'No, he lives alone. Out at Boorkhejm. Divorced several years ago. But he's been working at Rumford for ten years, and he hasn't collected any black marks.'

'Not until now,' said Reinhart.

'Not until now,' repeated Moreno thoughtfully. 'But we shouldn't get carried away. I only had time to speak to Leissne and one of the ward nurses – it didn't crop up until half past four.'

'How did it crop up?'

'Dr Leissne's secretary came and said she wanted to talk to me. I'd just finished one of these.'

She foraged in her handbag and produced three cassettes, which she put on the table.

'I see,' said Reinhart. 'Have you got any more information about him?'

Moreno handed over a sheet of paper, and Reinhart studied it for a while.

Personal details. Posts held and qualifications. A black-and-white photograph of a man about thirty-five years old. Short, dark hair. Thin lips, long thin face. A little birthmark on one cheek.

'Could be anybody,' he said. 'Is it an old photo?'

'Five or six years, I reckon,' said Moreno. 'He's just turned forty now.'

'Does he have any children? From that old marriage, for instance?'

'Not as far as Leissne knew.'

'Women? Fiancée?'

'Not clear.'

'And no black marks?'

'None that has been recorded, at least.'

'What about his ex-wife?'

Moreno went to close the window.

'Nobody knows. They didn't even know what she was called. But I've got the name of a colleague who Leissne thought might be able to give us a bit more information. Apparently he knocked around a bit with Clausen outside working hours.'

'And what does he have to say?'

'Nothing. I've only spoken to his answering machine.'

'Oh, bugger,' said Reinhart.

Moreno looked at the clock.

'Half past seven,' she said. 'Maybe we could drive out and take a look? To Boorkhejm, I mean. We've got his address.'

Reinhart knocked out his pipe and stood up.

'What are you waiting for?' he asked.

On the way out to Boorkhejm they were subjected to a hailstorm that made the suburban gloom even gloomier than usual. It took them a while to find Malgerstraat, and when Reinhart pulled up outside number seventeen, he felt even more sorry for the human race than he usually did. It must be difficult to find any sort of meaning of life when you live out here, he thought. In these grey boxes in this dreary climate. The street that God forgot. Grey, wet and narrow.

But it was middle-class even so. Standing outside each of the row of houses was a caravan of more or less identical small Japanese cars, and a blue television screen could be seen in every third window.

But number seventeen was shrouded in darkness. Both downstairs and upstairs. The house was one of a terrace of two-storey boxes in grey or possibly brown brick, with nine square metres of garden and an asphalted drive leading to the garage. A soaking wet flowerbed overgrown with weeds and a letter box made of concrete with black iron fittings.

Reinhart switched off the engine, and they remained sitting in the car for a while, looking at the house. Then he got out and lifted the lid of the letter box. It was fitted with a lock, but through the slit he could see several newspapers and rather a lot of mail. In fact, it was crammed full – he doubted if there would be room for another newspaper. He returned to the car.

'Would you like to go and ring the bell?' he said to Moreno.

'Not really,' she said. 'There doesn't seem much point.'

But she got out of the car even so and walked up to the door. Pressed the bell push and waited for half a minute. Tried again. Nothing happened. She went back to Reinhart, who was standing beside the car, smoking with the pipe upside down in view of the rain.

'Now what?' she said.

'We raid the house tomorrow morning,' said Reinhart. 'He has twelve hours in which to turn up.'

They crept back into the car and started trying to find their way out of the suburb.

31

'Who did you say?' said Constable Klempje, dropping his newspaper on the floor. 'Oh dear . . . I mean, good morning, Chief Inspector!'

He stood up and bowed solemnly.

'No, he's not in, but I saw Krause in the corridor two seconds ago – shall I shout for him?'

He stuck his head out of the door and was lucky enough to attract Krause's attention.

'*The Chief Inspector*,' he whispered when Krause came closer. 'On the phone . . . *The Chief Inspector!*'

Krause stepped inside and took over the receiver.

'Krause here. Good morning, *Chief Inspector* . . . What can I do for you?'

He listened and made notes for about a minute. Then he wished him a pleasant day and hung up.

'What did he want?' asked Klempje, scratching his ear with his index finger.

'Nothing you need bother about,' said Krause, and left.

Stuck-up ass, Klempje thought. I was only trying to help . . .

It took a few hours to prepare the necessary documentation for raiding the house, but at ten o'clock they were in place outside Malgerstraat 17. Reinhart, Moreno, Jung, and a car with four technicians and equipment worth a quarter of a million. If it's going to be done, we'd better do it properly, Reinhart thought. He had rung Clausen's number twice an hour since half past six; Rooth, deBries and Bollmert had been sent to the New Rumford Hospital to gather more facts, and it had stopped raining ten minutes ago. Everything was ready for the big breakthrough.

'It looks a bit better in daylight in any case,' said Reinhart. 'Let's go.'

The front door lock was opened by one of the technicians in thirty seconds flat, and Reinhart entered first. He took a look around. Hall, kitchen and large living room on the ground floor. Everything looked very ordinary: not all that clean, some unwashed cups, glasses and cutlery in the kitchen sink. The living room had a sofa group, teak bookcases, a hi-fi system and a substantial cupboard in what he thought was red oak. A television set without a video recorder, but with a thick layer of dust. On the smoke-coloured glass table was a fruit bowl with three apples and a few sorry-looking grapes. A copy of the *Neuwe Blatt* from last Thursday was lying open on the floor beside one of the armchairs.

Thursday? he thought. Four days already. Time to fly to the moon several times over.

He walked up the stairs. Jung and Moreno followed at his heels while the technicians carried in their equipment then stood in the hall, waiting for instructions.

Three rooms on the upper floor, one of which served as a study with a desk, a computer and a few rickety bookcases; another was a box room. The third was the bedroom: he walked in and looked around. Large double bed with pine head- and footboards. The bedding was primitively masculine . . . A bedcover with a large multi-coloured check pattern was draped over haphazard groups of pillows and blankets. A Van Gogh reproduction hung on one wall, suggesting a lack of interest in art. Reinhart had the impression that he had even seen the motif on tins of coffee. Various items of clothing lay about, both in and around a brown plastic laundry basket. Shirts and trousers were hanging on both white-painted chairs. Two books, a telephone and a clock radio were standing on one of the bedside tables . . . A dry cactus on the window ledge between half-drawn curtains . . . A series of dark stains on the beige fitted carpet.

He beckoned Jung and pointed at the carpet.

'There,' he said. 'Tell them to start up here.'

While the technicians were carrying their equipment upstairs, Reinhart and Moreno went through the kitchen and into the garage. There was a red Audi, probably a couple of years old, and about as ordinary as everything else in the house. He tried the door. It wasn't locked. He bent down and looked inside, first the front seat and then the back. Stood up again and nodded to Moreno.

'When they've finished upstairs I think they should take a look at this.'

He had left the back door open, and Moreno looked inside.

'It could be anything,' she said. 'It doesn't have to be blood . . . Neither here nor in the bedroom.'

'Don't talk crap,' said Reinhart. 'Of course it's blood. I can smell it. The devil be praised, we've got him!'

'Really?' said Moreno. 'Aren't you overlooking something?'

'What?'

'He doesn't seem to be at home. Hasn't been since last Thursday, as far as I can judge.'

'Thank you for reminding me,' said Reinhart. 'Come on, let's call on the neighbours.'

*

Reinhart and Moreno stayed out at Boorkhejm until half past twelve, which was when Intendent Puijdens, the man in charge of the technicians, finally announced – with a hundred per cent certainty – that the stains were in fact blood, both in the bedroom and in the car, the red Audi, which was indeed registered in the name of Pieter Clausen. Establishing whether the blood was from a human being, and possibly from the same human being, would take another hour or so of analysis, Puijdens reckoned.

Ascertaining if it was Vera Miller's blood, from both the afternoon and the evening.

'Come on,' said Reinhart to Moreno. 'There's nothing more we can do here. Jung can continue with the neighbours – let's hope he finds somebody who isn't both blind and deaf. I want to hear how things are going at the hospital, if there's anybody who can suggest where the bastard has run away to. If the blood turns out to be what I assume it is, he's already linked to the crime, for God's sake!'

'Don't you mean *crimes*?' wondered Moreno, getting into the car.

'Piffling details,' snorted Reinhart. 'Where is he? Where has he been since Thursday? Those are the questions to which you should be devoting your little grey cells instead.'

'All right,' said Moreno, and remained sunk in thought all the way back to the police station.

'A breech presentation,' said Dr Brandt. 'First child. It took some time – sorry to keep you waiting.'

'You can't rush a breech presentation,' said Rooth. 'I know all about that – it's how I was born.'

'Really?' said Brandt. 'Well, I suppose you were a bit smaller in those days. What did you want to talk to me about?'

'Maybe we could go down to the cafeteria?' suggested Rooth. 'I can treat you to a cup of coffee.'

Dr Brandt seemed to be about forty, but was small and slim, and moved with a youthful eagerness that reminded Rooth of a puppy. It was Jung who had spoken to him previously: Rooth hadn't got round to listening to the recording of the conversation, but he knew Brandt had said something about Dr Clausen. Assuming Jung hadn't simply nodded off, that is.

But now it was Clausen everything was centred on, only Clausen, and Rooth didn't beat about the bush once they had sat down at the rickety rattan table.

'Your good friend,' he said. 'Dr Clausen. He's the person we're interested in.'

'Clausen?' said Brandt, adjusting his glasses. 'Why?'

'How well do you know him?'

'Well . . .' Brandt opened his arms out wide. 'We socialize a bit. I've known him since I was a lad – we went to secondary school together.'

'Excellent,' said Rooth. 'Tell me about him.'

Dr Brandt looked at him with a sceptical frown on his face.

'I've been questioned by the police once.'

'But not about Clausen, I think?'

'Hmm. No, but I find it hard to understand why you want information about him. Why don't you speak to him instead?'

'Don't worry about that,' said Rooth. 'It will be easier if I ask the questions and you answer them. Believe me. So, let's hear it!'

Brandt sat demonstratively silent for a while, stirring his coffee. Come on, you little obstetric obstacle, Rooth thought, and took a bite of his ham sandwich while waiting.

'I don't know him all that well,' said Brandt eventually. 'A group of us meet now and again – we've all kept in touch since we left school. We call ourselves Verhouten's Angels.'

'Verhouten's what . . . ?'

'Angels. A maths teacher we used to have. Charles

Verhouten. A bit of a rum customer, but we liked him. And he was a damned good teacher.'

'Really?' said Rooth, and began to wonder if the doctor maybe had a screw loose. I wouldn't want to be delivered by him, in any case, he thought.

'But we usually just call ourselves The Brothers. There are six of us. We go out for a meal now and then, then sit and natter. We do have a few formalities as well.'

'Formalities?'

'Nothing serious. It's just a bit of fun.'

'I see,' said Rooth. 'Any women?'

'No, it's a men-only club,' said Brandt. 'That gives us a bit more freedom, if you see what I mean.'

He gave Rooth a knowing look, peering over his glasses. Rooth returned his gaze, his face expressionless.

'I understand. But enough of the other angel brothers, let's concentrate on Clausen. When did you see him last, for instance?'

Brandt looked a little put out, but scratched his head and seemed to be thinking.

'It was quite some time ago,' he said. 'We had a meeting last Friday – at the Canaille in Weivers Plejn – but Clausen was ill and couldn't come. I don't think I've seen him for about a month, come to think about it. No, not since the last meeting . . .'

'Do you never meet here at the hospital?'

'Very seldom,' said Brandt. 'We work quite a long way away from each other. Clausen is based in C Block, and I . . . Well, I work here in obstetrics, as you know.'

Rooth thought for a moment.

'What about his relationships with women?' he asked. 'Are you married, incidentally?'

Dr Brandt shook his head energetically.

'I'm single,' he said. 'Clausen was married for a few years, but it didn't last. They divorced. That was about four or five years ago, if I remember rightly.'

'Do you know if he's had any affairs with women recently? If he's met somebody new, for instance?'

Brandt suddenly seemed to cotton on to what it was all about. He took off his glasses. Folded them ostentatiously and put them in his breast pocket. Leaned forward over the table and tried to focus his short-sighted eyes on Rooth.

You should have kept your glasses on, little man, Rooth thought, and drank the remains of his coffee. That would have made it easier.

'Inspector . . . What did you say your name was?'

'Poirot,' said Rooth. 'No, I'm only joking. My name's Rooth.'

'My dear Inspector Rooth,' said Brandt impassively. 'I don't like having to sit here and listen to your insinuations about a colleague and a good friend. I really don't. I can assure you that Dr Clausen has nothing at all to do with this business.'

'With what business?' said Rooth.

'With . . . with that nurse. The one who's been murdered. Don't think you can fool me, I know perfectly well what you're after. You're completely wrong. She didn't even work at this hospital, and Clausen really isn't the type to go running around after women.'

Rooth sighed and changed track.

'Do you know if he has any close relations?' he asked.

Brandt leaned back on his chair and seemed to be debating with himself whether or not to answer. His nose was trembling, as if he were trying to smell his way to a decision.

'He has a sister,' he said. 'A few years older, I think. She lives abroad somewhere.'

'No children?'

'No.'

'And that woman he was married to – what's her name?'

Brandt shrugged.

'I can't remember. Marianne, perhaps. Something like that.'

'Surname?'

'I've no idea. Clausen, of course, assuming she took

his name . . . They don't always do that nowadays. But I expect she'll have retaken her maiden name in any case. I've never met her.'

Rooth thought while struggling with a little scrap of skin that had got stuck between two molars in his lower jaw.

'Why isn't he at work today?'

'Who?' said Brandt.

'Clausen, of course.'

'Isn't he?' said Brandt. 'How the hell am I supposed to know? I suppose it's his day off. Or that he's still on sick leave. He has flu, if I understand it rightly – it's quite wrong to think that just because you're a doctor you are immune to such things . . .'

'He's disappeared,' said Rooth. 'Have you no better explanation to offer?'

'Disappeared?' said Brandt. 'Rubbish. I don't believe that for a moment. Surely he can't just disappear?'

Rooth glared at him and took the last piece of his sandwich, despite the fact that the scrap of skin was still stuck between his teeth.

'The other angels – the ones in your little club – do any of them know Clausen a bit better than you do?'

Dr Brandt fished out his spectacles and put them on again.

'Smaage, perhaps.'

'Smaage? Could you kindly give me his address and telephone number?'

Brandt took out a little notebook, and shortly afterwards Rooth had details of all the members of the club. He took a lump of sugar from the bowl on the table, and wondered how best to thank him for his help.

'Okay, that's it, all finished,' he said. 'I think it's time for you to go and give birth again . . . Don't let me keep you any longer.'

Verhouten's Angels? he thought. Christ almighty.

'Thank you,' said Reinhart. 'Thank you for your help, herr Haas.'

He hung up and looked at Moreno with something that might possibly be interpreted as a grim smile.

'Let's hear it, then,' said Moreno. 'I think I can detect a degree of satisfaction in the bloodhound's facial expression.'

'And not without cause,' said Reinhart. 'Guess who was at the Spaarkasse last Thursday and picked up two hundred thousand!'

'Clausen?'

'Nail on the head, to quote one of his victims. He called in to collect it at the branch in Keymer Plejn shortly after lunch. In cash! Did you hear that? Two hundred and twenty thousand in fact . . . Every damned piece of the puzzle is falling into place.'

Moreno pondered.

'Thursday?' she said. 'It's Tuesday today.'

'I'm aware of that,' said Reinhart. 'God only knows what's happened, and God only knows where he's got to. But the Wanted notices have been sent out, so we'll have him here sooner or later.'

Moreno bit her lip and looked doubtful.

'I'm not so sure about that,' she said. 'What was he going to use the money for?'

Reinhart paused for a couple of seconds, staring at his pipe.

'He told them at the bank that it was something to do with buying a boat. A likely story! Huh, he was going to pay the blackmailer, of course.'

'And you reckon he did so?' asked Moreno. 'In that case, why has he disappeared?'

Reinhart stared gloomily at the piles of cassettes still lying on his desk.

'Enlighten me!' he said.

Moreno sat in silence for a while, sucking a pencil.

'If he made up his mind to pay,' she said in the end, 'and actually did so . . . Well, there would be no reason for him to run away and hide, surely? Something more must have happened, I don't know what, but it seems illogical otherwise. In any case, it can't have simply been that he just coughed up. For God's sake, two hundred thousand isn't exactly pin money.'

'Two hundred and twenty,' muttered Reinhart. 'No, you're right, of course – but when we catch him we'll no doubt discover the explanation.'

There was a knock on the door and Rooth came in, carrying a chocolate cake.'Peace be with you,' he said. 'Do you want to hear the one about the obstetrician and the angels?'

'Why not?' sighed Reinhart.

It took Rooth a quarter of an hour to report on his conversation with Dr Brandt. Reinhart made notes while listening, then ordered Rooth to find the other 'brothers' and collect more information about Pieter Clausen's all-round character. Plus what he had been doing and saying this last month.

'Try to get Jung and deBries involved as well,' said Reinhart. 'So that you've finished the job by this evening. This Smaage character first of all, of course.'

Rooth nodded and left the room. He bumped into Krause in the doorway.

'Have you got a moment?' Krause asked. 'I've spent the afternoon following something up.'

'Really?' said Reinhart. 'What kind of a something?'

Krause sat down beside Moreno and opened a notebook with a certain degree of ceremony.

'Van Veeteren,' he said. 'He phoned this morning and gave me a tip-off.'

'A tip-off?' said Reinhart, sceptically. '*The Chief Inspector* phoned and gave *you* a tip-off?'

'Yep,' said Krause, and couldn't resist a slightly smug smile. 'He was careful to stress that it maybe wasn't all that important, but I've done a bit of research in any case.'

'Can you come to the point, or would you like an ice cream first?' wondered Reinhart.

Krause cleared his throat.

'It was to do with a name,' he said. 'Erich Van Veeteren's fiancée – Marlene Frey – had found a name scribbled on a scrap of paper that she had forgotten to tell us about. Only a few days ago, it seems.'

'And what was the name?' asked Moreno neutrally, before Reinhart had a chance to interrupt again.

'Keller,' said Krause. 'Spelt like it sounds. It was only a surname on a small scrap of paper. Erich had scribbled it down in haste just a day or two before he died, apparently, and it wasn't a name in his address book. Anyway, there are only twenty-six people called Keller in the Maardam section of the telephone directory, and they are the ones I've checked up on . . . if for no other reason than that *The Chief Inspector* wanted me to. Hmm.'

'And?' said Reinhart.

'I think there's one that could be of interest to us.'

Reinhart leaned forward over his desk and gritted his teeth.

'Who?' he said. 'And why is he interesting?'

'His name's Aron Keller. He works in the orthopaedic department at the New Rumford . . . In the prosthesis workshop, if I've understood it rightly. And he lives out at Boorkhejm.'

Reinhart opened his mouth to say something, but Moreno got in first.

'Have you spoken to him?'

She could have sworn that Krause made a dramatic pause before answering.

'No. They don't know where he is. He hasn't turned up for work since Friday.'

'Christ almighty!' said Reinhart and knocked eighteen cassettes down onto the floor.

'His address is Malgerstraat 13,' said Krause.

He tore a page out of his notebook, handed it to Inspector Moreno and left the room.

32

The search of Aron Keller's flat in Malgerstraat 13 took place almost exactly twenty-four hours after the one at number seventeen.

As expected, it went quite quickly. The technical team had finished their work by as soon as half past twelve; after then there was no real reason why Reinhart and Moreno should stay on. But stay on they did for a few hours, in the hope (Reinhart insisted – and with no technical aids apart from our own five bloody senses, Inspector!) of finding clues that might possibly indicate what had happened to the loner of a tenant. And where he had disappeared to.

It was not an easy task. Everything suggested that Keller had not been in the flat since the previous Friday: he might even have gone off, or disappeared, as early as the Thursday night – he didn't subscribe to any daily newspaper, but a considerable amount of mail lay jumbled up in the metal cage on the inside of the door, and the potted plants were shrivelled and half-dead in both the bedroom and the kitchen. The two large hibiscus plants in the bay window in the living room seemed to have fared rather better, but they were fitted with a watering system that only needed filling once a week.

Or so Moreno maintained – she had a similar set-up in her two-roomed flat in Falckstraat.

Everything in the flat was more or less immaculately neat and tidy. There was no washing-up in the kitchen. No items of clothing lying around, either in the bedroom or anywhere else. No newspapers, no overflowing ashtrays, no odds and ends where they shouldn't be. The few books on the bookshelves, cassettes and CDs (three-quarters horse jazz, maintained Reinhart with distaste, the rest cheap versions of pop hits) were neatly lined up. Two pairs of well-polished shoes in the rack in the hall, a jacket and an overcoat on hangers. And the desk was as tidy as a display window for an office furniture firm. The same applied to cupboards, drawers and bureaux. The only thing Reinhart missed was small labels with the correct place and classification on every item – although if everything had been like this for the past twenty years, he realized after a little thought that such labels were not necessary.

What the flat told them about the man Aron Keller – apart from the fact that he had a fanatical feeling for order and neatness – was that he had an interest in sport. Especially football and athletics. There were a few books on football (yearbooks with red and green spines from as far back as 1973) in a prominent place in the bookcase, and several years of complete issues of the monthly magazine *Sport Front*, piled in a beer crate at the back of one of the wardrobes – the latest issue was lying on the kitchen table, and no doubt was the usual accompaniment to the Keller breakfast. In any case, that was the conclusion Reinhart drew, with an irritated snort.

Next to the telephone on the desk in the bedroom was an address book with a total of twenty-two people listed. Three of them were called Keller: none of them lived in Maardam (two in Linzhuisen, one in Haaldam) and Reinhart decided to postpone sorting out the precise family relationships until a bit later.

'The man must have a square head,' he said. 'Finding him shouldn't be a problem.'

Despite the obvious lack of leads, they stayed on until it turned three o'clock. Searched through every drawer and cupboard, examined every nook and cranny without really knowing what they were looking for. Reinhart also discovered a key marked 'Store-room', and spent an hour in the attic among old clothes, shoes and boots, tennis rackets, various items of furniture and some cardboard boxes full of comics from the sixties. Moreno found it a little difficult to understand why they were searching through the flat in this haphazard way, but she kept her counsel. She had no idea what the outcome might be, but knew that she would probably have made the same decision if it had been up to her . . .

'You don't know what you're looking for until you've found it,' Reinhart had explained, blowing smoke into her face. 'That applies to a lot of situations, Miss Police Inspector, not just the here and now!'

'The chief inspector is as bright as a poodle,' Moreno had answered. 'And I mean a bitch, of course.'

The reward came at a quarter to three. She had emptied the half-full waste-paper basket (which was under the desk, and contained only paper of course – nothing that could decay such as apple cores, teabags or banana skins) onto the living-room floor, and had started working her way half-heartedly through it when she found it. *It.*

A crumpled, ruled sheet of A4 paper, torn from a notepad. Presumably the one on the shelf to the right over the desk. She smoothed it out and read it.

Five weeks since you murdered the bo

That was all. Six words only. Six-and-a-half. Written in a neat, somewhat sexless style, blue ink. She stared at the brief, interrupted message and thought for a couple of minutes.

Bo? she thought. What does *bo* mean?

Could it possibly be anything else but *boy*?

She shouted for Reinhart, who had come down from the attic space and was cursing with his head in one of the bedroom wardrobes.

'Well?' said Reinhart. 'What have you found?'

'This,' she said, handing him the piece of paper.

He read the text and looked at her in confusion.

'Bo?' he said. 'What the hell is the bo? The boy?'

'Presumably,' said Moreno. 'You said something about not having the first link. I think we've got it here.'

Reinhart looked at the crumpled piece of paper and scratched his head.

'You're right,' he said. 'Absolutely bloody right. Come on, it's time for a bit of discussion.'

The run-through was brief and accompanied by neither wine nor sandwich layer cake. Such extravagances were no longer needed, now that the fog had started to lift, Reinhart explained.

The fog that had shrouded the cases of Erich Van Veeteren and Vera Miller. It was time now to see things clearly, and take action. No time-wasting speculations were necessary any longer. No theories nor hypotheses, they suddenly knew what it was all about and what they were looking for. It was time to . . . to tighten the noose round those involved.

Round Pieter Clausen and Aron Keller. The murderer and his blackmailer.

The only slight problem was that the noose would presumably be empty when they tightened it. Or so Rooth stated, as he unwrapped a Mozart chocolate ball.

'Yes, it's a real bugger of a case,' admitted Reinhart. 'There's a long way to go before we have them under lock and key, let's be quite clear about that; but we weren't all that far out in our guesses, were we? Keller had some sort of a hold on Clausen and demanded money for not exposing him. He sent young Van Veeteren to collect the money, and we all know what happened then . . . God knows how Vera Miller was involved, but we've found wisps of her hair and lots of other traces in Clausen's flat . . . Not least blood stains, in the bedroom and in the car. It's as clear as day. He killed her in the same way that he killed Erich Van Veeteren.'

'What about the link between Keller and Erich?' deBries wanted to know. 'There must be one.'

'We don't know yet,' said Reinhart. 'That's something we still need to find out. And it's not the only thing. Both Clausen and Keller have disappeared. Neither of them seems to have been seen since last Thursday . . . And it was also last Thursday that Clausen withdrew two hundred and twenty thousand from the bank. Something must have happened then, later that evening perhaps, and we've got to find out what. And we need to find them, of course.'

'Dead or Alive,' said Rooth.

'Dead or Alive,' agreed Reinhart after a moment's thought. 'They're pretty similar types, in fact, these gentlemen, when you look a bit closer at them. Middle-aged single men with not much of a social life. Keller is a real lone wolf, it seems. Bollmert and deBries can look into whether he has any friends and acquaintances at all. His colleagues didn't have much to say about him, at any rate . . . Isn't that right?'

'True,' said Rooth. 'There are only eight people working in the wooden leg workshop, but they all say that Keller's a bloody pig-headed mule.'

'Do they really say that?' asked Jung.

'They don't express themselves quite as colourfully as I do,' said Rooth, 'but that's the gist of it.'

Reinhart circulated a copy of the note Moreno had found in Keller's waste-paper basket.

'What do you say to this?' he asked. 'We found it in Keller's place.'

Nobody spoke for a few moments.

'Well, what do you reckon *bo* stands for?'

'The boy,' said deBries. 'There's no other possibility.'

'Of course there is,' Rooth protested. 'Loads of them . . . Bosun, boxer, bowmaker . . .'

'Bowmaker?' said Jung, 'What the hell's that?'

'Makes bows,' said Rooth. 'You use them for shooting arrows.'

'Very clever, Mr Sleuth,' said Reinhart. 'But I don't think I can recall a bowmaker being found murdered. Nor a bosun nor a boxer, come to that – not lately, at least. Nor a bodybuilder nor a bobble-hat vendor . . . Okay, there are several other possibilities. We can agree on that, but for the moment let's stick with *the boy*. There's no doubt that's the most likely. We can assume that Clausen killed a boy some time around the beginning of November, and that's what set the whole thing off. We don't know exactly when Keller wrote this note, but if we think in terms of an incident around the end of October-stroke-beginning of November – a week or so either way – let's see what we can come up with.'

'So it couldn't refer to Erich Van Veeteren?' wondered deBries.

Reinhart thought for a moment.

'Hardly,' he said. 'He was almost thirty. And the time doesn't fit in . . . "Several weeks since you murdered the bo" . . . No, that's out of the question.'

'All right,' said deBries.

'A murdered boy?' said Jung. 'Surely we must know if a

lad was killed around that time? It can hardly have escaped the attention of the police. Not if it was in this district, that is . . .'

'It doesn't need to have been in Maardam,' said Moreno. 'And there doesn't have to have been somebody suspected of a crime. It could have been something else. Something at the hospital he tried to brush under the carpet. Clausen, that is. And nearly got away with it.'

'Not the hospital again . . .' said Rooth. 'The very thought makes me feel ill.'

Nobody said anything for a while.

'He isn't a surgeon, is he, this Clausen?' said deBries. 'So he doesn't do operations?'

Reinhart checked the information he had on a sheet of paper.

'Internal medicine,' he said. 'But you can kill somebody in that line of business as well. If you're a bit careless, for instance. We must find out about deaths that took place on his ward during this period. Rooth and Jung can go back to the Rumford – it should be enough to speak to the doctor in charge. Or take a look at the journals, perhaps?'

'A boy who died unexpectedly?' said Jung.

'A young male patient who died during the night,' said Rooth. 'Despite enormous efforts to save him. They have a fantastic *esprit de corps*, don't forget that . . . And I think it would be best if you do the talking with Leissne. I seem to have got into his bad books.'

'You don't say,' said Jung. 'That's astonishing.'

'And what are you and I going to do?' asked Moreno when their colleagues had trooped off.

Reinhart placed his hands on his desk and straightened his back.

'I have a date with a certain Oscar Smaage,' he said. 'Convener of Verhouten's Angels. You stay here and see if we have any unsolved deaths. Missing persons as well . . . It's not certain that it has anything to do with the hospital, even if there's plenty to suggest it might have.'

'Okay,' said Moreno. 'I hope Smaage has something to contribute, though I can't see what. I think everything depends on one thing, in fact.'

'Thursday?' said Reinhart.

'Yes. What the hell happened last Thursday evening? It seems obvious that's when he was supposed to hand over the money. Or what do you think?'

'Definitely,' said Reinhart. 'It would be remarkable if nobody turns up who's seen or heard about them – or one of them at least – after the handover. We just need to bide our time. Have some patience – didn't somebody recommend that some time ago?'

'I think you're wrong,' said Moreno.

*

It took her no more than an hour to find what she was looking for. In any case, she felt instinctively that it was right, when the name came up on her computer screen. Her heart missed a beat, and the hairs on her forearms stood on end – those were usually sure signs.

Tell-tale signs of female intuition. Hers at least.

Wim Felders, she read. Born 17.10.1982. Died 5.11.1998. Or possibly 6.11. Found by a passing cyclist on road 211 between Maardam and the suburb of Boorkhejm at six o'clock in the morning. The investigation carried out by the traffic police (headed by Chief Inspector Lintonen) showed that he had probably been struck by a vehicle and died after hitting his head against a concrete culvert at the side of the road. A Wanted notice had been publicized in all the media, but no perpetrator had come forward. No witnesses of the accident. No suspects. No tip-offs. The guilty driver had disappeared and refused to make himself known.

She remembered the incident. Recalled reading about it, and seeing reports in news bulletins on the television. The sixteen-year-old-boy had been on his way home to Boorkhejm. He had been visiting his girlfriend somewhere in the town centre, and was assumed to have missed the last bus.

He had evidently been walking along the side of the road in bad weather, both fog and rain, and been hit by a driver who had fled the scene.

It could have been anybody at all.

It could have been Clausen.

Keller could have passed by shortly afterwards and seen it all. Or been sitting next to Clausen in the passenger seat, if they knew each other . . . Although so far there was nothing to suggest that they did.

A road accident?

That was certainly a possibility. When she began thinking about how probable it seemed, she noticed that she found it difficult to feel certain. Perhaps it was no more than a coincidence, a fleeting fantasy: but in any case, the thread needed to be followed up until it broke.

Intuitively, she knew that this was exactly what had happened. She had found the first link. No doubt about it.

She saw that it was now half past five, and wondered what to do next. Decided to go home and phone Reinhart later that evening. If it could be established that Clausen had been driving home from the town centre on that day, at that time – on evidence supplied by Wim Felders' girlfriend they knew that the accident had happened shortly before midnight – well, there could be no more doubts.

How it would be possible to establish or be certain that Clausen had been driving the car was another thing altogether: but as they had already linked him with two other murders, perhaps that didn't matter.

On the other hand, if he had indeed been in central

Maardam that evening, surely he must have met some-body? Somebody who could provide evidence.

Let's hope it wasn't Vera Miller, she thought. It would be better if it were those angels, whatever they were called. Verhouten's . . . ?

But more important than all that was finding Clausen. Naturally.

And Keller.

Having got that far, Ewa Moreno switched off the computer and went home. However she looked at it, she reckoned she had done a good day's work.

33

She had just completed the phone call to Reinhart when there was a ring on her door.

Half past eight, she thought. What on earth . . . ?

It was Mikael Bau, her neighbour in the flat directly below hers.

'Do you fancy a bite to eat?' he asked, looking miserable.

Bau was in his thirties and had moved into Falckstraat only a few months ago. She didn't know him. He had introduced himself when she bumped into him on the stairs the first time, of course, but since then they had merely said hello when they happened to pass each other. Three or four times in all. He looked rather handsome, she had decided from the start. Tall, blond and blue-eyed. And with a smile that seemed to have difficulty in suppressing itself.

But just now he was serious.

'I've made a beef stew,' he explained. 'A sort of boeuf

bourguignon – it's all ready, so if you've nothing against it . . . ?'

'It's a bit out of the blue,' said Moreno.

'I can understand that,' said Bau. 'Er . . . I didn't plan to invite you, but my fiancée dumped me just before it was ready to eat. Please don't think that . . .'

He couldn't find a satisfactory way of finishing the sentence. Moreno didn't know what to say either.

'Okay, thank you very much,' she said in fact. 'I don't think I've eaten today, as far as I can recall. Can you give me a quarter of an hour to have a shower first? It's not too difficult to keep stews warm.'

He smiled now.

'Good,' he said. 'I'll expect you in a quarter of an hour.'

He went back downstairs, and Moreno closed the door.

Is this how things happen? she wondered, but dismissed the thought immediately.

To add to his good looks and polite behaviour, Mikael Bau proved to be an excellent cook. Moreno was full of admiration for the stew, which she ate to her heart's content; and the subsequent lemon sorbet had precisely the subtle touch of tartness that the recipe usually promises, but the dish rarely delivers.

A man who can cook? she thought. I've never met one

of those before. He must have a skeleton in his cupboard. She would have dearly liked to ask him why his girlfriend had dumped him; but there was no real opportunity to get as intimate as that, and he didn't raise the subject himself.

Instead they talked about the weather, the block of flats and the neighbours. And their respective jobs. Bau was a welfare officer, so there were a few points of contact.

'God only knows why I chose to get involved with the seamy side,' he said. 'I won't go so far as to say that I don't enjoy it, but I don't think I'd make the same choice today. Why did you become a police officer?'

Moreno had asked herself that question so many times before that she no longer knew if there was an answer. Or ever had been. Things just turned out the way they did, that was all there was to it; she suspected the same applied to lots of people. Life just turned out the way it did.

'I think quite a lot comes down to pure chance,' she said. 'Or at least, to decisions made without an awful lot of thought. We have less control than we think we have . . . That we pretend we do have is another matter.'

Bau nodded and looked thoughtful.

'But it could be that we land up where we belong even so,' he said. 'I read the other day about the billiard ball theory – are you familiar with it? You roll along over a level, green surface among lots of other balls. The speeds and directions are fixed, but it's not possible to work out in advance what's going to happen . . . when we collide and change direction. Everything is predestined, but we can't predict it – there are simply too many contributory factors. Well, something like that.'

She came to think about what *The Chief Inspector* used to say, and couldn't help smiling.

'There are certain patterns,' she said. 'They say that there are certain patterns that we never discover – not until afterwards. Then they are perfectly obvious. It's reminiscent of a police investigation, in fact. Everything becomes clearer if you can approach it backwards.'

Bau nodded again.

'But you can't approach it backwards,' he said. 'Not in real life. That's the problem. A drop more wine?'

'Just half a glass,' said Moreno.

When she looked at the clock for the first time it was a quarter to twelve.

'Good gracious,' she said. 'Don't you have to go to work tomorrow?'

'Of course,' said Bau. 'We who work on the seamy side never rest.'

'Many thanks for a lovely evening,' said Moreno, standing up. 'I promise to invite you back in return, but I'll have to practise a few recipes first.'

Bau accompanied her out into the hall and gave her a carefully restrained hug by way of goodnight. A quarter of an hour later she was lying in bed, thinking about how pleasant it was to get on well with your neighbours.

Then she thought about Erich Van Veeteren. He must have been about the same age as herself and Mikael Bau. Possibly slightly younger – she hadn't thought about it until now.

And the others?

Vera Miller was thirty-one, and Wim Felders only lived to celebrate his sixteenth birthday.

When you raised yourself above the restricted horizons of good-neighbourliness, quite different considerations applied.

Reinhart was woken up by Joanna pulling at his lower lip. She sat on his stomach with a blissful smile on her face.

'Daddy's asleep,' she said. 'Daddy's awake.'

He lifted her up high. She screamed in delight, and a stream of saliva cascaded into his face.

Good Lord, he thought. This is marvellous! It's six in the morning, and life is pouring down on me already!

He wondered why it was so light in the room, then he recalled that his daughter had just learned how to flick switches on and off, and liked to practise this new skill. He tucked her in beside Winnifred and got up. Established that every single light in the house was switched on, and started switching them all off again. Joanna soon came toddling after him, babbling on about something to do with frogs. Or possibly dogs – she had a dummy in her mouth and it was difficult to make out what she was saying. He took her into the kitchen with him, and started making breakfast.

Halfway through he remembered what he had been dreaming about. Or rather, what had popped up in his mind at some point between sleeping and waking.

They had forgotten to send out a Wanted notice for Keller.

Oh, shit, he thought. Lifted Joanna up into her high chair. Put a plate of mashed banana and yoghurt in front of her and went to his study in order to phone the police station.

It took a while to get the message over, but Klempje, who was on call, eventually seemed to understand. The Wanted notice would be sent out immediately, he gave his word of honour.

I don't know how many words you know, or how many of them are honourable, Reinhart thought: but he thanked him even so, and hung up.

Careless, he thought. How the hell could anybody have forgotten a thing like that?

Two hours later he was ready to go to work. Winnifred had just got up, and he thought she looked like a thoroughly rested goddess. He toyed with the idea of staying at home for a while and making love to her instead. There was nothing to prevent it, in principle. It would soon be time for Joanna's nap, and the babysitter wasn't due until after lunch.

Then he remembered the situation. He unfastened his wife's dressing gown and embraced her. She gave him a bite on the neck. He bit her back. That would have to suffice. He fetched his overcoat.

'Are you going to have time off like you thought you would?' she asked as he stood in the doorway.

'*Nie ma problemu*,' said Reinhart. 'That's Polish and means that we'll have sorted out this business within the next three days. Three days at most.'

Chief Inspector Reinhart was deceiving her somewhat on that score, but it was not the first time. The main thing was that Winnifred didn't do that to him.

After Moreno had reported in more detail about the Wim Felders accident, Reinhart phoned Oscar Smaage, whom he had spoken to the previous afternoon. Smaage was news editor on the *Telegraaf*, and hence not all that difficult to get in touch with.

'There was something I forgot yesterday,' Reinhart explained. 'Regarding Clausen, that is. I wonder if you had one of those meetings of yours on . . .'

He gestured to Moreno, who handed over a sheet of paper with the relevant date.

'On the fifth of November? The Angels, I mean. It was a Thursday. Can you fill me in on that?'

'Just a moment,' said Smaage, and Reinhart could hear him leafing through some book or other. One chance in ten, he reckoned as he waited. At most. But nevertheless he knew that he wouldn't have hesitated to bet on it.

'You're right,' said Smaage. 'Thursday, the fifth of November. We were at Ten Bosch. All the brothers were present. It was an enjoyable evening. Why do you ask?'

'I realize that it's asking a lot,' said Reinhart, 'but we'd like to know when Clausen went home. Roughly, at least.'

Smaage burst out laughing.

'What the hell? . . .' he said. 'No, I haven't a clue. It would have been half past eleven-stroke-twelve o'clock – we don't usually hang around longer than that. I don't suppose there's any point in my asking you why you—'

'Absolutely right,' said Reinhart, cutting him short. 'Many thanks for the information.'

He hung up and took out his pipe.

'We get lucky sometimes,' he said. 'It fits. Bugger me if it doesn't fit! Clausen could very well have killed that lad, the timing's right . . . So that could be the root cause of it all. Hell's bells, it's just too awful when you come to think about it.'

'What's too awful?' wondered Moreno.

'Don't you see? What started this whole business off could have been a pure accident. Erich Van Veeteren's death. Vera Miller's . . . And God only knows what happened last Thursday. A bloody straightforward accident, that's all, and then the wheels started turning . . .'

Moreno thought about her discussions with her neighbour the previous evening. About accidents and patterns, billiard balls cannoning or not cannoning. Sudden changes of direction . . . 'The butterfly effect'?

'Yes,' she said. 'It's remarkable. But we need to investigate it all in more detail yet. It's still only a possibility at this stage . . . Even if I also think it all fits in. Do we still have people out at Rumford, by the way? Isn't it time now to pull people out and cut back on resources? As far as Clausen's concerned, at least.'

Reinhart nodded. Lit his pipe and started leafing through some papers.

'It's all about these two bastards,' he muttered. 'Clausen and Keller. Three dead bodies so far . . . And they've both vanished. What a bloody disaster.'

He eventually found the document he was looking for.

'Nobody has had anything to say about Keller,' he said.

'He seems to be a real hermit. Just the kind of background you need if you're going to become a blackmailer . . . Exactly the right type, come to think about it.'

Moreno had certain reservations about this broad generalization, but she had no chance to spell them out because Constable Krause stuck his head in through the door.

'Forgive me,' he said, 'but we've just had an important fax.'

'Really?' said Reinhart. 'Let's hear it.'

'From the airport,' said Krause. 'It looks as if Aron Keller left on a flight last Saturday afternoon.'

'A flight?' said Reinhart. 'Where to?'

'New York,' said Krause. 'Left Sechshafen at 14.05. British Airways.'

'New York?' said Reinhart. 'Hell's bells.'

34

Nothing happened the rest of the day, apart from the fact that it snowed.

At least, that was how it seemed to Reinhart. It snowed and something had slipped through his fingers. He spent hour after hour in his office, and every time he looked out of the window all he could see was those flakes drifting down over the town. Occasionally he stood by the window, watching the scene. Stood there smoking his pipe, his hands in his pockets, and thinking about *The Chief Inspector*. About what he had promised him at the beginning of the investigation, and how he had been so close to fulfilling that promise.

Or had he? Had he never been close, in fact?

And what was the situation now? What had happened between Clausen and Keller? He thought he knew the answer to that, but refused to dig it up and look at it. Not yet. Not just yet. Perhaps in view of *The Chief Inspector* and that promise he had made . . . Yes, on second thoughts that was precisely why, of course.

Shortly after lunch Moreno came back, now with Boll-mert and deBries at her heels. They sat down and began reporting on Keller's friends and acquaintances. Just as they had feared, there weren't any. None of the people in the address book they had impounded – the dozen or so they had made contact with – had claimed to be especially close to the man. Some of them didn't even know who Aron Keller was, and couldn't understand why their names and addresses were in the book. In toto there were only two people who admitted that they had any kind of deal-ings with him: his two sisters in Linzhuisen. Without hesitation they both – independently – called him a crash-ing bore and a hermit, but said that even so they took it in turns to visit their respective families.

About once a year. At Christmas time.

Sometimes he came, sometimes he didn't.

As for his life and way of living, there was hardly any-thing to say. He had been a bit odd ever since he fell off a tractor and hit his head when he was about ten. Perhaps even before that. He had been married to a woman just as pig-headed as he was, and they had split up after less than a year. She'd been called Liz Vrongel, and was probably still called that.

His only interest had been silence. And football.

'Hmm,' said Reinhart. 'Well, at least they won't need to send him an invitation this Christmas. He won't be going.'

'How do you know that?' wondered deBries, who was unaware of the message from Sechshafen.

'He'll be celebrating Christmas in New York,' said Reinhart with a sigh. 'The bastard. We'll get round to that in a minute. What about the other Keller in the book? I seem to recall that there were three.'

'His father,' said deBries, pulling a face. 'A seventy-five-year-old boozer up in Haaldam. Lives in some kind of home, some of the time at least. He hasn't been in touch with any of his children for twenty years.'

'A marvellous family,' said Moreno.

'Idyllic,' said deBries. 'The old man's a right pain in the arse, it seems. Perhaps his son takes after him?'

'I expect so,' said Reinhart. 'Any other information?'

'Yes,' said Bollmert. 'We think we know how Erich Van Veeteren knew him. Aron Keller worked as a probation officer for a few years.'

Reinhart produced something reminiscent of a snarl.

'Isn't that just bloody typical!' he said. 'It's scandalous that they let types like him become probation officers. Who do they think is going to be helped to fit back into society by an arsehole like Keller . . . ? The only meaningful relationship he can have is with a vacuum cleaner.'

'He hasn't had any customers for three years,' said deBries. 'If that's any consolation. We're not sure yet if he took care personally of Erich Van Veeteren, but it won't take long to check that out.'

'Why haven't you done it already, then?' asked Reinhart.

'Because you wanted us here at one o'clock,' said deBries.

'Ah,' said Reinhart. 'Sorry.'

He stood up and watched the snow falling for a while.

'I wonder . . .' he said. 'Yes, that's it, of course.'

'What?' said Moreno.

'He must certainly have had some kind of hold over Erich. They can hardly avoid it in that business . . . And then he must have used it to get the lad to go and collect the money for him. Damn and blast! Damn and bloody blast!'

'We did say that blackmailers aren't usually very nice people,' said Moreno. 'Keller seems to be no exception.'

Reinhart returned to his chair.

'I'll ring and look into that probation business,' he said. 'If it's true, and I assume it is, I reckon we can say that we're clear about most of what happened. You can all take the afternoon off.'

'Good,' said deBries. 'I'd thought of proposing that myself. I haven't had any time off since Easter.'

He left together with Bollmert. Reinhart sat in silence,

staring at the cassettes which would never be listened to. Not by him, or by anybody else.

'All that work,' he muttered, and glared at Moreno. 'All that blasted work and all that wasted time. If you can answer one question for me, I'll put a good word in for you to Heller and suggest he gives you a winter holiday.'

'Shoot,' said Moreno.

'What did Keller do to Clausen last Thursday evening? What the hell went on?'

'I need some time to think about that,' said Moreno.

'You can have all afternoon,' said Reinhart. 'Go and sit in your office and watch the snow. It makes thinking easier.'

Van Veeteren took out a newly rolled cigarette and lit it.

'So you know who did it?' he said.

Reinhart nodded.

'Yes, I think we've found the right man. It's not a pleasant story, but then it never is. It all started with an accident, more or less. This Pieter Clausen is driving along a dark road at night, hits a young boy and kills him. He drives off, but doesn't know he's been seen. He might have stopped to check what happened, that seems likely. He's on his way home to Boorkhejm, and so is a certain Aron Keller – probably on his scooter. It's foul weather, heavy rain and strong winds, but he recognizes Clausen. They are near neighbours. Keller decides he's going to make some money out of what he's seen . . . We're dealing with a very nasty piece of work, I think I can promise you that.'

'Blackmailers are rarely nice chaps,' said Van Veeteren.

'Too right,' said Reinhart. 'Anyway, he sends your son out to Dikken that Tuesday to collect the money. I don't know if you are acquainted with Keller, but he was the probation officer in charge of Erich for a few years . . . It's not even clear that Erich was going to be paid for what he did. Keller might well have had some kind of hold on him. Clausen doesn't know who the blackmailer is, he already has one death on his conscience, and doesn't want to find himself constantly under threat. He kills Erich, thinking he's killed the blackmailer.'

He paused. After five seconds which seemed like five years to Reinhart, Van Veeteren nodded and indicated he should continue.

'Then we have the murder of Vera Miller. Do you want to hear about that as well?'

'Of course.'

'I don't know why Clausen kills her, but it must have something to do with Keller and Erich. Clausen and Vera Miller were having an affair, they'd only started shortly beforehand. Anyway, we were finally beginning to understand what it was all about. You put us onto the blackmail motive, and Aron Keller. The annoying thing is that we were so late in catching on. Something must have happened on Thursday or Friday last week – presumably it was time for Clausen to pay up once and for all. He'd had a loan granted by the Spaarkasse. Withdrew two hundred and twenty thousand in cash – and then he disappeared.'

'Disappeared?'

'We know what that could imply,' said Reinhart curtly. 'It's not too difficult to guess what might have happened. Aron Keller flew to New York last Saturday. He's no longer in the hotel where he checked in – we've exchanged a few faxes with them. We don't know where Pieter Clausen is. There's no trace of him, but it doesn't look as if he's done a runner as well. His passport and even his wallet are still in his house. I have only one theory, and that is that . . . well, that Keller has done him in. Killed him and buried him somewhere. Unfortunately. I'm afraid . . . I'm afraid you might never come face to face with your son's murderer.'

Van Veeteren took a swig of beer and looked out of the window. Half a minute passed.

'What we can hope for is that we find his body in due course,' said Reinhart, and wondered immediately why he had said that. As if that would be some kind of consolation.

Making contact with the body of the man who has

killed your son? Absurd. Macabre.

Van Veeteren said nothing. Reinhart studied his own hands, and searched in vain for something to say.

'I have a photo of him,' he said in the end. 'So you can take a look at him, if you'd like to. And Keller as well, come to that.'

He took two photocopies out of his briefcase and handed them over. *The Chief Inspector* looked at them for a few moments, frowning, then handed them back.

'Why would Keller have killed him?' he asked.

Reinhart shrugged.

'I don't know. He must have got the money, otherwise he would hardly have been able to slope off to New York. That's what I reckon, at least. You can indulge in a bit of speculation, of course. Maybe Clausen discovered his identity somehow or other. Keller is a very odd customer . . . And he knew that Clausen wouldn't hesitate to kill. So he played it safe, as simple as that. If Clausen knew who the blackmailer was, Keller must have realized that he was living dangerously.'

Van Veeteren closed his eyes and nodded vaguely. Another half a minute of silence passed. Reinhart abandoned his awkward efforts to find something positive to say, and instead tried to imagine how *The Chief Inspector* must be feeling. Naturally enough he had been doing that all the time, more or less; but it wasn't any easier now that he started concentrating on it. Having his son murdered, that was bad enough; and then the murderer being swept out of the way by another evildoer, who in a way was just as guilty of Erich's death as the man who had actually killed him. Or was that not an acceptable way of looking at it? Did it matter? Did such considerations have any significance when it was your son at the heart of the matter?

He didn't find an answer. Didn't come anywhere near finding an answer.

Whatever, no matter how you looked at it, Erich Van Veeteren had been no more than a pawn in a game that had nothing to do with him. What a pointless way to die, Reinhart thought. A completely wasted victim. The only one who could have conceivably benefited from his death was Keller, who presumably raised the price for his black arts once Clausen had another death on his conscience.

What a bloody mess, Reinhart thought for the fiftieth time that day. The choreographer of the nether regions had struck again.

'What are you going to do now?' asked Van Veeteren.

'We've issued a Wanted notice in the USA for Keller,' said Reinhart. 'Of course. Maybe one of us will have to go over there sooner or late . . . But it's a big country. And he's got enough money to see him through for quite a while.'

Van Veeteren sat up straight and looked out of the window again.

'It's snowing hard now,' he said. 'Anyway, many thanks. You've done all you could. Maybe we can keep in touch – I'd like to know how things go.'

'Of course,' said Reinhart.

When he left *The Chief Inspector* alone at the table, he felt like crying for the first time in twenty years.

35

He spent Wednesday evening and half of Thursday in an old Art Nouveau-style mansion in the Deijkstraat district. Krantze had bought the whole of a private library on the owner's death: in round figures there were four-and-a-half thousand volumes to be examined, assessed and packed into crates. As usual there were three categories to be considered: books that would be hard to sell and of doubtful value (to be sold off by the kilo); books worthy of a place on the shelves of the antiquarian bookshop that would no doubt find a buyer in due course (no more than two to three hundred in view of available shelf space); and books he would love to see in his own bookcase (five at most – over time he had learned to transform moral questions into unambiguous numbers).

It was no unpleasant task, wandering around this old bourgeois mansion (the family had been lawyers and appeal judges for several generations, if he had read the genealogy correctly), thumbing through old books. He could take as long as he needed – the hereditary gout that now afflicted Krantze prevented him from doing work that could not be carried out while sitting down. Or lying down. Naturally he had first established that there were no scientific tracts from the seventeenth and early eighteenth centuries in the collection, the narrow field that, in the autumn of his life, had become his real passion (and his only one, Van Veeteren had unfortunately been forced to conclude).

When his Wednesday work was finished, he ate a solitary, lugubrious dinner, watched an old De Sica film on Channel 4, and read for a few hours. For the first time since Erich's death he found that he was able to concentrate on such matters. He didn't know if it had to do with the latest conversation with Reinhart. Maybe, maybe not. And in that case, why? Before he fell asleep he lay for a long time, recapitulating the grim series of events that had led to the murder of his son. And to that nurse suffering the same fate.

He tried to conjure up the murderer. Noted that he hadn't in fact been the motor driving the whole business. Rather, he seemed to have been dragged into a situation, an increasingly intense and infernal dilemma that he had tried to solve with every means available to him. He had killed and killed and killed with a sort of desperate, perverted logic.

And nevertheless, in the end, become the victim himself.

No, Reinhart was right. It was not a pleasant story.

That night he dreamt about two things.

Firstly about a visit he'd paid to Erich when he was in prison. It wasn't an especially eventful dream: he simply sat in Erich's cell, and Erich lay on the bed. A warder came in with a tray. They drank coffee and ate some kind of soft biscuit without speaking to each other – it was in fact a memory rather than a dream. A memory which perhaps had nothing more to say than what it portrayed: a father visiting his son in prison. An archetype.

He also dreamt about G. About the G file, the only case he had failed to solve over all his years as a police officer. Nothing actually happened in this dream either. G sat in the dock during his trial, wearing his black suit, and gazed at Van Veeteren from the depths of his dark eyes. There was a sardonic smile on his lips. The prosecuting counsel walked back and forth, firing questions at him, but G didn't answer, simply sat there looking at Van Veeteren in the public gallery with that characteristic mixture of contempt and mockery.

He felt much greater distaste at this short dream

sequence, but when he woke up he couldn't even recall in which order he had dreamt them. Which one had come first. As he ate his breakfast he wondered if they could have somehow been merged into each other, as if in a film – Erich in prison and G in the courtroom – and in that case what the message of such a parallel dream might be.

He didn't find an answer, perhaps because he didn't want to. Perhaps because there wasn't one.

When he had finished packing on the Thursday afternoon, and marked all the boxes, he took his own carrier bag of books to his car, drove to the swimming baths and spent a couple of hours there before returning home to Klagenburg at about six o'clock. There were two messages on the telephone answering machine he had been given as a present by Ulrike. One was from her: she intended visiting him on Friday with a bottle of wine and some morel pâté, she announced, and wondered if he could use his own initiative to buy a few small gherkins and whatever other accessories he felt would be appropriate.

The other message was from Mahler, who explained that he intended to set up the chess pieces down at the Society at about nine p.m.

At that moment *The Chief Inspector* was inclined to

give the inventor of the telephone answering machine – whoever that might be – half an acknowledgement.

It was raining when he emerged into the street, but it was pleasantly warm and he took the route through the cemetery as he had planned. The first week after Erich's funeral he had been there every day, preferably in the evening when darkness had wrapped its comforting blanket around the graves. Now it was three days since the last time. As he approached the spot he slowed down as a sort of sign of respect – it happened without his thinking about it: an automatic, instinctive bodily reaction, it seemed. The open area was deserted at this time of day, gravestones and memorials stood up like even blacker silhouettes in the surrounding darkness. All that could be heard were his own footsteps on the gravel, pigeons cooing, cars accelerating a long way away in another world. He came to the grave. Stood listening, as usual, his hands dug deep into his overcoat pockets. If there was any ever-so-faint message or sign to be perceived at this time of day, it would be a sound: he knew that.

The dead are older than the living, he thought. Irrespective of how old they were when they passed over to the other side, they have experienced something which makes them older than any living thing.

Even a child. Even a son.

In the darkness he was unable to read the little memorial placard that had been installed temporarily until the stone ordered by Renate was in place. He found himself wishing he could read it: he would have liked to see the name and the date, and he made up his mind to visit the grave in daylight the next time.

The rain stopped as he stood there, and after ten minutes he continued on his way.

Left his son for now with the words *Sleep well, Erich* on his lips.

If possible I'll come to you in due course.

The Society's premises in Styckargränd were packed. But Mahler had arrived early and secured one of their usual booths with Dürer prints and wrought-iron candelabra. He was sitting there, stroking his beard and writing in a black notebook when Van Veeteren turned up.

'New poems,' he explained, closing the book. 'Or rather, old ones using new words. My language ceased to transcend my brain thirty years ago – besides, I don't even know what transcend means any longer . . . And how are you keeping?'

'KBO,' said Van Veeteren, easing himself into the booth. 'Keep buggering on. I sometimes have the impression that I'll survive all this.'

Mahler nodded and took a cigar out of the breast pocket of his waistcoat.

'That's our lot,' he said. 'Those the gods hate are made to keep buggering on longest. Ready?'

Van Veeteren nodded, and Mahler started setting up the pieces.

The first game lasted fifty moves, sixty-five minutes and three beers. Van Veeteren accepted a draw, despite the fact that he had one extra pawn, because it was stranded on an outside file.

'That son of yours,' said Mahler after stroking his beard for a while. 'Have they caught the bastard who did it?'

Van Veeteren emptied his glass before answering.

'Apparently,' he said. 'Although it seems as if Nemesis has already put his oar in.'

'What do you mean by that?'

'He seems to be buried somewhere, according to what I've heard. It was a blackmailing lark. Erich was just a pawn in the game . . . No dirty hands in any case, not this time. Oddly enough that consoles me a bit. But I'd have liked to be able to look that doctor in the eye.'

'Doctor?' said Mahler.

'Yes. Their function is to keep people alive, but this one chose a different line. Slaughtered them instead. I'll tell you the whole story – but some other time, if you don't mind. I need to put some distance between me and it first.'

Mahler sat and thought things over for a while, then excused himself and went to the loo. Van Veeteren took the opportunity of rolling five cigarettes while he was away. That corresponded to his prescribed daily consumption: but it had gone up a bit during the last month.

What the hell? Five cigarettes or ten? So what?

Mahler returned, carrying new beers.

'I have a suggestion,' he said. 'Let's do a Fischer.'

'A Fischer?' said Van Veeteren. 'What are you on about?'

'Come on, you know – the BIG genius's final contribution to the game of chess: you set up the back line purely by chance . . . The same at both ends, of course. Then you avoid those bloody silly analyses right through to the twentieth move. The only must is that the king has to be between the rooks.'

'I've heard about that,' said Van Veeteren. 'I've read about it. I've even studied a game played on that basis – it seemed barmy. It never occurred to me that I'd have to play a game like that . . . Do you really analyse everything as far ahead as the twentieth move?'

'Always,' said Mahler. 'Well?'

'If you insist,' said Van Veeteren.

'I do insist,' said Mahler. 'Cheers.'

He closed his eyes and dug into the box.

'File?'

'C,' said Van Veeteren.

Mahler placed his white rook on c1.

'Good Lord,' said Van Veeteren, staring at it.

They continued with the whole back line: only one of the bishops landed in its right place. The kings were on the e file, the queens on g.

'Fascinating to see the knight in the corner,' said Mahler. 'Shall we begin?'

He skipped his usual long session of introductory concentration, and played e2 to e3.

Van Veeteren rested his head on his hands, and stared at the board. Sat there for two minutes without moving a muscle. Then he slammed his fist down on the table and stood up.

'Bloody hell! I'll be damned if . . . Excuse me a moment.'

He wriggled his way out of the booth.

'What the hell's the matter with you?' said Mahler, but he received no answer. *The Chief Inspector* had already elbowed his way to the telephone in the foyer.

The conversation with Reinhart took almost twenty minutes, and when he came back Mahler had already taken out his notebook again.

'Sonnets,' he explained, contemplating his cigar that had gone out. 'Words and form! We have a totally clear view of the world when we're fourteen years old, maybe sooner. But then we need another fifty years in order to create a language that can express those impressions. And in the mean time, of course, they've faded away . . . What the hell got into you?'

'Please excuse me,' said Van Veeteren. 'You sometimes get a flash of inspiration even in the autumn of your life. It must have been this daft set-up that sparked it off.'

He gestured towards the board. Mahler peered at him over his half-empty glass.

'You're talking in riddles,' he said.

But enlightenment had not yet dawned. Van Veeteren took a swig of beer, moved his knight out of the corner and lit a cigarette.

'Your move, Mr Poet,' he said.

SIX

36

Chief Inspector Reinhart landed at Kennedy airport at 14.30 on Friday, 18 December. He was met by Chief Lieutenant Bloomguard, with whom he had spoken on the telephone and exchanged half a dozen faxes over the last twenty-four hours.

Bloomguard was about thirty-five, a stocky, close-cropped and energetic man whose very handshake seemed to indicate the abundant generosity, open-heartedness and warmth of American culture. Reinhart had already declined his invitation to stay in his home in Queens during his New York visit, and had several opportunities to do so again in the car on the way to and through the increasingly dense traffic in Manhattan.

Reinhart checked into Trump Tower in Columbus Circle. Bloomguard gave him a pat on the back and three hours to wash away all the dust accrued during his travels: then he was required to be on parade outside the entrance in order to be conveyed out to Queens for a slap-up dinner with the family. Yes sir.

When Reinhart was alone he stood by the window of his room and looked out – the twenty-fourth floor with a view to the north and east of Manhattan. Especially Central Park, which was spread out like a frosty miniature landscape diagonally below him. Dusk was closing in, but as yet the skyline was grey and drab. As they waited for night to fall the skyscrapers seemed to be hiding away in an anonymity that could hardly be ascribed to Reinhart's lack of knowledge about their names and functions. Not entirely, at least, he told himself. He could identify the Metropolitan and Guggenheim towers in Fifth Avenue on the other side of the park, but then he was uncertain. In any case, it didn't seem particularly hospitable. Positively hostile, in fact. The temperature was a degree or so below freezing, Bloomguard had told him, and the forecast was that it would become colder during the night. No snow so far this year, but maybe they could hope for some soon.

It was fifteen years since Reinhart was last in New York. The only time he'd been there, in fact. It had been a holiday visit, in August. As hot as a baking oven: he recalled having drunk four litres of water a day, and that his feet had ached. Recalled also that what he'd liked best were walks along the river promenade, and the tumbledown state of Coney Island. And Barnes & Noble, of course, especially the premises on Eighth Street. The world's best bookshop, open more or less all day and night long, where you could read as much as you liked for free in the cafeteria.

It had been a pleasure trip that time. He sighed, and left the window. Now he was on duty. He took a shower, slept for an hour, then had another shower.

Lieutenant Bloomguard was married to a woman called Veronique who did her best to look like Jacqueline Kennedy.

With a degree of success. They had a daughter two weeks older than Reinhart's Joanna, and lived in a low hacienda-inspired house in north-west Queens which looked exactly like what he had always imagined an American middle-class home ought to look like. During the meal his host recounted selected tales from the family history (with occasional contributions by his hostess). His father, who had fought in both Africa and Korea and had half a dozen medals and a wooden leg for his troubles, had just undergone a triple heart bypass operation, and looked as if he was going to survive. Veronique had just celebrated her thirtieth birthday and came originally from Montana, where they used to spend long vacations enjoying the clear mountain air. Bloomguard's younger sister had been raped in Far Rockaway just over two years ago, but had found a good therapist who seemed able to get her back on her feet again; and they had switched to decaffeinated coffee, but were thinking of going back to the normal stuff. Etcetera. Reinhart recounted a similar tenth or so of his own journey through the vale of tears, and by the time they came to the ice cream he realized that he knew more about Lieutenant Bloomguard and his family than he knew about any of his colleagues in the Maardam CID.

When Veronique withdrew with Quincey (which Reinhart had always thought was a boy's name) after doing her duty most efficiently, the gentlemen detectives sat down in front of the fire, each with a brandy, and started serious discussions.

By half past ten Reinhart began to feel the effects of jet lag. Bloomguard laughed and slapped him on the back once again. Put him into a taxi and sent him back to Manhattan.

Apart from having been obliged to stand outside on the terrace to smoke his pipe, Reinhart thought it had been a pleasant enough evening.

He would probably have fallen asleep in the taxi had it not been for the fact that the driver was a gigantic, singing Puerto Rican (Reinhart had always thought that Puerto Ricans were small), who insisted on wearing sunglasses although it was the middle of the night. Reinhart remembered a line in a film he'd seen – 'Are you blind or just stupid?' – but although it was on the edge of his tongue all the way, he couldn't summon up the courage to say it.

Once in his room he telephoned Winnifred, and was informed that it was a quarter to six in the morning in Europe. He undressed, crept into bed and fell asleep.

There were five days to go to Christmas Eve.

It was Lieutenant Bloomguard himself who drove him to Brooklyn on the Saturday morning. They turned off Fifth Avenue after Sunset Park, and parked a short way up 44th Street. Only a few houses away from the premises they were intending to visit, on the corner of Sixth Avenue. A dirt-brown brick building, narrow with three storeys, no lights in the windows, and an exact copy of every other building in the area. A few steps up to the front door, a few tired-looking rubbish bags on the pavement outside.

Latinos and orthodox Jews, Bloomguard had told him. And Poles. These are the usual types in these parts – although the Jews live mainly a bit further up, around Tenth and Eleventh Avenue.

They remained seated in the car for a while, and Reinhart tried to make it clear how delicate an occasion the first meeting was. Extremely damned delicate. Bloomguard took the hint.

'I'll stay in the car,' he said. 'You go in on your own – I find it so hard to hold my tongue.'

Reinhart nodded and got out. Glanced over the park, the open, sloping expanse of grass and the low, greyish white, wall-less buildings in the middle. Something that looked like a swimming baths. It wasn't exactly a place for tourists to visit, Bloomguard had said. Hardly a place for honest folk at all. Not at night, at least. After nightfall Sunset Park changed its name to Gunshot Park. That's what the locals called it.

But just now it looked perfectly peaceful. A jogger was struggling up a tarmacked path while a bunch of obviously out-of-work gentlemen in woolly hats were sitting on a bench, throwing a bottle in a plastic bag from one to the other. Two fat women were pushing a pram and making ostentatious gestures as they talked. One of the bare trees at the side of the street had masses of shoes hanging from every branch – a motif Reinhart recalled from a picture postcard he'd once received, he couldn't remember from whom.

The air was cold. An icy wind was blowing from down by the Hudson River; it felt as if snow was on the way. The view was magnificent. To the north was Manhattan's skyline against steel-grey clouds, a little to the west was the whole of the entrance to the harbour with the Statue of Liberty and Staten Island. This is where they came to, Reinhart thought. This is what became the New World.

He walked past three houses and four cars – big, slightly rusty gas guzzlers – and came to number 602. The digits indicated the location – the second house between Sixth and Seventh Avenue, he had read. He mounted the eight steps to the front door and rang the bell. A dog started barking.

Delicate, he thought again. Extremely damned delicate.

The door was opened by a boy in his early teens, with glasses and protruding teeth. He was holding a chocolate sandwich in his hand.

'I'm looking for Mrs Ponczak,' said Reinhart.

The boy shouted into the house, and after a while a solidly built woman came puffing and panting down the stairs and greeted him.

'That's me,' she said. 'I'm Elizabeth Ponczak. What do you want?'

Reinhart explained who he was and was invited into the kitchen. The living room was occupied by the boy and a television set. They sat down at a small, rickety laminated table, and Reinhart began to explain why he was there, as he had planned it. In English, he didn't know why.

It took several minutes, and all the time the woman sat opposite him, stroking a yellowish-grey cat that had jumped up onto her knee. The barking dog evidently belonged next door: he could occasionally hear it howling or yelping at something or other.

'I don't understand what you saying,' she said when he had finished. 'Why he want to visit me? We have not had contact in fifteen years. I am sorry, but I can't help you a sniff.'

Her English was even worse than his, he noted. Perhaps she spoke Polish to Mr Ponczak, if there still was anybody of that name around. He didn't seem to be at home at the moment, in any case.

Okay, Reinhart thought. That's that, then.

He hadn't been speaking the truth. Had she?

He had no way of knowing. As he sat there spinning his tale he had paid special attention to her reactions, but seen no sign that she was hiding or suspecting anything.

If only she weren't so phlegmatic, he thought in irritation. Fat, sloppy people like this one never had any problem when it came to hiding something. He'd often thought about that in the past. All they needed to do was to sit gaping out into space, just like they always did.

When he came out into the street he recognized that that was an unfair generalization. Unfair and inappropriate. But what the hell, he'd only had one trump card with him over the Atlantic. One miserable little trump card: he'd played it and it hadn't won him anything at all.

He plodded back to Bloomguard and the car.

'How did it go?' asked Bloomguard.

'Nix, I'm afraid,' said Reinhart.

He flopped down onto the passenger seat. 'Can we go somewhere for a coffee? With caffeine.'

'Of course,' said Bloomguard, starting the engine. 'Plan B?'

'Plan B,' said Reinhart with a sigh. 'Four days, as we said, then we drop it. I'll take as much time as I can cope with. And it's definite that you can place people at my disposal?'

'Of course,' said Bloomguard enthusiastically. 'You don't need to sit here sleuthing on your own. We have plenty of resources in this village of ours – there's a different wind blowing compared with fifteen years ago. Zero tolerance. I was a bit sceptical at first, I admit; but the fact is, it works.'

'So I've heard,' said Reinhart. 'But I don't want to feel like a tourist. And we need to work round the clock, or there's no point.'

Bloomguard nodded.

'You'll get a car for your own use,' he said. 'Let's go to the station and work out a timetable, and you can pick out the times you want to have. Then I'll look after the rest. Okay, compadre?'

'No problem,' said Reinhart.

★

In fact he delayed his first shift until Sunday. Bloomguard made sure that there was a car with two plain-clothes police officers parked at the junction of 44th Street and Sixth Avenue out in Brooklyn from four o'clock on Saturday. Reinhart spent the afternoon and evening wandering around Lower Manhattan. Soho. Little Italy. Greenwich Village and Chinatown. He eventually ended up in Barnes & Noble. That was more or less inevitable. Sat reading. Drinking coffee and eating brownies, and listening to poetry readings. Bought five books. It was half past nine by the time he left and managed to catch the correct subway train to Columbus Circle. When he came up to street level he found it had started snowing.

I wonder what I'm doing here? he thought. There are over seven million people in this city. How can I imagine that I'll ever find the right one? There must be better odds on my getting lost and disappearing than on discovering anything.

As he travelled up in the lift he reminded himself that it had in fact been *The Chief Inspector* who had convinced him he would be successful in his quest, but that wasn't much of a consolation. Not for the moment, at least, in the loneliness of Saturday evening

When he phoned and woke Winnifred up for the second night in succession, she told him it was snowing in Maardam as well.

37

Moreno met Marianne Kodesca for lunch at the Rote Moor. According to Inspector Rooth the Rote Moor was very much a place for women between the ages of thirty-four-and-a-half and forty-six, who lived on carrots and bean shoots, read *Athena* and had kicked one or more men onto the rubbish dump. Moreno had never set foot inside there, and was quite sure that Rooth hadn't either.

Fru Kodesca (she had remarried a year ago, to an architect) could only spare forty-five minutes. She had an important meeting. Had nothing to say about her ex-husband.

She had said as much already on the telephone.

They ate Sallad della Piranesi, drank mineral water with a dash of lime, and had a good view of the Market Square, which was covered in snow for the first time since Moreno could remember.

'Pieter Clausen?' she said when she thought the preliminaries were over and done with. 'Can you tell me a bit about him? We need a rather more clear psychological portrait of him, as it were.'

'Why, has he done something?' asked Marianne Kodesca, her eyebrows raised to her hairline. 'Why is he wanted by the police? You really must fill me in.'

She adjusted her rust-red shawl so that the designer label was a little more obvious.

'It's not completely clarified as yet,' said Moreno.

'Really? But you must know why you want him, surely?'

'He's disappeared.'

'Has something happened to him?'

Moreno put down her knife and fork and wiped her mouth with her napkin.

'We have certain suspicions about him.'

'Suspicions?'

'Yes.'

'What kind of suspicions?'

'I'm sorry, but I can't go into details about that.'

'He's never displayed any of those kind of tendencies.'

'What kind of tendencies?'

'Criminal. That's what you're saying, isn't it?'

'Do you still meet at all?' asked Moreno.

Kodesca leaned back and looked at Moreno with a smile that seemed to have been drawn with a pair of compasses on a refrigerator door. She must have toothache,

Moreno thought. I don't like her. I must be careful not to say anything stupid.

'No, we don't meet at all.'

'When did you see him last?'

'See?'

'Meet, then. Exchange words . . . However you'd like to put it.'

Fru Kodesca breathed in a cubic metre of air through her nostrils, and thought that one over.

'August,' she said, blowing out the air. 'I haven't seen him since August.'

Moreno made a note. Not because she needed to, just to tame her aggressions.

'How would you describe him?'

'I'd rather not describe him. What are you after?'

'A rather more detailed picture, that's all,' said Moreno. 'A few more general characteristics, that kind of thing.'

'Such as?'

'Such as what could happen if he became violent, for instance.'

'Violent?'

She fished the word up at the end of a very long line, from a different social class.

'Yes. Did he ever hit you?'

'Hit me?'

The same long line.

'If you'd rather come to the police station to conduct

this conversation, that's fine by me,' said Moreno in a friendly tone. 'Maybe this isn't the right kind of milieu?'

'Hmm,' said Kodesca. 'Sorry, I was gobsmacked, pure and simple. What do you take us for? I can imagine Pieter being subjected to something, but that he himself would . . . No, that's out of the question. Totally out of the question. You can write that down in your little book. Was there anything else?'

'Do you know if he'd had any new relationships since you divorced?'

'No,' said Kodesca, looking out of the window. 'That's not my problem any more.'

'I understand,' said Moreno. 'So you have no idea where he might have gone? It's ten days since he disappeared . . . He hasn't been in touch with you at all?'

A disapproving wrinkle appeared between fru Kodesca's right nostril and the corner of her mouth, and made her look five years older at a stroke.

'I've already told you that we have absolutely no contact with each other any more. Have you problems in understanding?'

Yes, thought Moreno. I have problems in understanding how you managed to find yourself a new husband.

But then, perhaps she hadn't seen Marianne Kodesca from her best side.

*

Half an hour later she met Jung in his office in the police station.

'Liz Vrongel,' said Jung. 'Disappeared without trace.'

'Her as well?' said Moreno.

Jung nodded.

'But twenty years ago. She was married to Keller for a year . . . Well, ten months if you want to be finicky . . . Then they divorced and she moved to Stamberg. A mixed-up devil, obviously. Took part in all kinds of protest movements, and was kicked out of Greenpeace after she bit a police officer in the face. Joined various sects and is said to have gone to California at the beginning of the eighties. After that the trail goes cold. I don't know if there's any point in looking for her.'

Moreno sighed.

'Presumably not,' she said. 'We can start thinking about celebrating Christmas instead and hope Reinhart comes home with something from New York.'

'Do you think that's likely?'

'Not very,' said Moreno. 'To be honest.'

'And what was the former fru Clausen like?'

Moreno wondered how best to put it.

'A different type from the former fru Keller at any rate,' she said. 'Discreet bourgeois fascism, more or less. And not all that discreet, in fact, come to think of it. But she had nothing to offer us, and I don't think I want to talk to her again.'

'Rich bitch?' said Jung.

'You could say that,' said Moreno.

Jung checked the time.

'Anyway,' he said, 'don't you think we can allow ourselves to go home now? Maureen has started going on
about how I ought to get a new job. I'm beginning to
agree with her.'

'What would you become if you did?' asked Moreno.

'I don't really know,' said Jung, pulling thoughtfully at
his lower lip. 'A cinema usher sounds attractive.'

'Cinema usher?'

'Yes. One of those people who show customers to their
seats with a little torch, and sell goodies in the intervals.'

'They don't exist any more,' said Moreno.

'That's a pity,' said Jung.

Chief Inspector Reinhart drove himself out to 44th Street
in Brooklyn on the Sunday morning. He arrived exactly
half an hour late: the night shift had just packed up,
but the brown house numbered 602 was not unguarded.
Bloomguard had decided to post an extra car there in
addition to Reinhart's – in view of his European colleague's knowledge of the city that was no doubt a good
move.

He parked between 554 and 556, where there was a
space, got into the car on the other side of the street – a

3-metre-long Oldsmobile – and greeted the police officer inside it.

Sergeant Pavarotti was small and thin and looked unhappy. Reinhart didn't know if that was because of his name, or if there was some other reason behind it.

Having to spend a whole Sunday sitting in an old car in Brooklyn, for instance.

'I've considered changing my name lots of times,' said Pavarotti. 'I sometimes get to a point where I'd much rather have been called Mussolini. I sing worse than a donkey. How are things in Europe?'

Reinhart explained the situation, then asked if Pavarotti had any special interests.

Baseball and action films, evidently. Reinhart stayed with him for another five minutes, then returned to his own car. He had asked Bloomguard if it wouldn't look suspicious, sitting behind the wheel of a stationary car for hours on end, but Bloomguard had merely given him a knowing smile and shaken his head.

'People never look out of the window in the houses out there,' he had explained. 'Besides, there are always lots of men sitting alone in their cars – go for a walk round and see for yourself.'

A little later on Reinhart actually did go for a walk around the block, and discovered that it really was true.

Oversized cars stood parked on either side of the street, and in every fifth or sixth sat a man chewing gum or smoking. Or digging into a packet of crisps. Most of them were wearing dark glasses, despite the fact that the sun seemed to be further away than the Middle Ages. What's going on? Reinhart wondered.

It was cold as well, certainly several degrees below freezing, and the same inhospitable wind as yesterday was blowing up from the river.

I don't understand this society, Reinhart thought. What the hell do people do? What lies are they living that we haven't discovered yet?

He told Pavarotti to go off for an hour and have a coffee: Pavarotti seemed to doubt if he ought to take an order like that from this dodgy chief inspector, but in the end he did as he was bidden.

Reinhart clambered over the low stone wall surrounding Sunset Park and went to sit down on a bench. There was just as good a view of number 602 from there as from inside the car, and he didn't think there was any risk of fru Ponczak recognizing him. In his woolly hat, long scarf and old military parka he looked just like any other tramp, or so he told himself: one of those drifters who couldn't even afford a car to sit in while they were waiting for death to catch up with them.

It was ten minutes to eleven when fru Ponczak came

out. Pavarotti still hadn't returned, even though it was over an hour since he had left. Reinhart wondered what to do, and decided to follow the woman.

She walked down as far as Fifth Avenue and turned left. Waddling gently and with a slight limp, it seemed. For a moment he thought she was going to the subway station on 45th Street . . . But he didn't need to decide what to do in that case, as she went into a mini-market on the corner instead. Reinhart walked past and stationed himself on the other side of the street. Started filling his pipe with fingers as supple as icicles.

After five minutes she came out with a plastic carrier bag in each hand. Started walking back along Fifth Avenue the same way as she'd come. Turned back into 44th Street and was home in number 602 a minute later.

Reinhart sat in his car again. Ah well, he thought. That was presumably today's dramatic high point. *Mrs Ponczak goes shopping*. It sounded like an English kitchen-sink film.

However, it turned out to be a correct diagnosis. Neither fru Ponczak nor her layabout son bothered to go out any more on this icy cold, windy, December Sunday – and why should they have done? There was always the telly, for instance. No sign of any possible herr Ponczak, and Reinhart guessed that if he existed at all, he was lying down in a back room overlooking the courtyard, reading the paper or sleeping off his hangover. That's what he would have done if he'd been herr Ponczak.

For his own part, he hesitated between wandering around Sunset Park, lying back in his car, and sitting next to the cheerless Pavarotti. He also took up the question of what they should do if the object of their reconnaissance should leave her house once again. Pavarotti maintained that the object of their reconnaissance was in fact the house and not its occupier – that's what Bloomguard had ordered him to do. Quite specific orders. In order to avoid any falling out between them, Reinhart phoned Bloomguard in his home in Queens and asked him to issue new instructions. In the event that the object of their reconnaissance Ponczak (Mrs) should again leave the object of their reconnaissance Ponczak (House), it was Pavarotti's duty to shadow the former. No matter what the circumstances Reinhart should stay put near the street corner in question, since he was not considered to be one hundred per cent suitable for shadowing duties in a city with seven million inhabitants in which he knew the names of six people, two parks and five buildings.

At about two Pavarotti went to fetch a shoebox of junk food for each of them, by four o'clock Reinhart had finished reading the first of the books he had bought at Barnes & Noble – *Sun Dogs* by Robert Olen Butler – and at precisely 18.00 they were relieved by the night shift.

Nothing else happened, either in number 602 or any-where in the vicinity.

If I don't have a crash or get mugged on the way back to the hotel, Reinhart thought, I suppose one can say it's been a quiet Sunday.

Neither of these things happened. After bathing up his body temperature to something approaching normal, he phoned Bloomguard and invited him to a meal, but was declined. He went for a long walk through the darkness of Central Park instead (still without being attacked or run over), had an evening meal at an Italian restaurant in 49th Street, and returned to his hotel and the next book at about eleven.

I don't think I've ever followed a more slender lead than this one, he thought. Three more days to go. Just as point-less as giving roses to a goat. If it weren't for *The Chief Inspector* and his damned intuition, well . . .

He set his alarm clock for 02.15, and when it rang he had slept for one-and-a-half hours. It was some time before he remembered what he was called, where he was and why. And why he had been woken up.

Then he phoned across the Atlantic and heard his daughter's early-bird voice in his ear.

38

Monday was rather more eventful than Sunday had been.

But only a little. Reinhart had only just arrived at Sunset Park when both mother and son Ponczak came out into the street. Pavarotti had the day off and was replaced by the significantly more optimistic Sergeant Baxter, who looked like a successful cross between a bulldog and a young Robert Redford: after a brief discussion he slid out of the car and began following Mrs Ponczak down towards Fifth Avenue. Her son set off in the opposite direction, eastwards towards Seventh Avenue, but Reinhart judged him to be of only minor interest (presumably kids go to school in this country as well, he thought) and remained in Baxter's car.

It was an hour and ten minutes before anything happened. Baxter rang from a department store down on Pacific (still in Brooklyn) and said he was drinking coffee (with caffeine) in a cafeteria directly opposite the bodyshop where Mrs Ponczak apparently worked. Today, at least.

As number 602 seemed to be deserted (Mr Ponczak's existence seemed to become more improbable with every hour that passed), Reinhart decided that Baxter might just as well stay where he was, drinking coffee and keeping his eye on the mobile object, while he looked after the somewhat less mobile house in Sunset Park.

Good Lord, he thought as he closed down the call from Baxter. Was this the kind of thing I used to do twenty-five years ago?

By half past twelve he had read seventy pages of James Ellroy's *My Dark Places*, and started asking himself once again what sort of a country this was that he'd come to. At one o'clock he left the car and went to buy some provisions at the mini-market on the corner of Sixth and 45th. He bought bananas, a bottle of mineral water, a bar of chocolate and a few bagels. Apparently there was a mini-market on every other street corner, you could take your pick. As he walked back to the car he noticed that it had become a bit warmer, and a quarter of an hour later it started raining. He continued ploughing on through Ellroy's morbid world, and spoke to both Baxter and Bloomguard on the telephone a few times. At half past three Ponczak junior returned home in the company of a red-headed schoolmate, and half an hour later Reinhart was relieved.

Monday, he thought on the way in to Manhattan. Two days left. What the hell am I doing here?

Despite the fact that a smoggy dusk was already in the air, he took the ferry over to Staten Island. Managed to catch the right bus to take him to Snugg's Harbor, where he wandered around for an hour among rotting leaves – it was the same place he'd wandered around with a young woman fifteen years ago: that was why he was repeating the experience now, but it didn't feel the same at all. Then it had been plus thirty degrees, and the leaves had still been hanging on the trees.

Her name had been Rachel, and he hoped it still was: he recalled having loved her passionately for four days. With his head, his heart and his sexual organs. By the fifth day his head (perhaps also his heart, come to that) had vetoed the relationship, and after the sixth they had gone their separate ways.

He spent the evening with Bloomguard in an Asian restaurant in Canal Street. Bloomguard would have liked to take him up to 1 Police Plaza as well, to show him the latest technical advances in the fight against crime (electronic bugging devices, laser-sweepers etc.) but Reinhart declined the invitation as politely as he could.

He was back at his hotel by midnight. Winnifred had sent him a fax with the outlines of both Joanna's hands and a message to the effect that they had use of Professor Gentz-Hillier's house in Limbuijs for a fortnight from the 27th.

He slid the fax under his pillow and fell asleep without having rung home.

When he came to Sunset Park on Tuesday morning, he didn't understand at first what Sergeant Pavarotti said to him.

'The fucker's in there.'

'Eh?' said Reinhart.

'In there. That bastard. In the house.'

He pointed over his shoulder.

'Who?'

'That guy you're looking for, of course. Why the devil do you think we're sitting here?'

'What the hell are you saying?' said Reinhart. 'What . . . I mean, what have you done? How do you know he's in there?'

'Because I saw him go in, of course. A quarter of an hour ago. He came down from Fifth Avenue. Presumably he'd come with the R-train to 45th Street. He came walking past me, up the steps and rang the bell . . . Then she appeared and let him in. The boy had left for school just five minutes beforehand. They're in there now, as I said.'

'Jesus fucking Christ,' said Reinhart, to show that he had understood the local lingo. 'What measures have you taken?'

'In accordance with orders, of course,' snorted Pavarotti. 'I rang Bloomguard. He's on his way here with a posse. He should be here any minute now.'

Reinhart felt as if he had suddenly woken up out of a three-day-long hibernation.

'Good,' he said. 'Damned good.'

'It'll be a straightforward operation,' said Bloomguard, 'but we mustn't take any risks. Two men go round to the back. Two cover the street and the windows at the front. Two go and ring the doorbell – me and Chief Inspector Reinhart. There's no reason to think he's armed, but we'll follow the usual procedures even so.'

The usual procedures? Reinhart wondered.

Two minutes later everybody was in place. Pavarotti stayed in the car with his mobile in one hand and his gun in the other. When Bloomguard gave the signal Reinhart walked up the eight steps and rang the bell. Bloomguard followed twelve centimetres behind him. The door was opened by Mrs Ponczak.

'Yes?' she said in surprise.

Three seconds later there were four men inside the house. Sergeants Stiffle and Johnson took the upstairs floor, Bloomguard and Reinhart stormed into the living room and kitchen downstairs.

He was sitting in the kitchen.

When Reinhart clapped eyes on him he had just turned sideways on his chair and seen the two hefty-looking police officers on the kitchen terrace, each of them aiming their 7.6 millimetre Walthers at him. Bloomguard was standing shoulder to shoulder with Reinhart, aiming his own gun at him as well.

Reinhart put his gun into its holster and cleared his throat.

'Dr Clausen,' he said. 'I have the doubtful pleasure of arresting you for the murder of Erich Van Veeteren and Vera Miller. You have the right to remain silent, but anything you say might be used in evidence against you.'

He shrank back slightly, but not a lot. Put down the mug of coffee he'd been holding in his hand. Looked Reinhart in the eye without moving a muscle. His dark face looked haggard – a few days of stubble and bags under his eyes. Hasn't had much sleep, by the look of it, Reinhart thought. No wonder.

But there was something else about his appearance, something that looked completely fresh, he noted. As if it had only landed on his face a few seconds beforehand. A sort of relief.

That's probably what it was. Perhaps that's what he felt, at last.

'Keller,' he said in a low voice, hardly more than a whisper. 'You forgot Keller. I killed him as well.'

'We suspected as much,' said Reinhart.

'I'm sorry.'

Reinhart said nothing.

'I'm sorry about it all, but I'm pleased I killed Keller.'

Reinhart nodded.

'We'll take the rest at the station. Take him away.'

Mrs Ponczak hadn't said a word since they stormed in, and she didn't say a word when they led away her brother. Reinhart was the last one to pass her in the vestibule: he paused for a moment and tried to think of something to say.

'Sorry to intrude,' was the best he could think of. 'We'll be in touch.'

She nodded and closed the door behind him.

He interrogated Pieter Clausen for three hours in a light-blue room in the police station of the 22nd district. Recorded it all on tape, but postponed the transcription and signatures in view of the language problem. When he had finished he left Clausen in his cell, securely guarded, and went to Bloomguard's office in order to telephone Maardam. After a short pause he was put through to Moreno.

'I'll be returning with him tomorrow evening,' he said. 'He's confessed to everything – I think he's relieved that it's all over.'

'What happened to Keller?' asked Moreno.

Reinhart took a deep breath and began to explain.

'Clausen killed him. He'd worked out who he was . . . Ambushed him and killed him, just like that. More or less the same method as he'd used for Erich and Vera Miller. Just outside his home in Boorkhejm, in the centre of the estate – but it was the middle of the night and nobody saw anything . . . It was just as Keller was about to set off to collect the money. If there's anything he doesn't regret, it's doing Keller in. He claims Keller knew that he was on his trail because he was armed with a big knife that evening. But Clausen was quicker. Anyway, he put the body in his car, drove out towards Linzhuisen and buried him among some trees. I've got a description of the location, but maybe we can leave him there for a few more days.'

'Certainly,' said Moreno. 'The ground frost will keep him in check. Winter has set in over here. How did he manage the role change?'

'It was straightforward, it seems. Before burying the

body he took Keller's keys and wallet. Drove back to Boorkhejm, let himself into Keller's flat and . . . well, stole his identity, I suppose you could say. They were quite similar in appearance, that was what *The Chief Inspector* had caught onto, and anyway, who the hell looks like his passport photo? On the Friday he rang and ordered a ticket to New York, took the scooter around lunch time and rode out to Sechshafen. Stayed one night at one of the airport hotels, then flew out here. No problems at passport control – a two-month tourist visa and white skin solves all the problems, I expect. Checked in at that hotel in Lower East – you know the place. Then moved out after just the one night. Rented a little flat among all the Russians on Coney Island – saw an advert in a shop window and followed it up. I don't understand why he didn't find something better, he had plenty of money after all. But in any case, it wasn't as good as he'd thought . . .'

'Alone with his conscience?' said Moreno.

'Presumably,' said Reinhart. 'He contacted his sister and told her he'd got problems – that was before I went to see her. She phoned him and warned him, but she probably didn't realize who I was and he couldn't stand being on his own any longer. He didn't tell her what he'd done, just that he had problems. So he came to visit her when he thought the coast was clear – but of course it wasn't. He must have felt really cut off. The more people who live in a city, the more space you have to feel isolated. I think he'd been taking quite a lot of medication as well – that's presumably what enabled him to go through with it all . . . It's only just beginning to sink in that he's killed four people.'

'So he's on the edge of a breakdown, is he?' wondered Moreno.

'I suspect so,' said Reinhart. 'We can go into more detail when I get back. Can you inform *The Chief Inspector*, by the way? I'll be arriving with Clausen tomorrow evening . . . It will be good if he can let us know how he wants to go about things. What do you think?'

'All right,' said Moreno. 'I expect he'll be wanting one last round.'

'It looks like it,' said Reinhart. 'Anyway, over and out.'

'See you soon,' said Moreno.

It snowed again on Wednesday morning. There were four of them in the car out to JFK: Bloomguard and Reinhart in the front seats, Clausen and a gigantic black police constable by the name of Whitefoot in the back – the two latter were linked together by handcuffs for which Whitefoot had a key in his back pocket, and Reinhart had another in reserve in his wallet. It was obvious that Christmas was coming: the journey took only half an hour, but they managed to hear 'White Christmas' twice and 'Jinglebells' three times on the car radio. Reinhart was feeling home-sick.

'It was great to meet you,' said Bloomguard as they stood outside the security check. 'We plan to make a little trip to Europe in three or four years' time, Veronique and I. And Quincey, of course. Perhaps we can meet over a cup of coffee? In Paris or Copenhagen or somewhere?'

'Sure,' said Reinhart. 'Why not both? You've got my card.'

They shook hands and Bloomguard vanished into the departure hall. Clausen seemed to have become more life-less with every hour that passed since they found him, and Whitefoot had to more or less drag him onto the plane. Reinhart was deeply grateful that he wasn't the one who would have to sit handcuffed to the murderer for the seven hours of the flight. He had offered to take the doctor back home himself, but there had been no question of the offer being accepted. Whitefoot had been on this kind of mission before, and knew what it was all about. Without a word he dumped Clausen into the window seat, sat down next to him and left the aisle seat for Reinhart. He explained to Clausen that he would be allowed one toilet visit, no more, and that he should regard his right arm as having been amputated. Everything – eating, turn-ing the pages of a book or newspaper, picking his nose, the lot – would have to be done with his left hand. It was no problem, said Whitefoot, they had more time than in fucking hell.

Reinhart was deeply grateful, as already said. Read some more of the Ellroy, slept, ate, listened to music, and at 22.30 local time they landed at Sechshafen in a foggy Europe. Whitefoot said his goodbyes. Checked in for one night at an airport hotel, handed Clausen over to Reinhart, Rooth, Moreno and Jung, and wished everybody a Merry Christmas.

'Three of you?' said Reinhart. 'There was no need for all three of you to come, for Christ's sake.'

'DeBries and Bollmert are waiting in the cars,' said Moreno.

There was one day left to Christmas Eve.

39

Reinhart had not issued orders for a run-through, and neither had anybody else.

Nevertheless, a quartet was assembled in his office at ten o'clock the next day, which was Thursday, 24 December. Christmas Eve. Moreno and Jung were each sitting on a window ledge, trying to avoid looking at the rain which had started falling in the early hours of the morning and rapidly washed away any vain dreams of a white Christmas. Grey, wet and windy: Maardam had resumed normal service.

A little further away from the rain, Reinhart was half-lying behind his desk. deBries and Jung had flopped down on the visitor's chairs on each side of the impressive array of Christmas flowers that somebody (presumably fröken Katz, as instructed by the chief of police himself) had brought in to decorate the room.

'So, that's that, then,' said deBries. 'Pretty good timing, one has to say.'

Reinhart lit his pipe and enveloped both the flowers and deBries in a cloud of smoke.

'Yes,' he said, 'you're right there.'

'What time's he coming?' asked Jung.

Moreno looked at the clock.

'During the morning,' she said. 'He didn't want to be more precise than that. But perhaps we ought to allow him a bit of leeway in view of . . . Well, in view of everything.'

Reinhart nodded and sat up a bit more on his chair.

'We have very little to preen ourselves on for once,' he said, looking round at his colleagues. 'But as we are all sitting here, perhaps we might as well sum up . . . Before it's time, that is.'

'Before it's time,' repeated Rooth. 'Huh.'

'The starting point of this case was the murder of *The Chief Inspector*'s son,' said Reinhart, 'and it was *The Chief Inspector* who made the biggest contribution towards solving it. There's no denying that. He was the one who dug up the blackmail motive, he gave us the name Keller, and he suspected that it was in fact Clausen who had gone off to New York. Don't ask me how the hell he did it. The last bit came to him while he was playing chess, he maintains . . .'

'Have they found Keller?' asked deBries.

Reinhart nodded.

'Le Houde was out with his team and dug him up this

morning. Clausen didn't need to accompany them, it was enough with a map and the description. Mourners are going to be pretty thin on the ground when it comes to burying him properly. Nobody seems to lament the passing of Aron Keller, that's for sure.'

'Hardly surprising,' said Moreno.

'What about the doctor? How's the murderer himself?' asked Rooth. 'Full of Christmas cheer, is he?'

Reinhart smoked for a while without speaking.

'It's hard to say,' he said eventually. 'I don't think he'll be able to hold himself together for much longer. And what will happen when he meets . . . No, I've no idea. I just hope it isn't a bloody disaster.'

The telephone rang. It was Joensuu ringing from the front desk.

'He's here now,' he declared solemnly. '*The Chief Inspector* is here.'

You could hear that he was standing to attention as he spoke.

'All right,' said Reinhart. 'Ask Krause to take him down to the cells. I'll be there in a minute.'

He hung up and looked round.

'Well, here goes,' he said, standing up. 'Detective Chief Inspector Van Veeteren has just arrived to interrogate his son's murderer. What the hell are you all hanging around here for?"

The room was pale grey and rectangular. The furnishings were simple: a table with two tubular steel chairs, two more chairs along one of the walls. No windows. A fluorescent tube on the ceiling spreading a clinical, democratic light over every square centimetre.

No ashtray on the table. Only a carafe of water and a pile of plastic cups.

Clausen was already there when Van Veeteren came in. Sitting at the table with his hands clasped in front of him, looking down. Simple white shirt, dark trousers. He had been sitting motionless for several minutes: *The Chief Inspector* had watched him for a while through the peephole before gesturing to Reinhart and Krause to let him in.

He pulled out the chair and sat down at the table. Clausen didn't look up, but Van Veeteren could see the muscles tightening in his neck and cheeks. He waited. Clenched his hands in the same way as his son's murderer, leaning forward slightly over the table. Half a minute passed.

'Do you know who I am?' he asked.

Dr Clausen swallowed, but didn't answer. Van Veeteren could see his knuckles turning white and his head trembling. Small oscillating shakes, like the fluttering of leaves before a storm. He still didn't raise his gaze.

'Have you anything to say to me?'

No reply. He noticed that Clausen was holding his breath.

'I have a meeting with Elizabeth Felders in an hour,' Van Veeteren said. 'The mother of Wim, the boy you also killed. Have you any message you'd like me to pass on to her?'

He waited. Thank God I don't have a gun, he thought.

Eventually Clausen took a deep breath and looked up. Looked *The Chief Inspector* in the eye, and seemed as if he wanted to disappear into his head.

'I'd like you to know . . .' he began, but his voice wouldn't function. He coughed a few times and looked here and there. Then tried again.

'I'd like you to know that I was a normal human being two months ago . . . Perfectly normal, I'd just like to say that. I shall take my own life as soon as I get a chance. As soon as I get . . . a chance.'

He fell silent. Van Veeteren looked into his lifeless eyes for five seconds. Felt something suddenly beginning to happen inside himself. How his awareness of the room round about him seemed to shrink, and how he was slowly but surely being drawn into something dark and swirling, something sucking him in, something irrevocable. He closed his eyes tightly and leaned back.

'Good luck,' he said. 'Don't wait too long. If you do I'll come back and remind you of what you said.'

He stayed there for a few more minutes. Clausen was staring at his hands again, the trembling continued. The air conditioning hummed. The fluorescent tube flickered once or twice. Nothing else happened.

Then Van Veeteren stood up. Signalled that he wanted to be let out, and left the room.

He didn't say a word. Not to Reinhart or to anybody else. Walked straight through the foyer, opened up his umbrella and wandered out into the town.

If you enjoyed Hour of the Wolf *you'll love*

THE WEEPING GIRL

the new mystery from Håkan Nesser, out Spring 2013

A community is left reeling after a teacher – Arnold Maager – is convicted of murdering his female pupil Winnie Maas. It seems the girl had been pregnant with Maager's child.

Years later, on her eighteenth birthday, Maager's daughter Mikaela finally learns the terrible truth about her father. Desperate for answers, Mikaela travels to the institution at Lejnice, where Maager has been held since his trial. But soon afterwards she inexplicably vanishes.

Detective Inspector Ewa Moreno from the Maardam Police is on holiday in the area when she finds herself drawn into Mikaela's disappearance. But before she can make any headway in the case, Maager himself disappears – and then a body is found. It will soon become clear to Ewa that only unravelling the events of the past will unlock this dark mystery . . .

An excerpt follows here . . .

1

Winnie Maas died because she changed her mind.

Afterwards there were those who maintained that she died because she was beautiful and stupid – a combination acknowledged to be risky.

Or because she was gullible, and relied on the wrong people.

Or because her father was a shit who had abandoned his family long before Winnie had stopped using nappies or a baby's bottle.

And there were others who claimed that Winnie Maas used to wear skirts that were rather too short and blouses that were rather too tight, and that in fact she had only herself to blame.

None of these explanations was totally without justification; but the thing that clinched it was that she changed her mind.

The moment before she hit the ground and smashed her skull on the steel rail, she even realized that herself.

She wiped away a tiny bit of extra lipstick and contemplated her image in the mirror. Opened her eyes wide and wondered if she needed a bit more eyeliner. It was a nuisance to have to keep remembering to open her eyes wide – easier to apply a bit more liner underneath. She drew a thin line with the pencil, leaned towards the mirror and checked the result.

Pretty good, she thought, and transferred her attention to her mouth. Showed her teeth. They were even and white, and her gums were hidden behind her lips, thank goodness – not like Lisa Paaske's, who was very pretty with her green, slanting eyes and high cheekbones, but was condemned to wander around looking serious all the time, or at best to give an enigmatic smile, all because her upper gums grew down so far. Huh, Winnie thought. That must be hard to keep up.

She checked her watch. A quarter to nine. High time she was on her way. She stood up, opened the wardrobe door and checked how she looked in the full-length mirror. Tried out a few poses, thrusting out first her breasts, then her pelvis. She looked good, both high up and low down – she had just plucked out four strands of hair that had been sticking out dangerously close to her bikini line. Light-coloured, but even so . . .

Perfect, Jürgen had said. I'll be damned if your body isn't perfect, Winnie.

Smashing, Janos had suggested, she recalled that clearly. You really are smashing, Winnie – I get a hard-on every time I walk past your house.

She smiled when she thought about Janos. Of all the boys she'd been with, Janos was the best. He'd done it in just the right way. He'd somehow managed to combine sensitivity and tenderness, just as they said it should be in *Flash* and *Girl-zone*.

Janos. In a way it was a pity that it wasn't going to be Janos.

But so what? she thought, slapping her buttocks. No point in crying over spilled milk. She dug out a pair of lace panties from the dressing-table drawer, but she couldn't find a clean bra and so didn't bother. She didn't need one, after all. Her breasts were quite small, and firm enough not to sag. If there was anything about her body she would have liked to improve, it would be slightly bigger breasts. Not much bigger, just a little bit. To be sure, Dick had said that she had the prettiest titties the world had ever seen, and he'd sucked and squeezed them so thoroughly that they'd hurt for several days afterwards – but let's face it: a few extra grams wouldn't have done any harm.

But that'll come, she thought. Pulled her T-shirt over her head and wriggled her way into her tight skirt. Yes indeed, it was only a matter of time before she started putting on weight. Unless she . . .

Unless she . . .

For God's sake, she thought, lighting a cigarette. I'm only sixteen. Mum was seventeen when it happened to her, and look how she's turned out . . .

She made one last check in the dressing-table mirror, licked carefully round her lips, then set off.

Frieder's Pier, half past nine, he'd said. He came on the train that arrived at half past eight, but wanted to go home and have a shower first, if she didn't mind. Of course she didn't: she approved of men who kept themselves clean. Washed their hair and removed the dirt from under their fingernails – that showed they had a touch of class, she felt. It would be the first time they'd met for three weeks: he'd been up in Saren, staying with an uncle. A mixture of work and holiday. They'd spoken on the telephone a few times, and discussed 'the project', but she hadn't told him that she'd changed her mind. She was going to do that now, this evening. Best to do it face to face, she'd thought.

It was a warm evening. When she came down on to the

beach, she felt almost sweaty after the short walk. But it was cooler down here. There was a pleasant, gentle breeze blowing from the sea; she slipped off her canvas shoes and started walking barefoot over the sand. It was nice to feel the tiny grains rubbing against her toes. It was almost like being a child again. It didn't do her nail varnish any favours, of course, but she would put her shoes back on before she got there. Before she met Him. She liked to think about him having a capital H. He was worth that. Mind you, if he wanted to have sex with her afterwards, it struck her, he would probably want her to be barefoot. But maybe it didn't matter – in those circumstances it wasn't usually her toenails that he was most interested in.

And why would he not want to have sex with her? They hadn't seen each other for ages, after all!

She paused and lit another cigarette. Moved closer to the waterline where the sand was more tightly packed and it was easier to walk. The beach was pretty deserted at this time in the evening, but there were a few people around. An occasional jogger came running past, and she met an occasional dog-walker; she also knew that there would be quite a few young people necking on blankets in among the dunes – they always did that in the summer. She often did it herself, and maybe they would end up there this evening as well.

Maybe, maybe not.

It would depend on how he reacted. She started thinking about it. Would he be angry? Would he grab hold of her and give her a good shaking, as he'd done that time in Horsens when she'd been as high as a kite on hash, and rambled on about how she thought Matti Frege had nice muscles.

Or would he understand, and agree with her?

Perhaps he'd be able to talk her round. That wasn't entirely out of the question, of course. Perhaps his unparalleled love for her would make her think again? And the money, naturally. Was that a possibility?

No, she didn't think so. She was feeling strong and certain about the decision she'd made, goodness knows why. Maybe because she'd been on her own and able to think things over in peace and quiet for a few weeks.

But she knew that his love for her was all-consuming. He kept on telling her that, more or less every time they met. They were going to become an entity, they'd known that for a long time. There was no doubt about it. They didn't need to hurry things.

But what they certainly did need was money.

Money for food. For cigarettes and clothes and somewhere to live, perhaps. Especially in the longer term: they'd need lots of money then – after all, that's why they'd done what they'd done . . .

Thoughts had started wandering around inside her

head, and she realized now that it was difficult to keep track of everything. There was so much to take into account when you started thinking along these lines, and in the end you didn't know if you were coming or going. That's the way it nearly always turned out – it would be nice if somebody else could make the decisions, she used to think. Make decisions about difficult matters, so that she could think about what she liked to think about instead.

Perhaps that's why she was so much in love with him, of all people? *Him*. He liked to make decisions about things that were a bit complicated and major. Such as this plan they'd thought up. Yes, no doubt that was why she loved him, and wanted to be his. Yes indeed. Even if this last project had gone off the rails a bit, and she'd been forced to change her mind. As already said.

She came to the pier, and looked around in the gathering gloom. He hadn't arrived yet, she was a few minutes early. She could have continued walking along the beach – he lived out at Klimmerstoft and would be coming from the opposite direction; but she didn't bother. Sat down instead on one of the low stone walls that ran all the way along each side of the pier. Lit another cigarette, despite the fact that she didn't really want another one, and tried to think about something pleasant.

*

He turned up after another fifteen minutes or so. A bit late, but not all that much. She saw his white shirt approaching through the twilight long before he reached her, but she remained sitting there until he came up to her. Then she stood up, put her arms round his neck and pressed the whole of her body against him. Kissed him.

She could taste that he'd taken a drop of the strong stuff, but only a little.

'So you're back.'

'Yes.'

'Did you have a good time?'

'Great.'

There was a moment's silence. He was grasping her arms tightly.

'There's something I have to tell you,' she said eventually.

'Go on.'

He loosened his grip slightly.

'I've changed my mind.'

'Changed your mind?'

'Yes.'

'What the hell do you mean?' he said. 'Explain.'

She explained. She had trouble in finding the right words, but in the end he seemed to understand what she was saying. He didn't respond at first, and she couldn't see his face clearly in the darkness. He'd let go of her altogether now. Half a minute passed, perhaps a whole one, and they just stood there. Stood there, breathing in time with the sea and the waves, as it were, and there was something vaguely disturbing about it.

'Let's go for a walk,' he said, putting his arm round her shoulders. 'And have a little chat. I have an idea.'

2

July 1999

Helmut had been against it all from the very start.

Looking back, she had to give him that much. 'Daft,' he'd said. 'Bloody silly.'

He'd lowered the newspaper and glowered at her for a few seconds with those pale eyes of his, slowly grinding his teeth and shaking his head.

'I can't see the point of it. It's unnecessary.'

That was all. Helmut wasn't one to waste words. As far as he was concerned, all in all, it wasn't a case of from dust thou art – stone more like.

From stone thou art, and unto stone thou shalt return. It was a thought she'd had before.

There are two sides to every coin, of course. She knew when she decided on him that she was not choosing storm and fire – not love and passion – but solid rock. Grey, primary rock on which she could stand safely, without any risk of sinking down into the mire of despair once again.

Something like that.

That's more or less what she'd thought fifteen years ago when he knocked on her door and explained that he had a bottle of Burgundy he'd bought while on holiday and wouldn't be able to drink it all himself.

And if she hadn't thought that as he stood there on the doorstep, she'd have done so shortly afterwards in any case. Once they'd started bumping into each other.

In the laundry room. In the street. In the shops.

Or when she was sitting on her balcony on warm summer evenings, trying to rock Mikaela to sleep, with him standing on his own balcony, leaning on the rail that separated them, smoking his pipe and gazing out into what remained of the sunset in the vast western sky over the polders.

Next-door neighbours. The thought came into her mind.

A godlike figure, solid and secure, holding out a hand of stone towards where she was drifting around in a floundering boat on a turbulent sea of emotions.

To her and Mikaela. Yes, that is in fact what the situation had been like: looking back, she could sometimes smile at the thought, sometimes not.

Anyway, that was fifteen years ago. Mikaela was three.

Now she was eighteen. She celebrated her eighteenth birthday this summer.

Mark my words, he had declared from behind his newspaper. As I told you, this won't make her any happier.

Why hadn't she listened to him? She asked herself that over and over again. During these days of worry and despair. When she tried to get a grip on herself and look back over the links in the chain. To think back and try to find reasons for doing what she had done . . . Or simply to let her thoughts wander freely; she didn't have much strength to speak of just now. These hellish summer days.

But she'd done the right thing, as she saw it. All I've done is what is right and proper. I haven't betrayed the decision I made all those years ago, then let it lie. In a way that's another stone – a murky boulder sunk down at the muddy bottom of the well of memory, but one that she'd promised herself she would fish up again when the time was right.

Carefully and respectfully, of course, but bring it up into the light of day even so. So that Mikaela could see it. No matter how you looked at it, that was necessary. Something that had remained in abeyance for many years, but now needed to happen to put things into perspective.

Her eighteenth birthday. Even if they hadn't discussed

it, Helmut had known about it as well. Been aware of the situation all the time, but had preferred not to confront it . . . The day would have to dawn when Mikaela was told the truth, one had no right to deny a child knowledge of its origins. One couldn't hide away her roots under mundane everyday happenings and the detritus of time. One couldn't send her out into life on false pretences.

Right? Life? Truth? Afterwards, she couldn't understand how she had been able to fit such grandiose concepts into her thoughts. Wasn't it this very pretentiousness that was hitting back and turning upon her? Wasn't that what was happening?

Who was she to go on about right and wrong? Who was she to make such hasty judgements and shake off Helmut's morose objections without giving them more than three-quarters of a second's consideration?

Until later. When it seemed to be too late. These days and nights when everything seemed to lose every ounce of significance and value, when she had become a robot and didn't so much as glance at these old thoughts which were drifting past her consciousness like tattered remnants of cloud over the blue-grey night sky of death. She simply let them sail past, on their disconsolate journey from horizon to horizon.

From oblivion to oblivion. Night to night and darkness to darkness.

From stone thou art.

From your gaping wounds your silent fury seethes up to a dead sky.

The pain of stone. Harder than anything else.

And madness, insanity itself was lying in wait round the corner.

Her eighteenth birthday. A Friday. In July, as hot as hell.

'I'll tell her when she comes back from the gym,' she had said. 'So you don't need to be present. Then we can have dinner afterwards in peace and quiet. She'll take it well, I can feel it in my bones.'

At first merely a sullen silence.

'If it's really necessary,' he'd said eventually. When she was already at the sink, washing the cups. 'It's your responsibility, not mine.'

'I have to,' she said. 'Remember that I promised her this when she was fifteen. Remember that it's a gap that needs to be filled. She's expecting it.'

'She's never said a word about it,' he said. From the side of his mouth. With his back to her.

That was true. She had to grant him that as well.

'Daft, but do whatever you like. What's the point?'

That's all. Nothing more. Then he left.

Daft?

Am I doing it for her sake, or for mine? she asked herself.

Reasons? Motives?

As blurred as the borderline between dreams and consciousness.

Unfathomable as stone itself.

Nonsense. Verbal sticking plaster. She probably knows anyway.

3

When Detective Inspector Ewa Moreno stopped outside
the door of Chief Inspector Reinhart's office, it was a
quarter past three in the afternoon and she was longing
for a cold beer.

If she had been born into a different social class, or
blessed with more imagination, she might have been
longing for a glass of cold champagne instead (or why
not three or four?); but today any possibility of thinking
straight, any ability to think at all had been sweated away
in the early hours of the morning. It was over thirty
degrees, and had been about that all day. Both in town
and inside the police station. A forgotten manic flat-iron
seemed to be pressing down from above, overheating
everyone and everything, and apart from chilled drinks,
there seemed to be only two possibilities of surviving: the
beach and the shade.

There was a noticeable absence of the former in the Maardam police station.

But there were Venetian blinds. And corridors where the sun was certain not to be shining. She stood there with her hand on the door handle, struggling with an impulse (that in itself was sluggish as a bluebottle high on Coca-Cola, so that the outcome could go either way) not to turn it. To retreat discreetly.

Instead of entering and finding out why he wanted to talk to her. There were good reasons for not going in. Or one, at least: in less than two hours' time she would be going on leave.

Two hours. One hundred and twenty suffocating minutes. If nothing unexpected happened, that is.

Moreno's intuition told her that he probably hadn't asked her to come in order to wish her all the best for her holiday. It hadn't sounded like that, and in any case, to do so wouldn't be Reinhart's style.

If nothing unexpected happened . . . ?

In a strange way, the unexpected didn't seem to be all that unexpected. If she'd been offered decent odds, she might well have bet on it. That's the way it was when you were in the lacklustre police business, and it wouldn't be the first time . . .

So, to beat a retreat, or not to beat a retreat: that was the question. She could always explain that something had turned up. That she hadn't had time to call in, as he'd put it.

Call in? That sounded a bit dodgy, surely?

Call in at my office some time after lunch. It won't take long . . .

Bugger bugger, she thought. It sounded as potentially deadly as a hungry cobra.

After a brief internal struggle, the drugged-up bluebottle drowned, and her Lutheran-Calvinistic copper's conscience won the day. She sighed, turned the handle and went in. Flopped down on the visitor's chair with her misgivings dancing around in her head like butterflies greeting the arrival of summer. And in her stomach.

'You wanted to see me,' she said.

Reinhart was standing by the window, smoking, and looking ominous. She noticed that he was wearing flip-flops. Light blue.

'*Salve,*' he said. 'Would you like something to drink?'

'What do you have to offer?' Moreno asked, and that cold beer floated into her mind's eye again.

'Water. With or without bubbles.'

'I think I'll pass,' said Moreno. 'If you don't mind. Well?'

Reinhart scratched at his stubble and put his pipe down on the window ledge beside the flowerpot.

'We've found Lampe-Leermann,' he said.

'Lampe-Leermann?' said Moreno.

'Yes,' said Reinhart.

'We?' said Moreno.

'Some colleagues of ours. Out at Lejnice. In Behrensee, to be precise, but they took him to Lejnice. That was the nearest station.'

'Excellent. And about time, too. Any problems?'

'Just the one,' said Reinhart.

'Really?' said Moreno.

He flopped down on his desk chair, opposite her, and gave her a look that was presumably meant to express innocence. Moreno had seen it before, and sent a prayer flying out through the window. 'Not again, please!' was its essence.

'Just the one problem,' said Reinhart again.

'Shoot,' said Moreno.

'He's not really prepared to cooperate.'

Moreno said nothing. Reinhart fiddled with the papers on his desk and seemed uncertain of how to continue.

'Or rather, he is prepared to cooperate – but only if he can talk to you.'

'What?' said Moreno.

'Only if he can talk to—'

'I heard what you said,' interrupted Moreno 'But why on earth does he want to talk to me?'

'God knows,' said Reinhart. 'But that's the way it seems to be – don't blame me. Lampe-Leermann is prepared to make a full confession, but only if he can lay it at your feet. Nobody else's. He doesn't like policemen, he says. Odd, don't you think?'

Moreno contemplated the picture hanging above Reinhart's head. It depicted a pig in a suit standing in a pulpit and throwing television sets to a congregation of ecstatic sheep. Or possibly judges wearing wigs, it was difficult to say which. She knew the chief of police had asked him several times to take it down, but it was still there. Rooth had suggested that it was symbolic of the freedom of thought and level of understanding within the police force, and Moreno had a vague suspicion that it could well be an accurate interpretation. Although she had never asked Reinhart himself. Nor the chief of police, come to that.

'My leave begins two hours from now,' she said, trying to give him a friendly smile.

'They're holding him out at Lejnice,' said Reinhart, unmoved. 'A nice spot. It would take just one day. Two at most. Hmm.'

Moreno stood up and walked over to the window.

'Mind you, if you would prefer to have him brought here, that wouldn't be a problem,' said Reinhart from behind her back.

She gazed out over the town and the ridge of high pressure. It was a few days old, but it seemed to be here to stay. That's what fru Bachman on the ground floor had said, and the meteorologists on the television as well. She decided not to respond. Not without a solicitor present, or a more detailed instruction. Ten seconds passed, and the only sound was from the bustle of the town down below, and the soft tip-tap from Reinhart's flip-fops as he shuffled about.

Flip-flops? she thought. Surely he could get himself a pair of sandals at least. A chief inspector in light-blue flip-flops?

Perhaps he'd been to the swimming baths at lunchtime and forgotten to change? Or maybe he'd been to see the chief of police and put them on as a sort of irreverent protest? It was hard to say as far as Reinhart was concerned: he liked to make a point.

He gave up in the end.

'For Christ's sake,' he said. 'Get a grip, Inspector. We've been after this bloody prat for several months now, and at last Vrommel has caught up with him . . .'

'Vrommel? Who's Vrommel?'

'The chief of police in Lejnice.'

Reluctantly, Moreno began to consider the possibility. Remained standing with her back turned to Reinhart as the image of Lampe-Leermann appeared in her mind's eye . . . Not much of a name in the underworld, quite small fry in fact: but it was true that they had been on his tail for quite a while. He was strongly suspected of being involved in a few armed robberies in March and April, but that wasn't the point. Or at least, not the main point.

The big thing is that he mixed with certain other gentlemen who were much bigger heavyweights than he was. Leading lights in so-called Organized Crime, to use a term that was heard all too often nowadays. There was no doubt about his links, and Lampe-Leermann had a reputation for grassing. A reputation for being more concerned – in certain difficult circumstances at least – about his own skin than that of others, and willing to inform the police authorities of what he knew. If doing so would serve his own ends, and could be treated with appropriate discretion.

And it could be in this case. At least, there was good reason for thinking so. Reinhart was inclined to think so, and Moreno tended to agree with him. In principle, at least. That was why they had made a bigger effort than usual when it came to tracking down Lampe-Leermann. That was why they had found him. Today of all days.

But the news that he was only prepared to unburden his mind to Inspector Moreno had come as a bit of a surprise, no question. That was something they hadn't reckoned with. Neither her nor anybody else. Just some malevolent little gremlin, no doubt . . . Damn and blast, you can never . . .

'He likes you,' said Reinhart, interrupting her train of thought. 'That's nothing to be ashamed of. I think he remembers when we were playing a game of good-cop bad-cop with him a few years ago. Anyway, that's the way it is. He wants to talk to you, and nobody else. But there's the minor matter of your leave, of course . . .'

'Exactly,' said Moreno, returning to her chair.

'It's not so far up to Lejnice,' said Reinhart. 'A hundred and twenty kilometres or thereabouts, I should think . . .'

Moreno said nothing. Closed her eyes instead and fanned herself with yesterday's *Gazett* that she had picked up from the pile of newspapers on the desk.

'Then I came to think of that house you're going to – didn't you say it was in Port Hagen?'

Oh my God! Moreno thought. He remembers. He's been doing his homework.

'Yes,' she said. 'Port Hagen, that's right.'

Reinhart tried to look innocent again. He'd be good as the wolf in *Little Red Riding Hood*, Moreno thought.

'If I'm not much mistaken it's quite close by,' he said. 'It must be only ten kilometres or so north of Lejnice. I used to go there when I was a kid. You'd be able to . . .'

Moreno threw away the newspaper with a resigned gesture.

'All right,' she said. 'Don't go on. I'll sort it out. Damn it all, you know as well as I do that Lampe-Leermann is the nastiest, creepiest piece of work that ever wore a pair of hand-sewn shoes . . . or a signet ring. Apart from anything else he always stinks of old garlic. Note that I said old garlic – I've nothing against the fresh stuff. But I'll sort it out, you don't need to strain yourself any more. Damn it all once again! When?'

Reinhart walked over to the flowerpot in order to empty his pipe.

'I told Vrommel you'd probably turn up tomorrow.'

Moreno stared at him.

'Have you fixed a time without consulting me?'

'*Probably*,' said Reinhart. 'I said you'd *probably* turn up tomorrow. What the hell's the matter with you? Aren't we playing for the same team any more, or what's going on?'

Moreno sighed.

'Okay,' she sighed. 'I'm sorry. I'd planned to set off tomorrow morning anyway, so it won't involve a lot of disruption. In fact.'

'Good,' said Reinhart. 'I'll ring Vrommel and confirm that you're coming. What time?'

She thought for a moment.

'About one. Tell him that I'll be there at around one, and that Lampe-Leermann shouldn't be given any garlic with his lunch.'

'Not even fresh?' wondered Reinhart.

She didn't answer. As she was on her way out through the door, he reminded her of how serious the situation was.

'Make sure you squeeze out of that bastard every bloody name he can give us. Both you and he will get a bonus for every arsehole we can put behind lock and key.'

'Of course,' said Moreno. 'But there's no need to swear so much. I like the colour of your shoes, though – it makes you look really young again . . .'

Before Reinhart could respond she was out in the corridor.

extracts reading groups
competitions books new
discounts extracts
competitions
books new
events books
extracts
new titles reading groups
interviews
events extracts
discounts
new books events
events new
discounts extracts discounts

www.panmacmillan.com

extracts events reading groups
competitions books extracts new